Radical Extreme

by

James Schaefer

2008

Published by Cocoon Tales, LLC
12000 Carmon Street, Richmond, VA 23233

Printed in Bangladesh
First Edition
0 9 8 7 6 5 4 3 2 1
Library of Congress Control Number: 2008907611
ISBN 978-0-9817478-0-4

This is for Ann

"Love Never Dies."

PROLOGUE

In the years before September 11th, 2001, a Saudi exile named Usama Bin Ladin issued his interpretation of Islamic law through an Arabic newspaper in London. In his Declaration of War, he called for "...the murder of any American, anywhere on earth, as the individual duty for every Muslim who can do it in any country in which it is possible to do it."

During an ABC television interview, Bin Ladin claimed "...it was more important for Muslims to kill Americans than to kill other infidels... We do not have to differentiate between military or civilian. As far as we are concerned, they are all targets."

Of course America was concerned about terrorism. In Europe and the Far East, small scale terrorist attacks were expected, but so far they had always happened to someone else. Kidnapping, bombings, bank robberies, assassinations, and just general mayhem could always be expected from the more formalized terror groups and a few self-styled groups with an axe to grind.

The greatest problem after 911 was that many groups broke into smaller groups, renamed themselves, and went underground. Over the years, some groups used a series of different names for each type of criminal action they undertook. Mainly, their goal was to obtain money so they could invest in more destructive terrorist initiatives.

In the Middle East, one such group, carefully and secretly set up several small cells, each wholly unknown to the other, but controlled by a single individual with a unique idea on how to destroy America from within.

To carry out his attack would take a number of years, scientists, engineers, medical specialists, and, most of all, a select group of fanatics that would give their lives in a heartbeat to destroy America.

Chapter 1
Hot Stuff

A slight shiver ran through Leonid as he watched the lights on the ZIL delivery truck fade into the night. Inside, Abdullah and Fahid headed north towards Kakhovka on the Pivdenny Buh River.

Leonid had done some stupid things in his career to keep the Ukrainian missile industry alive, but knowingly selling enriched uranium to terrorists now topped the list of the dumbest things he had ever done.

In a well practiced move learned during his first year at Moscow State University, Leonid shook a pack of Java cigarettes, carefully released one into the air, caught it in his mouth and had it lit without any conscious thought. After taking a drag he slowly exhaled a thin stream of smoke toward his feet. With a final drag, he flicked the butt away and lowered the entrance gate to the Russian ICBM dismantling facility at Pervomaysky in the Ukraine.

As he walked back to the Low-level Enriched Uranium Storage building he began wondering how long it would be before he and Oleksandr would face a firing squad.

Sure the terrorists could have bought the ton of nuclear material from at least a dozen other sources in the world. Hell, maybe even the highly enriched uranium grade used in nuclear weapons. But, they bought it from him. And the only thing that might save his ass was the skillful way Oleksandr had blended this particular batch down to the twenty percent level so it would appear as if it had come from the French experimental facility at CERN in Geneva, Switzerland.

Before Leonid opened the office door he could hear Oleksandr inside laughing and talking to himself like a drunken bum who had just been pushed out the back door of a bar at closing.

"So they think they have the best of us, do they, old friend. Come. Come. Have a drink of Stolichnaya. I've already poured the glasses," Oleksandr said looking like a schoolboy with a secret he just couldn't wait to tell.

After clinking their glasses together and downing the slurry of nearly frozen vodka, Leonid slammed his glass down on the table indicating that he was ready for a second. "I've seen that impish look in your eyes before, Oleksandr. What the hell are you up to this time, my old friend?"

Oleksandr put his left index finger to his lips and laughed. He refilled their glasses, raising his high in the air. "I'm not going to tell you anything until this bottle is empty."

Leonid had known Oleksandr for over half his life and he knew that he wasn't going to be able to get anything out of him until they had drained the bottle dry. Flipping another cigarette into his mouth he tossed the pack to Oleksandr. "Okay, you old fox, I give up. Let's get drunk."

A half-hour later found them sitting across from each other at a workbench as Oleksandr emptied the last of the vodka into their glasses. Leonid tossed his drink down and waited for Oleksandr to finish, eager to get down to the business at hand while he could think straight.

In contrast, Oleksandr enjoyed prolonging his friend's agony as long as possible, so he deliberated at length about exactly where to set the bottle before picking up his glass. Unfortunately, his judgment was off and set the bottle down against the edge of the ashtray they had been sharing – flipping it into the air. When it miraculously landed right side up a shower of sparks blossomed, igniting the little puddles of vodka that had accumulated on the table.

As the blue flames twinkled, Oleksandr picked up his glass, saluted his friend, and swallowed his drink. A spasm of laughter blocked its descent and sent vodka hurling out of his mouth in a mist, bursting into a ball of fire.

Stumbling back, Leonid began a long belly laugh that drained any remaining tension from his body. Soon he was sitting there with tears running down his face. "You stupid shit, you're going to kill us before the government does."

After recovering from his first attempt at fire eating, Oleksandr smoothed back what remained of his eyebrows and hair and began laughing at himself. "Not too bad, maybe I can get a job with the Moscow Circus if things don't work out here."

When they had both settled down and were almost breathing normally, Leonid poked at the table and said, "Okay, now it is time to let the cat out of the bag. What did you have to get me drunk to tell me?"

2

"Well, if you must know then I will get serious for a moment. You know that I was trying to mix up a batch of LEU that looked like it came from CERN."

"Yes, of course," Leonid said as he got up from the table and returned with the case of uncut diamonds.

"You know, I really thought I might be able to do it too, but circumstances brought me a better solution." Oleksandr said as he turned the front of the case toward him and opened it up.

"This doesn't sound good. What kind of 'better solution' are we talking about here?" Leonid asked rubbing his temples in an effort to sober up.

Oleksandr scooped up a big handful of diamonds and let them trickle through his fingers before continuing. "Well to me it seems like the perfect solution. I actually traded some power generation rods for Plutonium two thirty-seven."

Now Leonid was as sober as any man who consumed half a liter of Stolichnaya in half an hour could be. He realized what they had unleashed on the world. "What the hell are you talking about? How could you give them Plutonium? Now they will go out and make a couple of bombs, and we will be blasted straight to hell when they catch us."

"No, I think you are wrong. They will probably be dead before they get that crap back home. Hopefully, found floating in the Black Sea or rotting in the mountains where the Americans will find them and point to the treasure they have been looking for all these years. If they do manage to get it back to their manufacturing facility, it will kill anyone that gets close enough to work the metal. Hell, they could single-handedly kill more terrorists than the United States just lugging it around."

Leonid's mind began to bombard itself with questions and answers: "how the hell could Oleksandr get rods from CERN? Oleksandr never lied, but how did he get it? You can get anything if you have the right connections. Oleksandr knew everyone." He shook his head, got up and wandered over to the refrigerator. Opening the freezer compartment he grabbed a bottle of Stoli Zinamon.

He stood there staring at the drawing of the Hotel Moskva under the gold script. Remembering happier days as a youth in Moscow where he had first met Oleksandr at the university, it had been a time of innocence, hard work, and heretofore unknown pleasures. Most of all he remembered how Oleksandr could get anything from the latest American music to French chocolate. Not to mention the scores of eager young women that followed him back to the room they shared.

Returning to the table with new resolve he poured another round, sat down and raised his glass. The more he thought about it the better it sounded. "That stuff really came from CERN?"

"Yes, I absolutely guarantee that it is one hundred percent CERN generated. So if they do get caught, they will not be looking toward us. They will be focused on Geneva," Oleksandr said pointing westward.

•••

Seventy-five minutes after they left Pervomaysk, Abdullah and Fahid reached Kakhovka and headed toward the docks. Since they had just handed over twenty million dollars in uncut diamonds to the ex-president of the Ukraine, they were pretty sure the word was out to leave them alone, but their instincts told them to be aware.

Just as they began to relax, a blue VAZ 2107, complete with police lights and distinctive markings in black over a white hood entered the street ahead of them. Then a second unit pulled up close behind their ZIL truck and began blowing its horn. Abdullah's first reaction was to mash down hard on the gas pedal, but a sharp look from Fahid convinced him to slow down and pull over to the curb.

The car behind stopped, the officer got out and walked slowly to the back of the truck.

"A little problem," he shouted, as his flashlight pointed directly on the side view mirror - illuminating the interior of the cab.

He waited until his partner walked up and began talking with the driver. Taking a step back, he pulled back the canvas flap and began scanning the boxes piled inside the cargo area.

Upfront, Fahid was pulling papers from the glove compartment and handing them to Abdullah without saying a word.

"Out, Out! Both of you," the Captain said.

First Abdullah slid out, followed by Fahid who slid across the seat and exited on the driver's side.

Meanwhile, the officer with the flashlight had climbed into the back of the truck and was rummaging around to see if there was anything that would be more valuable than the ten Euros he was planning on getting from the driver.

Just then he spied what looked like a large metal cooler and thought it might contain something to quench his thirst. However, when he tried to pull it toward him, it didn't budge, which instantly made him even more disagreeable. Determined, he knelt down and after a few seconds had managed to get the lid opened. His mood changed again when he saw a couple dozen mini-kegs of premium German beer chilling in the misty water.

Up front, the second officer flashed a little smile as he tucked the ten Euro note, Fahid had just handed him into his shirt pocket. Then a series of things happened in rapid succession.

First, the rather large police radio, complete with a hand-fashioned set of external batteries attached to it with a generous amount of blue electrical tape, began to emit a rather loud hum. A loud scream rose from inside the truck's cargo area as the officer bounded out the back. This was followed by the sound of the metal cooler lid closing and the abrupt silencing of the hum.

The screaming officer displayed his gruesome right hand - now covered with blisters. And pleaded with his partner to get him to the hospital forgetting about the two idiots they had just stopped. Without hesitation, the officer loaded his injured partner into the lead vehicle and raced away.

This left Abdullah and Fahid standing alone beside their truck a few seconds later blindly staring at each other. After what seemed like forever they broke for the back of the truck, jumped inside and knelt beside the cooler.

Fahid grabbed a rag from his pocket and twisted the metal fasteners to secure the lid. Touching the side of the cooler with the back of his hand, he quickly realized that they had been set up in a most ingenious way.

"Fucking Ukrainian assholes," he blurted out. Dropping the rag on a small spots of water, Fahid smeared it around with his boot, and then kicked it out the back of the truck.

Chapter 2
The Volvo Ocean Race

Inside the Volvo Financial Services building in Geneva, Switzerland, the monotonous review of financial reports had droned on for hours. To an outsider the almost imperceptible changes in Derrick Parker's body language would have been hard to read as he sat at the head of the table, but to those who knew him, he was not a happy man.

As president and CEO of the Volvo Car Corporation, Derrick had worked hard to get where he was today and he knew better than most how tenuous his position was. It only took two or three slow quarters for the stockholders to begin looking for a new champion and it was beginning to sound like this quarter was dangerously close to being flat.

The single quality that had enabled him to rise to the position of CEO was his ability to visualize what each item on the financials meant to the overall health of Volvo. As each member of the board spoke he saw: plants opening and shutting down; new machinery being installed and old machinery being carted off; the smiling faces of new employees and the tearful goodbyes of employees caught in forced reductions. Worst of all, he visualized whole cities rising and falling as the numbers projected on the screen to his right rose and tumbled. Finally all was quiet and Derrick focused on the people sitting around the table.

"Not what I would call something to write home about," he said looking down at the screen of his Blackberry Omega III, which was flashing a message from his personal secretary.

He clicked the remote he had been holding in his palm since the meeting began. Before anyone realized what was going on behind them, the walls at the far end of the room slid open, revealing what would have passed as an elegant restaurant in other parts of Geneva.

"Lunch apparently has saved us for the time being," Derrick said with the slightest of smiles.

Once everyone left the conference room, the walls closed again. Derrick dropped the remote in his pocket, grabbed his Blackberry and headed for his office.

He paused in front of the door and looked at his secretary Linnea, who nodded. He opened the door and disappeared inside. As he stood there surveying the six people seated around his large circular conference table he smiled, but was wondering how he was going to get out of this mess.

Of the six people, Derrick knew four: Moritz, head of Volvo trucking and heavy equipment; Ali from the Saudi Oil Ministry; Sheik Saud who had been in negotiations for over six months to enter the Volvo Ocean Race; and Abd Atwa, the technical mastermind who ran all the electronics on the Saudi II.

As Derrick moved down the line with Moritz making introductions, he learned that the two strangers were Aziz from the Saudi Chamber of Commerce and Industry and his assistant, Ayman.

After introductions and greetings they sat down and Derrick punched a button on the Blackberry that was preprogrammed to text message his secretary with a request for lunch. He sat back into his chair and closed his eyes for a second.

He knew that Saud was determined to enter this year's boat race despite the fact that he had missed several deadlines and filed his application a week late. Derrick also realized that if he did make an exception and word leaked out it would cheapen the prestige of the race that he had worked so hard to build over the years. So he was prepared to say no in the most diplomatic way he could, despite the fact that Saud had brought an impressive contingent of allies.

"Gentlemen, we all know the reason we are here is to discuss whether or not the Saudi II should be allowed to enter this year's Volvo Ocean Race. From the start, I have to tell you that I'm against it, but willing to listen, open mindedly, to your arguments concerning the granting of an exception."

Ali was the first to speak. "Good afternoon Derrick. I'd like to thank you for allowing us to meet with you. After reviewing the Annual Report you delivered in Goteborg last month, it looks like Volvo is doing very well. I compliment you on your success. I've brought along a presentation that I'd like to share with you, if you don't mind."

Derrick smiled. He was the master of presentations and was interested in what the Saudis had cooked up. So he didn't hesitate to lower a projection screen from the ceiling while Abd hooked Ali's laptop into the system.

As Ali began to speak, pictures of Saudi Arabia's bustling cities began flashing on the screen. "Just as you, I must take care of my people in the best way possible. As I look to the future, I see a day when

7

the wells will be dry and my nation's economy will dwindle. So while I sit on our treasure chest, I must carefully choose how best to invest in Saudi Arabia's future."

"As everyone in the world knows, we are lacking in water." Ali continued as pictures of vast desert wastelands flashed on the screen. He paused and for a second a large aerial map of his country displayed stars placed at various places along the Red Sea and Persian Gulf. "To alleviate that problem I am proposing that we build desalination plants at strategic points along our coastline. This project is vital for our future, but the problem is the reverse osmosis process used in such plants requires huge amounts of power."

As he built to his conclusion, simulated construction site sketches flashed across the screen each containing at least one vehicle or piece of construction equipment manufactured by Volvo. The inference didn't escape Derrick, who had used similar ploys when he was trying to change behavior or negotiate a union contract. Despite himself, Derrick was beginning to like Ali's style.

"This plan is a long way from fruition, but research shows nuclear generating stations would be the best alternative to oil-powered stations that are destined to become obsolete in another fifty years. Besides generating the enormous energy required for desalination, nuclear plants could also provide electrical power for our industries and our people."

Ali continued with a series of slides showing the construction of the Saudi II. The first slide showed early conceptual drawings, which set the overall dimensions at eighteen feet wide and sixty feet in length, but computer simulations eventually lead to the slimming and lengthening of the lady to enhance performance. Several unique contours in the Kevlar hull helped provide the lift necessary to raise the fifteen ton racer out of the water and into a plane. Once it was skimming across the water, the computer simulations of the model suggested it was capable of reaching forty knots, which was faster than any of the other boats.

Even the six ton counterweight at the bottom of the keel had lifting wings that could be trimmed. In fact if you were swimming upside down and the Saudi II came at you, the keel would look very much like the tail of an aircraft that bulged at the top. This design was unique among the ocean racers that had applied to enter the Volvo Ocean Race. It meant that the helmsman didn't need to worry about pumping water from one holding tank to another to trim the boat as the force of the wind pushed against the sails attached to the eighty-seven foot mast. The last slide showed the Saudi II as she headed for the finish line in the last race and then a fifteen second video played showing her plowing through rough seas under full sail - her green hull blending to white as the mast silhouetted against the setting sun.

As Ali motioned to Abd to switch off the laptop he smiled at Derrick. "Every dream has a beginning - one point in time can be looked back on as the start of a new beginning. I believe that Saudi Arabia is about to embark on that journey --a journey driven by fresh water. The water is all around us, but to use it we need to build nuclear generator and the generators are the problem. Saudi Arabia is in a very precarious part of the world and many forces are working against us as we seek to enter the nuclear age."

Pausing, Ali took a drink of water. "That is one reason that Sheik Saud is so interested in entering the Volvo Ocean Race. In order to show the world that we are a peace-loving country and to gain support of our generators, we need to build good will. He has convinced us that this can be the first step as there is much publicity and prestige associated with your race. I leave it up to you to decide whether or not you will allow a few minor mistakes in filings to hold us back."

As the presentation ended, Derrick used his Blackberry to summon lunch, so he would have some time to think about the presentation before he had to respond.

A second later the doors swung open and a staff of four presented food carts laden with the best Geneva had to offer. While Abd unplugged Ali's laptop and stuck it back inside his leather bag, a silver plate of warm hand towels was circulated. Plates were set, glasses filled, and a Swiss Braiser Chef waited for his first order.

All in all, Derrick's little plan had worked better than he hoped. It looked like he had arranged a special party just for them. Little did they know that the directors, Derrick had left twenty minutes ago were almost finished eating the exact same fare down the hall. Soon they would head back to the conference room for the second half of their meeting.

When he had finished eating, Derrick slid a small data-stick across the table to Ali and asked him for a copy of the presentation and video. Once he had a copy he excused himself and left the room saying,

"Thank you all for coming. I would like you to join the second half of our board meeting this afternoon. I'll send my secretary in to escort you when it starts. In the meantime, please enjoy coffee and dessert."

Gliding past his secretary, Derrick handed her the data-stick. "Have someone in design grab an appropriate shot of the sailboat on this, make a poster like the others and bring it to the board room. Priority one. "

Once that was done, Derrick headed for the only place in the whole building where he could think without interruption: his private bathroom. After checking his Blackberry to make sure the special shielding was working and his Blackberry was disconnected from the Wi-Fi wireless network, he dropped his pants and sat down to think.

He knew that he had the power to allow the Saudis to enter their sailboat in the race, but should he? Never once had he granted an exception if every item on the checklist had not been ticked off in the correct order and at the proper time. He had ordered the poster to be printed as a contingency, but did he seriously believe he was going to put it up on the wall alongside the other qualifying sailboats?

He didn't know. His first impulse was just to say no and his first impulse was usually the way he went, but the pictures of the construction sites floated before him. He dreamed of the revenue that could be produced, the factories, the workers, and the shareholders. Still Ali hadn't actually promised to order anything. He had dealt with the Saudis before and knew that they had a tendency to place large orders on a whim and that their checks never bounced.

Ten minutes later and feeling much better, a confident Derrick Parker slipped into the boardroom through a back door. Surveying the transformation that had taken place while everyone enjoyed lunch, he smiled. Looking up he saw eight posters of boats covered by white cloth connected to a release string hanging along the windowed side of the rectangular room.

On the wall opposite the posters stretched a physical 20-foot X 40-foot map of the world. A cartoon cannon, labeled #1 sat over Vigo, Spain and a black and white checkered flag with #10 flew over Gothenburg, Sweden.

Other ports of call included: #2, Cape Town; #3, Melbourne; #4, Wellington; #5, Rio de Janeiro; #6, Baltimore/Annapolis; #7, New York City; #8, Portsmouth, England; and #9, Rotterdam. Great white arched arrows connected the ports which marked the 31,200 nautical mile course that would take the sailboats eight months to complete.

A looping video of the company's own entry, the Majestic, was running on a screen strategically placed in the corner by the desserts and coffee. Nearby, models from the Elaine Modeling Agency on Rue de Diorama lined up for inspection in front of a line of replicas of the winners from previous races. Each girl was between nineteen and twenty-four, blonde, and tastefully dressed in navy outfits with shorts to show off their long legs.

"Okay ladies, when the door opens I don't want you standing around in little groups chattering. You are here today to provide a little eye candy for the guests who are awaiting the official announcement of the sailboats that will be competing in this year's Volvo Ocean Race. Remember, the press will be photographing for the trades and videoing for the local and international news, so be professional." A curt nod of their heads, a few rolling eyes at these words, and a shuffling of feet was all the response expected, and that was what he received.

They were professionals, and would act as such. He knew it, and they knew it. Derrick turned off the microphone system to the room, then turned away and left as quickly as he had entered to make his announcement.

Each member of the security staff was dressed in a brown suit with a tiny gold pin on the left lapel to identify them. Everyone that worked in the building knew who they were and gave them a wide berth as they passed in the hallways. Their expertise in combat was proven two or three times a year when someone unlucky enough to cross the line was dragged through the building and handed over to the local police in the lobby.

Derrick knew the directors and sailors would enjoy the photo opportunity even if they didn't make it to publication. And for those lucky enough to make it into the public eye it would be a topic of conversation around their towns, offices, and homes for months to come.

"Okay. Here we go," he said raising his hands and announcing, "Let them in."

Seconds later the doors swung opened and the crowd of two hundred Volvo executives, crewmembers, journalists and guests streamed into the room. Derrick was pulled into more group photos than he expected.

11

When he saw that everyone, including Ail and the Saudis, were in the room, he gave the girls a signal and they began passing out tall thin glasses filled with champagne.

Standing under the center of the poster Derrick said, "I'd like to have the board come stand with me over here under the boats that made this year's cut." As the board assembled the rest of the guests moved closer and photographers checked their equipment one last time.

"Please gentlemen grab a string and prepare to unveil the winners on my count. One, two, three."

As the cloth coverings fell, the room was filled with the strobes of a dozen flash units as the photographers clicked away and scurried around the room searching for the best angle. As a few hands began to clap, Derrick held up his arms.

"Wait. Wait. I'd like to propose a toast to the new captains, crews and sponsors assembled here today. May God bless and keep you safe in your endeavor this year, both on the seas and in the ports where many an uncharted danger lurks in the guise of such beautiful women, as we have here," he said, pointing to the hostesses who had formed a line between the directors and the others.

A burst of laughter filled the room followed by tilted glasses and thunderous applause that lasted for over a minute. Being a good host, Derrick circulated around the room and was photographed with each of the crews. When he finally got around to Sheik Saud's group they were lining up for a photo so Derrick walked over beside the photographer.

"Come, come, my friend, get in the picture too." Saud said motioning Derrick over with his hand. As Derrick joined the group, Sheik Saud held up his hand again. "Wait. Where is Abd? I want all the crew here."

"If you like I can come back." Derrick said.

"No. No. Don't be ridiculous. I just thought he would have liked to be in the picture since he worked so hard to get us where we are. No, go on," the Sheik said and the camera flashed.

Chapter 3
Stinger Down

As Mark walked down the passageway holding his helmet in the crook of his left arm, his subconscious kept a wary eye on the pipes, valves, and electrical boxes protruding from the bulkhead. Even though he was a seasoned veteran with six tours of duty aboard carriers, a little piece of his mind still remembered the embarrassment his fellow pilots inflicted on him when something ripped his helmet out of his hand and sent it rolling down the passageway, with him scampering after it like a dog after a ball. But today, as he slipped on his aviator glasses and stepped over the lip of the water-tight door onto the flight deck of the USS Ronald Reagan (CVN 76), you would never guess that anything so trivial still echoed in his brain.

Mark stepped aside and let a couple of pilots pass so his best friend Luke could catch up with him. They headed for their Hornets parked on the opposite side of the flight deck. Luke was two years older and an inch taller than Mark, standing six foot two and weighing in during the shipboard boxing matches at one ninety-five. Though they came from completely different backgrounds, their light brown hair, strikingly blue eyes and lean bodies often got them mistaken for brothers.

Since it was their last mission before their squadron rotated back to the States, most people would have thought the pilots would have been excited, but as launch time drew near, most of them were a lot quieter than usual.

Mark and Luke had met at the Naval Academy during their senior year and attended had flight school and carrier landing classes together before they were assigned to the same squadron. After taking their finals they had spent the last week in Annapolis bar hopping each night, finally connecting with two young coeds who had their own apartment early on Friday night.

From the beginning there wasn't any question of who was going to hook up with whom when they met Amy and Wendy. Mark had an attraction for dark hair and Amy, besides having an outgoing personality, and a laugh that could be heard for a mile, also had been the Miss Maryland runner-up the previous year. Amy was also almost six feet tall and in heels she was clearly taller than Mark.

Wendy, on the other hand, was three inches shorter with a tiny frame, blonde hair and a reserved nature that appealed to Luke. After a few failed attempts at getting her to laugh, his good natured humor finally penetrated her defenses and it wasn't long before she was enjoying his company.

After the four of them were totally smashed on various concoctions they had dared each other to drink, the bartender called them a cab. They ended up back at the girls' apartment and slept until Saturday morning. Once awake the couples spent the rest of the weekend making love in bedrooms separated by the thinnest of walls until one of them called for a meal break. That weekend bonded them together in a way that few people ever experience.

So it was no surprise that a year later, when Mark and Luke returned from their first tour of duty, they stood together on the altar of the Naval Academy Chapel looking out on five hundred faces they had tried in vain to memorize, while waiting for Amy and Wendy to make their appearance.

Contrary to the outward appearance as heroes, the boys were literally shaking in their shoes. No one was ever more relieved than Mark and Luke when the first few notes blasted from the organ and the crowd turned around toward the back of the chapel. As the girls became visible and the cameras began clicking, each best man quickly pulled out a handkerchief and wiped away the beads of sweat that had begun running down the pilots' faces.

By the time Amy and Wendy had fallen in step with the Wedding March and relaxed the grip on their fathers' arms the boys were standing tall and proud in bright rays of light that streamed through sculptured windows set in the capitol-like dome high over the altar. In what seemed like a second, Amy and Wendy walked down the white satin runner spread over the ocean-blue carpet. In a daze they passed rows of faces they couldn't quite focus on until they were standing in front of Mark and Luke. Their fathers pulled back their veils, gave them a kiss and presented their hands to their soon to be husbands.

The ceremony lasted about half an hour and was better remembered by watching the videos than by what they personally experienced. Soon the two couples were ushered into the Bride's room as the chapel emptied. It was the only time since they had met eighteen months ago

14

that nobody seemed to want to say anything, instead being merely content to look into their spouse's eyes and dream about the future.

Then came the knock at the door and soon they were walking outside where five pairs of officers faced each other, swords drawn in an arch with the blades facing into the wind.

"Mr. and Mrs. Mark Baker, Mr. - Mrs. Luke Brisbane. Passage for a Kiss," echoed off the stone walls and across the crowd that was busy snapping pictures.

After the new brides each kissed their husband, the next set of swords was lowered and the set behind them was raised until they had exchanged five long kisses and they had navigated the gauntlet.

"Welcome to the Navy, Mrs. Baker. Welcome to the Navy, Mrs. Brisbane," echoed off the stones again as each was greeted with a round of thunderous applause that didn't diminish until the photographers ushered the newlyweds away to the Super's Gardens for shots.

What was unexpected was the spectacular reception that followed at the Officers Club with guests continually tapping their glasses until the couples were taunted into a full makeout session, complete with "Love by the Dashboard Lights" blasting through the building. Finally, in an attempt to quiet the well-wishers, the couples jumped up on a nearby table and began lip-syncing the words and taunting each other suggestively until the metal legs gave way and sent the four spilling across the hardwood floor.

This excited the crowd even more as they tapped their glasses louder and began shouting "Crash and Burn, baby. Crash and Burn!"

•••

Those memories were thirteen years old now and didn't break the two pilots focus today as they continued across the flight deck toward their F/A-18 Hornets.

Once there, Mark climbed the curved metal ladder designed to wrap around the fuselage without touching its shiny aluminum skin. Stopping on the fourth step, he looked aft at the twin tails. Like usual, his maintenance crew had pulled an all-nighter patching up his baby and the ragged cut on the starboard tail from yesterday's mission.

Satisfied, he reached into the cockpit and dropped his helmet on the ejection seat, which was an engineering nightmare he hoped he would never have to test. Since it sported more red warning tags than anything else on the plane it was easy to figure out that it was dangerous.

15

In fact, one of these seats had killed a tech on the last cruise when the seat he was kneeling on blasted him into the overhead of the hangar deck. The investigative board that convened after the accident had some hunches about what had happened, but the only thing for certain was that the poor kid was turned into applesauce. Knowing that it could kill you as quickly as it could save your life, Mark always treated these seats with respect.

After climbing back down to the deck, he started his inspection of the engine intake on the port side and watched the turbine blades spinning slowly - powered by the wind blowing down the deck. Next on his list was the forward landing gear and tire assembly. Not much to look for except leaking hydraulic fluid from the massive shock absorbers, cut electrical wires, and tire wear. Everything looked okay here, but Mark knew that if the pressure in the catapult was set too high, the whole assembly could be ripped right off the plane on takeoff.

Next on his list was the M61 Vulcan Gatling gun and ATFLIR targeting pod. After satisfying himself that everything was in order he walked back and checked the leading edge of the port wing and the AGM-88 HARM air-to-surface missile attached under it.

Mark ducked under the belly and pushed against the thousand-pound CBU-97 cluster bomb on the center line to insure it was snug. When he sure it wasn't going to fall off on launch, he walked to the rear of the plane. While he was there he duck- walked over to the rear landing gear that looked strangely like the bent leg of an Imperial Walker. On landing it was built to withstand the Hornet's loaded weight during a dead drop from twenty feet. Walking aft of the plane gave Mark the perspective of a gnat looking directly down the business end of a double barrel shotgun with twin poly-chokes.

The slightly concave stripes on the Hornet could be pushed together to constrict the flow of exhaust gasses, giving the plane more control than conventional static exhausts. Considering the abuse these plates took it was amazing that only a slight discoloration caused by carbon buildup marred their surface.

Moments later the carrier turned into the wind and a thirty-five knot wind began buffeting him as he completed his check. As he walked back to the ladder, the wind blowing through his hair reminded him of zipping along atop his Harley on his daily runs between Silver Spring and the Naval Academy at Annapolis where he taught when he was stateside.

Soon he was sitting in the seat while his crew chief held his helmet and helped him get strapped into the Hornet. Once done he switched on the electronics and began listening to the tower bark orders to the Search and Recovery helicopters.

Looking through the cockpit plexiglass, Mark saw his chief giving him the thumbs up signal and waving at him. Now that he had a couple of minutes before the launch sequence started he focused on a picture of Amy with their two children, Samantha and Josh, now four and twelve, respectively. The picture was taken almost a year ago, but it was his favorite and destined to remain glued to the bulkhead until he returned home and began teaching again.

He knew that being married to a Navy pilot hadn't been easy for Amy since he was away as much as he was home. Hopefully in another eight years they could move away to some quiet rancher by a lake and he would be there to make up for all the birthdays and anniversaries he'd missed.

As he heard the planes ahead of him checking in, Mark pushed those thoughts away and focused on today's mission. Looking farther down the line, he saw a heat plumb build on the last SAR helicopter.

"Six Two Zero. Cleared to lift. Spot 3. Report established SAR, Say REDLIGHT. Cleared to lift, REDLIGHT, three plus zero." The pilot answered back as the Search and Recovery helicopter lifted off.

As the plane next to him began firing up the first of its two jet engines, Mark checked in. "Tower. Stinger 24 Up on Deck. Ship's heading 230. Final bearing 220. Using Daytime Procedures. Altimeter 29.97." Engine Start Approved," the Air Boss replied.

In the old days, a Huffer would have been connected to the plane and compressed air would have been used to bring the engines up to starting speed, but the Hornets were self-starting and soon the screams of his F404-GE-402 engines joined in with the other twenty-two Hornets.

Before the wheel chocks were pulled. Mark punched 29.97 into his navigation computer and signaled the Boss. "Tower, Stinger two-four, up and ready, slot eight."

After watching Luke, who was two ahead of him, launch, the chocks wedged against his wheels were pulled out and a Blue Shirt began guiding him out of his parked position toward the white line that

17

marked the approach to catapult four. He stopped about 30 feet behind the plane and waited. As soon as that plane was hooked-up and ready, the foot-thick blast plate separating the two aircraft was raised to keep Mark from being cooked by the blast of the jet about to takeoff. As the plane disappeared, Mark counted off the seconds, and then relaxed when he saw it begin climbing and banking left.

The blast plates were lowered and it was his turn. Mark applied some thrust and pulled forward until a raised fist from the yellow shirted Director told him to stop. Sitting there like a kid waiting for the best rollercoaster in the world to start, Mark smiled as he watched the wheel locking mechanism glide back down the track in the deck toward him until it disappeared.

Unseen from the cockpit a Green Shirt connected the launch bridle to the front wheel assembly of Mark's Hornet. Then he watched carefully as the Yellow Shirt called for tension that jerked the nose of the jet down and a couple of inches forward. Once he was convinced that the jet was ready for takeoff, the Green Shirt sprinted off to safety as the Yellow Shirt motioned for Mark to rev up his engines. Before pushing the throttles forward he moved the twin swept-back tail fins quickly through their maximum ranges then set them for takeoff. Doing the same with the tail rudder, he settled back into the seat and waited for the quick salute and kick in the pants that meant he was on his way.

Unfortunately just before Mark was launched a gust of wind blew the hat off one of the pretty new female officers who was standing with a small group of newly assigned officers observing flight operations. As she bent over and began chasing her hat the motion caught Mark's attention and caused him to turn his head slightly. This moved his helmet off-center and an inch away from the foam cushion behind him. When the Hornet began to accelerate down the last three hundred feet of the carrier in two seconds his head was thrown back hard giving him a dull headache.

By the time he reached the refueling rendezvous point sixty miles away the pain in his head had traveled down and settled in his neck. Inside his helmet he rocked his head quickly back and forth in an attempt to relieve the tightness, but it didn't help much. He knew the only thing that would help would be to take his helmet off and administer some quick chiropractic adjustments himself, but that wasn't going to happen until he took on the first of two fuel loads.

Luke had already leveled off at 5,000 feet and was hooked up to the port basket trailing the tanker when Mark arrived. So Mark lined up the vacant starboard station. He flipped the switch that extended the stinger's refueling nozzle and began slowly moving in until he was hooked-up and fuel began flowing into his tanks. This was a lot trickier than the movies made it look as he constantly had to keep tweaking the controls as the Hornet's weight increased. Luke unhooked and drifted back then maneuvered his plane around Mark's to patiently wait for his buddy. When Mark was fueled they veered off and began a climb to twenty-five thousand feet looking for their marker pilot.

Commander Robb Jackson in his Tomcat watched the two coming up from the tanker on his computer screen and verified they were both squawking the correct code.

"Striker two-four, open your data link for a weather update."

"Roger, Jack-o One, data link opened." Mark replied.

By the time they leveled off at 25,000, Mark's neck was really beginning to bother him again so he tried snapping his head back and forth a couple of times before giving up on that technique. Next he tried leaning forward and then banging his head back against the seat, which actually seemed to help until he heard Luke's voice over the radio.

"What the hell are you doing in there – dancing the Watusi?"

Mark looked over and waved. "No, I got a crick in my neck from watching one of those new females chase her hat down the flight deck. She looked Bangkok hot from my angle."

"You keep banging against that seat and you may end up blasting yourself into history, as the first pilot to ever auto-eject in the middle of a dance at twenty-five thousand. Remember that fucking AIMD tech who ejected himself into the overhead of the hangar deck last month?"

Mark finally gave up, took a deep breath, removed his helmet and placed it on his left knee. Then he grabbed his chin with one hand and the top of his head with the other and pushed on his head until he heard a loud pop.

After gently pushing his head back into the helmet, he smiled at Luke and gave him the thumbs-up sign. "Damn that feels a lot better."

Forty-five minutes later they passed Baghdad and began descending toward the second tanker. Soon they were connected and taking on fuel that would give them an hour of combat time over Mosul. Today they were there to support ground troops hot on the trail of a local rebel leader claiming that he was responsible for shooting down a fighter in the area last week.

•••

Oblivious to the plans of the Americans, Jaber and two fellow terrorists were setting up operations twenty-eight miles south of Mosul in hopes of shooting down another jet.

While the United States relied on the world's most sophisticated equipment, the terrorists had done quite well with the triangular "listening ears" they had created by simply digging out dry dirt to create a concave hole much like an old wooden bowl. To make it lethal all they needed was a couple of shoulder-launched missiles nearby. Each pit was carefully measured to be 60 feet in diameter and hemispherical in shape, with the equilateral points of the triangle roughly 1,000 feet apart.

The terrorists had learned how to do this by reading books about the Vietnam War. The North Vietnamese Army had done this to target U.S. fighters and bombers. Some simple reading of history and what was old was new again.

A battery-powered telephone system had been set up between each pit so that no radiation would be given off that could be detected by the Americans.

On a calm day this allowed the terrorists to hear a plane 20 miles away. By moving around inside a pit it was easy to calculate the plane's direction and know which way to aim the missile. Another added advantage was that each pit was relatively deep, which offered protection from everything except a direct hit.

As an added incentive the terrorists had pushed and pulled together some wrecked military vehicles into what looked from the air like a small group of juicy targets. They had even created some stick figures and dressed them up to look like rebels to entice the Americans closer. Next was the gray smoke flares stuffed into the exhausts of each vehicle that gave the appearance the convoy was starting the engines and about to move out.

Wires from the flares had been buried in the dirt and ran to a simple board with nails sticking out of it that had been connected to the positive side of an old truck battery. Jaber only had to run a short piece of wire from the other terminal down the row of nails to ignite the flares.

20

It was late afternoon and Jaber was lying on a dirty old blanket enjoying the cool shade half asleep, when he heard the faint sounds of the jets coming in from the south. Without getting up, he rolled over and reached for the battery powered handset nearby then pressed the ringer. When he got two short buzzes back from the other two "Listening Holes" he knew they were ready.

"Isnilon. Turn on one of those emergency radios for one minute then turn it off again."

Inside the blockish building at the center of the triangle, Isnilon smiled as he set the phone down and walked back toward the center of the room where two American pilots, suspended from the rafters by ropes binding their wrists and ankles, cringed at the sound of boots coming closer.

Switching on one of their AN/PRC-149 Personal Location Beacons he spoke to them in an overly friendly voice. "Looks like you two may be getting company today."

•••

Within seconds the beacon was picked up by a SARSAT satellite and relayed to the United States Mission Control Center (USMCC) in Suitland, Maryland. From there it was automatically relayed to the Air Combat Command's Combat Search and Rescue at Langley Air Force Base in Virginia where Timothy McFadden was on duty.

Timothy had just snapped a rubber band at his buddy sitting at the desk in front of him when he noticed that an emergency locator signal alert began flashing on his monitor in bright red letters. Immediately becoming very serious he turned the volume up on his headphone and listened as the voice synthesizer built into the AN/PRC-149 back in Iraq began mechanically reading out coordinates.

"PLB A1279-7924-6214 Coordinates: 35 degrees, 54 minutes, 20.7 seconds North; 43 degrees, 11 minutes, 40.47 seconds East."

Timothy punched the beacon's serial number into his computer and smiled when it confirmed it belonged to one of the missing pilots. When the picture of the pilot popped up on his display, he grabbed the image and passed it into the Incident Report Form that the computer had begun filling out when the information first started coming in. Then he punched in the latitude and longitude and turned his attention to a third monitor that showed a view of Earth as seen from a geo-synchronous orbit 22,000 miles out in space.

As it zoomed in and stopped a big red X flashed on the top of the roof of a very white building. The view was too tight for Timothy to see much more than that one building, so he maneuvered the mouse and zoomed back out. He was now looking at a small farming settlement built along the western side of a small creek that flowed south until it finally disappeared.

The red X flashed over the smaller white building as Timothy stood and caught the eye of his supervisor. "Captain Davis, over here, ma'am."

As the attractive blond tucked tightly into her Air Force uniform turned and walked toward Timothy she wondered what the hell was going on as he danced from foot to foot with of look of anticipation. The young corporal could barely contain himself and started speaking before she got close enough to actually hear his first few words. ". . .and I worked a double shift to help find those pilots?"

"Timothy, calm down and take a breath," she said trying not to smile.

"Remember last week when that Hornet went down and I worked a double shift to help find the pilots?" Timothy said anxiously.

"The Super Hornet attached to the Regan?" Davis asked to be sure she was locked into the conversation.

Timothy was so excited that he actually reached out and took her hand, pulling her over to his station. "Yes, the one that went down south of Mosul."

Since he was so excited she thought it was best to forgive the transgression Timothy had just committed when he had touched her. "Damn it Timothy. What the hell are you talking about?"

"I just got a beacon flash from one of their PRC-149. They are right here," he said pointing to the display.

"Do you still have the signal?" Davis asked as she bent over the desk and stared at the red X flashing on the white building.

A look of disappointment flashed on Timothy's face. "No, it only lasted long enough for me to punch the information into the report form, but it's on the log if you want to hear it."

Without waiting Timothy jumped into his seat and opened the audio log looking for the exact time the message had first arrived. By the time he found it and playing the first few seconds through the computer's speakers, Captain Davis was convinced that this was the real McCoy.

After verifying the numbers had been entered correctly, Davis sprang into action.

"Timothy, bring it up on the big board. People, we've got a situation here. An emergency beacon transmission was just received and verified. Let's get in gear. "

●●●

Minutes later the information had been passed up the line and preparations for a joint rescue mission had been put together. The information hopped around the world to the Regan, then bounced up to the Hawkeye communications plane with its disc-shaped antennae and back down to Jacko's Tomcat.

As the two Hornets hadn't been able to find anything to shoot at around Mosul, Mark and Luke had begun flying low and fast hoping someone on the ground would take a shot at them - thus giving them a perfect excuse to blast the hell out of them.

After verifying the message from the Hawkeye Jacko clicked on his transmit button. "Striker 24, you and Luke get back up here. I've just gotten a message that puts downed pilots thirty five miles south of here. We've been ordered to take a look and hold over the area until the extraction team arrives."

Five minutes later they arrived at the coordinates, pulled back the throttle and began to slowly circle the area at 25,000 feet.

"I'm going down to take a closer look," Luke said.

He cut in his after burners and headed off toward the southeast. A minute later he executed an inverted power dive, pulling out level 500 feet above the dusty brown farmland. Traveling at Mach 1.1, he checked to be sure he was still headed for the coordinates he'd punched into his navigation computer on the way to the site.

Then he took a quick peak in the convex mirrors giving him a distorted view aft. He laughed as he saw shockwaves traveling along the ground behind him. Like the wake behind a boat on a calm lake, it kicked dirt a hundred feet into the air. Thinking that more is always better, Luke nudged the throttles and watched the dust cloud grow a little higher.

As Jaber lay on his blanket about to light a cigarette the sky was turning from dark blue to a lighter purple.

"Maybe another day." He muttered, striking a match.

From above, Luke's plane looked like a tiny silver splinter stuck into the handle of a beautiful brown fan that obliterated everything behind it. As it moved across the compound toward the white square, its target seemed to vanish. The splinter became a point and began to grow bigger as it powered straight up and the fan it was dragging slowly melted - revealing what it had covered.

The Listening Hole did exactly what it had been designed to do and amplified the sonic boom – focusing its power to the bottom of the pit. When the dust finally settled, Jaber regained consciousness. As he steadied his head with his hands, little streams of blood from his ears and nose ran down his face. Then the silence hit him and he clapped his hands together, but heard nothing.

Inside the building, Isnilon had faired much better. Even though the dirt inside made it impossible to see for more than a few feet, he had managed to find the stack of Anza MKII shoulder launched missiles. Racing against time, he opened a case, grabbed the contents and ran outside.

Ten seconds later he was ready and waiting as the glint off Mark's plane coming in from a slightly different angle caught his eye. Knowing his best chance was to wait until the plane passed, Isnilon stepped back inside the building and closed the door.

After the sonic blast shook the building again, Isnilon ran outside, hoisted the forty pound launcher to his shoulder and pressed the trigger. Three seconds later the eleven pound MKII missile fired and he threw the useless launcher to the ground.

Jacko, who had been watching the two planes buzz the compound, got a launch warning from his thermal imaging system. "Striker Two Four. You've got company hot and fast on your tail. Get the hell out of there."

By the time Mark got the message the MKII missile's dual band infrared seekers had passively locked onto his Hornet. Since the MKII didn't use active pinging, Mark would have never known death was on the way without Jacko's message.

Looking back in his mirrors, he spotted the smoke trail from the solid fuel sustainer rocket, which meant the rocket had already attained its Mach two cruising speed and was closing on him. Pushing his Hornet to the limit gave him some more time, but even then the MKII

24

would eventually reach him unless he could keep it in the air until it ran out of fuel.

Running out of options fast, Mark pointed his Hornet at the sun and accelerated to full throttle. Then he killed the after burners, reduced power and dove toward the ground. For a second the MKII continued flying straight as the fuel inside the Pakistani manufactured missile continued to burn, but as soon as the Chinese electronics realized its target was the Sun, it started looking for the signature left by the Hornet.

Mark pulled up a hundred feet from the ground. He could see where the exhaust trail from the MKII had stopped. A couple of seconds later he relaxed when it self-destructed. By the time he realized that he was heading directly back toward the compound, it was too late. A moment later a second MKII raced past him and the three pound HE fragmentation warhead exploded 100 feet behind the Hornet, taking out the electronics and both engines. The crippled jet began a slow roll that increased quickly pinning, Mark against the right bulkhead. As he reached for the ejection lever his arm became useless as the G-forces increased. The last thing he saw before blacking out was the picture of Amy and his two children smiling back at him.

Chapter 4
Arlington

As Amy and her family sat in the green velvet chairs provided by the staff at Arlington National Cemetery, she could hear the crowd behind them talking in low voices and snapping pictures. On the way in she had been greeted by many she recognized and several she'd never seen before.

It was the last day of June, but felt more like the middle of July as Amy sat there with Samantha on her left and Joshua on the right between her and her father, Duke. Together, the three represented all the family she had left in the world now that Mark was gone. During the two weeks she had time to think about their life together. She had expected to be sad, but slowly became more and more angry.

Amy was angry at herself for not insisting more strongly that Mark get out of the Navy. Ever since 911, she had felt it was just a matter of time before those crazy assholes struck again. But no, whenever she had pleaded with him he just smiled and made some kind of lame joke. Hell, sitting here wasn't even safe. She remembered the debris from the Pentagon had fallen on the cemetery after the 911 attack.

All she wanted from that day on was for Mark to become a professor at some Podunk little college out in the boondocks. Some place where they could swim and fish with the kids without worrying every time they heard a jet. But now it was too late to do that with Mark.

As she felt a trickle of sweat run down her back she took a quick look at her watch, which seemed to be stuck at one twenty-five. Why wouldn't the damned thing get to one-thirty?

Behind the crowd a ground controller using a discrete frequency keyed the microphone button on a rather large transceiver with a two foot antenna. "This is Arlington GC to Honors one. What's your status?"

"Arlington GC Honors One is up and away. We'll be in your vicinity in twenty"

When Amy heard the radio conversation behind her a flash of anger whipped through her as the ground controller continued to chatter way with the pilot. Pulling herself back together, she realized it wasn't the military that was the problem. It was her.

As she went through a long list of grievances she'd been carrying around for the past two weeks, Amy began eliminating the trivial ones, paring down the items until she began getting closer to the problem that had been eating at her core.

It wasn't the fact she would never be able to hold Mark in her arms again. Hell, she'd gotten so accustomed to doing things over the past thirteen years by herself that it took her a couple of days just to get use to having him around when he came back from a tour.

When she finally hit on the answer she was surprised. She was raging inside because she hadn't had the chance to say goodbye. Hell, even Luke must have had a few seconds to do that. But she never would.

Leaning over Josh, Amy whispered into her father's ear. "God damn it Dad, when are they going to get this show on the road?"

Her father looked back at her and squeezed her hand a couple of times. "It'll just be another minute or two, Baby."

Then he turned back and looked at the empty hole in front of him and closed his eyes to keep the tears inside. Sitting there in his white dress uniform with four rows of ribbons, he looked hard as nails. No one in the crowd who didn't know him would have ever guessed that he had retired from the Navy over twenty years ago. Or that the only thing he got to fly these days was model airplanes with his grandson, Josh.

Still he hadn't won all the ribbons he was sporting for just flying around Vietnam in his Phantom. He had killed hundreds from the air by dropping napalm and low-level release bombs with airbrakes, which usually gave him time to get away before they hit the ground. He had engaged in aerial dogfights and blasted enemy tanks, trucks and outposts with missiles to protect the ground troops. And during all that combat he had only received a couple of injuries.

Sitting there next to Josh, he wondered what it had felt like for Mark. Was it quick or painfully slow? As he reached up and brushed his eye he knew one thing for sure. He was going to have to step up to the plate and become more like a father and less like a grandpa to Amy's children.

Putting his arm around Josh, he asked "How are you doing?"

"Fine Pop-pop, but I'll be glad when it's over and we can go home."

Secretly, Josh wondered how his grandfather could have so many metals and still be alive when his dad only had a few and was dead. It

27

was a question that many adults would have asked in anger, but to him it was just a question – nothing more.

In fact Josh was excited his dad was going to receive the Navy Cross, the Nation's second highest metal during the ceremony. It was for his part in helping the two pilots who had been captured and tortured. It meant, at least in that respect, that his dad had caught up to his grandfather.

Samantha on the other hand was too young to understand very much of what was going on. She knew it was important and had promised to be on her best behavior, but when the bagpipes began playing "Amazing Grace", she spun around in her chair to watch the piper.

Before standing up, Amy pulled her gently back around. "Best behavior, remember? Now stand beside me and put your right hand over your heart."

"Yes mommy, best behavior," she replied with a giggle. Then she pulled her legs back under the chair, swung them out and jumped down beside her mother.

"Mommy, I hear the horses coming," She said a little too loudly and immediately drew her hands up to cover her mouth. "Sorry."

The caisson with Mark's flag draped casket was being pulled toward them by a matched team of six black horses. Army soldiers sat atop the three horses farthest away from the crowd gathered at the funeral site.

When the caisson finally settled to a stop, the Non-Commissioned Officer in Charge (NCOIC) yelled "Present Arms." The Navy Chaplain snapped a salute that was mirrored by all of the military in attendance. Most of the civilians put their right hand over their hearts, but a few couldn't resist snapping photos as the ceremony began.

The chaplain waited for the six uniformed pallbearers to slide the casket out of the caisson and grip it firmly before he turned and led them to the grave site. After making a few minor adjustments to the flag the NCOIC barked "Order Arms," as the music ended.

As Amy listened to the chaplain it seemed as if she had Attention Deficit Disorder because the words from one sentence triggered thoughts that didn't quit fit together with the next. In fact by the time it was over she couldn't remember anything he had said.

When the benediction began, the Arlington ground controller contacted the Honors leader again. "Arlington GC to Honors One. Fly over in three minutes."

"Honors One. Roger. Three Minutes. Give me three one second clicks when you're ready."

"Arlington GC, roger - three clicks."

When the chaplain finished the benediction he backed away and the NCOCI stepped forward and saluted. Then the NCOIC barked orders to the seven seamen holding rifles "Firing Party, Port Arms. Prepare to fire."

The Arlington ground controller began keying his microphone as each volley rolled across the cemetery. "Ready, aim, fire." Not even a half-second, then, again. "Aim, fire. Aim, fire." Then, "Present Arms." On the final shot, the NCOCI stopped saluting and Taps began to play as the casket slipped slowly into the ground.

Amy and the children looked up as the sound of jets raced toward them. A moment later four Hornets, flying in a V formation, appeared over the tree line, which caused Samantha to forget all her promises about acting like a lady. She pulled away from her mother, and before Amy could react, Josh caught up with his little sister and stopped her from going any farther. He reached over and held her hand as the jets became bigger and noisier.

As they watched, the second plane from the left cut formation and raced straight up, disappearing in the puffy white clouds high over head.

When its sonic boom crashed to the ground a few seconds later, Amy thought, "That's got to be Luke." And she smiled for the first time that day, as she imagined the anxiety that would cause the locals and the reprimand that would no doubt appear in his service jacket.

When the flyover ended, Samantha broke away from Josh and ran back to her mother squealing in her most excited voice. "Did you see daddy up there? He's flying up to heaven."

Those few words acted like a trigger that finally released all the emotions that had been bottled up inside Amy for the past two weeks and her eyes filled with tears as she hugged Samantha and began sobbing.

By the time the flag had been folded she had regained some of her composure, but was still shaking when the NCOIC bowed and handed the folded flag to her.

Josh sat very still as he was presented with his own pre-folded flag and he couldn't hold back a tear that fell from his right eye onto one of the stars.

Samantha was almost dancing when she was handed her flag. "Mommy, I got one too," she whispered holding it up for Amy to see.

"Yes you did. Now you need to put it in a special place so it won't ever get lost," Amy said before leaning over and kissing her.

Samantha hugged the flag. "Yes I will always keep it safe for daddy."

Before the crowd began to disperse the Arlington Ladies gave each of the family members a special card of condolences to mark the end of the ceremony.

Normally the service would have been over in ten to twelve minutes, but the presentation of the Navy Cross and the flyover stretched it to almost half an hour.

"Amy, I have to go home and pick up the kids and Luke - if he isn't in the brig, before we come over. So I was thinking that you might want to be alone with your Dad on the way home." Wendy said picking up Samantha.

"Oh, Mommy, can we? I want to show Megan my flag," Samantha asked with a smile.

"Well I don't know. What will the neighbors say when I come home without my kids?" Amy said smiling back at Samantha.

Josh walked up beside his mother and put his arm around her waist. "It's okay. I'd kind of like to see Ethan. That flyover was great and besides you need a break before all those people show up for the party."

Amy gave him a big kiss, which he didn't even pull away from as he grabbed her and squeezed his arms around her.

Pulling him back so she could look into his eyes, she asked "Are you sure it'll be okay?"

"I'll be fine Mom. You take care of Grandpa. I saw him crying today. He needs you right now."

"What about you? I could have sworn I saw a few tears from you, too."

Josh flashed her one of his best freckle face smiles. "What do you expect, I'm a kid. Old men aren't supposed to cry."

"That does it," Wendy said as she grabbed Josh's hand and began walking toward her car. "I'll see you around three."

When Amy turned around she saw that the crowd had thinned out and the ones that stayed expected to talk to her before they departed. As she walked over and begin accepting condolences, she kept an eye on

30

her father who was standing with a few of his buddies exchanging stories of long past glories.

Ten minutes later, after Amy said her last goodbye, she turned and saw her dad standing by the grave looking down. When she walked over and put her hand on his shoulder, he flinched.

"Sorry dad, I didn't mean to sneak up on you." Amy said rubbing his neck.

"You could have given an old man whiplash yanking him back from forty years in the past like that," Duke said. He turned and gave her a great big hug, rocking back and forth on his feet.

When Amy closed her eyes and felt the love from her father she was transported back in time herself. She was five or six standing on her father's shoes as he danced her around the kitchen to a tune playing on the radio. Life was so simple then, she thought as she let go and just enjoyed the memory.

Kissing him once more, she took his hand and they walked silently back to the limo that was waiting to drive them back to Silver Spring.

After one last look back as they rolled down Memorial Drive, Amy turned to her father with a serious look on her face that the old man recognized all too well.

"Listen Dad, you know how I feel about living here and that I've wanted to move for years. The only reason we're still here is because every time I tried to light a fire under Mark's ass, he'd come up with some silly excuse until he was off on a tour again. Well, now he's gone, and I'm begging you to help me find some place in the middle of nowhere where the kids and I can be safe."

Duke took her hand and sighed. "I don't think there are too many places left that are as safe as you imagine. Sure Washington and New York were hit the last time, but who's to say one of the sand fleas won't dump a bottle of poison in some unprotected reservoir out in the middle of Nebraska or in a water park in Orlando. There just isn't any place left that's really truly safe."

Amy withdrew and said. "God damn it, Dad I'm begging for you to help me." Then she started crying.

When he reached for her she began flailing her arms at him, but as he continued to block her punches they slowed and in the end she grabbed hold of him and sobbed.

Twenty minutes later the limo stopped in the driveway at the end of the Burnt Mills cul-de-sac and they emerged. Amy's makeup and hair were a mess and Duke's left shoulder was painted a pale pink.

As they looked at each other they both said "You're a mess," at the same time and laughed.

From the cars Amy spotted she knew that Nicole and Tom had arrived early and the food would be laid out and waiting when they walked in. For a Navy SEAL, Tom was an excellent cook and for years he had talked about opening his own restaurant when he retired. Nicole, her second best friend from college, always kidded him about it – usually ending the conversation with, "Who's going to buy hors d'ouevres from a black man. We need to open a rib joint."

As they walked in the side door it smelled like Tom had taken Nicole's advice today. The smell of barbecued ribs permeated the house. Hearing voices in the dining room, Amy snuck over to the stove, grabbed the tongs and dropped four ribs on a plastic plate.

"Dad, you've got to try one of Tom's ribs."

Seeing the barbeque sauce dripping from the rib Amy was eating, he backed away. "Those things look messy as hell," he whispered backing up as she advanced toward him like Frankenstein smacking her lips.

"Come on, Dad. You already look like you've spent the night with some floozy. Enjoy."

Defensively, Duke grabbed a rib, then bent over and took a small bite.

Before he could give his opinion, Nicole and Tom walked in carrying some half-filled bags of assorted chips.

"See Tom, I told you. Ribs are your specialty," Nicole said as she threw her bags on the counter and rushed over to Amy.

"These are pretty good. I thought the only things SEALS could cook were rats and monkeys," Duke said as he took the plate from Amy.

"No monkeys today, but if you hear any of your neighbors complaining about a missing cat or small dog, don't pay any attention to them." Tom said grabbing two iced beers from a large plastic tub in the corner.

Twisting the caps off, he handed one to Duke. "You'd better take one of these, 'cause once the spices start working you'll want something to put out the fire."

"Good idea." Duke went to the stove and piled some more ribs on the plate.

"Let's sneak out to the sun room and polish these babies off before everyone else gets here. You two all right with that?" Duke asked turning his head back toward the girls as he started walking away.

"Sure Dad, you and Tom enjoy yourselves. I've got to change clothes anyway."

When Amy turned around, Nicole had disappeared, but soon returned with two glasses filled with white wine. "From the looks of you, you better have one of these before you go jump in the shower and relax a bit."

Amy tilted the glass and enjoyed the cool wine as it flowed down her throat. "Better get me another glass. This one seems to have a hole in it," Amy said waving her empty glass at Nicole.

Nicole took the glass and was about to go back and refill it when Steve walked in through the door carrying a case of beer in each hand.

"I picked up a couple more cases on the way over. Where do you want them?"

Nicole pointed toward the tub. "Just sit them down over there. We'll stick them in when it starts to get low."

Steve strolled over to the corner and put them down. Then he picked over the bottles and cans in the tub until he found one he liked.

"Got a bottle opener?" he said walking towards them.

Amy grabbed one from a drawer, opened the bottle and then ushered him into the sun room.

"Daddy, you remember Steve from Georgetown, don't you?"

Duke looked up and immediately felt his belly jiggle as he stifled a laugh. He wiped the barbeque sauce off his hands, stood up, and shook Steve's hand. "How could I forget the flame of your freshman year? Come on in and relax, you old dog. How have you been? This is my friend Tom…"

As Amy turned back toward the kitchen she saw Nicole standing in the doorway with a big smile on her face holding two full wine glasses. Amy took her glass. Nicole nodded her head, and then the two headed for the bedroom talking in whispers.

Once inside the room, Nicole jumped on the bed and Amy closed the door, leaning back against it. Then they both burst into laughter.

Nicole was the first to regain her composure. "Old dog is right. Steve had been sniffing around you like an old hound dog ever since you dumped him for Mark."

"Come on now. I only run into him at church or at the mall once in a while." Amy said trying to maintain a straight face.

"Sniff! Sniff," Nicole blurter out, as a new wave of laughter spread through her.

"Didn't you tell me he stopped over after that big storm in March?"

"Yes, but he only wanted to make sure that the electricity was back on and the pilot light on the water heater was on," Amy said with conviction.

By the time Amy had gotten her shower and dressed most of the guests had arrived. She spent the next hour mingling, as best she could, as couple after couple waited for the proper moment to offer their condolences.

Suddenly Wendy and Luke appeared with the kids and the celebration started in earnest. Amy gave Samantha and Josh each a big hug and listened to their stories of what they had done with Megan and Ethan.

She stood up and gave Wendy a big hug, saying "I'm so glad you took the kids."

"And you," she said giving Luke a kiss on the cheek, "I thought you would be in the brig for a week after that stunt this afternoon."

"He did make the afternoon news," Wendy said proudly.

"Local?" ask Amy.

"Oh yes. The incident made all the local stations. CNN too!" Wendy said as she poked him in the ribs.

"CNN," Amy said pursing her lips, "I guess that marks the end of a promising career."

"He's already resigned his commission," Wendy announced. "But I don't think they'll accept it, since the news piece spent more time talking about the rescued pilots than they did about the gridlock at the 911 communications center."

"Hope not. Still, he'd look so cute in one of those little commercial airline outfits." Amy teased.

"That does it. Where's your Dad hanging out?" Luke said grabbing a beer.

"He's in the sun room, Captain. When do we get to Orlando?"

"Come on boys. Let's go join the real men." Luke said tossing them each a soda and giving Amy a disgusted look.

The boys didn't have to be asked twice. They wanted to join the group of military heroes camped out in the sun room and didn't waste any time scampering after Luke who had already disappeared.

By eight o'clock everyone except the military encampment in the sun room had once again expressed their condolences and departed. When Steve finally couldn't stand listening to another war story, he said goodbye to Duke and the others and went to look for Amy.

He found her slouched down on the couch drunk as she tried to direct Wendy and Nicole, equally plastered, in their vain attempt to tidy the living room.

Pulling Amy up, Steve hugged her goodbye and whispered in her ear. "If you need any help cleaning up in the morning, give me a call and I'll come over," he said with a smile and left.

Amy stood there for a few seconds before collapsing back to the couch, calling to her father, "I want to go to bed."

"Okay guys, looks like the celebration is over." Duke said. Then he thought for a minute and continued. "Everybody get one last beer. I want to make a toast."

"Is there any more wine?" Nicole yelled at the top of her voice.

When everyone had a drink in their hand, Duke raised his bottle high and began, "I'd just like to say that the best years of my life began when Mark came into our family. He was a little wild and rough around the edges, but he gave me two of the best grandkids in the world and always looked out for his friends. I'm really going to miss that old bastard. And by the looks of her, Amy will miss him in the morning when she sobers up again."

After clinking their drinks together and downing the contents, the girls took Amy into the bedroom and dumped her into a pair of pajamas. While they were tending to Amy, Luke made an executive decision. He put all the sleeping kids in his SUV and announced that they were spending the night at his house. The house emptied, until only Duke and Amy were left.

As he sat on the side of the bed looking at her, he brushed the hair away from her face and kissed her.

"Dad, I'm drunk."

"That's the best way to be on a night like this, baby. Luke and Wendy have the kids. I'll pick them up and bring them home tomorrow. Do you understand?" he said kissing her forehead.

"Yep, Pop I got it. See you tomorrow. But you better make it in the afternoon the way I feel," she said pushing herself up on her elbows.

"And you better help me get out of this fucking town like you promised in the car today."

Duke smiled, resigned to the fact that he would do anything to make her happy. "Yes, baby, don't worry about that. A promise is a promise. Sweet dreams."

Chapter 5
War Driving

When they arrived in Mexico, Ahmed and Saif lived for several weeks in a low rent apartment on the north side of Mexico City. The first thing they did after renting the apartment was to shave off their beards. Ahmed laughed every time he remembered how silly they looked without them, but it was important to cultivate an even tan before continuing north.

Each day was the same as the last and consisted of spreading sun screen on the tan parts of their bodies then laying in the sun for longer and longer periods of time until they didn't need to use the sun screen any longer. They began to look more and more like the locals.

At night they would go out to dinner and hang out in a couple of low class bars - working on their Spanish and picking up the local slang from the hookers who were glad to grab a beer and joke with them between tricks. Finally, they were ready and boarded a bus for the long ride to Nuevo Laredo on the Texas border.

It didn't take them long to befriend an old man named Juan Garcia. Soon the three of them could be found in one of the brothels, cantinas, or bars in La Zona de Tolerancia section of the city almost any night. Within a week they had supplied Juan with enough cheap beer and rides on the local prostitutes to become trusted friends. So he wasn't surprised when he learned that they were interested in crossing the border into the United States.

The next Friday, Juan introduced Ahmed and Saif to a mysterious acquaintance of his. This friend supplied counterfeit documents to anyone wanting to cross the border and lacking the proper papers. Three days later Ahmed and Saif each paid a thousand dollars –American-- for an envelope containing a Border Crossing Card, birth certificate, and Texas driver license.

Knowing that they wanted to find work once they were in Texas, he promised them jobs driving cabs for his cousin in San Antonio if they were willing to work for a month without pay. Having heard the stories of the bodies found cooked in trucks that were left unattended; they were a little hesitant at first. After finding out that all they had to do was walk through the border crossing as common laborers, they agreed.

37

The plan was a little sketchy, but called for them to go to the corner of San Francisco and Hidalgo in Laredo, where a car would be waiting to drive them to his cousin's company in San Antonio. Since the two had enough money at their disposal to buy the cab company, they thought it was a good deal and plunked down another thousand to seal the deal.

Early the following Wednesday, Juan pulled up in a beat-up old Chevy. He drove them down San Dario Avenue toward the bridge leading to the border checkpoint until the car slowed to a stop in traffic.

"Listen, when we get closer you will need to get out of the car. Then I will drive through the inspection line and disappear. It is important for you to be close to the gate at seven-thirty, but do not try to cross through until the diversion starts," Juan said passing them a picture of the car and driver that would take them the rest of the way.

Then Juan pulled the car over and they got out.

"You think Juan is setting us up?" Ahmed asked as they watched the car pull away.

"Well, we are about to find out. It's either America or Guantanamo for us today," Saif said as he began to move into the crowd.

With their dark skin and worn clothing they blended in with the Mexican workers heading North, but inside they were each sure they were going to get caught. Watching the large clock at the checkpoint, they adjusted their pace and kept moving forward as others moved around them.

Ahead of them seven gates were opened for cars and three for foot traffic as the minute hand on the clock ticked to six. Suddenly a dozen people began shouting "Run for it. Now! Now! Now!"

In an instant something inside the usually well mannered workers clicked and they became a mob running through the checkpoints and disappearing down the streets and alleys on the other side.

Saif and Ahmed pretended to resist the crowd, even holding their Border Crossing Card high in the air as if trying to comply. A few minutes later, hot and sweaty, they jumped into an older model Ford sedan and were whisked away from the area.

•••

After six months of honing their driving skills in Texas, they moved on to Washington, DC.

•••

Today, as they sipped coffee in the break room of Independent Capital Cab Company, there was nothing to distinguish them from the other drivers waiting to start the morning shift. They had worked hard to stay inconspicuous. Not wanting to be the best or the worst drivers in the company they worked hard, never complained, and always came to work early.

They loved the idea of getting paid for driving around the nerve center of the nation that had put them on the Most Wanted List. They were still amazed that after all this time no one had come up and slapped a pair of handcuffs on them. The old adage of never looking right under your nose had certainly proven true in their case, so far, and they hoped it would continue until the end of the year.

"Have a good day, my brother," Saif said as Ahmed finished his coffee and tossed the paper cup into the trashcan at the end of the table.

"You too," Ahmed answered, as he picked up his metal briefcase and headed towards the door leading to the taxicabs parked behind the old brick building.

After checking his cab, Ahmed drove towards the Washington Monument where the pickings were usually good. As he drove along, the GPS antenna installed in the bubble on the roof constantly radioed his position back to dispatch center so they could track his every move. This lack of freedom was the reason that the seasoned professionals back at the company were not too anxious to get two new replacement vehicles on the road. In fact the company was finally forced to offer a cash incentive to drivers in order to get anybody inside the new vehicles.

Ahmed laughed every time he thought about how the two of them were getting paid an extra fifty dollars a week to let big brother watch them drive around the city. When the next light turned red, Ahmed stopped and slipped his laptop out of the briefcase, plugging one cord into the GPS system's USB maintenance port and the power cord into the cigarette lighter. Then, he opened the cover and pressed the power switch. Before the computer powered up the car behind him honked and he started moving again.

At the next red light he launched his Wardriving program and watched the display as it began searching for Wi-Fi wireless networks in the vicinity. The program's name was derived from the War Games movie, in which a telephone modem connected to a computer randomly dials phone numbers in hopes of connecting with another computer.

In Ahmed's case the program was searching for wireless network IP addresses. When it found one it recorded the latitude and longitude then matched the coordinates to the actual street address. Like a high-end version of the navigation systems available in cars, it worked flawlessly for the past six months. Together he and Saif had mapped eighty percent of the city inside the beltway, while on duty.

On the weekends when they weren't using their own cars to gather data they would drop their laptops into briefcases or backpacks and pretend they were tourists. After coming back from a tour, they were always surprised at how much additional data they had collected.

Each night they would drive to a coffee shop or bookstore offering free Wi-Fi connections and send their 'PointsOfInterest' data file to Mohammed in Jakarta. Some days the file contained thousands of unique IP Address location pairs. Other days might only contain a few hundred. But as the heat of summer baked the capital, they knew they had plenty of time to completely cover the thirty-mile circle radiating from the Capitol Building before the end of the year.

Chapter 6
The Recruiter

Fahid had taken the assignment partly to protect Abdullah, but mostly because he knew he was a better recruiter. After all, if it weren't for him, Ramzi would have never gone to Jersey City and built the bomb used in the first attack on the World Trade Center in ninety-three.

Fahid was always a little nervous in Baghdad, now that the Americans patrolled the streets. Sipping coffee in a small kiosk, he smiled to himself every time a convoy rolled by because he could tell by the look on their faces that they were more afraid than he was. As the war dragged on, each side discovered new ways to kill its enemy and appropriate countermeasures to minimize the effectiveness of the other's new strategies.

Tactics started out as 'hit and run' then progressed to 'lure, trap and shoot' and finally evolved into burying old munitions along streets, highways and mountain trails - Improvised Explosive Devices (IEDs), as America's President was so fond of calling them in his speeches.

Now soldiers rode around in Mine Resistant Ambush Protected vehicles. The V-shaped hulls under these vehicles deflected a blast from an IED under it to the sides. Convoys patrolled the streets with Counter Remote Control IED Electronic Warfare (CREW) devices, creating a dead zone around the vehicles that cell phones and toy controllers couldn't penetrate. To counter these the Al Qaeda leaders had simply moved the IED's into the walls and returned to using strings and wires to set them off; penny solutions to billion dollar improvements.

Fahid laughed when he read the American and British newspaper accounts of the IED attacks because they made it sound as if the Jihadist groups weren't fighting fairly. To him, that always sounded like a lot of crap. The school children in America were taught that one of the reasons the colonies beat the British was because the American colonists didn't march around in brightly colored uniforms in lines waiting for the Americans to come out and fight fairly. Instead the Americans snuck around in clothing that blended in with the forest and picked off the British one at a time.

Now it was American's turn to walk around and get picked off one at a time. In fact it was Fahid's sworn duty to be sure that happened. America faced a similar situation fighting a war far from home in unfamiliar territory with limited resources. In fact, since World War II, America had proven time and time again that it wasn't ready to fight a protracted war. As he sat there sipping coffee, Fahid prayed they would fail again in Iraq as they had in Cuba, Korea, and Vietnam.

Back in the early days it was easy to recruit people for Osama's global Jihad. All you had to do was ask, and hundreds would volunteer. It was so easy in fact, that Fahid had sometimes felt a little guilty taking advantage of their religious fervor to further bin Laden's war.

Today it was different. The war had come to his homeland and the Americans were there in full force - so the tactics had changed. Since many of the early fighters were either dead or too scared to fight, Fahid had begun recruiting young boys and women. Each group, eager to please, gladly donned explosive vests or pulled strings to blow up trucks and themselves.

Sitting in the kiosk today, Fahid was looking for a new type of martyr. Motivated by information that Adam had reported, he was willing to sit there all day if necessary. Fortunately it wasn't going to take that long. He looked up and saw Hamoodei coming down the street.

Fahid got up and greeted him as he walked slowly to the table. "Hamoodei my friend, how are you doing today?"

"The same as yesterday, I'm afraid, living from hand to mouth, like most of my brothers here." Hamoodei said gesturing out toward the crowded street.

Fahid ordered some more tea then turned his attention to Hamoodei. "I have heard something of your plight from others, but I would still like to hear it from you."

Hamoodei waited for the tea before he started. "I have lived in Baghdad for all of my fifty-two years. After marrying and having our second child, I opened a small bookstore. With my wife and daughter taking care of our modest home and my three sons working with me, we lived well by Iraqi standards and enjoyed simple and uncomplicated lives."

Waving the waiter over and ordering food, Fahid continued listening.

"During the first attack on Baghdad, the building where my bookstore was located was partially destroyed and what the American bomb left behind was quickly taken by looters and the weather. Not long after that bomb attack, two of my sons joined the Taliban to fight

42

the invaders. Since I have not seen or heard from them since they left, I assume they are dead. Yet, I still cling to the hope they will return one day."

Taking a sweet roll, Hamoodei tried not to eat it quickly, but it disappeared in three quick bites. "When the Americans began their second offensive on the city, my house was hit by a missile and reduced to a pile of bricks. On that day I managed to dig my wife and daughter out of the rubble with my bare hands. By the time I got them to the hospital my daughter was dead. My wife died an hour later."

Fahid filled the man's empty tea cup and passed him another sweet roll. "And your son?" He asked.

"I never found a trace of him." Hamoodei said as tears began trickling down he cheeks, "now I have nothing."

Fahid smiled sympathetically. "It's a sad story I've heard over and over. In another year the number of innocent civilians killed by the Americans will reach a million – and they complain about four thousand."

Hamoodei looked at Fahid with anger flashing in his eyes. "I hate them. But what can I do? They have everything and I don't even own a gun."

Fahid reached over and placed his hand on Hamoodei's shoulder. "What would you be willing to do in order to seek revenge?"

Hamoodei laughed like a madman. "There is nothing I can do. Should I attack them in the streets with a stick?"

Fahid moved around the table and pulled a chair close to Hamoodei. "There is a plan underway that will bring America to its knees. It is so much more than knocking down a couple of buildings and yet simple enough to succeed."

Hamoodei looked astounded. "What can I do to help?"

Fahid looked away for a few seconds before he continued. "In order for this plan to succeed I need to find a few people who are willing to die."

Hamoodei laughed. "I'm already dead. I've lost everything. I have no place to live and nothing to eat."

Fahid looked deep into the old man's eyes. "Before you agree you must know what is ahead. Before you hear more you need to decide if you are willing to die today or would rather simply walk away and forget about our meeting."

"Where am I supposed to go? I have nothing." The old man said quietly.

"Then come with me and I'll explain." Fahid stood and held out his hand.

Twenty minutes later they entered a safe house. While Hamoodei sat on a long couch, Fahid walked to the kitchen and poured coffee into two cups. Joining Hamoodei on the couch he reached under it and retrieved a large binder which he placed on the coffee table.

Opening the cover, Fahid pointed to the picture on the first page. It showed the head of a man that looked like he had been badly burned in a fire. His face was bright red and large patches of his hair were missing. Blood was oozing from his gums and mouth and it was plain to see he had been vomiting.

Hamoodei pulled the rings apart, took the picture out, and studied it closely. "Is this what the Americans will look like after the attack?"

"No, they will probably look quite a bit better than that. This is what you will look like a week after you begin powdering the material that will kill them."

Fahid reached behind him and put his hand on the pistol tucked under the cushion that he was sitting on and waited to see what Hamoodei was going to do next. If he tried to leave, Fahid would shoot him and have one of his underlings dump the body. On the other hand if he agreed to give up his life now to kill Americans later, he would take him to the stone quarry with the other six volunteers he had recruited over the past week.

"This will be painful?" Hamoodei asked.

"Yes, very painful," Fahid said.

"The plan will move ahead whether or not I participate?" Hamoodei asked tilting the photograph back and forth.

"I am sure we will get enough volunteers to continue." Fahid answered getting a better grip on the gun.

"And you are sure that many Americans will die?" Hamoodei asked putting the picture back into the binder and snapping the rings closed.

"Thousands will die." Fahid answered.

"Then I will do whatever you tell me to do," Hamoodei said as he relaxed and smiled.

Chapter 7
I Spy With My Little Eye

Over the next two weeks Abdullah and Fahid had managed to get the nuclear material into Iraq with a lot less trouble than they had experienced the first night in Kakhovka.

The original plan was to grind the material into a fine powder which could have been accomplished with a minimal loss of life by supporters of the Taliban. All this changed when they received the Plutonium. Now Fahid calculated that it was going to require an additional fifty volunteers/martyrs to process the material. Getting the bodies was not the problem that concerned him. The real problem was getting them to the bombed-out remains of the remote cement plant where they would be working - without attracting the attention of the Americans.

There was little they could do, except move between the passes of the spy satellites that swarmed over Iraq like mosquitoes at a summer picnic.

If they had been in a lab grinding operation it would have been as safe as sanding a piece of wood. Here, with little protection, the workers would begin exhibiting spontaneous symptoms from the radiation in half an hour. Then for the remainder of the first day when they weren't sleeping they would be vomiting until they emerged from the makeshift infirmary as "walking ghosts". They lasted about a week after that and seemed relatively happy and willing to give their lives for the purpose at hand.

By the time the powder had been loaded into the spreader units and packed inside the four cylindrical pods, teeth littered the floor and one hundred forty-two bodies had piled-up inside a small shower room. Long before that day arrived, however, Abdullah and Fahid had given orders to Jamel on when, where and how to deliver the device, and then he had departed for America.

•••

There is something to be said about the fog of war when you are participating in the fighting that cannot be felt by those far removed from the battle. Such was the case inside the National Reconnaissance Office (NRO), an agency where spy satellite information was collected, cataloged, analyzed and many times overlooked.

45

That would be true on many days, but today was not going to be one of them. As Cindy Andrews electronically fanned through a sequence of photographs, something caught her eye. Re-sequencing the photos returned by Space Imaging and Digital Globe, both companies under contract with the Pentagon, she spotted a truck moving towards the partially destroyed cement facility high in the mountainous region in the far northeast corner of Iraq.

Cindy reexamined the set of 48 photos representing a two-week period. She noticed a total of nine vehicles had entered the area and disappeared inside one of the larger structures. What was unusual was the fact that not a single vehicle had been snapped leaving the area.

She knew the two 'birds' that had supplied the photos passed over the area twice a day and this type of intelligence was mostly hit or miss, but now she was interested. After expanding the set of photos to cover the past sixty days, Cindy found one image that showed a small vehicle leaving and eleven more that disappeared inside.

So just to satisfy her curiosity, she shot off emails to the National Imagery and Mapping Agency in Virginia and the National Photographic Interpretation Center in southeast Washington requesting a confirmation.

A week later, after the report had been received by the Joint Command, it was routed to their Intel Analyzer, who confirmed Cindy's identification. Deeming it worthy of closer scrutiny, the report made its way to the Joint Chiefs of Staff after another week. It sat with the JCS yet another week before it was forwarded on to SAC Euro, South Command. Finally the AIC Intel Command requested an unmanned flyover within the next fourteen days.

The Predator RQ-1B was being piloted by airmen at the Balad Air Force Base in Iraq, but since it was using the K-band satellite for communications it could have been piloted from anywhere in the world that had a CGS system.

Tonight Staff Sergeant George Winslow was piloting and Senior Airman Weston Peters was operating the sensor pod located under the front belly of the drone. Since this RQ had been borrowed, after it completed another mission, it had only five hours of flight time left.

"I've been working the numbers and it looks like this one may go down before it gets back to base." Winslow said without looking up from the display.

"Well, that will be two this month. I don't think Lieutenant Max is going to buy us a round of beers for that. Do you?" Peters said as he reached out toward a row of switches, "Going to thermal."

"You never know he might buy you one - because you're so cute." Winslow said letting go of his joy sticks and relaxing back into his seat on the left side of the control unit.

"That's funny. There's nothing down there." Peters said sitting up in his chair.

Winslow turned his seat around to look at the display. "This is Iraq at 0200, what did you expect, a marching band?"

"I don't know what I expected, but there is absolutely nothing alive down there at all." Peters adjusted several controls, but nothing seemed to help.

Winslow reached over and switched to the hi-def black and white camera and panned around until he found something. "There you go - a dead horse."

Peters zoomed in on the horse and sucked in air. "Yea a dead horse surrounded by dead vultures, with a few dead rats thrown in for good measure."

After Staff Sergeant Winslow's report was reviewed by Lieutenant Max, he forwarded it along with the video his team had shot to the JCS, who informed the Navy and SEAL Team Six. They wanted them to take a closer look at the quarry and obtain samples before sending in the HAZMAT Team for a full breakdown.

•••

Tim McGovern loved HAHO jumps. Nothing could beat one in the middle of the night, he thought as he ran down the loading ramp toward the darkness at the rear of the C-130. A list of all the things that could go wrong went through his mind. As he closed the distance, the thumping of his Danner boots against the aluminum grew fainter and completely disappeared two steps before he left the plane, as his adrenalin spiked. A second later he arched his body into position and felt the wind-chill at 32,000 feet.

Once he was in the air he became a bird - able to do anything except climb. After checking the altimeter, oxygen flow, and compass heading on the nifty little readout strapped to his left wrist, Tim did a quick radio check. He popped his chute at 26,000 and immediately the straps of the MT1XS cut into his crotch as he slowed down.

For an instant the gear that had been weightless transformed into a massive weight before settling back down to its normal ninety pounds. Once his team had formed a stack above him, he used his compass and headed for the target twelve miles north of Dubardan.

His night vision goggles showed a few lights burning below as they glided over the sleeping town. A few minutes later the quarry complex, if you could still call it that, came into view. It had been hit so many times in the past that it was hard to distinguish between what was manmade and what was just rock.

Tim was glad they were using the newest version of night vision goggles that gave them some depth perception as they neared the ground. In the old days he would just close his eyes and let his body instincts control the impact, but now he could almost land as easily as he did in the daytime. About fifty feet above the ground, he pulled down on the control handles flaring out his chute for a standup landing. Tim gathered up the fabric while consciously ticking off the sounds of seven controlled crashes around him. As he waited for his squad, Tim wondered why Naval Special Warfare Command had been in such a hurry to get SEAL Team Six in here to snoop around this old bombed complex. It was hard to imagine that any of the highly enriched uranium from the tens of thousands of nuclear weapons formerly controlled by the post-dissolution of the Soviet Union could have ended up in this god- forsaken place. There hadn't even been any electricity running to this place for the past three years. Everything Tim had ever learned kept telling him this was just another exercise in futility.

But he knew that the one thing you had to give the Al Qaida and the Jihadist network was the fact that they seemed to be able to obtain a never-ending stream of followers that would gladly give up their own lives just to stick it to America and other freedom-loving countries around the world.

Tim waited for everyone to gather around him, and then led them quietly down the steep slope until they were on level ground.

Greg Tyson took out a set of binoculars and ranged the targets. "Two clicks to the complex and one to the nag," he said without a hint of emotion.

"Anything moving out there?" Tim asked as he and the others began opening the large pack they each carried.

"Nothing, just like the report said. There's nothing in any mode," Greg said. Holstering his binoculars, he dropped down on one knee and began opening his pack like the others.

In the dark it was hard to make out what they were doing as they unpacked and powered up the small remote controlled surveillance vehicles they had brought with them. A LCD monocle that rotated down from their helmets gave each of them the same perspective from the vehicle's onboard camera. When all the vehicles were on the ground each SEAL grabbed a controller and pushed the joystick around to test the drive units and onboard monitors.

"Okay you all have been briefed. Let's go," Tim said. Soon the SEALS were standing like giants over the remote vehicles as a small cloud of dust and gravel peppered their boots when the cars raced off, silently into the night.

It was more or less an even race until the cars were about half way to the pile of dead animals, then one car slowed to a stop. "Relay one in position" a voice whispered.

Then at the carcass two more cars slowed – one stopping and one slowly circling an oval path around all the dead animals. "Relay two in position" another voice whispered, as the second vehicle raced back to join the pack.

Half way between the animals and the complex another car stopped. "Relay three in position - The counts are getting hot," The controller said with some excitement.

"It a good thing the rest are shielded" Tim said as he pushed forward leading the remaining four cars.

When they reached the complex the four cars stopped and Tim activated the radiation sensor, which popped up in the center of the vehicle and began rotating. "You all stay put - I'm going inside. Everyone else start taking samples. I'm setting the timer on this baby for five minutes. If you hear a bang inside, Franklin, come in and see what happened."

Tim's vehicle moved slowly away from the other cars and disappeared inside the building with the hottest reading. Though his monocle, he could see some metal fabrication equipment like lathes, milling machines and foundries placed along various walls. As he proceeded along the room the car began vibrating as it ran over bits of metal and debris. When he saw what appeared to be a finely shaped jewel attached to a piece of wire he stopped the car and raised the camera angle to get a better view. He was a little surprised when he finally recognized a human tooth which had been drilled through and slid on a wire large enough to be worn as a necklace.

When he started moving again, he noticed that someone had begun painting the floor up ahead. As he reached the reflective paint, he slowed and followed it down a passageway into a small room off the side. The room appeared to have been used as a dumping area for old work uniforms. Then a hand passed in front of the camera as it reached toward the vehicle.

As another lifeless hand dropped out of nowhere, Tim flinched and yelled, "Shit," as he pulled back on the stick.

Chapter 8
The Moon Cake Festival

The day of the Moon Cake Festival in Hong Kong found Halley with her parents, Petter and Haiwei Andersson, in the Lucky Dragon restaurant enjoying the yueh ping she had ordered for dessert. Initially, she decided to try the less filling sweet cake made with lotus seed paste, but finally opted for the traditional one made with egg yolks that was much richer. Ever since she was a small child, they had been coming here to visit her grandmother Jai Li, but this year was different. Her grandmother had passed away unexpectedly a few days before they arrived.

Of course, Halley had loved her grandmother a great deal, but being half Chinese she had been taught death was not something to be afraid of or shunned; it was accepted as part of the natural cycle. The fact that she only saw her grandmother for a few days once a year also insulated her from the grief her mother felt.

Halley's mother had escaped from China to Hong Kong with her parents when she was five. Her father, Kaili, died a few days after they arrived, the responsibility of raising Haiwei fell totally on Jai Li's shoulders. During the twenty years they lived together, Haiwei never once heard her mother complain about how long and hard she had to work to provide for them.

In fact the only thing Jai Li ever complained about was one poor report card that came home during Haiwei's first year in school. When she saw how upset it made her mother, she vowed it would never happen again. Haiwei more than made up for that report card when she graduated with honors from high school. After that she worked two and three part- time jobs on the side while she attended business school and landed a job as a secretary at a small engineering company owned by Ericsson.

"Let me look at grandma's pictures again, while you try your cake." Halley said slipping the envelope out of her mother's hand.

"Okay." Haiwei answered softly, as she passed the photos to Haiwei and slowly picked up her fork.

To keep from crying, Halley turned inward as she leafed through the prints remembering all the stories her grandmother had told her about growing up in Huizhou, Guangdong Province and the grandfather she never met.

Thinking about the stories, Halley realized how fragile life's circumstances are. According to the stories, Jia Li was born in Huizhou City in China near Hong Kong in 1927. At sixteen, she married Halley's grandfather, Kaili, and soon presented him with a daughter they named Haiwei. During the early years of their marriage Kaili was rarely home. He worked many jobs to keep his family fed and to save a few coins each month for their future.

Kaili's main job was working at the White Dragon Martial Arts Institute. This required much time and dedication to keep both his master and students satisfied. This undertaking provided the family with the barest of essentials. If it weren't for the money he received for performing dances at the many festivals held throughout the year, it was doubtful the family would have survived.

Halley, who had continued the tradition, smiled as she thought of the enjoyment she got from learning and teaching martial arts herself. Like most students, she imagined that it would have been fun to go back in time and learn from the masters of her grandfather. However, the past is not always as we would like it to be.

Besides his respectable jobs, her grandfather also worked part-time as a messenger and bodyguard for Jiao-long, the leader of the largest gang in Huizhou. Occasionally, Kaili was asked to collect overdue payments or negotiate a sales transaction when more drastic measures were required. And Kaili never failed to provide a solution. It was from this work that he made most of the money he was able to save.

By 1948, when Halley's mother Haiwei was five, rumblings began to be felt in China. Mao pushed for reform, and restrictions began to tighten. Kaili knew that if he didn't move his family soon it would be too late to leave China. He took the biggest gamble of his life and bet half of his life's savings on the Dragon Boat race. The fates smiled upon him the day of the final race. Finally, he had enough money to move his family. However, Jiao-long wouldn't let him go.

Kaili faced the choice of paying the gang ten times more than he had saved or fighting a duel to the death. He had little choice. Figuring that he had nothing to lose he had stipulations place in the blood certificates, guaranteeing him two things. First, free passage to Hong Kong for him and his family if he won the match. His second request amused Jiao-long as it expressed his wish to be buried with his ancestors in a small cave on Luofu Mountain.

After much wrangling, the final agreement was ready for Kaili's signature. Jiao-long had placed stipulations of his own that required Jia Li and Haiwei to become the property of the winner. It was the hardest decision that Kaili had ever made, but with his years of training he was confident that he would win – so he signed. What he didn't foresee was that his opponent would choose the short sword, his least favorite weapon.

On the day of the match, with his family watching, he walked to the official and bowed. He presented his short sword for inspection and flexed his body as hard as possible as two gang members moved in and patted him down to be sure he wasn't concealing any additional weapons.

Unlike the fights staged for movies, this contest was over in twenty seconds with Halley's grandfather standing over a body with its nearly severed head and blood dripping off his elbow from a small cut he received on his blocking arm.

Disgusted, Jiao-long signed the certificate and handed it to Kaili, who demanded that the family be transported immediately. True to his word the boss gave a short nod and the next day they were standing outside the immigration station peering at Hong Kong for the first time.

It wasn't until they had secured an apartment and had their saving tucked into a reputable English bank that her grandfather revealed to his wife the serious wound he had received during the fight. When she saw that the cut had already become infected, she insisted he go to the hospital, but he refused.

Jai Li stayed up for two days and nights feeding Kaili medicine from a nearby herb shop, but he became weaker by the hour. Before he died two days later he made her promise to work hard, keep their daughter safe, and make sure she got a good education.

"Halley. Halley. " Her father Petter called, snapping his fingers in front of her face. "Where have you been?"

"Sorry Dad, I was just thinking about Grandma and that this will be the last time we come here. It's really sad when you think about it."

Halley's mother reached over and gave her a hug. "It is sad, but your Grandmother wouldn't want you moping around on your last visit to Hong Kong."

Just then their waitress Jin Wang came over to check on them. "Is everything okay? Would anyone like more tea?"

"No, just the bill, please," her father said.

When the waitress returned with the bill her father handed over his credit card and took the plate of sliced oranges and fortune cookies.

Halley quickly cracked hers open and announced. "Mine says 'Love is just around the corner, '"

Then she coaxed her mother into opening hers. "What does it say?"

Haiwei smiled. "I will have a long and prosperous life."

"Come on Dad, open yours."

Petter decided it would be fun to tease Halley a little so he intentionally stalled as she begged him to hurry.

"Well, my little princess, this one says: 'a huge fortune at home is not as good as money in use."

He looked at his watch and faked a frown. "Looks like it's time to grab a taxi and pick up our bags. We've got exactly enough time to get to the airport for the Annual Andersson Jakarta Jamboree." As the family got up, Petter took a bill out of his wallet and slipped Benjamin Franklin's chubby face under the fruit plate.

Chapter 9
Fortune Smiles on Ning Wang

When Jin Wang came back to the table lugging a square plastic tub half filled with dirty dishes, the pleasant smile she had flashed at her customers was gone. It was late afternoon and she still hadn't made enough in tips to get the phone in her apartment turned back on. It looked like all the promises she had made to her husband, Ning, about making extra money during the festival had been empty.

Her heart sank even further when she picked up the signed credit card receipt and saw that the tip line was blank. But all that changed in an instant when she picked up the empty fruit plate and saw the brand new one hundred dollar bill staring up at her. This was the biggest tip she had ever received at the Lucky Dragon. In fact it was probably the biggest tip the Lucky Dragon hanging on the wall had ever seen. This was so much better than a credit card tip which had to be divided with the staff. All she had to do was slip it into her pocket without one of the other workers seeing her and it was hers. The problem was that Jin was as honest as the day is long and had never done anything dishonest in her life.

If the business her husband ran from their small apartment hadn't taken a turn for the worse and the pile of bills had been less high, she would never have thought about taking the money for herself. As Jin stood there, wrestling with her conscience every eye seemed to be turned on her and every sound rang in her ears like a giant temple bell.

"Hurry up Jin. We have customers coming in," the owner shouted.

"Okay boss," she said as she slipped the bill into her inside pocket and began clearing the table.

An hour later, after obtaining special permission from the owner to leave for an hour, she walked down the street toward the drug store. When she was out of sight, she hailed a cab to travel the half mile to the phone company. Once there, she paid the delinquent bill.

When Jin returned home that night she found her husband, Ning, busy putting together a model airplane kit that had been ordered before the phone and computer link had been shut down.

"That's the last one," he said closing the box and slipping it into a shrink-wrap envelope.

"Maybe not," his wife said presenting him with the receipt from the phone company, "Everything should be back on tomorrow afternoon."

Ning jumped up and gave her a big hug and grabbed a bottle of whiskey and two glasses. "It's time to celebrate."

After sharing a drink with Ning, Jin began pulling him towards the corner of the room where the bed was rolled up in the corner. "Let's really celebrate" she said coyly.

When she came to work the next day she was already worn out, but managed to get through the busy lunchtime before Ning came running into the restaurant.

"I've got a big meeting in thirty minutes here with a representative of a company who wants me to build a thousand special kits for a promotion his company is doing. A thousand."

"Sit down and I'll bring you some tea." Quickly returning with a pot and two cups his wife sat down across from him.

"How did you get such an offer?"

Ning quickly gulped down the hot tea, then fanned his tongue to cool it off. "When the phone came back on, I had the message. Very mysterious, I don't know how he got my name, but he knew all about my little business and you working here. Do you remember talking to anyone about my airplane models?"

"Well, I talk about you all the time, so that could have been anybody. Wait, there were a couple of guys - Eastern I think. Anyway, I showed them the picture that I took at the park last summer of you holding your red plane with the white stripes."

"That must have been it. What did they say?" Ning asked as he poured himself another tea.

"Nothing really. They did ask if you ever built anything bigger." Jin said. "That's all I remember."

"Okay, bring me some noodles, so I can finish before he gets here." he said waving her away with his hands.

Jin came back with noodles and another clean tea cup. "Here are your noodles. I need to get back to work. Good luck," she said taking the cup of tea she had been drinking with her.

Ning ate very quickly and spent the next twenty minutes watching the front door. Every time someone came in his heart raced a little, but soon returned to normal as they were seated and began to order.

He was just about to go to the restroom when two men came in and talked with the owner who pointed in his direction. As they got closer, Ning stood up and bowed.

"You must be Ning Wang. I'm Ali and this is Mr. Din" the bigger of the two said holding out his hand.

"Yes, I am Ning. I am very pleased to meet you Mr. Ali and you too, Mr. Din. Please sit down." Before Ning sat down he motioned to his wife to bring another cup, which soon arrived.

Ali thanked the waitress then poured himself a cup of tea and began. "Listen Ning, Mr. Din is sponsoring a contest for large model planes in Japan next summer and expects a thousand entrants to participate. In order to test the skills of the pilots, but not their models, he wants each kit to be fully assembled, except for the wings, which need to be built so they can be quickly snapped into place. Is this something you can do?"

Ning did some quick mental calculations. He quickly realized even if the planes were the size of the one in the picture, that he would never be able to get the money to even start such a project.

"Without knowing the exact specifications of the model you are talking about, I cannot say." Ning said stalling for time and hoping for a miracle.

Din, who had been very quiet, pulled a few folded sheets of paper from his pocket and opened them on the table in front of Ning.

"You will get a general idea of what we are looking for from these, but the actual design is up to you. I want something with an approximate five foot wingspan that is equipped with a high performance engine. The model must be able to fly for one hour at thirty miles per hour and carry a load of three pounds plus whatever fuel is required."

Ning had never built such a plane, but had seen pictures of them in model magazines and two or three times at the competitions he had attended. Realizing what it cost to build such a model, he could see no way to do it.

"I am sorry gentlemen, but building such a plane is above my means. I live in a small two room apartment with no machinery and do not have the facilities to build the plane you are describing. This is something best left to the large companies with the machinery and capital necessary for such a project." Ning said as he shook his head and looked down disappointedly at his cup of tea that was now definitely half empty.

Din leaned in a little closer to Ning. "I know exactly your circumstances. That is why I am here. You will be supplied with whatever you need: wood for the frame; plastic covering; servo motors and batteries; engines, two or four cycle; everything. In exchange for keeping this a secret, so that others in the industry don't catch on to my promotional plans, I am willing to pay you what it would cost me to have it done at a large company. That figure breaks down to $1,000 US dollars a plane, which I believe you will find most generous."

Ning couldn't believe what he was hearing. That added up to one-hundred thousand US or nearly a million HK dollars. "But where would I even keep the inventory and finished kits?" he blurted out before he realized it.

"Nothing to worry about, Mr. Ali will act as my representative. Each week he will stop in the restaurant on Tuesday for lunch and ask for your wife to serve him. She will pass him a list of materials and keep him abreast of your progress. When you have the final design finished there will be a test to ensure the model meets our expectations. If the model works well, you will be given a $2,000 bonus. Then it will be a simple matter to begin constructing the kits in an assembly line fashion. If you agree, a package will arrive for you tomorrow, which contains enough to get you thinking about the design. What do you say?"

Ning was still in shock, but found himself holding out his hand and accepting the proposal. "I will do my best to meet your needs."

Now, it was Ali's turn to talk. "To make things a little easier I have a basement apartment near here, which is at your disposal. Remember you do not need to buy anything, just have your wife pass me a list of whatever you need. Here are the directions and key to the workshop. I think you will be very happy when you see it."

After they left, Ning stood by the table shaking. When Jin hurried over to find out how the meeting went he found it hard to speak. "I can't believe it. One minute we can't pay the phone bill and the next minute we are rich beyond my dreams."

"What are you talking about?" his wife asked.

"I have just gotten a contract worth a fortune," Ning said as he fell back into his chair, "a million dollars."

Ning spent the next morning drinking tea, going to the bathroom, and pacing back and forth as he watched the street below. Just before noon a delivery truck pulled up and the driver got out carrying a box that seemed much too small.

Crossing the room, Ning waited next to the door, like a small boy, as he heard footsteps climbing the stairs and coming down the hall towards him. He nearly gave the delivery man a heart attack when he pulled the door open an instant after the first knock.

"Ning Wang?" the delivery man asked holding out a clipboard.

"Yes." Ning said trying to take the package.

"Not so fast. You need to sign this receipt first."

"Yes. Yes." Ning said signing the paper quickly.

After checking to be sure everything was in order, the man handed the box to Ning who quickly closed the door and raced to the table. After opening it he brushed away the layer of packing material and discovered it was filled with smaller boxes that had been tightly packed together.

Prying the first one out proved to be somewhat difficult, but once it was out the others on that layer came out easily. Eventually, he had them all out and arranged on the table according to size.

The largest was also one of the lightest and this is the one he opened first. It contained a molded piece of plastic with several compartments and instructions that it was to be used to hold the plane's electronics, servos, batteries, and test weights. It was about five inches across and a foot long with a slight taper that Ning guessed would point to the tail.

Since it was designed to hold the weights, Ning picked up the heaviest box next and guessed correctly. This box contained three weights, which fit perfectly into the molded plastic. Once he had the weights inserted, he realized what a challenge it was going to be to get the plane off the ground. Fortunately the weights were positioned along the center of the plastic with one in the front, middle, and back to distribute the weight evenly.

The next three boxes he opened contained a single cylinder two-cycle engine with tuned exhaust, a single cylinder four-cycle engine with normal exhaust, and a two cylinder four-cycle engine.

The only other large box contained a one liter plastic fuel tank. "Shit," Ning said aloud to no one, "that's another two pounds. This thing has to be able to lift five pounds."

Opening the rest of the boxes produced an assortment of servo-motors to control the rudder, flaps, and retractable landing gear, and wiring harnesses connected to small PDA computers.

Ning poured himself another cup of tea and looked at the parts on the table. This new opportunity was quickly turning into a nightmare. He picked up the large box to start cleaning up the mess he had created, but he noticed an envelope stuck under the bottom flap.

He opened it and the nightmare got even worse. In one month he was to bring his completed prototype to Tai Tong to demonstrate his progress. As he let out an agonizing groan his head fell to the table and he cursed.

Chapter 10
Jakarta Junket

Petter Andersson had spent so many wasted hours flying in first class, he didn't even wakeup as Haiwei stood over him cleaning up the mess he'd left on his tray.

"Sleeping like a baby," the flight attendant beside her said as she held out a plastic trash bag, "he must have a clear conscience."

"After all these years, I'm pretty sure it's because he has no conscience," Haiwei said returning across the aisle to her seat next to Halley.

"I swear, your father can sleep through anything," She said taking the containers Halley had stacked together and passing them to the attendant.

"Oh Mom, leave Daddy alone. He'll be up soon. Besides this gives us a chance to talk about how we're going to spend his money this year."

"I just want to get to the hotel and relax," Haiwei said rocking her shoulders back and forth against the plush seat.

"Well, I'm heading over to the Pasaraya Department Store and getting something for Kathy. We were so busy in Hong Kong I completely forgot to even text message her before we got on the plane. She must think we're dead."

Before Haiwei could respond a little click echoed from the speakers then the captain's voice come on. "Flight attendants, make final preparations for landing."

A few seconds later they touched down and taxied to the terminal. After buying three visas at 25 U.S. dollars each, and passing through customs, they headed for the baggage claim.

Petter spotted the driver he had ordered and got mad. "They always get my name wrong," he said pointing at the little sign a well dressed man was holding that read, "Mr. Anderson"

Petter made a mental note to lower the tip. By the time they arrived at the Mulia Senayan Hotel, he had forgotten all about it and passed the driver a hundred dollar bill.

For the next two days Halley enjoyed visiting the National Museum and shopping with her parents before they returned home.

Now that her parents were gone, Halley was on her own. She went over the list of things she wanted to do before flying back to MIT. She really wished her cousin Kathy could have accompanied her, but she had already committed to a Yosemite getaway with some of her sorority sisters.

Doing some mental arithmetic, Halley calculated that it was 2 a.m. in California, but quickly composed a message: kathy wuzup u zzz smaim. She attached a couple of photos she snapped of her parents as they were leaving the hotel and sent it anyway.

Five minutes later her phone chirped. Halley laughed when she read, "im2bz2p hbib gg h&k." She imagined what a hot but inappropriate boy might be doing with Kathy at 2 a.m. and responded with, "Hugs and kisses to you too."

Since it was only four in the afternoon, Halley decided to try on the skimpy bikini she had kept hidden away for the past week. When she had slipped it on she walked into the bathroom and looked at herself in the mirror. "Why not get it wet?" she thought as she grabbed the white robe hanging on the back of the closet door.

Chapter 11
Jakarta Coolers

Mohammed sat comfortably in a well padded chair facing the large swimming pool. He always enjoyed watching the girls in skimpy bathing suits. That would have gotten them severely beaten, if not killed in Iraq. Of course being a man living on the controlling side of power, he saw nothing wrong with enjoying the spectacle. As he sat calculating the probabilities of getting one of these beauties to come back to his room on the thirty-eighth floor, Ramadan strolled over and sat down in the chair next to him. Stroking his graying beard, Ramadan followed Mohammed's gaze out to a young girl swimming lazily on her back. She was headed in the direction of the large steps built into the blindingly bright white pool. Once there, she rolled lazily over and stood up to her waist in the deep blue water.

When she reached up with both hands and began ringing the water out of her long dark hair, both men stopped breathing. They followed her every move as she slowly walked up the wide steps and emerged from the pool. Not a single drop of water from her well-shaped body or a wet footprint she left on the white cement escaped their attention.

As she reached her chaise lounge, she laid down and began moving around looking for just the right position to fall asleep, both men felt a tightening in their groin. Then a few seconds later as she settled in, both men sucked in a lung full of air and began laughing.

"Don't worry my brother. Soon you will be enjoying a harem of your own," Ramadan managed to wheeze out.

Just then a waiter came over and Ramadan ordered each of them a drink, he looked at Mohammed seriously and asked, "How did it go today?"

"There's really no way for me to know until Abdullah or Fahid contacts me, but I'm not too worried about this initial phase. Planting the bait is obvious and will surely set off some kind of alarm, but this kind of thing happens so often that it shouldn't be a problem."

When the waiter came back with their drinks, Mohammed handed him a hundred rupiah note and pointed at the girl they had been watching. "Take that girl under the palm a mint tea. If she asks who sent it, tell her it was from the man in thirty-eight-twelve, who won't be back until ten tonight."

Ramadan gave Mohammed a puzzled look as the waiter hurried away. "What was that all about? You're still in thirty-eight eleven aren't you?"

"Of course I am, but that room is empty. If she does show up, I'll hear her knocking on the door across the hall. Besides, the chances of that happening are less than one percent," Mohammed said picking up his drink. "But if she does show up, I'll be sure to take a nice video for your collection."

He took a drink and saluted, "Now that I've done my part on both ends. How are you doing?"

Ramadan chuckled and leaned in over the table. "For my part things are going extremely well. We have been working with the H5N1 RW4 strain, but just got our hands on some chickens infected with RK7, which looks even more promising."

As Mohammed listened to Ramadan's much too technical explanation of how all the magic connected with the bird flu was going, he watched the waiter carry a small silver tray with the mint tea over to the girl who was now sleeping. He looked toward Mohammed and placed the tray on the ground. Scribbled something on the back of the receipt, he stuck it under the edge of the glass and walked away.

"All that stuff is too complicated for me. It hurts my brain just to listen to you. All I want to know is will it kill people and when will it be ready to ship to our brothers in Los Angeles?"

Ramadan couldn't hide his disgust for Mohammed's inability to marvel at the excellent science he had been performing, but decided that he'd dummy down his explanation so this moron could understand.

"As you know, Mohammed, we have been working on this avenue of attack for almost a year. While it is a slow and cumbersome process, we are beginning to see some promising results. Let me review the process again in a manner that may help you to understand better. In the beginning we worked with two dozen chickens from Jakarta carrying the H5N1 strain. We froze sixteen of the carcasses and threw the other six dead chickens into a sealed room containing one hundred healthy hens. On the seventh day when the last chicken died, we knew we had cultivated the virus."

Mohammed, who seemed to be paying attention, moved forward in his chair. "That doesn't sound that complicated."

"Of course not, any fool could have done that, but we had to be sure the virus could be transmitted to humans, which of course didn't seem very likely as the children snatched from the Bantar trash dump proved when we threw them into the room and they all survived." Ramadan said with disgust.

"But as we gathered other strains like 7B, 9A, and L33 and began throwing more and more infected chickens into the room, a most marvelous thing happened." Ramadan looked skyward then continued. "The children started to die"

"Praise Allah," Mohammed said with a smile.

Before Ramadan left the table, he invited Mohammed to come out to the facility to observe the progress he was making. Mohammed assured him that he would visit in a week or two. They both stood, embraced, then parted company.

As Mohammed made his way back to his suite in the hotel, he stopped by the gift shop and picked up some soap and three large bottles of shampoo before taking the elevator up to the thirty-eighth floor. Once inside the room he tossed his laptop on the bed and carried the small bag of toiletries into the bathroom, placing it on the marble counter between the two inlaid sinks.

He pulled up on the lever that closed the drain and began slowly filling the gold embossed king-sized tub with warm water. He unpacked his purchases – storing the soap and two of the shampoo bottles in the cabinet under the sink. He began undressing, throwing his clothes into a hamper until he was down to his boxers.

Walking into the bedroom, he grabbed the laptop off the bed and headed towards a large glass-topped table next to the picture window that overlooked the pool far below. From this distance it was hard to tell, but it looked like she was still sleeping in the lounge chair. Mohammed sighed as he reached back and flipped the computer on. "I guess it's all in the hands of God now."

When he sat down and began reviewing his email, he was pleased that the first few emails from America had already begun to arrive, indicating that at least some of the software had been accepted and installed itself.

Satisfied that the first part of his plan was operational, he got up and returned to the bathroom. He took the remaining bottle of shampoo from the counter and slowly poured it into the churning water under the spigot. It took about a minute before the bottle was empty and he turned the water off. He threw the bottle into the trash can, producing a loud bang. Then he turned around and looked at himself in the wall-to-wall mirror. At thirty-eight he was still hard as a rock from years of fighting and living on the run. Over the past six months he had been using extreme sun block religiously and now could pass as a vacationer from Italy or Greece. Pulling out the top of his boxers he inhaled and let them fall to the floor, kicking them in the direction of the hamper.

Mohammed who was usually very self-controlled couldn't get the picture of that girl out of his head. Before he realized it, he was standing by the window in his bedroom looking down at her still sleeping quietly. His thoughts were interrupted by a special ring tone from his cell phone. He had not anticipated this call and his hand shook as he answered.

"Yes this is Mohammed. The sun shines invisibly in the night sky - like a beacon to lead those who can see."

On the other end Abdullah countered "The rain falls equally on the good and evil in the world, quenching their throats for another day."

Then he waited the prescribed fifteen seconds before continuing. "I just left the dragon's lair. His powers travel with me to visit Cindy as he watches over his children." After another fifteen seconds, he finished with "All the stars must align at the beginning of the New Year or we have wasted our chance for paradise."

As each second that Mohammed waited to respond ticked by a little bead of sweat rolled down his left temple. "All is well as the lovers embrace and Cupid's arrows bring down the wounded dove circling above." He ended the call and sat down on the bed, weakened by the ordeal.

It was the first time he had spoken to the leader of the operation and he wanted to be sure he hadn't made a mistake. He retrieved his copy of the Koran sitting next to the prayer blanket folded neatly in the corner of the room before going into the bathroom and returning with a double edged razor blade.

After arranging himself in the chair and pushing the laptop out of the way, he flipped the Koran open to the last page and skillfully split the leather binding open with the blade. He then held open the little pouch that he had created and pulled out a thin piece of tracing paper. It was covered with notes he had made soon after he was first recruited.

He scanned down the paper with his finger until he found what he was looking for and smiled when he confirmed he had not missed a single word during his conversation. Once done, he crumpled up the paper dropped it in the ashtray sitting on the table and lit it with his silver lighter. The specially treated paper burned quickly with a bluish flame without creating a trace of smoke and disappeared into nothingness.

Now that this unexpected ordeal was over, Mohammed walked into the bathroom and got into the tub to relax. As he lay dozing he raised his left arm to check the time. When the frothy bubbles rolled off his Rolex, it showed that it was a quarter till five in the afternoon, making it just before two in Iraq.

Relaxing he settled down into the water until it filled his ears and popping bubbles tickled his nose.

Chapter 12
Addicted to Love

Stewart woke up five minutes before the alarm clock would have begun to beep and got out of bed, careful not to wake up his wife Cindy who was still sleeping soundly. When he opened the door, his wife's mangy old cat, Fig, was waiting on the other side. The cat walked beside him all the way down to kitchen until Stewart put some dried food in his bowl. Truth be told, the cat would have been gone a long time ago, but Stewart just couldn't figure out how to get rid of the disgusting creature without hurting Cindy.

Once the cat was fed, Stewart flipped on the television hanging under the counter and tuned in CNN, which he particularly liked. Living in Washington, he really didn't care about what little store got robbed or who drove their car through the side of a house or who won an award for helping the seniors at the Shady Lane convalescent center. The only thing he was really interested in: Will we all still be here tomorrow? That also seemed to be CNN's main focus. When the coffee machine reported a final deep hiss, he automatically got up, poured a cup of coffee and headed to his computer room.

Stewart pulled the black leather office chair away from the custom made table, sat down and punched on the computer. He spent the next five minutes playing Blackjack on an antique handheld from the 80's, while the collection of security programs that protected his machine fired up and checked every nook and cranny inside the beast he used to surf for porn.

When the machine beeped he smiled and put the Blackjack game down, but when he saw the big red X flashing on the icon bar at the bottom of the display his eyes narrowed.

"God Damn it. This is the fourth time this week this thing has been infected," Stewart said as he clicked on the security icon – bringing up a page titled "Error: Program has a license problem..." After about thirty minutes he had reinstalled his Internet Security package and the red 'X' reverted back to the well behaved green checkmark he needed to see before continuing.

By that time however, it was too late to do any surfing for new porno clips and all he could do was turn off the computer and go to work.

When he returned home, Stewart found out that Cindy had made a dinner date for them with two other teachers from the high school where she taught math. Changing his plans again, he switched into his let's party mode. They drove his wife's car to one of the popular sports bars where he had an enjoyable time sharing jokes with the other men while the girls talked mostly about troublesome students, teacher indiscretions, and the end of semester failure notices they would be sending out next week.

Once home, Cindy went to bed so she would be ready for school the next day. Stewart took his customary shower, brushed his teeth, and changed into gym pants and a t-shirt. When he was ready for bed he noticed that Cindy had fallen asleep, so he retreated to his computer again and fired it up.

"Shit. This thing is getting to be a real pain in the ass," he said when the persistent red 'X' began flashing once more. "It must have been that 'Harsh Teen Tarts in Heat' website that screwed this thing up so bad."

This time Stewart uninstalled all the security software and then reinstalled it and the full sweep program. In a little over an hour, he was pretty sure all the problems he had experienced over the past week were behind him.

Once that was done he was surfing his favorite sites and finally zeroed in on one of his favorite little Spanish beauties. He clicked on her image, which brought him to another web page that had three twenty-second clips of her doing what she did best.

Stewart moved the mouse over the first of three photos and right-clicked the mouse. This brought up a pop-up dialog where he selected the 'Save File As' option, which brought up another 'Save As' window. That window already had the directory where Stewart stored his porno collection and the file name the hosting website had given to the link for the video clip he wanted to download.

In the early days, Stewart had just taken the default names, but soon learned that it was better to store the clips as numeric files with letters at the end designating the order they should be played in. Once he typed in the name, a little pop-up kept track of the progress of the download, giving him the progress percentage and download speed, which usually ran between 128 and 500 kilobytes per second.

After downloading his first set of video clips for the night he was off and running. Within an hour he had downloaded twelve groups of new clips.

It was now about one in the morning and Stewart decided to take a break and edit the clips in the morning. Before he shut down the machine he scanned the last clip from each group to be sure he would have something interesting to do when he got up. When he was satisfied he clicked on the 'Start' and two 'Shut down' icons, waited for his machine to shut down, clicked off the lights and went upstairs to bed.

What Stewart and the other million or so porn surfers in the greater Washington, DC area never paid much attention to were the little green lights blinking away on their wireless network connection modules, twenty-four hours a day, seven days a week.

Since he regularly downloaded video porn from sites around the world, he was use to the kind of erratic behavior he had experienced over the past week, but all that would change the next time Stewart switched on his machine. The tiny program that Mohammed had launched from poolside in Jakarta, begin compiling a list of all the wireless connections Stewart's machine could reach.

Once the list was complete it would be stored until a random trigger would send it back to Jakarta to be sorted and collated with the pairs of addresses and URL's that Abdullah and Fahid had so painstakingly collected from their vehicles as they swept though the interstates, highways, and major streets.

The next morning when Stewart powered-up his computer the green checkmark appeared, and he was ready to start editing his videos. He launched his video editing program and waited for it to load his current project. Stewart added the clips from last night to the media directory and slid the first group up to the video channel, placing it at the far right end of the project for viewing.

After watching the six fifteen minute clips of two lesbians kissing and probing each other with a transparent pink vibrator, he smiled and went to work locating the appropriate section, sliding the movie apart and adding the new video.

When he had slid the movie back together and watched the transitions at each end of the new section, he smiled.

"Acceptable."

As soon as Stewart loaded the second group into his editor, he could tell by the graphs displayed in the voice channel under each clip that it was trash. It was easy to see that the original editor had taken one thirty-second clip and cut it into four ten-second clips, each starting at different points. This was clever, in a way, as it produced different stills on the hosting website that made it look a lot more tantalizing than it really was.

"Crap," Stewart said as he highlighted the clips in the media bin and removed the clips from the project as well as deleted them from the computer.

The third video was a single clip format that sometimes proved interesting, but this one featured a dark-haired sword swallower gagging on drool that screamed to be deleted. "Very disgusting," Stewart said clicking the mouse and sending her to oblivion.

By this time Mohammed's software had created a list of all seven wireless modems in the vicinity of Stewart's home. It then combined that with the address it had glommed when he was working with his internet security software download and reinstall the day before. Once that was done, it went back to sleep and waited for the signal from its random trigger to signal that it was time to send the information back to Jakarta.

During the short time it was working, Stewart never noticed that anything unusual was going on, which meant that Mohammed had created quite a nifty little program that didn't attract attention even when it was running at the same time as the processor intensive video software was fighting for every clock-cycle it could grab.

The fourth group was pretty good, and a few months ago, Stewart would have kept it, but there was no happy ending, so it had to go.

The fifth set was shot in someone's back yard and showed a busty blond in a sunbathing outfit rubbing herself for thirty seconds. Since she looked more like she was working a 50's crowd at a strip club than creating state of the art porno; click-click, and she was gone.

The other clips were completely unusable and removed. That left his latest masterpiece with a run time of twenty-two minutes and thirty seconds.

After auto-adjusting the volume levels and saving the program, Stewart wandered back to the kitchen to refill his coffee cup and as luck would have it that was the exact time that the random generator fired.

Before he returned the program had generated an email with the attached list of IP addresses and sent it to Mohammed's email account. Then it erased all traces of the email and the list from the computer.

Chapter 13
Chip Off the Old Block

Twelve-year old Josh Baker's tongue slipped out from between his teeth, as he concentrated on the bright red and white remote controlled aircraft flying down the third base line along a row of trees. Executing a tight left-hand turn 50 feet over home plate, the plane raced back down the first base line in the empty baseball field behind the Saint Bernadettes School that he and his sister Sam attended. Once it was flying straight and level, he let his eyes dart over to the folding chairs where his grandfather was sitting in the shade with his feet propped up on a beer cooler. Josh had just enough time to notice that his grandfather's Navy buddy, Tyrone, had given him the thumb's up sign before the pitch of the engine changed slightly requiring some quick adjustments of the control box in his hands.

Behind the dark aviator glasses his grandfather wore, Duke's mind had once again drifted back to the cockpit of his F-4J Phantom as he made a wide turn to line up with the ball of the USS Constellation cruising in the South China Sea off Vietnam. It was June 15th, 1972 and Duke and his Radar Intercept Officer, Irish, had just blasted two MiG fighters out of the sky with Sidewinder missiles, bringing their total up to five to become Aces.

Duke was snapped back to the present as Ty pushed his legs off the cooler to grab another beer. "You want one?"

"No better not. You know I catch hell every time my daughter catches the slightest whiff of that stuff on me when I bring Josh home."

Ty smiled and leaned back in his chair, "I know just what you mean. I can still remember my first wife complaining about most everything I did, but the new one knows when to leave me be."

Duke took a look at his watch and smiled. "He's had her up for almost half an hour now. She'll be down soon."

"Well when that bandit comes down, I think I'll be heading out. I have to hand it to you, Josh is a lot better than the last time I watched him," Ty said as he leaned back against the canvas chair to rest his shoulders.

"I was hoping that if I let him crash his trainer enough, he'd get all that anger out of his system. A couple of weeks ago it had been put back together so many times it was almost flying sideways, but he's doing a lot better today. I just wish his father could be here to see him."

Without thinking Duke leaned forward, opened the cooler, and soon had a half empty can of beer in his right hand.

Ty laughed and gave Duke a friendly slap on the back. "You're going to catch hell now."

"You're probably right." Duke said before downing the second half of the can, "just didn't think about it. Automatic Stress Reflex, beer dulls the mirror."

Just then the engine on the model sputtered and quit, which caused them both to sit up. As they watched, Josh pushed one of the control knobs forward causing the model to go into a steep dive. The plane plunged toward pitcher's mound picking up speed until it was about twenty-five feet above the ground. Then Josh pulled the control back and executed a perfect little loop-the-loop before setting the plane down gently half way between second and third.

"For a second there, I thought you were going to have another repair job on your hands," Ty said as they hustled out to help Josh with the plane.

"That was some pretty fancy flying you did up there champ", Ty said as he knelt down and tussled Josh's hair."

Duke smiled, took the controller and patted Josh on the shoulder. "You're doing a lot better today. I guess you wanted to impress your adopted Uncle Ty."

As Ty and Josh gently lifted the aircraft by its wingtips, Duke grabbed the controller and pretended to fly the model back to the chairs. Once he folded the chairs he carried them and the cooler in the crook of his left arm, while continuing west to the parking lot where his bright red Dodge truck sat cooking in the hot autumn sun.

After setting everything down on the blacktop, he reached into his pocket and pulled out his gigantic key-ring and unlocked the fiberglass bed cover. After lifting it up an inch or so, he let go and pretended he was using his magical powers to open it as two hydraulic cylinders pushed it open like a clamshell. Duke always preferred the streamline look of the cover, but since it was only a couple of feet high at the far end he was glad Josh still enjoyed climbing inside.

As usual, the cooler was the last thing to go into the truck and they each grabbed a can of soda before Josh tied down the plane with bungee cords. As they relaxed, Ty's phone rang. He looked at the caller ID and made a terrible face before walking about twenty feet away and answering it.

"Grandpa, do you think I can fly at the competition next month?" Josh asked.

"Well you keep practicing every weekend like you have been and I bet you'll be right there with all the other kids in your age group. In fact, when I tell your mother how well you did today, we might even get her to come along." Duke said with a big smile.

"I don't think she'll come." Josh said looking down, "she told me that if she never saw another airplane she'd be the happiest woman on the planet."

As they continued to talk, Ty wandered back toward the truck shaking his head. "If it isn't one thing, it's something else. Now I have to drive back to Homeland Security before I can go home."

Duke gave him a pouty face. "Sounds like you're in fifth grade instead of Josh."

"Sometimes I wish I was. It's getting ridiculous down there. Every time the slightest thing happens, they call another meeting," Ty said, heading towards his car.

"Anything you'd like to share with your old Top Gun instructor?" Duke asked with both arms held out.

"Just some crap about internet traffic - nothing as exciting as chasing your ass around the hills at Miramar," Ty shouted back as he jumped into his Atomic Orange Metallic Corvette and chirped the tires all the way to Woodmoor Drive before he turned left and disappeared.

"Ty is really cool. Someday I'm going to have a car just like his," Josh said slipping down off the tailgate.

"Yea, before you do that you better learn how to drive better than he does or the police will come and take it way," Duke said. Then he pulled up the tailgate and lowered the metal cover back into its locked position and escorted Josh around to the passenger side of the truck, making sure he was securely belted in before locking the door.

Duke walked around the truck inspecting it like it was one of his old fighter planes before opening the driver's side door, jumping into the seat and starting the engine. He watched all the instruments for a few seconds until they all stabilized within normal ranges. Then he pulled around the school and turned right on University Blvd.

After taking another right on Colesville Road, it only took a few minutes before he reached the reservoir bridge, but that was enough time for Josh to have fallen asleep. Normally, he was a bundle of energy; but since his father died, he'd acted a little different. Josh's manic-depressive behavior would have bothered Duke a lot more if he hadn't seen it begin to improve slowly.

Slowing down for the turn onto Lockwood, Duke took his foot off the accelerator and coasted down the street and into Amy's driveway at the end of Burnt Mills Court.

When Amy heard the truck approaching she put the real-estate magazine she was reading down beside her on the cushion of the double size white wicker swing she was sitting in, got up and walked down to meet her dad.

"He's sleeping," Duke said in a quiet voice, "go open the door and I'll carry him to his bed."

They moved as a team: Amy moving to the front door and Duke getting out, moving around to the passenger door, opening it and slowly unbuckling the seatbelt; then gently lifting Josh up into his arms and carrying him inside the house to bed.

Closing the door to Josh's room, Duke walked back to the kitchen where he knew Amy would be waiting for him with a freshly brewed cup of coffee.

"How did he do today?" Amy asked as she pushed the pitcher filled with two percent milk toward him.

"You should have been there. He was fantastic. Even Ty noticed how much he improved," Duke said as he reached for a packet of sweetener and sprinkled it into his cup.

"How is Ty? I haven't seen him since the funeral," Amy said with her voice trailing off.

"He's fine. Always asks about you and how you're doing. He'd probably stop by if the OHS didn't call him every ten minutes." Duke patted Amy's arm then took a sip of coffee.

"By the way, I wanted to ask you to do Josh and me a favor and come to the model competition next month."

Amy pulled her arm back and her eyes welled up almost to the point of tearing. "Do you know what you are asking me?"

Duke reached out and took her hand then pulled it back toward the center of the table. "Look I know how hard everything is with Mark

76

gone, but Josh has come such a long way. I was hoping you would be there for support. Hell, maybe it would even do you some good to watch the kids having a great time."

A single tear rolled down Amy's cheek and fell onto the table. "I'm not sure I can stand watching one of those planes crash. It's just too soon."

"I know it's a hard thing to do, but it would mean so much to Josh. Besides I promise there won't be a single crash." Duke half stood and cupped her chin in his hand then began laughing as he said, "There will be dozens."

Amy tried to turn away, but he held her head so she had to look at him and soon, against her will, she began laughing too.

"Damn you, old man, I never could resist you - even when I was a kid," she said getting up and moving around the table to hug her father. They stood together for a long time. Father and daughter, hugging and laughing and crying, but most of all releasing buckets of pain they had both kept inside hiding the loss of someone they both loved.

When Amy had cried her last tear she led her dad out to the swing on the porch. Slowly pushing the swing with her feet she looked at Duke. "Okay, I'll go, but you have to do something for me in return," she said as she picked up the magazine she had been reading. "You have to help me find a new place to live as far away from here as I can get."

Duke gave her that look he always used when he knew he was going to have to do something he didn't want to. "I know you never liked the life style here, but maybe you should reconsider now that Josh is beginning to settle down."

"No you don't. I've been talking about moving someplace safe for years. You know the only reason we stayed here was because Mark loved all the intrigue and he always wanted to be where the action was. But I hate the constant feeling that another attack is on the way. Every hour of every day that's all I can think about. You've got to help me get away."

This had been a road they had been down before, but this time Duke couldn't think of anything to say except, "All right I'll help you find a nice safe place for the kids and you, but you've got to promise me that you won't jump the gun and do something crazy while I'm looking around. Deal?"

Amy held out her hand, smiled, and they shook on it.

Chapter 14
Worms and Rats

Ty pulled onto the George Washington School of Engineering campus in Ashburn, Virginia, forty-five, minutes after he left Duke and Josh. Driving toward the computer science building, he wondered what type of catastrophe it would be this time.

As he walked into the building, Ty looked down at his watch and knew Dr. Noah Shipman had finished teaching, which meant he'd probably retreated to the computer complex under the building. Walking towards the specially constructed elevators in the center of the main hallway, Ty passed Shipman's office and saw that the lights were out, confirming what he already suspected.

When he was within five feet of the elevator door the RF security card in his wallet activated the entry program and the door opened. A second later, the piezoelectric scale sensors built into the floor confirmed his weight was within specifications. Watching the door close, Ty got a firm hold on the handrail then leaned back against the wall and waited for the bottom to drop out of the universe.

As the elevator dropped, Ty's mind jumped back to the day he had received his access badge for the facility. They checked his identification—twice, then verified everything against the clearance and special accesses he would require for the facility, had his thumb and first finger scanned into a reader, took an eye scan, then his weight was calibrated, once in basic clothes, then again with a heavier coat on, 'for cold weather climates,' he was told. Next, a sound bite was taken using words from a random selection list. Just a few of them, and finally, the sergeant had Ty write several different variations of his signature with a special stylus pencil on an electronic sensor pad. It seemed like an awful lot of different things had to be done, but the sergeant pointed out that only under extreme circumstances would more than two or three be used for verification. Each time he entered the facility, and at certain points within the facility, for access, a reader would ask for one of the items, then a second. If there were more, he must understand that the security level had jumped, thus an increase in verification. Seconds later, he relaxed when the plummeting elevator slowed as it neared the OHS internet monitoring complex.

When the elevator gently stopped, the doors opened and Ty walked out into a small ten by ten foot room. It was rather plain except for a camera hanging on a small bracket, a brass button, and the chromium-steel blast door built into the opposite wall. The door had a small bulletproof window built into it which showed a room on the other side that was identical to this one, except that it was missing the elevator door.

Ty pushed the button beside the door and waited for Dr. Shipman or one of his grad-students to let him in. A minute later the locks inside the door were pulled back and it swung open about thirty degrees. As Ty walked into the room the eighteen-inch thick door slowly closed behind him and relocked. The second door unlocked and swung open. He walked into an enormous room twenty feet high and the area of three football fields.

Inside this complex sat the American node of ECHELON, the greatest surveillance computer system ever built. The National Security Agency (NSA) had poured billions into the project that was started back in 1948. Today the United States, England, Canada, Australian and New Zealand still worked together under secret agreement. Their mission was to monitor all satellite, microwave, cellular and fiber-optic communications traffic looking for words and phrases that it deemed to be threatening to democratic societies.

Since it was humanly impossible to listen to every simultaneous conversation going on at any moment in time, the system employed voice recognition and optical character recognition that was capable of sifting through terabytes of intercepted information per second. In theory the design was simple. It was like placing a very coarse sieve on top of hundreds of other sieves that kept getting finer until only the finest powder poured out at the bottom.

Somewhere near the top sieve, languages were identified and routed to specific computers that translated them into a common language the rest of the system could understand. After years of experimenting and several overhauls the designers had chosen Sanskrit for the common language. Sanskrit is unique among Earth's languages. Its perfect grammar and scientific characteristics make it the most unambiguous language on Earth. And that is exactly what the scientists working on the phrase matching portions of the system needed.

Of course keeping the computer systems up to date and editing the translation algorithms kept hordes of professors and grad students busy. Plumbs like this didn't come along very often, and the board at George Washington University jumped at the chance of having the complex built on their campus.

While some scientists objected to using the system for domestic eavesdropping on real-time intercepts of Senators, Congressmen, Amnesty International, Greenpeace and the Christian ministries, others couldn't resist the chance to work with the newest technology and the unlimited budget available here.

Since no one was there to greet him, Ty walked over the row of Segways and unplugged the last one in line. He grabbed the handle, stepped onto the platform and leaned forward. Soon he was cruising past offices, potted palms and endless cabinets of electronics as he headed towards Dr. Shipman's office in the center of the complex.

On arrival, Ty rolled over to another row of Segways, jumped off, and attached the charger. When he walked into the office, Shipman was watching data and graphs scroll by two computer monitors. His assistant, Sarah, sat in front of him playing the computer keyboard like she was performing at Carnegie Hall.

"Why did you call me today?" Ty asked.

Shipman nervously adjusted his glasses and wiped his right nostril with his forefinger before answering. "At first we thought it was an unannounced Penetration Test, but that's not scheduled to begin until sometime in February."

Sarah chimed in. "I knew that didn't seem logical this early, then it started to look like a denial-of-service attack. But wait, I've got it now."

She laughed. "It's some kind of spam or phishing campaign aimed at internet users interested in porn."

"So it is a penetration test after all," Ty said with a big smile.

Sarah looked back at Ty and blushed. "Not so surprising when you think about the statistics. The revenue generated in the Unites States by internet porn is up to about three billion dollars. Every second, eight thousand people are watching it (roughly a seven to three ratio of men to women), and the good old U-S-of-A produces ninety percent of the almost four-hundred million porn web pages in the world."

Ty was about casting about in his mind for something clever to say, but before he could come up with it Shipman derailed his thought processes.

"Funny the attack seems to have come from Indonesia, but they're one of the few countries with a ban on pornography," Shipman said walking over to the printer.

"The problem with banning anything is that it just makes it more irresistible to the people who aren't supposed to use it. Nothing is worse than a reformed person. They forget about everything they did and start telling anyone who will listen how they're a better person now that they have quit. It doesn't matter if it's sex, drugs, or rock-n-roll. They're hypocrites," Ty said sitting down in Shipman's chair.

"Good thing I've only sworn off one of your big three," Sarah said looking up from her terminal.

"Which one is that?" Ty asked.

"That's for me to know and for you to figure out," she bantered back.

"You two stop it or I'll have to give you both a timeout," Shipman said taking the printout and walking back to his desk. "Get out of my chair!"

"Sorry boss, I forgot how obsessive you are about that old thing," Ty said sliding out of the way just as Shipman sat down.

Looking over the printout Shipman removed his glasses and tilted back in his chair. "This email originated in Jakarta from a wireless connection located in the Mulia Senayan Hotel. The CPU's serial number and Ethernet adapter IP Address lookup makes it a Dell Latitude D610 shipped to Virginia three years ago."

"Seems a long way from home," Ty said looking over Shipman's shoulder.

"Yes since it was reported stolen from a CompUSA warehouse and never registered," Sarah said walking over with another printout.

"I guess pornography is out, and receiving stolen property is in over there," Ty said as he walked over to Sarah and peeked over her shoulder.

As Ty stood behind her, Sarah could feel his warmth radiating across the air conditioned space between them. When his shoulder touched her, an electric spark shot through her body. "Give a girl some room, will you," she said sitting back down at the keyboard.

81

Chapter 15
Delta Lake

A week after the funeral, Duke had gotten a large envelope from Ajax Jet Models Incorporated. The cover letter explained that they were testing a prototype model of the Phantom jet he had flown in Vietnam and wanted to know if he would be interested in helping them promote the product. The envelope also contained: a limited non-disclosure agreement that precluded him from talking with other model manufactures, a five-year endorsement agreement, and a request for any of his photos that could be used in advertising the model. That alone would have been enough to get Duke onboard, but the icing on the cake was the letter of intent, which promised him $1,000 plus expenses for every regional, national and international competition he attended to promote the model.

When he wasn't helping Amy or his grandkids he was busy sorting through his memorabilia from Vietnam and emailing his old buddies about the offer from Ajax, sometimes remembering to mention that his daughter is looking to move to a more rural location. He received an email from an old Air Force buddy, whose ass he had saved from the North Vietnamese.

Durwood, who had taken an early retirement from the Pentagon after the 911 attacks, was getting bored living in Sticksville. He had been offered his old job back with a substantial increase in pay. So, he had his house on the market and wanted Duke to bring Amy up for a look-see.

Durwood had attached directions to the Home Owner's Association and Marina, where he would meet them if they decided to come up. He included a photo he thought Duke might want to use for his Ajax promotions.

After a call to Amy, Duke emailed Durwood to ask if it would be okay to come up the following weekend and to thank him for the photo of Duke making a treetop bombing run on the radar installation that had shot Durwood out of the sky.

•••

Once Amy, Samantha, and Josh were buckled into Duke's Dodge Ram, he punched in the address of the Home Owner's Association and Marina at Delta Lake, New York into the GPS and their weekend adventure began. Heading north on 83, Duke started telling Amy about the new Phantom jet model he was working on with Ajax and didn't stop until he rolled onto 81. By the time he reached the New York State Thruway the kids were asleep and Amy was finding it hard to stay awake herself, so Duke stopped talking and she quickly fell asleep, too.

Waking everyone up when he turned off the Verona/Route 365 exit onto Erie Blvd, Duke thought it was about time to start bragging about completing the trip in five hours and thirty minutes. No way anyone would believe him if they hadn't been sitting in the car. He must have broken every speed law numerous times, and luck had been with him as he hadn't seen a single cop along the way.

"Not too bad for an old fart," Duke announced as he pulled into a parking space near the door of the Marina.

When they walked inside the single story building, Duke saw Durwood waving at him from a table in the corner that was surrounded on two sides by large picture windows. He stood up as they approached and held out his hand to greet Duke.

"Well, long time - no see," Durwood said and he took Duke's hand and gave it a strong squeeze and vigorous shake.

"Let's see, I don't remember if you ever actually met my daughter Amy", Duke said as he put his left arm around her shoulder.

"Don't think so, I'd remember a face as pretty as this – if I had." Durwood said as he relaxed his grip on Duke and reached out towards Amy.

Amy extended her hand then emitted a little squeal as Durwood clamped down on it. "No I don't think we ever met, but Duke always tells the story about how he helped you evade capture until the SAR team rescued you when he was partying with his buddies."

Durwood relaxed his grip and a genuine smile appeared on Amy's face as she extracted her hand from his vice-like grip. "I guess it was a good thing you two were so into golf."

"Yep, no telling what would have happened to me if your dad hadn't figured that out we both played the same golf course so quickly," Durwood said giving Duke an appreciative nod.

"Usually I'd get a match on baseball or football, but Durwood here was lucky. Golf was the last thing on my list of directional topics that we both had a flare for," Duke said drifting back to that day.

•••

"Air Force, you've got Charlies all around you. Which do you like better baseball or football?" Duke radioed as he circled the smoking radar installation he had just obliterated."

"I'm more of a golf type, Navy. Over," Durwood radioed back.

"Play anything around Washington, Air Force?" Duke said pulling away to gain some maneuvering room.

"Got into Congressional Blue a couple of times the year Ernie Els won the Open. Over," Durwood radioed back, as he watched the Phantom disappearing to his east.

"Air Force, whatever you do, don't move. I'm flying towards the pin on six," Duke said just before pulling a vertical loop and roll, heading back toward the downed pilot.

"Air force, follow the bullets. Now, now, now," Duke said pulling the trigger on the control stick.

The next thing Durwood heard was the whine of fifty caliber bullets drawing a line through the jungle to his right. A second later he was up and running as fast as he could through the green mist of chewed up debris falling around him.

"Stop and drop," Duke radioed down to him. "When you hear the blast, you're the ball on eighteen. Get across the lake and drop."

Durwood waited for what seemed like an eternity before a missile exploded behind him. Then quickly jumped up and ran two yards due north and dropped to the ground waiting for more instructions.

•••

As Duke's focus returned to the present he chuckled. "Good thing you could run like a rabbit back in the day."

Durwood smiled back at him without saying a word, knowing that had been the luckiest day of his life.

A few seconds later Durwood turned to Duke's grandchildren. "You must be Josh. I've heard you can fly a plane with the best of them," Durwood said as he reached under the table and pulled out a big package. "Here's something I picked up for you to wear the next time you fly in competition."

Josh took the package and began tearing away the wrapping paper. Durwood turned toward Samantha and presented her with a somewhat smaller package wrapped in pink paper.

"I'm never sure what to get for little girls," He said, "but I'm pretty sure you don't have one of these."

"You didn't need to get the kids gifts, you old conniver. I told you we'd be coming up to see the house. Looks like you've been reading Guerrilla Marketing again," Duke said as he bent down to help Sam open her present.

A few minutes later Josh was wearing a leather aviator's jacket and Sam was inspecting an electric pink puppy with long purple hair around its head and on the tip of its tail.

"Let's sit down and enjoy some of the finest food you can get on the lake until this place opens again next spring." Durwood said as he signaled the waiter to come over.

During the lunch Duke and Durwood caught up on old friends who had died and how, something Amy wished she could have stopped, but knew she couldn't. By the time the coffee was served and all the information in the two men's databases had been brought up to date and synchronized, it was time for Durwood to get down to the business of trying to sell his house.

"Can you see the house over on the other side of the inlet?" Durwood said as he pointed to a row of houses that ringed the lake's north shore.

"Well, I see a lot of houses over there. Which one is yours?" Amy said as she shielded her eyes from the bright rays of the setting sun that had crept across the floor while they were eating.

Durwood reached behind his chair and pulled on the cord that adjusted the blinds to give her a better view. "Which one catches your eye?"

Amy adjusted herself in her chair and scanned the houses for one she thought she might be able to afford. "I don't see anything over there that I can afford, but I like the one with the copper roof, windmill, and boat elevator that goes from the back yard down to the lake. Whoever lives there must be rolling in dough."

"Why isn't the windmill turning?" Samantha asked.

"Neighbors kept complaining, said it made too much noise, so I had to shut the thing down." Duke answered.

"You mean that's your house." Amy exclaimed.

Durwood laughed. "If you play your cards right you and the kids could be living there."

Amy was stunned, angry, and hurt all at the same instant. "You mean you brought me all the way up here to see something I could never afford."

Durwood sat back in his chair and smiled. "Listen Amy, believe it or not, there aren't many people in Oneida County that could afford that house, but if you're interested in living in the middle of what some might call nowhere. I think we can work something out."

•••

As they walked down the driveway Amy was dumbfounded. "This thing is huge."

Durwood, who was leading the way with Duke by his side responded over his shoulder, "Ten thousand square feet, if you don't count the basement and underground blast shelter."

Since Josh really didn't have any idea what ten thousand square feet had to do with a house, but knew perfectly well that the word blast had to be something cool, he ran up to Durwood and asked, "What's a blast shelter?"

"Well, I'll show you after the house lets us in," Durwood said with a smile.

"What do you mean after the house lets us in?" Josh squealed as he began to immediately take a liking to this one.

When they were about ten feet from the front door the alarm system inside responding to the RF Security card in Durwood's wallet emitted three little beeps and unlocked the electronic front door. Then it went through its checklist of 'things to do when the boss comes home,' turning on appropriate lighting and the satellite radio receiver.

Once they opened the door and everyone was inside, the HOME (Holistically Optimized Monitoring Environment) computer asked, "Would anyone like a fire tonight?"

"Not if your mother lit it. HOME," Durwood responded harshly. Explaining that if he had not responded with the correct phase the computer system would have locked the house up tighter than a drum. Then the surveillance system would begin recording, while the local and state police were called in.

"That's crazy," Josh said as he began laughing. "All you have to do is break a window and you'd be out of here in a second."

Without a moment's hesitation Durwood picked up a heavy paperweight from the writing table in the foyer. Took a few steps into the living room and threw the heavy object as hard as he could against the large picture window. It made a peculiar sound when it loudly ricocheted off the glass. As paperweight slid across the floor and stopped, Josh's mouth dropped open in amazement.

"It's Bullet Proof, so I'm pretty sure the windows will stop the common criminal," Durwood said. He retrieved the paperweight and returned it to the writing table. "Let's go into the library and I'll show you the rest of the place on the computer."

Amy sat between Duke and Durwood with the children in leather recliners on either side. Durwood picked up what looked like an elaborate TV tuner and pressed a couple of buttons. A few seconds later a giant screen began lowering in front of them. At the same time a projector emerged from the ceiling behind them and clicked on when the screen was fully extended.

"Since Josh was so interested in the blast shelter, I'll start there," Durwood said as he brought up a diagram on the screen.

"During the Cold War there was a SAC, the Strategic Air Command installation at Griffith's Air Force Base over in Rome, and this area was a primary Russian target. So, one of the eggheads working in Research and Development decided he needed to build a blast shelter, if he wanted to live on after the nuclear war cooked the world."

"I guess you're talking about the fallout shelters that the government got everyone to build back in the 50s and 60s?" Amy asked.

Duke chuckled. "No I'm afraid that a fallout shelter here wouldn't do you much good. If you were living here when a bomb hit the base your standard fallout shelter would just collapse and crush you to death."

Seeing Samantha had changed her position and was now sitting in her mother's lap, Durwood stopped for a moment then smiled at her, pushed out his lips and shook his head from side to side and said, "Nothing to worry about today, little miss."

He picked up two chocolate kisses wrapped in shiny foil from a bowl on the coffee table in front of the couch and handed one to Samantha and tossed the other one to Josh before he continued.

"This engineer got hold of a section of twelve foot diameter pre-stressed concrete pipe that was twenty feet long, and then he buried ten feet under the front lawn. You can see that the only way to get into or out of it is from the basement."

He stopped again handing the candy dish to Amy. "You can be in charge of parceling out the goodies."

"The basement is a basement, although the kids might enjoy the pool, pinball machines, and pool table. Then there's the main floor, we're on now. It boasts three bedrooms, each with its own full bathroom. There is another full bathroom near the breakfast room by the back door. Also a kitchen, dining room, library, and equipment room for all the electronics in the place."

"If we somehow manage to move in, I don't even want to know what's on the second floor," Amy said in wonder.

"I'm not sure that's true." Durwood said as he continued. "The second floor has an observatory with a twenty-inch telescope, garden, where I grow some mighty fine vegetables and flowers and a little lab where I tinker when I'm not out on the boat taking friends water skiing or fishing."

Duke, who had been silent throughout the whole presentation, cleared his throat, leaned forward put his hands on his knees and stood up. "Well this is a lot more than I bargained for when I came up here. I'm beginning to think that Amy was right back at the club when she said she could never afford something like this. I'm afraid we might be wasting your time."

"Well give me a minute to complete my sales pitch before you go off half cocked like usual. Tell you what. Let's all get something to drink and take a walk around the place before I tell you what I want."

By the time the tour was over and they had all topped off their glasses at the wet bar. Durwood led the tired little band out to the sunroom. Everyone except Durwood seemed to be glad they could sit down and enjoy the new moon reflecting off the water some forty feet below.

"Now that you've seen everything, I'm hoping you can appreciate my many problems," Durwood said, as he took a long drink of cola.

"The only problem I can see is how you are going to find someone to buy this place. It's a palace," Amy said saluting him with her glass.

"A palace it may be," Durwood replied, "But that is only one of the many problems I have. No one around here can afford to buy a place like this. Besides who wants to live in the middle of nowhere, if you need to drive for an hour to get to some place where you might be able to make a decent salary. I need just the right person to be interested in

88

this house. Another thing is, I need to sell it in the next thirty days so I can go back to Washington before the offer expires. If I want my old job back I need to find a house in the Silver Spring area."

"We live in Silver Spring," Samantha said smiling proudly.

"Is that so?" Durwood replied as a sly grin began to form in the corners of his mouth.

Chapter 16
Thanksgiving Past

After another afternoon at the pool, Halley had returned to her room on the eighth floor of the hotel and took a quick shower before taking a nap. Lying there she could have easily been mistaken for a young teenager, but she had been conceived in 1984 during the approach of Halley's Comet and named after it the following year as it retreated back into deep space.

As the old saying goes, "Good things come in small packages" and Halley was a remarkable package with long dark hair that spilled over her shoulders and half way to her waist, deep brown eyes and the hint of a smile always peeking out from an adorable face. On the inside however she was hard as nails holding black belts in several martial arts.

All this had started at the age of five at the insistence of her mother who thought it was important to hold on to a few of her family's traditions. However, tradition soon transformed itself into a ritual to attract the attention of her father, who never missed one of her belt tests.

Her martial arts training, coupled with the fact she had just graduated from Swarthmore College with Highest Honors in Liberal Arts and a BS in Engineering was the reason Halley's parents had been convinced to let her extend her stay in Jakarta an extra week, after they returned home.

As Halley slept a slight sound vibrated from her throat and her head moved slowly as her neck muscles stretched and relaxed. Under closed eyelids her eyes darted back and forth as she was transported back to two thousand and one and the annual Thanksgiving family gathering at her Uncle Jorgen's horse farm in New Jersey.

It was a confusing time, one marked by tragedy and disbelief. Halley remembered sitting beside her mother on the couch in Cambridge, Massachusetts listening to the one-sided conversations as her father phoned his two younger brothers, Jorgen and Kettil.

Since the week-long family reunion was always held at her Uncle Jorgen's, Halley's parents decided to play it safe and drive down, but Kettil's family lived in San Diego and would have to fly if they were coming. Halley felt helpless listening to the conversations that would go on for hours, but sat through them all so she would eventually get a chance to talk to her cousin Kathy.

Halley and Kathy had been born a month apart and ended up being the only children in their families, which gave them something in common. This may have been responsible for their bonding on the first Thanksgiving they spent together at the farm.

The only difference between the two girls until they were seven was the color of their hair and eyes. Halley had taken after her mother and had jet-black hair and eyes so brown they seemed black. Kathy on the other hand had inherited the best parts of her parents' Scandinavian physicality and sported long straw colored hair and light blue eyes.

Except for those two differences the girls could have passed for twins, but when they were seven Kathy began inching up a little each year until she was now almost a foot taller than Halley.

As they got older Kathy took up surfing while Halley studied martial arts. They both had discovered boys at the same time and constantly shared secrets over the internet – also discussing the latest fashions and makeup tips. Since their fathers both worked for Ericsson, they knew better than to write anything too juicy on their computers, which were undoubtedly monitored.

Of course they had come up with a couple of coded references while they were on the phone together, but were anxious to get together now that they were sixteen and share their secrets privately. That's why they were both so happy when Kathy's father changed his mind at the last minute and booked the family's flight to Newark.

On Wednesday they had spent most of the day riding horses and playing with their Uncle Jorgen's three girls. Finally they had slipped away to the basement rec room while everyone was busy putting together dinner upstairs. It seemed like they had only been sitting at the card table a minute when Petter and Kettil found them.

Expecting to get a lecture on how they should be pitching in upstairs, the girls got up and began to huff off. They were called back and told politely to sit down. As their fathers joined them at the table, Kathy noticed that her father was carrying a box under his arm and nudged Halley with her elbow.

It was apparent whatever he was carrying was intended for them so, they began to get excited each imagining what was in the box.

"I've got something here you may be interesting in using until we go home," Kettil said taking out two smaller boxes and handing one to each of the girls.

Kathy was the first to get hers opened and saw what looked like a small radio with re-charger and a flesh colored earpiece.

"These look like something the boys would like." Halley said as she took hers and examined the controls carefully.

Since the device didn't have a conventional tuner listing the AM/FM bands, she figured it wasn't a radio. The volume control looked normal, but the other switches marked: 'Single & Dual' and 'Monitor On & OFF' didn't give her much of a clue about what this contraption was.

"What's this little piece of plastic on the cord for?" Kathy asked.

"That's the microphone," her father stated. He took them back and set them up for the girls and handed them back. "Now, see if you can talk to each other."

After a few seconds of chattering back and forth the girls began to lose interest and were ready to hand them back.

"I know they seem lame, don't they." Kettil said as he reached into the first box again.

When the girls started to protest, he held up his index finger and put it to his lips. He opened a small plastic case and took out a translucent disk of plastic about the size of a pencil eraser. Holding it in the palm of his hand he passed it slowly before the two girls so they could get a good look at it. This maneuver produced a quizzical look from the girls as they looked at each other and made a funny face.

Undiscouraged, Kettil continued, knowing the best part was coming. Picking up the disk he peeled off the paper covering the adhesive and stuck it on Petter's face by the center of his ear where it seemed to disappear. Then he pointed to his brother and motioned for him to go upstairs.

As Petter climbed the steps, Kettil reached over and flipped the 'Monitor On' switch. Instantly the girls flashed a smile as they heard Petter's footsteps on the rug and the voices from the kitchen getting louder as he arrived there.

"Has anybody seen Halley and Kathy? I've been looking all over for them," Petter said getting himself a glass of water and walking outside.

Down in the cellar it sounded like the girls were right beside him and they giggled.

"These things are pretty cool," Kathy said.

"Yes they are, princess," Petter answered as he disappeared around the corner of the farm house and headed for his car.

"Are you trying to make us believe this that tiny disk transmits too?" Halley asked with a puzzled look on her face.

Kettil laughed and leaned closer to Kathy's monitor and spoke slightly louder than usual, "Petter, I see that your money wasn't totally wasted. Halley seems to be catching on."

While this was going on Petter retrieved a pack of cigarettes from under the driver's seat and lit one.

"You are supposed to be quitting, Daddy," Halley said when she figured out what he was up to.

"Well that's the beauty of these little Digital Obscure Transceiver Systems or DOTS, as we like to call them. They let you know what's really going on behind your back. Might be fun to play with for a few days, don't you think, Princess?"

While Petter finished smoking, Kettil took the units from the girls and placed them each back into their small cases along with two plastic disks. "These things need to be charged for a couple of hours before you start using them. I don't care what you do with them, but keep a record of how they work and the distances involved. You know, kind of like you were doing a report in school. The DOTS are all on the same frequency, so only use one at a time. They only last for about an hour, but might cut out sooner since they're prototypes. Enjoy."

Kettil got up and began to walk away, but he stopped and turned around. "One more thing, if you don't want the person wearing the DOTS to be able to hear you, switch to the 'Single' mode." Then he bounded up the stairs to grab a cigarette with Petter.

When Petter saw his brother coming around the corner of the house, he reached into the car, smiled and grabbed the cigarettes. When Kettil reached his brother, he took a cigarette. Then reached up and peeled the plastic transceiver off his brother's face and stuck it on the tip of the cigarette before lighting it.

"I never thought $5 million dollars could taste so bad," Kettil said tossing the smelly cigarette away and taking another one.

Since Petter and Kettil were working on part of the ECHELON project for the National Security Agency, they both had access to some pretty interesting prototypes and DOTS was one of them. But in truth, neither of them knew what DOTS or anything else they had been building actually cost.

What Kettil had hoped for, when he volunteered to test the equipment over the Thanksgiving holiday, was that Kathy would somehow use them and get a good dose of reality when it came to boys. So far the hook had been baited and they just had to wait for a fish to take it.

Oblivious to the fact that what Kettil had just handed them was actually $20 million dollars worth of equipment, the girls had managed to get the chargers hooked up before their mothers finally caught up with them and dragged them back to the kitchen to help prepare dinner.

One of the things Halley and Kathy could never understand when they visited their uncle was how much food his kids could pack away. Tonight as they sat down at the large dining room table set for sixteen they were amazed by the size of the bowls piled with enough food to feed their families for a week or more.

After their Uncle Jorgen said grace, pandemonium broke out when his kids attacked the food like they hadn't eaten for a week. If their Aunt Janet hadn't pleaded for everyone to slow down, the girls doubted there would have been anything left for them by the time the bowls and platters made it to them.

A friend of the two oldest boys came in through the back door and made his way to the dining room.

"Grab a chair, Hunter. Looks like you showed up right on time to eat again," Janet said grabbing an extra plate and some silverware.

"Regular as clockwork, I see," Kettil said passing him an ear of corn.

"Jason and Jimmy told me it would be okay to stop over," Hunter said in his defense as he grabbed a pork chop with his fork.

Since Hunter lived down the road and had been hanging out with the older Andersson boys for years, Halley and Kathy had met him before. Over the last year he had shot up another four or five inches and put on a lot of muscle. This didn't go unnoticed by Kathy, who thought he looked a lot cuter than she remembered.

When dinner was over, Hunter started cleaning up the table while Halley and Kathy helped their aunt Janet clean up the kitchen.

"So what's new in San Diego?" Hunter asked Kathy when he brought in the last pile of dirty dishes.

"Nothing much, I spent most of the summer surfing and hanging out at the beach. I'm on the cheerleading squad again." She said.

"How about you, Halley?" Hunter asked flicking a little glob of bubbles at her.

"Well, we visited my grandmother in Hong Kong in August and I learned some really neat bendy twisty joint locks at a dojo there. Would you like to see?"

"No thanks. The last time you showed me something, I ended up getting tossed across the barn. The only thing that saved me was landing on a pile of hay."

A little laugh escaped from Halley as she remembered him arching through the air into the hay. He landed exactly where she had been aiming him. "I'm sorry. Sometimes I don't know my own strength."

Kathy gave him a little kiss on the check. "You poor thing Hunter, always abused by beautiful girls."

For a second neither of them seemed to know what to do, but they quickly went back to rinsing off the plates in the sink.

"What kind of move was that?" Halley asked poking Kathy in her side.

"This kind," Kathy said poking at Halley until she was laughing so hard she couldn't breathe.

Kathy continued chasing Halley down the hall and up into their room until they both finally collapsed on the bed giggling.

"I think Hunter likes you," Halley said sitting up and seeing the DOTS equipment was now fully charged.

"Let's try this thing out." Halley continued as she reached for the box of translucent disks. "I paste one of these things on him when he leaves and we'll see what happens.

Kathy squirmed a little on the bed then propped herself up on one elbow. "What have we got to lose?"

When the girls returned to the kitchen, Hunter had finished loading the dishwasher and was heading out the back door to go find Jason and Jimmy.

"You're quite a guy Hunter. Have fun." Halley said as she slapped him on the shoulder.

"Goodbye, Hunter. Will we see you tomorrow?" Kathy asked.

"No, I've got to go to my grandmother's for Thanksgiving, but I'll be back on Friday. Will you two still be here?" Hunter asked as he pushed the back door open.

"We'll be here till Saturday. See you." Kathy answered.

As Hunter started walking toward the barn the two girls raced up stairs to get the monitors. They each grabbed their jacket and raced downstairs and out toward the barn. When they got there, all the Andersson kids were playing ping-pong on a table set up under a bright light.

"Where's Hunter?" Kathy asked.

"His father just drove over and picked him up. Guess they're leaving tonight instead of tomorrow," Jimmy said. "You want to play the winner?"

"No, I'm not very good. I think Halley and I will go up in the loft and look for shooting stars.

"Suit yourself, but if you change your mind, we'll be here until I've beaten everyone else." Jimmy said with a note of confidence.

Up in the loft, the girls pushed the earpieces into their ears and began listening to Hunter and his father talking.

"...You know Kathy is really cute, Dad. I wish we lived in California so I could go to the ocean and learn how to surf," Hunter said.

"You can surf right here. We're only a half hour away from the shore." His father said.

"Yea, but the waves around here suck. They're huge out there and it's warm all the time..."

Halley smiled as she woke up at the hotel in Jakarta. It was a pleasant dream; one that she always enjoyed when it popped into her head. As she walked slowly into the bathroom she somehow felt closer to her cousin Kathy, who married Hunter and now lived in Washington, DC with their two daughters.

Chapter 17
Jakarta Twist

As Halley rode the elevator to the 38th floor she fingered the silver good-luck locket that Kathy had given her for being her maid-of-honor. When it stopped she reached out a finger to press the lobby button, but stopped herself and walked out into the hallway. Each step she took toward the door opposite Mohammed's suite seemed to happen automatically without her control and soon she was knocking softly on the hard wood.

After a minute she knocked again and was about to return to the elevator when the door behind her opened. She dropped down into a fighting stance and spun around instinctively holding her hands out for protection.

Mohammed held up his hands and smiled. "Sorry. Sorry. I didn't mean to startle you. I just thought you might me looking for the man who sent you the tea by the pool."

Halley tried to regain her composure, but felt a little embarrassed by the defensive pose she had automatically taken. "Sorry I was expecting you to be in that room." She said pointing back over her shoulder.

"Well it's hard to get good help anymore. Maybe the waiter wrote down the wrong number. Please come in if you like or we could go down to the bar or restaurant if you prefer more public surroundings."

As Mohammed opened the door wide and bowed, Halley couldn't see anyone else inside and she was pretty sure she could take out one guy by herself, as she had proved on countless occasions during training and matches over the years. Still she had this little tingle on the back of her neck that wouldn't go away.

"Maybe you're right. I'd love to go down and have a bite to eat."

"I'll be right out. I have to get some things before we go," Mohammed said as he left the door opened and disappeared inside.

A few moments later he returned, locked the door and accompanied Halley to the elevators. As they rode down, Halley decided to avoid ending up in one of the formal restaurants and suggested they eat at her favorite spot so they could listen to the jazz quartet.

The hostess guided them to a table near the center of the room. Just walking in here with a stranger that she had met only moments ago made her feel excited, grownup, and happy for the first time since her parents had left.

"I just love the atmosphere here," she said sarcastically pointing to the ornate paper fern pretending to grow out of a large hand-thrown pot serving as the centerpiece of the room.

She pointed to the red, gold, and blue piece at the end of the bar and finally to the large one sitting on a shelf behind the base player – directly in front of them. "I call them space plants because they look like all those weird things they put in science fiction movies to make you think you're someplace else."

Mohammed smiled at her kindly and leaned forward. "I don't get to watch many movies, but I agree that they do look like something from outer space."

He spotted the waiter coming in their direction and winked at him. "When the waiter arrives I would like to order for the both of us, but I don't know what you like to drink."

This presented a problem for Halley, as she only had had a couple of drinks with her parents on special occasions and one glass of champagne at Kathy's wedding. "I really don't know. Why don't you surprise me?"

As soon as she said that, she regretted it. Pictures of flaming concoctions designed to get someone drunk enough that they could easily be manipulated back to the bedroom and raped flashed into her eyes.

Halley pulled herself back from the nightmare she had created in her head and blurted out. "I would love a club sandwich."

Just then the waiter pulled up between them with his pad raised and ignored Mohammed as he addressed Halley like an old friend. "And what would we like to eat tonight, Miss Halley?"

"Oh Jackie, I think you better ask my friend, he's ordering for us tonight." She said hoping that this wasn't going to get back to her parents.

"Excuse me Miss Halley. I assumed that this gentleman was someone the family was entertaining." Then he turned toward Mohammed. "A thousand pardons sir. What can I get for you?"

Mohammed laughed out loud. "It appears that you have been here before."

Mohammed hadn't expected Halley to be so well known here and was a little taken aback by the last fifteen seconds as he paused to consider all the possibilities that had just presented themselves. "I think the lady will have a champagne cocktail - on the light side. And I will take a screwdriver along with two club sandwiches."

The waiter scribbled something in his book then was about to see if they wanted anything else when he caught a look from Mohammed that sent him quickly scurrying away.

"It would seem that you are pretty popular here in Jakarta," Mohammed said as he unfolded his cloth napkin across his lap.

Halley's smile beamed back at him. First of all, because he had ordered a drink that sounded interesting and second because she didn't want him to go running off, just because she wasn't as alone as she appeared. "Well we've been coming here every year in late August forever. First while I was at boarding school and then in college. Dad is so busy working I hardly ever get to see him. But that's all going to change now that I've graduated. I'm going to intern at his company and start working on my Masters in Computer Science at MIT."

Before Mohammed could reply the waiter was back with their drinks. When he left Mohammed raised his slender glass, waited for Halley to do the same then clinked them together. "This must be my lucky day, catching you between school and work. Maybe we can have some fun together before you leave."

After taking a sip and finding it much to her liking, Halley put the glass down and tossed her head slightly to the side sending a dark wave of hair cresting toward her lap. "Yes, I would like to have some fun. What did you have in mind?"

A very serious looked appeared on Mohammed's face as he leaned forward again. "That depends entirely on you," he said as he sat back up, tilted his head and smiled.

"I don't know when you are leaving, but tomorrow I'm going out on a sailboat with some friends; and Saturday I'm off to visit another friend who runs a research facility. I'd love to have company," Mohammed said after he finished the first quarter of his dinner.

"I'm leaving the Friday after next so I'm free until then," Halley said finishing the cocktail. "What kind of research does your friend do?"

Mohammed caught the waiter's eye and held up two fingers before continuing. "Ramadan is into animal research, but I don't pretend to understand what he does. I just like to go up there and ride his horses. Besides he treats me like a king while I'm there."

"I love horses," Halley said, "and sailing too. I might just take you up on your offer."

By the time they had finished eating both had consumed three more cocktails and Halley was feeling totally relaxed and strangely attracted to this mysterious man.

"Would you like some dessert before we leave?" Mohammed asked brushing away the last crumbs from his mouth.

"Sure, that sounds fantastic," Halley said as she listened to the jazz tune playing in the background.

Before she knew it, she was eating chocolate covered strawberries and sipping brandy. An hour later, Mohammed was helping her toward the elevator and back up to his room.

Chapter 18
Trial Run

The next morning, Halley awoke slowly alone in a strange bed with the softest sheets she had ever felt. Tiny vortexes of air danced across her face and tickled her toes. It took her a minute to focus on the ceiling fan and another to realize that she was totally naked. When she tried to sit up it felt like something hit her in the back of her head and she melted back down into the bed for a few more minutes.

Lying there, she heard a soft knocking then the door opened. When she managed to open her eyes again, Mohammed was peeking in. "What the hell happened last night?" Halley blurted out pulling the sheets closer.

"Why, don't you remember dancing naked around the room for hours last night?" he said laughing.

"No. Definitely no dancing that I can remember," she said maneuvering up to a sitting position using her shoulders to drag her body up against the pillows behind her.

"Unfortunately, I can assure you that nothing happened last night except that I got to see the most beautiful girl in the world naked for about ten seconds as I tucked her safely into bed," Mohammed said as he crossed his heart.

Then he walked over and sat the silver tray down at the foot of the bed. "If you still want to go sailing with me today, you need to get up. I bought you some appropriate clothing this morning at one of the shops down stairs." Seeing that Halley was about to speak he raised his hand and continued. "Sorry, but now I know all your secrets, as I read the labels before sending out your articles to be laundered."

Mohammed excused himself and Halley looked at the tray of food and almost got sick. She did manage to get the two aspirins down with the orange juice before struggling into the adjoining bathroom for an extra long shower.

She emerged in much better shape than she had entered and found the clothes Mohammed had bought fit perfectly. The deck shoes on the other hand were a tad too big, but Halley fixed that by stuffing a tissue into the toe of each one.

An hour later when she walked into the living room, Mohammed was sitting by the window working on his computer.

"Just checking up on a few loose ends before we leave", he said switching off the machine, "are you ready?"

Despite a really bad headache, Halley smiled and held out her hand toward him. "Ready when you are."

By the time they pulled into the parking area of the marina, Halley was feeling much better. The ride in the Mercedes convertible had breathed new life into her. She sat in her seat as Mohammed walked around and opened the door for her. She took his hand, touching him for the first time that she remembered.

As Mohammed led her though the maze of walkways and down a long pier, they didn't talk. When they reached the Saudi II, Halley leaned her head back following the eighty-five foot mast up into the sky.

"Jesus Christ," Halley exclaimed, "I thought you meant something a little smaller."

"Yes, quite impressive. Today we have a crew of six taking her out for their last practice run before leaving to compete in the Volvo Ocean Race. It should be great."

Once they were aboard and Halley had been introduced to the crew, they sat back out of the way and watched as the mooring lines were cast off and the MD22 Penta diesel pulled the boat away from the dock. Once they had cleared the other ships anchored in the harbor, the crew raised the sails and they headed for the open ocean at twelve knots.

Mohammed put his arm around Halley and whispered into her ear. "Not bad for a $12 million dollar investment."

"This thing cost $12 million dollars?" Halley asked dumfounded.

"Not the boat, but the whole project from beginning to end. The boat by itself only cost three."

"Only three! I'll have to get dad to buy me one," Halley said cuddling back against his side just in time to avoid the mist from a large wave.

After an hour of zigzagging around, the helmsman cut the wheel hard and headed toward a small island they had skirted a few times during the training session. As they got closer, Halley stood up and noticed another boat anchored a couple hundred yards off the beach. As the Saudi II raced toward it, she saw two men on the other ship waving at them, so she waved back.

Below deck another member of the crew sat at the navigation console. Abd had purposely stayed below when Mohammed and Halley had come aboard because he didn't want her to be able to identify him if something went wrong. As he watched the sandy bottom began to rise, he grabbed the sail-by-wire joystick in his right hand and switched control over from the auto-trim computer to the console. Watching the monitors connected to the underwater cameras, he began moving the joystick. Triple redundancy motors on the keel-wing responded in concert with the boat's main rudder, and the Saudi II leaned forty-five degrees into a hard left turn.

Up on deck Halley grabbed the rail to steady herself as water began lapping at the port gunnels. Mohammed, attempting to standing up beside her, was thrown against her by the sudden change of direction. He grabbed the rail before being thrown to the deck. Instead he ended up with his left arm wrapped around Halley's waist, pressing his muscular body against her.

For an instant Halley tensed, but quickly relaxed and settled back against him. Twisting herself around in his arms she hugged him without looking up. "That was a close one," she exhaled as she lifted her head and kissed him.

When the boat was halfway through the turn, Abd raised a red plastic cover and pressed buttons numbered: four, five, six, and seven. At the bottom of the keel-wing, four spring-loaded emergency weight pods shot out into the water reducing the weight of the ship by 2,500 pounds. Immediately a shudder ran through the Saudi II, and it seemed in danger of tipping over on its port side until the wheel spun back and the boat regained an upright position.

"What was that?" Halley asked as she pulled away from Mohammed.

"They are just showing off for you," he said as the crew began lowering the sails.

After allowing the boat to drift about a quarter of a mile along the beach there was a loud splash as the anchor dropped. When it caught the bottom the boat jerked to a stop and swung around. The breeze pushed the hull until it was pointing upwind.

"Last one in is an old maid" Mohammed said as he pulled off everything except his shorts and dove over the side. As he began swimming toward the shore, Halley kicked off her shoes and threw her life vest on the deck before jumping in after him.

By the time she got to the island Mohammed had walked up the dunes and was propped against one of the many palms that covered the island. "What took you so long?" he asked, patting the sand next to him.

"You cheated," she yelled back at him. "And cheaters never win." Then she smiled and walked slowly over to him, seeing his hard body for the first time. He was definitely good looking. For a second her eyes blanked out as she fantasized about making love with him by the beach while the waves crashed against the shore. She heard Mohammed call her name and she snapped back to the present.

"I guess that can't be true. After all here we are alone on this island and who knows if the boat will wait for us or just sail off into the sunset?"

Halley snapped her head around quickly to check the boat. Then felt silly as she watched the crew disappearing below deck, knowing that he was just teasing her. "It looks like we don't have anything to worry about yet. They're all going below to eat."

"I'd rather think they are going to polish off the four bottles of wine I brought them in my knapsack," Mohammed said taking Halley's hand and pulling her down beside him.

He pulled her face toward his and they began kissing each other softly. Halley drifted back and forth between fantasy and reality for almost an hour before she realized that things weren't going to go any farther unless she instigated the next move. She reached around and guided his hand toward her breast.

She felt his arm stiffen as his hand brushed the hard nipple, before he pulled away and leaned back against the palm.

"Before we go any farther, I need to talk to you about something rather delicate," Mohammad said in a quiet voice. "One of my brothers died of HIV and I made him a promise that I would never make love to a woman unless I was sure that we were safe."

Since Halley was still a virgin, she felt like she didn't have anything to prove. She was rather insulted at the thought of him thinking she could pass such a terrible thing on to anyone. As she started to get up she reached for her hand with a look that melted her back to the ground across from him. Before she could speak he took her hands in his and began telling her how hard it was to watch his brother die day by day

104

until he finally gave up and passed away after a year of fighting the disease.

The more she thought about it the more she realized she didn't know anything about him either. He could have had STD, AIDS, or any of a dozen other things infecting him, too. The worst part of that realization was the fact that a few minutes ago she would have let him do anything he wanted to her without even thinking about the repercussions. After all she wasn't even on any kind of birth control, and it didn't look like either of them came there prepared for safe sex.

"You're right. Who knows what we could be carrying around?" She kissed him again and said, "I'm sorry about your brother."

He gave her a long, long kiss before they walked back to the beach and sat down together looking out to sea.

"Look, I need to get a physical before I start working for my dad anyway. Maybe I can make an appointment here and get the physical before I go back home," Halley said without looking at him.

"I appreciate the way you are taking this. The last time I asked a girl to get checked, she threw an ashtray at me and cursed at me while she walked away." Mohammad said laughing.

"Another girl, you cad! How many girls have you tried this with?" Halley said theatrically holding her hand against her heart. Before he could answer she ran toward the water and began swimming back to the boat.

Mohammed caught up to her about halfway back and pulled her underwater where they embraced in another long kiss before their air ran out and forced them back to the surface. When they popped up together they continued toward the boat smiling at each other whenever their eyes met.

Mohammed climbed aboard first then pulled Halley up easily with one arm. Not wanting to disturb the crew members who were laughing below, they cuddled up in some towels. He drifted off to sleep while Halley enjoyed watching the gulls drifting along the tops of the waves.

Later, as the wind changed direction, the Saudi II slowly swung around pointing out to sea, and Halley saw the same small boat she had seen earlier.

It was hard to make out what the two men onboard were doing, but it looked like their anchor was stuck on something. Halley watched the activity onboard. Every now and then the bow of the boat dipped dangerously into the water. A few seconds later the sound of an overstrained electric winch, spinning past its torque, drifted over the calm sea.

After about half an hour the men had looped a rope under their boat and tied each end off to the ship's handrails. The whole ship dropped about half a foot lower as the winch growled and the anchor finally sprung free. The instant it came loose the sailboat sprang back up to its normal depth with a shiver that sent a ripple up the mast - snapping the flag at the top like a wet towel.

Chapter 19
The Clinic

That night, as Halley lay alone in Mohammed's bedroom enjoying the seductive silk sheets that seemed so strange only hours ago, she wondered what would happen at the clinic Mohammed had contacted for their AIDS tests the following morning.

The tension from the last twenty-four hours eased and she fell into blackness without so much as the hint of a dream until she awoke to the tapping on her door.

Mohammed peeked in and then pushed a cart overflowing with a breakfast befitting a queen into the room. They enjoyed breakfast together before heading to the clinic.

When they arrived, Mohammed ushered Halley through the waiting room and into a private office of what turned out to be another of his close friends.

"Dr. Imad this is my special friend Halley, the woman I phoned you about last night," Mohammed said as he scooted her toward the young man who didn't seem old enough to have graduated from medical school.

Nevertheless, Halley smiled and held out her hand. "I'm pleased to meet you under such peculiar and I must admit embarrassing circumstances," she said blushing a little as she turned her head back over her shoulder and made a face at Mohammed by wrinkling up her nose and pursing her lips.

"Never mind about that Miss Halley, there isn't anything to be embarrassed about here. The only problem is I had to squeeze you in with a small group of locals who volunteered to be Guinea pigs in exchange for free medical checkups. That means you are in for a long list of tests that you probably not interested in getting. But don't worry it will only take an hour or so."

Before Halley could respond she was whisked out of the room by a pleasant looking girl who didn't seem to understand anything that was said to her. She smiled and nodded all the way to a dressing room where she ushered Halley inside. To her surprise it was filled with a dozen attractive teenagers who probably would have had a tough time getting served at a bar back home.

As she stood there Halley felt a little self-conscious as those around her seemed to be having a great time striking seductive poses as they undressed - all the time chattering away in Betawi Malay with a little English thrown in now and then.

One of the girls smiled at her. "Hi, I'm Ahnu. Better hurry up, they will be here in a minute and expect us all to be ready for the exams."

"Halley," she responded as her shoulders relaxed. She began to get undressed the same way she did in high school when her gym teacher was on her way to the locker room.

Just as she finished and joined the back of the line, a male technician came in and sat down at a little table next to a chair that had a strip of foam rubber taped to the right armrest. As he opened a little cabinet and began setting up, he cocked his head and motioned to the first girl to come over.

As he rubbed her arm with an alcohol swab, she pretended to bite her lip in fear and gave him her best shy little schoolgirl look. The pose had the desired effect, freezing him like a statue looking blankly into her eyes. This caused everyone, except Halley, to burst into laughter, which freed him from her charms.

Seconds later they burst out again when he stabbed the needle into her arm and pretended to fish around vigorously while the girl contorted her face and moaned in pain. This scenario went on until Halley had moved up to the front of the line and she sat down in the chair.

Then a hush filled the room as the girls moved in closer to get a better look. After watching the other blood tests being taken, Halley was expecting the worst. But after the rubber tubing was tied around her bicep and alcohol applied to the inside of her forearm she was pleasantly surprised when the needle slid into her arm vein with nothing more than a pinprick of pain and blood squirted into the first vacuum vial. There wasn't even any discomfort when the vial was removed and the second vial was filled. In fact the only thing that caused her to jump was when the technician reached up and pulled the rubber tubing from her arm and it snapped against her breast as he put the last vial into place.

Halley contorted her face and rubbed her nipple gently, which caused the other girls to burst into a fit of laughter. Handing her a cardboard form with a serial number in red across the top that matched the numbers on the blood kit, the technician got up bowed and walked out amid the applauding and catcalls of the girls.

No sooner had he left than three nurses came in to check their height, weight, and blood pressure, recording each statistic in the appropriate place on their cards.

Next they were marched down the hallway and into X-ray. Halley was surprised to see that the hospital had a digital machine, but figured it had probably been donated by some larger hospital that had bought something even more expensive and donated this one to the clinic as a tax write-off. When her turn came she was placed against the cold apparatus and told to stop breathing and hold still as full scans of her head, chest, pelvis and legs were recorded.

As they left X-ray and headed to the last door at the end of the hallway the demeanor of the girls changed noticeably, signaling something unpleasant was about to happen. Dreading whatever had changed their mood, Halley slipped to the end of the line again and immediately knew the reason for their concern. She spotted the examination table with stirrups extended at the far end of the room.

Dr. Lisa Ben, accompanied by dykish assistants, Elaine and Bella, walked in and began looking in each girl's eyes, nose, and throat. They were individually ushered into a small alcove protected by a curtain and given very intense anal and vaginal inspections.

It was at that point Halley had nearly bolted from the room. She tried to pull her feet from the stirrups and stand up, but before she could escape the assistants grabbed her feet and yanked her back into position.

"Relax, bitch, or you won't be getting your medical card stamped today and you know what your pimp will do to you when he finds out, You'll be out of work for a month," the larger one barked at her.

The only thing that saved the assistant from one of Halley's swift kicks to the head was the fact that she couldn't believe that Mohammed had arranged for her to be inspected with a bunch of local hookers. It just wasn't possible! He would make his friend pay for treating her like trash once he found out what had happened.

As quickly as it had started it was over and she was back in the dressing room surrounded by local prostitutes, acting as if they had just had the best time of their lives. The more they cavorted and pranced around, the angrier Halley got. By the time she had finished dressing, she was seething.

109

Not wanting to spend another minute in this hellhole, she ran to the door, but found it was locked. This caused Halley a little panic until she heard someone on the other side jiggle a key into the lock. When it opened the girls rushed past her, surrounding their benefactor who gave them each a long stemmed rose and a kiss on the forehead.

Halley was angrier than she had ever been. All she wanted to do was deliver a groin kick to Imad for putting her through all that. A simple blood test should have been enough. The nurse opened the door to the office and left her standing there like some raging lunatic while Mohammad and Imad talked together in a foreign tongue

Mohammad could tell in an instant she was really upset and managed to jump between Halley and Dr. Imad before she could launch an attack on his old friend. Once they were alone, Mohammed held her at arm's length with a look of concern on his face.

"What the hell were you thinking when you put me in a room full of whores who get their nasty asses checked, so they can turn tricks for another month?" Halley screamed at the top of her voice.

A look of pain shot through Mohammed's eyes, as he dropped his head and looked at the floor. In a flash, Halley moved into his space, grabbed his chin, and pulled his head back up until she was looking him directly in the eye. "Exactly how long before we know that we aren't diseased? I think I may have caught something in here."

Mohammed began babbling quickly. "Well the Rapid HIV takes about thirty minutes, but the ELISA test can take up to a week or more. That's all according to Dr. Imad. I'm just telling you what he said. I really don't know. But he said he'd rush it through the lab himself, and we should know in a couple of days."

Halley punched him in the solar plexus with just enough energy to make him taste his breakfast, but not quite hard enough to cause any permanent damage. She did became a little concerned when it took him a full minute to recover, but then relaxed when he stood up and look at her sadly. "Now we're even, but no more bullshit," she said.

She hugged him for a long time and he slowly began to realize that he wasn't going to lose his prize. He bent down and kissed her. It was a long passionate kiss that conveyed more than words could, and they walked out of the office with their arms around each other.

Absorbed in each other, they rounded the corner at the end of the hall and literally bumped into Dr. Imad. As their bodies collided,

Halley's right hand instinctively shot out for protection. She delivered a quick snapping hook punch to the B-10 pressure point at the base of his skull and Dr. Imad blacked out. After everyone had recovered from the collision, apologies were exchanged and Mohammed and Halley left the clinic.

As Imad continued on to the lab he felt a catch in his neck and cocked his head up and to the right, which produced a little popping sound and cleared the problem. Because this is the type of normal adjustment everyone's body makes automatically, Imad didn't connect it with the kyusho jitsu technique Halley had delivered.

On Friday morning Dr. Imad tried to reach Dr. Ramadan at the Research Center, but when no one answered he had to leave a message with the desk operator. He got up from his desk, and as he walked over to this fax machine the papers slipped out of his hand. He cursed quietly as he bent down to retrieve them. Once he had them in the machine he punched in Ramadan's personal number and clicked the send button before returning to his desk.

As he sat there listening to the machine transmit the sheets, Dr. Imad became conscious of a tingling in his right arm. During the next two weeks this would develop into a cold numbness, and he would begin dropping his pen more often. As he scheduled himself for more and more tests that showed nothing out of the ordinary, he began to worry and to have trouble sleeping. Then exactly four weeks after the collision in the hallway, his retina separated from the back of his left eye and panic set in. Two weeks later he died of massive hemorrhaging of the brain. The autopsy results revealed nothing out of the ordinary and the only legacy he passed on was a large insurance settlement, which his wife used to catch another doctor twenty years her senior.

Chapter 20
Headed South

Oblivious to the problems about to befall Dr. Imad, Halley and Mohammed spent the rest of the week enjoying each other's company without anything more romantic than an occasional make-out session between extravagant dinners, tennis matches, and swimming.

On Thursday night they each packed a suitcase for the trip to the research clinic and slept together for the first time with nothing more than a goodnight kiss.

Friday dawned bright and cooler than normal. They were in the elevator when Dr. Imad's call came in and had passed the deck before the operator had finished taking down the message.

As they waited for the Land Rover to be delivered they looked at each other with anticipation. When the car pulled up, the valet jumped out, grabbed their bags and put them into the back before handing Mohammed the keys, waiting with a practiced pause for a tip. He wasn't disappointed as Mohammed laid a $20 in his hand.

Leaving the hotel Halley slid over next to Mohammed and settled into a comfortable position for the two-hour drive to the biological research center operated by Ramadan. When they turned into the facility and drove up the long road to the complex, Halley heard a pounding next to the vehicle and sat up. On the other side of a three-rail fence running alongside the road, a small herd of Arabian horses kept pace with them.

"They're beautiful," Halley said as she leaned out of the window watching them.

When they reached the top of the hill there was a signpost pointing left to the center and right to the stables.

"Go that way," Halley said pointing toward the stables.

As soon as the car stopped, she was out and running toward the fence. She climbed up and held out her hand waiting to see what would happen. The horses stopped ten feet away and began milling around keeping an eye on her without much intention of getting any closer.

"Here, try this." Mohammed said tossing her an apple from his backpack.

Before she could turn around the lead stallion moved quickly forward a few feet with his ears pointed back and fire in his eyes.

112

"I'm not going to hurt you. Boy, come on over here," she said holding the apple out.

The stallion pawed the dirt with his right hoof. Then he pointed his ears toward her, sniffed the air, and let out a long whinny. Finally, he gave in to the smell of the apple and trotted over to her. Halley pulled the apple back so she could pet him with her other hand and the horse pulled his head back.

"No, you don't," she said holding the apple out a little more.

After a few seconds of deliberation the horse gave in and allowed her to pet him. In a sudden move he lunged forward and took a big bite out of the apple, nearly pulling the whole thing out of Halley's hand.

"Hey," she said pulling the apple away. This spooked the horse, which darted away until he was again drawn back by the irresistible lure of the apple.

"I've got your number--now," Halley said waving the apple in front of her. She put the remaining apple in the palm of her hand and waited. Slowly the horse moved forward, shook his head and pawed at the ground until he suddenly grabbed the apple and trotted off.

"Just like a man. Hangs around until he gets what he wants then it's off to brag about his latest conquest."

Mohammed laughed. "How does snatching an apple compare to having twenty girl friends running after you?"

"Ah. The girl friends are always there, but apples come by only once in awhile, "Halley said jumping down and holding her arms out toward Mohammed.

Like an animal that is obedient to the rules of the universe, Mohammed ran to her, swept her off her feet, twirling her around in the air. "Where's my apple?" he said as he put her back down.

"Ah, ah, ah," she said shaking her index finger back and forth at him. "We don't know if it's safe yet. Remember, you are the shy one."

She reached down and poked his belly before running back to the car and jumping into her seat. Mohammed looked down, laughed out loud, shook his head for a few seconds and raced to the car to join her. Once he was inside he began playfully poking her in the ribs until she squealed for him to stop. He grabbed her and pulled her into his arms, giving her a warm tongue kiss that lasted forever.

"What are you two up to?" a guard said tapping on the door with the barrel of his MAC10.

It took Halley's brain a few seconds to decode the words and realize that they were not alone. When she opened her eyes and saw the boxy end of the weapon pointed at her, she gasped and readied herself for a fight. Before she could do anything, Mohammed put his hand on her arm and whispered for her to relax. He turned around in his seat and faced the guard.

Halley saw the guard go white when he saw Mohammed, immediately pointing the weapon toward the ground and babbling like small child who had been caught with his hand in the cookie jar.

"Dr. Ramadan is expecting you. Please go to the clinic's main parking lot and I will radio ahead so he can meet you." The guard then bowed a little without looking directly at them and backed away.

Mohammed started the Land Rover and quickly took off, spraying a little gravel and dust at the guard as they sped away.

When they turned into the parking lot, Halley saw a man standing on the steps, reminding her of an old actor she'd seen several times. As he began walking toward the car, Mohammed parked. She realized that this must be the mysterious Dr. Ramadan.

"Welcome my old friend. I trust things are going well for you?" Ramadan said kissing both of Mohammed's cheeks.

"Very well, indeed. Our internet project is coming along nicely. I hope you are doing equally well with your research?" Mohammed said returning Ramadan's greeting.

Halley had walked around the car by the time they were finished exchanging greetings and waited to be introduced.

"And this must be Halley," Ramadan said looking deeply into her eyes.

Mohammed laughed as he took Halley's left hand. He raised it high over her head as he slowly turned her in a pirouette for his pleasure. When she was facing the doctor again, she blushed slightly and smiled up at him. "I'm very happy to meet you."

"The pleasure is all mine," Ramadan said as he stroked his short graying beard.

As the two men laughed together, Mohammed slipped his right arm around Halley's waist and gave her a little squeeze. "Yes, she is truly remarkable."

"Follow me and I'll give you a tour of our little Research Center before we decide where you are going to stay," Ramadan said as he turned and led them up the steps and inside.

They walked through a lobby and down glass-walled hallways that amazed Halley. Each room they passed contained equipment that made her Swarthmore College labs look like they should have been in the Smithsonian.

"This place must have cost a fortune," she finally blurted out when they turned a corner and she saw three scanning electron microscopes with small groups of technicians working the controls.

"Yes, several fortunes – actually," Ramadan said with pride. "It's amazing how much my people are willing to sacrifice in the hope that tomorrow will bring peace."

As they reached the end of the hallway, Ramadan ushered them into a little reception area set up for lunch. "Please make yourself comfortable. As you can see there is plenty to eat."

At that moment Halley was more excited by the elegant bathroom she spotted a few feet away than she was by the mountains of fruit and cheese laid out in a fancy arrangement.

"I hope you won't mind if I borrow Mohammed for a few minutes before we join you for lunch?" Ramadan said smiling at her.

"No problem. I'll just make myself comfortable here until you get back," she said hoping they would leave quickly.

Chapter 21
Paybacks are A Bitch

Ramadan, who was seated behind his desk, slid a folder toward Mohammed. "I don't expect you to understand all the results printed there, but the tests done by Imad show that Halley is in perfect health. Another interesting fact is that she was still a virgin last Wednesday morning, which is quite remarkable considering her age."

Mohammed smiled. "No wonder she was so mad at getting stuck in with a bunch of whores."

"No wonder at all when you realize that the lesbian trio who gave her the pelvic exam actually raped her," Ramadan said pounding his fist on the table.

"What are you talking about?" Mohammed asked with a puzzled look.

"From what I managed to get out of the three of them yesterday, Halley was about to walk out of the exam because the doctor was getting a bit too personal. So the two assistants masked her with nitrous oxide, to keep her quiet and subject to their commands. Once that was done they took turns enjoying the irresistible pleasures offered by a virgin. When they were finished they sprayed Xylocane into her to mask the pain and convinced her that she had merely passed out during the examination."

"I'll kill those bitches," Mohammed screamed.

"No need for that, my friend," Dr. Ramadan said turning one of the external flat-panel computer displays around and increasing the volume.

Inside a large hermetically sealed isolation chamber loud buzzers and horns blasted randomly every few seconds causing hundreds of caged chickens and ducks to react violently. On the floor a few of the two dozen pigs that could still move kicked up liquid nutrient covering the floor, which the flashing strobe lights captured as color stills on the monitor.

"What the hell is that?" Mohammed asked as he leaned forward.

Dr. Ramadan chuckled. "That is my little Petri dish, Mohammed. The noise and lights keep the animals from getting much sleep. Their immune systems are weakened and the bird flu establishes itself more easily in the uninfected birds. Of course we have H5N1, with all its various strains – the R12, RW4, RK7, X1 through X3. I've even thrown in a dozen or so that aren't even very nasty."

"And the pigs?" Mohammed questioned.

"The pigs act as a conduit. You probably never heard of the "Barking Pig Syndrome?" Dr. Ramadan asked waiting for a response.

Mohammed shook his head.

"Not many outside the research field have. It started in Nipah when a bunch of fruit bats began slobbering and peeing on the pig pens. The pigs developed a loud cough. Soon after the cough began, infected animals became paralyzed and died a day later. It spread to the other farm animals and eventually to the farm workers. When an autopsy was performed, it showed their brains were swollen with fluid."

Inside the chamber, one of the more energetic pigs jumped up on top of a cage and got its legs stuck in the chicken wire. When it finally wiggled loose it fell onto the floor, spraying one of the cameras with white liquid.

Dr. Ramadan watched the video clear, as water was automatically sprayed on the lens. "The liquid is a growth medium made primarily from monkey kidney cells and chicken embryos. We are at the point now when we can start dehydrating the solution and make a powdered form of the virus that can be re-hydrated at a later time."

"Despite what you may believe, science is twenty percent hard work and eighty percent luck. While everyone else has been busy trying to figure out how to stop the bird flu, my efforts have created a strain that will kill humans."

Mohammed, who had been half listening, was finally bothered enough by Ramadan's babbling to break away from the display. "What the hell does this have to do with the way Halley was treated at the clinic in Jakarta?"

Ramadan smiled and leaned back in his chair. "It has everything to do with the sexually twisted doctor, the disease, and getting the virus through customs and into the United States."

Ramadan leaned forward again and switched to a camera covering the back of the room, where he zoomed in on Dr. Lisa Ben's dead assistant Bella who was floating face up in the water. "She only lasted a couple of hours before she went into convulsions and dropped."

Mohammed refocused on the display. "So what killed her? Bad air?"

"No, the air inside that room is as pure as the air in this room. Although, I'm sure that it doesn't smell quite as nice with all that death and decay."

Slowly zooming into the far corner of the room, Ramadan continued," as you can see the deviant doctor is quite a cavewoman when all the right buttons are pushed."

As the darkly lit section grew on the monitor, Mohammed caught sight of Dr. Lisa Ben, who had examined Halley, standing on the carcass of a large pig. She was swinging what appeared to be a long stick at one of her assistants who was trying to pull her off her somewhat dry pig perch.

Judging from the size of the pig, Mohammed calculated the water to be about six inches deep. With her shoulder wedged into the corner, the lecherous doctor appeared to have the upper hand as she stood on the only island visible in the room.

Ramadan pressed the chat button then spoke. "How are we doing today, ladies?"

"Let me out of here you miserable freak," Dr. Ben screamed, looking directly into the camera bolted to the wall ten feet to her left.

"I have an old friend of yours here who would like to speak to you," Ramadan said as he motioned to Mohammed.

"So you like playing with girls when the curtains are pulled?" Mohammed blurted out before he could stop himself.

The doctor didn't think she knew that voice, but in her present state she couldn't be sure. Concentrating to make a connection she lowered the stick, which was the opening her assistant Elaine, had needed. Elaine lunged toward Lisa, grabbed the end of what now was clearly a human thigh bone. With a quick jerk she pulled the doctor off her feet.

With the doctor on her side in the liquid, Elaine wasted no time kicking her in the face, causing her to release the knobby end of the bone she had been using as a handle.

While Mohammed and Ramadan watched the action unfold three stories below, the assistant connected with the side of Lisa's head and she slowly sank back in a heap on the pig. As Elaine continued to beat her, a few drops of blood spattered the camera.

Just as they thought Dr. Ben had been beaten to death, she sprang up and punched Elaine square in the face causing her to fall backward into the filthy brew. Lisa staggered forward and threw herself on top of

118

Elaine's abdomen. In a sitting position with her knees on Elaine's shoulders, Dr. Ben wrapped her hands around her assistant's neck and slowly pushed her head under the liquid. After a few heroic attempts to escape, Elaine was dead.

Crawling back to the safety of the carcass, the doctor sat down facing the camera. She inched her way back up the wall until she was standing.

As soon as she was on her feet, she wailed. "Please let me out of this hellhole." Each sob became uncontrollable.

Ramadan smiled, and then said, "My good doctor is that any way to beg for forgiveness?"

He picked up the phone. "Please retrieve that piece of shit from the incubator and give her the best regimen of drugs available. Don't forget to have the team record every detail. I want it all on video."

As the sound of an airtight door echoed through the chamber two technicians dressed in positive airflow HAZMAT suits carefully waded through the liquid toward the doctor. When they reached her, one shot her in the neck with a portable gas-powered syringe rendering her unconscious. They dragged her out the door which closed behind them. Switching to another camera they watched as she was disrobed and scrubbed with disinfectant. When she moved on to the next station, Ramadan switched off the computer and leaned back in his chair.

"I'm not going to bore you with all the details of how I've recreated the conditions responsible for the 1918 Spanish Flu Pandemic. Suffice it to say, after three years of trying both the very scientific and the shotgun approach – the shotgun has won. Now I have a viable strain of the Bird Flu killing one hundred percent of the subjects placed in that chamber."

"So how long does that miserable doctor have to live?" Mohammed asked with a hiss.

"Considering we filled her full of all the drugs designed to prevent the virus from being contracted, I would say she might live another day," Ramadan said smiling. "But I guarantee she will not enjoy it as she drowns in her own fluids."

Chapter 22
Things that Go Bump in the Night

When Mohammed and Ramadan returned to the reception area, Halley was in the middle of her favorite t'ai chi form and the two men stood silently in the doorway until she closed at a relaxed attention with her arms at her sides.

After taking in three long slow breaths, she sprang toward Mohammed. "I was wondering when you two were going to get back here."

Mohammed held her at arm's length, looking deeply into her eyes, pulled her closer and kissed her on the forehead. "I'm so truly sorry," he said pushing her back so he could see her eyes again.

As she gazed back at him, Halley's heart began to race until she could hear it pounding in her ears. "Don't be so silly," she said slipping away from him and running to the table. "Let's eat, I'm starved."

As they enjoyed the food, their conversation turned towards Halley's life in America and her Master's program at MIT. From the conversation the two men gathered she worshiped her father and hoped to join his engineering company when she graduated.

After the three had eaten as much as they wanted, Ramadan got up and walked around behind Halley and put his hands gently on her shoulders. "Mohammed tells me you love horses. I've arranged for the two of you to stay at a lovely little place a few miles away. I think you will enjoy it. It has a barn where I keep my very best Arabians."

He smiled at Mohammed and turned his head around so Halley could see him out of the corner of her eye. "If that is all right with you?"

Halley, who didn't often blush, felt her cheeks warming up, "I think it would be perfect," she said. Then she smiled at Mohammed until she was sure he knew exactly what she expected when they got there.

The sun had set by the time they pulled onto the dirt road leading to the house. As they drove the house came into view. It was easy to see that it was much bigger and more expensive than anything they had passed along the way.

When the car stopped, Halley leaned over and kissed Mohammed. It was a long hot kiss and soon they were lost in each other. When they finally broke apart, each was damp with sweat and anticipation.

120

Mohammed got out of the car and walked around to Halley. Then he scooped her up in his arms and carried her to the front door. When he sat her down on the porch, she reached up hungrily and pulled him down for another kiss, which lasted longer than the first. She wanted him like she had wanted nothing else in her life and she wanted more than anything to pull him to the floor and give herself to him there.

But Mohammed had other intentions. He slowly guided her toward the door until she was leaning against it with her hips pressed hard against his. Standing on her tiptoes, she felt his right arm tighten around her waist. He reached into his shirt pocket and pulled out the magnetic card opening the door behind her.

Halley heard a buzz behind her as he opened the door. She felt herself being lifted up into his arms and carried inside. As she floated up the steps a slight breeze brought the smell of horses and hay through the open windows on the second floor. Another kiss and she was moved through the master bedroom into the marble bathroom and sat down gently next to a huge walk-in shower.

Mohammed left her side only long enough to adjust the water temperature. Before returning to her arms, he gave her a few seconds to enjoy the cooling breeze blowing from the large double windows at opposite ends of the room. The breeze made thin silk curtains dance like angels. But, before long he was back pulling her inside the glass enclosure.

Slowly they began undressing each other as their lips met again. As the warm water trickled down Halley's back she felt pulsating warmth inching up inside her. When it stopped moving, she reached down and felt a familiar slipperiness that took her back to New Jersey, so many years ago and she shuddered. She could see Kathy smiling at her and heard her unmistakable voice saying, "Yes."

It was almost two in the morning when Halley was finally satisfied, and she drifted to sleep in the soft king-size bed. Lying there next to her, Mohammed wrestled with his conscience for an hour before grabbing his cell phone and getting out of bed.

Safely downstairs, he dialed a number and waited. "Yes, she's asleep." Then he walked to the front door and waited.

Five minutes later an ambulance arrived with Ramadan behind the wheel. He got out carrying a small black bag, and quietly walked over to Mohammed. "Are you sure she is asleep?"

121

"Yes, there is nothing to worry about. I think you could shoot a canon off next to her and she wouldn't even move. Come on. Let's get this over with," Mohammed said leading Ramadan up the stairs and into the bedroom.

Ramadan set his bag on the floor. He watched Halley for any signs she might be waking up. Seeing none he took out a small empty-looking syringe with a long needle that was rounded at the end. "I need to get this into her nose without disturbing her. If anything happens, be ready to grab her."

When Mohammed was in position, Ramadan took out his nasal flashlight and began sliding the needle up into Halley's nose. When he had it correctly positioned, he pushed the plunger and a single drop of liquid dripped onto her nasal membrane. Ramadan returned the syringe to his case and motioned for Mohammed to follow him.

When they were downstairs in the living room Ramadan smiled, patted Mohammed on the shoulder and gave him two bottles of pills he was carrying in his jacket pocket. "Take one from each bottle every four hours until they are gone. If Halley begins to show any signs of the flu, bring her back to the center immediately. Other than that, you can enjoy the rest of your time together."

Chapter 23
Aftershocks

At eleven the next morning, Halley was still half asleep as she cuddled against Mohammed's protective body. Outside the horses had been fed and were cavorting in the pasture near the back of the house. When the wind changed direction a gentle puff of air blew through the curtains and cooled the room.

Her mind surfaced just in time to catch the sweet smells and a slight shiver ran through her as the tiny hairs on her body danced in the breeze. Moving closer to Mohammed, she wiggled until she had maximized the contact area and drifted back toward sleep, enjoying dreamy clips from last night.

A half hour later, her internal alarm clock rang and she was fully awake and managed to slip out of bed without waking Mohammed, who was still quietly snoring. After taking a quick shower, Halley slipped into a tight pair of cotton shorts and an old college T-shirt before going downstairs and finding her way out to the horses.

It wasn't long before she had climbed between the rails of the fence and was standing face-to-face with the most beautiful horse she had ever seen. He was jet black and had a shine to his coat that seemed to reflect the sun like a mirror. Halley could tell by his stance he wasn't exactly sure what to do about her invasion of his territory and decided just standing quietly would be the best approach.

A few minutes later the stallion had walked within an arms length of her and began sniffing the air. They remained in that position for several more minutes before the horse took another step and brushed her shoulder with his chin.

Halley smiled and watched the horse as he pulled his head back. She twisted slowly around and raised her hand up in front of her until it reached the middle of her chest. The horse's ears moved back and forth as he carefully turned his head a little from side to side to watch her.

At the same slow speed Halley lifted her palm up and out, stopping when it was an inch away from the stallion's chin. The horse seemed hypnotized by these strange movements. After feeling the horse's breath three times, Halley began slowly withdrawing her hand, which had a magnetic effect on the horse as he moved his head forward to follow it.

Half an hour later, Mohammed stood on the back porch, amazed to see Halley practicing her t'ai chi form, while the horse moved with her a few feet away. Deciding to let her enjoy her morning exercises, he went back inside.

While he waited for the coffee to finish brewing, he punched Ramadan's number into his cell phone and waited for him to answer. "Good morning. I'd like to report Halley is up and practicing her forms in the pasture."

There was a slight pause before he continued in an irritated tone. "No, I don't think that stupid horse of yours is going to be a problem. She's got him following her around like a puppy. When she's done with him, he may be able to open his own studio."

Despite Ramadan's concern on the other end, Mohammed brushed his warnings aside. "Look, nothing is going to happen with that damned horse. Let her enjoy herself while she still can. . . . Yes, I'm taking the pills. Going to have my second set when I get off. . . . See you soon."

True to his word after the conversation had ended, Ramadan filled a glass with water and had tossed the capsules into his mouth when Halley walked through the door. "What's that you're taking?" she asked with a smile.

After washing the pills down, he answered. "Just vitamins I take every day." Then he held out his arms and Halley moved across the room towards him. She was a little surprised when he grabbed her and swung her around putting her down on the spot from which she had been lifted.

"Morning breath," he said running playfully away from her toward the coffee pot where he managed to fill two cups before slipping toward the refrigerator narrowly escaping her clawing hands like a Sunday afternoon quarterback. By the time he was back she was ready for him. After allowing him to pour the cream into the coffee, she grabbed him and began kissing him all over his face.

Together they walked to the table, each holding the other's waist to be sure neither could escape. They parted and settled down in separate chairs.

"Not bad for an old man," Halley said after sipping her coffee.

"Old man, hell," Mohammed shot back at her. "I'll kick your ass from here to Timbuktu if you say that again." Then he hung his head and put on a pouting face – watching her in the reflection of the table.

"I'm sorry, Mohammed. You're not an old man. You are a very old man. And you should be ashamed of yourself for seducing someone so young and innocent," she said. She got up and ran out to the porch before he could grab her.

When Mohammed walked to the door, he saw her swinging in a hammock pretending not to notice him.

"Well, well. Hello little girl. What are you doing here?" he said as he walked over next to her.

Still doing her best to sound innocent she flopped over on her back and shielded the sun from her eyes with her left hand. "I'm waiting for a handsome prince to come and rescue me from a terrible dragon. Do you know any handsome princes?"

"I know one that lives up in the hills by a big lake, but the only way to get there is on horseback," Mohammed said playing along.

Halley smiled and twisted her body back and forth in the hammock. "Well then we better get ready to go see him."

"Are you sure you want to go? We may have to spend the night there," he said pushing the edge of the hammock with his knee.

"Oh yes. I think it would be fun to camp out by a lake." Then with a scolding tone in her voice, she added, "And you are sure there is a handsome prince there, too?"

"Yes. At least the last time I was there he was," Mohammed said sitting down next to her.

After showering together, Halley packed some food. Mohammed collected a couple of sleeping bags from the barn and led two horses up to the house and tied them off on one of the porch railings.

As soon as Halley came out, she insisted she wanted to ride the stallion. It wasn't long before she had ridden the horse Mohammed had selected for her back to the barn and made the exchange herself.

"That's much better," she said as she pulled the horse to a stop beside the porch.

"I don't know if it's such a good idea for you to ride that one. Ramadan thinks he's a bit too spooky to trust," Mohammed said handing her a canvas bag of food.

Halley just smiled and put her finger beside her chin. "There's nothing to worry about. The horse assured me he'd be a real gentleman. Besides he says he's been to the lake and met the handsome prince too."

With nothing more to say, Mohammed unwound the reins from the rail, swung up onto his horse and led the way south.

They rode slowly side by side for a couple of hours until they climbed a rise and Halley saw a deep blue lake in the valley below.

"Is that where the handsome prince lives?" she asked in a somewhat normal voice, with just the hint of the little girl.

"That is the place," Mohammed said pointing to a bit of land that jetted out from the north shore, "right down there."

An hour later, as the sun dipped low over the water Mohammed led Halley towards a tiny cottage nested in the middle of a grove of trees about forty feet from the lake.

Pulling her horse next to Mohammed's, Halley smiled, "This looks like something out of Sleeping Beauty."

Mohammed laughed and pulled his horse to a stop. "I see a beauty, but hopefully she won't be getting too much sleep tonight."

Halley's face took on a serious look as she stood up in her stirrups and began looking around. "Why? Is this where the handsome prince lives?"

Before Mohammed could answer, she fell back onto the saddle, tapped the stallion lightly with her heels and jetted off toward the lake so the Arabian could get a well deserved drink. Despite all his urgings, Mohammed's mount slipped further behind with each step and soon Halley had disappeared as the ground ahead tilted toward the water's edge.

He continued on, the sound of the Arabian's hooves pounding on firm ground changed as it raced down the pebbly slope ahead. Suddenly there was an explosion of water and a loud scream.

Knowing how quickly the water deepened, he imagined the worst as he encouraged his horse on with his heels. He didn't start breathing again until he reached the crest and saw Halley brushing wet hair out of her eyes while the stallion meandered around drinking, about twenty feet into the lake.

Mohammed released the reins and let his horse carefully move into the water where it instinctively moved close to its companion.

Halley blew the last bit of hair away from her face and laughed. "God, this water is cold."

Mohammed shook his head and let the tension that had built up over the past few seconds escape in a contagious laugh that started Halley laughing too, until tears rolled down their cheeks.

"You scared the shit out of me," Mohammed managed to wheeze out as he began to calm down and enjoy the view of Halley's breasts pasted against her waterlogged clothing.

When she realized she was being stared at, Halley looked down and began seductively unbuttoning the sheer white blouse that she had been wearing over a tight pair of black jeans, careful not to expose too much.

When the last button had been freed, she grabbed the fabric and began pulling it down slowly until the hard nipples seemed to push straight through the fabric.

In all his years, Mohammed had never seen such a delight as Halley. Sitting there proudly on the magnificent black Arabian with her wet hair pasted wildly around her face, she was silhouetted in the deep orange sun sparkling off the water all around her. He fell in love for the first and last time in his life. That moment in time would be his fondest memory, carried with him until the day he died.

Later as they lay together in the cottage, entwined in love, Mohammed cursed his life and what he had become. He wished with all his might he had never seen Halley at the pool, had never made inquires of the hotel personnel about her background, and had never selected her for a part of such a dirty operation. But despite his lack of medical training he knew one thing for certain, within a week she would be dead.

After they reached their final climax that night he waited until she was asleep, slowly turned away from her, and drifted into a restless sleep.

A few hours later he was awakened by a spasm of coughing behind him. When he rolled over and touched Halley, he knew immediately that it was time to call Ramadan. An hour later the sound of the pontoon equipped helicopter could be heard inside the cabin. Mohammed held Halley in his arms and sponged her hot forehead with a wet towel.

On the way back to the research center Mohammed didn't say a word as he sat next to the stretcher and held Halley's hand. Two doctors monitored her vitals and administered various medications.

When he knew she was safely tucked away in one of the isolation rooms and there was nothing else he could do, Mohammed walked back to Ramadan's office and waited for him to return. He was sleeping when the scientist returned.

"Mohammed. Mohammed, Wakeup," Ramadan whispered.

Mohammed slowly sat up on the couch and rubbed his eyes. "When will it be over?"

Ramadan handed him a cup of coffee then sat down behind his desk. "I'm not sure. She was a perfect specimen, in top physical condition and I only inserted one tiny speck of the virus into her nasal passage. Quite frankly, I'm surprised it happened so quickly.

Mohammed took another big gulp of coffee set it down and pressed his palms against his eyes until tiny sparks danced in his brain, "Will she feel anything?"

"No, I doubt it, not unless she recovers, and that is doubtful, since she became infected so quickly. It does however prove I can dehydrate the virus then reconstitute it with a nutrient solution without it losing its potency."

Convinced that Mohammed wasn't going to snap, Ramadan relaxed and moved over to the couch, sitting next to Mohammed. "I know you really liked Halley and I will do everything I can to save her. The one thing I will not do is allow her to suffer. Under these circumstances, it's the best I can do."

In spite of himself, Mohammed couldn't control the tears welling up in his eyes and running down his cheeks.

Ramadan allowed Mohamed a few minutes to regain his composure before he put his arm around his shoulder, "Are you okay?"

"I'm functional," Mohammed said after taking a long sip of coffee. Then he stood up. "Is there anything else I need to do here?"

Ramadan led Mohammed out of the office and down to an examination room where he administered three different experimental doses of drugs that had killed the virus in laboratory animals and four more bottles of pills with strict instructions to take them religiously until they were gone.

He walked Mohammed out to the helicopter pad, waited for him to board and lift off before waving goodbye as the aircraft turned and headed back to Jakarta.

Chapter 24
Plane Delight

Josh always loved flying with his grandfather, but today was special because Ty had been able to reserve the twin-engine Aztec, Josh was going to get to fly it for the first time. After lifting off from the College Park Airport, Duke climbed to 7,500 feet, leveled off, and headed for the Municipal Airport at Marion, Ohio, three hundred miles away.

"I guess you're ready for a nap by now," Duke said as he switched on the autopilot.

"Come on Pop-Pop, you promised I could fly this thing after we got over Pennsylvania," Josh pleaded with Duke.

"Well you keep looking for the state line and when you see it you tell me," Duke said grabbing a diet soda out of the cooler strapped into the seat behind him.

"Don't start that again. I fell for it once when I was six. You're not getting away with that one again," Josh said smiling.

Ty looked out the side window from behind Josh. "I don't know it looks like some kind of white line down there," he said reaching over the seat and messing up Josh's hair.

"Come on you two. I'm getting too old for this stuff,"

"Okay, let me get out of the pilot's seat and you can fly her for awhile. Just don't touch anything until we both get situated," he said sliding up out of the seat.

Duke pulled a thick cushion out of a storage compartment and placed it on the left seat. Then he helped Josh strap his seatbelt on before he sat down sideways on the passenger seat so he would be ready to take over quickly if anything went wrong.

"Can you see out the front okay?" Duke asked, trying to judge the angle by bending over until their eyes were about the same height.

Josh sat up as tall as he could, keeping his hands in his lap and away from the controls. "I can see fine."

"Good. I guess I can take a nap now and dream about the model of my old Phantom that we're going to see when we land in Marion," Duke said as he sat back in the passenger seat and closed his eyes.

Josh knew his grandfather was pretending, but it still made his stomach tighten a little, thinking about what would happen if he really did go to sleep. "Stop it right now."

"Are we there yet?" Duke asked as he rubbed his eyes and yawned.

"Grand Pop, come on," Josh begged, giving the old man a scowl.

"Okay, when you're ready turn the autopilot off," Duke said pointing to the instrument panel.

Duke let go of the controls and the plane steadied and began flying straight and level. "See, the thing is built to fly itself. All you have to do is point it in the right direction and keep the altitude steady."

Josh looked a little skeptical. "There's got to be more than that to it or everyone would be flying."

"There's a lot more to it than that, but basically once you're up, it's pretty easy. That's how the terrorists managed to fly into the towers on 911. The pilots did all the hard work getting the planes up in the air. After that, the flying was all pretty easy."

Josh looked proudly at his grandfather. "I'll bet if you were still in your jet, you could have stopped them."

"Don't think so buddy. Nobody was prepared for that day."

Josh looked at the computer navigation map. "We're not too far from the place where the plane crashed in Pennsylvania, are we?"

Duke punched a couple of numbers into the computer. "It's about twenty miles northeast of here."

"What's there now?" Josh asked.

"Not much, just a grassy field and a lot of broken hearts," Duke answered quietly. "Okay, she's all set now. Just keep her on course and holding at seventy-five hundred feet," Duke said sitting back and watching Josh closely.

When Josh took the controls the plane responded and began yawing left and right as he overcompensated for each deviation. Concentrating on the compass, his tongue peeked out from between his teeth and his breathing started to become more rapid.

"Josh you're trying too hard. Remember the plane will fly itself. Just nudge her in the right direction," Duke said.

As Josh relaxed, the yawing left and right began to disappear. A few minutes later, Josh had a big smile on his face and they were both feeling proud.

Watching Josh, Duke remembered the night he almost got shot down in Vietnam. When he landed and looked at what was left of his starboard wing he was amazed that he got back to the ship at all. Ten minutes later, after he had heaved his guts up in the bathroom, he started wandering around the ship trying to shake off the jitters.

It was two in the morning when he found himself standing on the bridge watching the helmsman steer the carrier through the South China Sea. Thinking it might relieve his tension, Duke had convinced the second class petty officer to let him take over the wheel for a few minutes.

Funny now, he remembered feeling just like Josh did piloting the plane. It only took a minute for his throat to get dry and for little beads of sweat to form on his forehead. He remembered leaving the bridge and looking aft. Instead of the razor straight neon line created by the props exciting the luminescent algae in the water, there was a wavy line that began when Duke started steering and stopped when the petty officer took over again. Proving to him once again that nothing is as easy as it looks.

Ten minutes later Josh was getting tired. "It's you turn now, Pop-Pop."

"Are you sure?" Duke asked.

"Yep, I need a rest," Josh said as he carefully unbuckled the seatbelt and squirmed out of the seat.

"Why don't you change seats with Ty so he and I can talk while you get some sleep," Duke said slipping into the pilot's seat.

"Okay Pop-Pop. Thanks for letting me fly. Some day I'm going to be just like you and Dad," Josh said.

"I hope so, Josh. That would make your daddy very proud," Duke said watching him climb into the seat diagonally behind him.

By the time the plane crossed into Ohio, Josh was asleep and Ty was pouring coffee from a thermos into a plastic cup. "You want some?"

"No thanks. I've still got half a soda left. I really appreciate you getting this plane." Duke said.

"Don't worry about it. That's one of the nice things about being a member of the Blue Skies Flying Club. We were just lucky nobody was using the Aztec this weekend or else we would have been in one of the single engine birds. I thought this would be better if Ajax decided to give you a model to bring back," Ty said sipping his coffee.

A big smile appeared on Duke's face. "That would be nice. Dick Berry, the VP who set this whole thing up, said they just wanted me to come up for a face-to-face, but you never know."

After checking to be sure Josh was sleeping, Ty loosened his seatbelt and leaned back against the bulkhead. "Listen Duke, I need some advice about a girl I met over at Ashburn."

"Don't tell me you finally want to have a serious relationship with a woman. I thought you were always going to be the wham bam thank you ma'am type," Duke said laughing.

"Come on, man. I'm serious," Ty said sorry that he had even brought it up.

"Sorry. I guess I'm a little jealous that you have more confirmed kill markings painted on your love life than anyone I know. Okay let me hear the story," Duke replied.

"You're not making this easy, but here goes. There's this woman working with Shipman in the dungeon complex. She seems to like me. Every time I go over there she's always there. In fact, I wouldn't be surprised if she sleeps there most of the time."

"Maybe she's in love with that old fart Shipman," Duke interjected.

"Come on now. Be serious. He's old enough to be her grandfather," Ty shot back.

"Careful," Duke said, "don't malign grandfathers."

"Sorry old man, I forgot. Anyway she's one of those women who seems to be scared to go out into the sun."

"Now, I've got it. You can't get her out to the parking lot to show her your new car," Duke teased.

Ignoring the last comment, Ty continued. "We've had coffee a couple of times and I can tell she likes me, but how the hell do I get her out of her shell?"

"Puppies," Duke answered.

"Puppies?" Ty questioned.

"Yep, puppies. If I wanted to make a million dollars I'd start a puppy rental store. Girls can't resist puppies," Duke said smiling.

"How does having a puppy help me out?" Ty questioned.

"Think about it man - the next time you go over there take a puppy along. What's her name?" Duke asked.

"Sarah." Ty said.

"Tell Sarah you're watching it for a friend and that you don't know much about dogs. Then, if she seems to like it, get her to get it some water. Twenty minutes later it will have to pee. Then invite Sarah outside to help you walk it," Duke said triumphantly.

"Sounds a little contrived to me," Ty countered.

"Like driving around in that big Corvette of yours isn't contrived?" Duke said.

"Come on now, don't start in with my car again," Ty said.

"Okay. Okay. What's going on over there now? Got any good stories?" Duke asked.

"Off the record?" Ty said.

"But of course," Duke answered.

"Not much. The traffic from Indonesia has picked up lately. Someone's spamming the east coast with porno advertisements every few days that keeps tripping the wire. So far we haven't been able to track down the culprits because they're using wireless connections. Terrorist chatter has picked up a little lately about another attack using passenger planes, dirty bombs, and attacks on tunnels and bridges. All the usual stuff that keeps us up at night," Ty said grabbing the thermos and pouring another cup of coffee.

"In other words, nobody knows anything," Duke said.

"That's about right," Ty said. "The ball just keeps rolling until it hits something. Then, we're pretty good about figuring out how it all happened."

Satisfied they were going to live long enough for him to see his model; Duke radioed the tower and started his descent into Marion.

After landing it didn't take long for them to find the vice president of Ajax. Soon the four of them were on their way to the Ajax facility ten miles outside of town. While Ty and Josh sat in the back seat, Dick was telling Duke how excited everyone was to have him on their team.

When the car pulled through the gate, Dick drove past the main building and continued down a narrow road for about a mile. When he reached a large field with a blacktop landing strip in the middle, he parked the car and got out.

As they walked towards a small group of people standing between two vans, Duke noticed they were all wearing silly looking wraparound sun glasses and leaning back and forth in unison.

"Charlie," Dick said in a loud voice, when they were about ten feet away.

A tall man in the center of the group took his glasses off, and looked at Dick. He nudged the man next to him and handed the controller to him. Walking towards the newcomers he blinked to clear his eyes. "Hello, Dick. I see you found our war hero."

"Yes. Let me introduce you. Duke this is Charlie our chief engineer." Dick waited for the two men to shake hands, and then continued. "And this is his grandson Josh and a good friend named Tyrone. Oops, I mean Ty."

"Glad you could make it today. We're giving the prototype a workout. Come on over," Charlie said motioning them to follow him.

"I'll give you some goggles in a minute, but first I want you to see this thing in action," Charlie said allowing Duke, Josh, and Ty to get in front of the others.

Duke looked around the sky, but couldn't see anything. "You sure there's a plane up there?"

"Coming in on your left in five, four, three. . . " Charlie said.

Hearing a faint whine to his left, Duke turned just in time to see a small silver speck coming towards them. A second later the model jet flew past them at two hundred and fifty miles an hour and was gone.

"I hope it goes slower than that or nobody will want to buy it," Duke said a little dejected.

"Don't worry about that. She can stand on her tail if you want," Charlie said bringing the model back for another pass. This time it came in much slower from the right and slowed down as Charlie pitched up the nose and brought the jet to a halt in front of them. As it hovered about five feet off the ground he kept goosing the throttle just enough to keep it almost stationary. After a few seconds, he slammed the throttle to full and the model shot skyward like a rocket until it disappeared over head.

"Now, that's impressive," Duke said itching to get his hands on the controller.

"So you'd be willing to plunk down five thousand for that?" Dick asked.

"Why would I pay five thousand for that when I can get one for half that much that's ready to fly out of the box?" Duke questioned.

"Gosh, I don't know?" Dick said. "Charlie, land that baby at the far end of the runway and we'll see if there's anything that would make it worth the price."

Dick tapped a couple of other people on the shoulder and asked them to help him. A moment later a row of folding chairs sat in front of the engineers. Duke, Josh, Ty and Dick took their seats.

When they were comfortable, Charlie came over with four pairs of the thick sunglasses and handed them each a pair. "I've already powered them up. Just put them on and focus them with those slider bars over each lens. You don't need to worry about leaving your regular glasses on. These can be adjusted like binoculars."

As Duke fiddled with the glasses, he finally got them adjusted and could see himself sitting in the chair between Dick and Ty. He waved and Ty and Josh waved back.

"Pretty cool," Josh yelled.

"Yep, pretty cool," Dick agreed. "Just don't fall out of your chair when the show starts. Okay, Charlie, let's get this thing airborne."

The 3-D streaming video that had been so clear when the jet was sitting on the runway began to shake around as the model rolled down the runway. And the noise from the turbine engine seemed like it was getting much too close to them when the jet lifted off and rocketed over their heads.

Once it was in the air, the picture became rock steady and a big grin stretched across Duke's face. Charlie kept applying power until the model reached its maximum speed of two hundred fifty mph, then he guided the jet through a series of rolls and tight turns. Soon Josh was feeling like he was about to barf.

"Take it easy, Charlie, I didn't pass out any vomit bags today." Dick said as his body moved back and forth, trying to compensate for what it perceived to be real motion.

"I'm going to switch to the aft view," Charlie said. As he flipped a switch a small mirror popped up in front of the camera lens, which showed the reverse angle.

"Go over to the lake and show them the strafing run," Dick suggested with a chuckle.

Charlie flipped the mirror out of the way and pressed another button popping up a targeting radical in front of the camera. They watched as the plane headed for a model boat anchored in the lake and began firing at it.

Duke had come to grips with the sensations the glasses produced and started laughing out loud. "Blast the hell out of that thing."

As the plane skimmed a foot over the lake little missiles began shooting out from under the model and exploding all around the boat.

A minute later the jet was gliding toward the runway and made a perfect three point landing.

"Still think you'd buy something else now?" Dick asked as everyone removed their glasses.

Duke was so excited he jumped up and down a couple of times before he turned and shook Dick's hand. "Not on your life. Everybody that hears about this is going to want one."

Let's go back to the office while the team takes care of business out here," Dick said walking back to his car.

"Man that was cool," Ty said looking at Duke.

Josh, who was sticking to his grandfather like glue, looked up with a big smile. "When you get one of those, can I fly it?"

Duke stopped and bent down. "You're going to be the first one I let touch it," he said patting Josh on the shoulder.

Once they were back in the main building, Dick led them to a conference room next to his office. "Come on in and make yourselves comfortable. Charlie will be here shortly to go over the specifications and the lawyers want you to sign a few dozen papers."

"Not a problem." Duke said leaning back in the soft leather chair. "That model is the next best thing to actually flying I've ever seen."

"Yes it is, and we're proud to have you onboard to promote it."

While they continued to talk, Charlie came in and dropped five large binders on the table. "Okay let's get down to the brass tacks," he said passing them each a copy of the owner's manual.

"Flip to page eight, titled Wireless VR Goggles. The standard ones that we're shipping with the model are equivalent to watching a fifty-two inch television at optimal distance. They're rechargeable and will run for about four hours before you need to plug them in again. They also only need fifteen minutes to charge back-up. There is a high end model at the lab that will last longer and also provide sound, but who knows if anyone is going to be willing to pay an extra hundred bucks to listen to the engine whine?" Charlie paused for questions, but nobody asked any.

"Okay, the controller supports eight electric servo motors to control the jet engine and move the control surfaces. The prototype you saw today used all of them. Of course, the speed will be limited to the two hundred mph the law allows, which is not a bad idea because the box only has a range of one and a half miles."

"You were flying a lot farther than that today," Duke said.

"Yes, the test area is a ten mile rectangle. We use digital repeaters along the east-west corridor to boost the range, but you won't have that once they leave the factory." Charlie flipped to the next section.

"The plane itself is a one-eighth scale model of the Phantom you flew in Vietnam. It weighs in at twenty-five pounds and produces a maximum of thirty-five pounds of thrust. The plane configured for maximum air time will stay aloft for an hour at sixty percent power – cruising at 110 MPH." Charlie closed the manual and put both hands on the table waiting to see their reactions.

"What about the missiles?" Josh asked.

"Well, you can probably understand why they're not included in the package. We are trying to work on something less lethal that the government might allow us to sell as an option, but don't hold your breath," Charlie answered.

Duke leaned forward. "What the hell were you using today?"

"You may not remember the guns that came out during the 60s that used little rocket-propelled bullets. They had no recoil and twice the power of a forty-five. The only problem was you could put your finger over the barrel and stop the thing before it got going." Charlie could tell by the blank looks on their faces none of them knew what he was talking about.

"Anyway, that's what we were using today. Thought it might have some military value if we ever decide to go in that direction. When designed correctly they have a straight trajectory. The ones the Army tested in the 60s were defective, which is one of the reasons they never became popular. If you don't have any more questions, I have to get back to work."

Standing to shake Charlie's hand Duke said, "I have a million questions, but can't think of any I can't ask later."

After Charlie left, two lawyers came in and led Duke through the paperwork one page at a time. They were followed by a photographer hired to snap some publicity shots.

When it was over, Dick loaded them into one of the company vans and headed back toward the airport. He stopped at a local restaurant that he knew would have something on the menu that would appeal to Josh.

Leading them all inside, Dick was greeted by name as the hostess led them to a large table off to the side. After ordering, Dick used the time to once again tell Duke how happy he was that he had decided to help promote the new plane.

"I don't want to throw cold water on the party Duke, but I think you should know there's probably going to be a fair amount of pushback from the government on this new jet," Dick said.

"You mean because of 911 and everything?" Duke asked, his smile flattening into a line.

"Since you're involved in R/C flying, you know after the attacks all the industry leaders were called down to Washington and grilled as to why the government shouldn't just make radio controlled models illegal," Dick said taking a drink.

"Sure. It was a topic in every modeling magazine for over a year after the attack," Duke replied.

"I figured you'd remember, but what a lot of people forget is we were only one signature away from being shut down for good that week. It took a lot of convincing to get them to understand r/c flying is line-of-sight. Flying a model into someone or something isn't as dangerous as using a rifle or crashing a gas truck," Dick said getting more worked up.

"So what's the problem?" Duke asked. "Isn't that all water under the bridge by now?"

Dick leaned forward. "If this were just another model, I wouldn't have ever brought it up, but this model is state-of-the-art. Hell, the thing could just as easily be sold to the government for recon over in Iraq. The only problem is it's a toy compared to the million dollar R/C's they're using now. If you set them side by side, nobody would pick our model because it just isn't big enough to do much damage. But the government may see it another way."

Duke sat back in his chair and thought about it for a second. "So what do you want me to do?"

"I want you to promote the product. Just wanted to let you know there may be some pushback," Dick said as dinner arrived.

When they were finished eating, Dick picked up the bill and drove them to the airport where the Aztec waited on the tarmac.

Turning off the van's engine, Dick swiveled around in the seat so he could see them all. "Charlie thinks I'm crazy, but before you go, I want to give you each a plane. I've included some promotional jackets for you and a box of hats to give away. And remember, there's no guarantee, so try not to crash them."

Five minutes later after loading three large boxes and two smaller ones containing the Ajax wearing apparel into the Aztec, Duke started the engines and waved out the window to Dick. He radioed the tower before he began to taxi toward the runway.

Chapter 25
A Sure Thing

Although Mohammed had known that pornography was king of the Internet, he was amazed when he got back to his suite in Jakarta to find he had received over a million hits from the symbiotic ping-bot virus he'd emailed a week ago. Before going to bed that night, he launched a program designed to strip the IP addresses out of each email and append it to the IP_Porn.txt file on his hard drive. With any luck it would finish collating the information before he woke up. Then he took a very long shower and downed two large glasses of brandy before flopping on the bed and dropping into a dreamless sleep.

He was awakened by the ringing of his cell phone the next morning and was afraid the call would end before he found the phone. After a wild hunt, he finally zeroed in on the bathroom hamper and grabbed the phone from his pants pocket. He was surprised to hear Ramadan on the other end.

"Mohammed, she's gone", said the quiet voice on the other end pausing for a reaction.

Mohammed shrugged his shoulders a little, walked over to the window and looked at the trees beside the pool where he had first decided Halley was a target of opportunity. "I thought she would last a few days. In fact I was planning on coming up on Wednesday to see her again – but no use now, I guess."

Ramadan's speech accelerated a bit. "It was very fast, almost too fast. I just wanted you to know. I'm going to start dehydrating the virus today. It should be ready by the time I contact her family. How are things going on your end?"

"I'm doing better than expected. I will be ready for my first trial run in a few weeks," Mohammed said proudly. "I just need to wait for Ahmed and Saif to finish collecting all the data. The farther they get away from the Capitol Building, the longer it takes, so it will be a while. It looks like we can both cook up a pretty mean virus when we put our minds to it."

After hanging up the disposable phone, Mohammed walked over to his computer and looked at the drive light that was now totally dark. "That's my baby," he said sitting down and moving the mouse to activate the display.

Bringing up another program he had written, Mohammad set it up to match the data in the IP_Porn.txt file and LatLong.txt file he had created from the PointsOfInterest.txt files provided by Ahmed and Saif. In the end he would have a file that contained a list of the physical locations where those little wireless servers the Americans were so fond of installing in their homes, coffee shops, and offices were located.

As the program began to run, a map of the Washington, DC, area appeared on the display. Once the first red dot appeared, Mohammed got up and changed into his bathing suit. Grabbing a towel, and headed down to the pool to see if any beauties were there today.

When he returned three hours later the map was covered with thousands of dots as the program continued to process the data. It was easy to see that by the time all the data had been processed every major roadway leading to the Capitol Building would be covered by long red lines.

After a quick shower, he sat down at the computer again. He took a deep breath and began what he considered the most boring part of his assignment. Especially bothersome to him was the fact that he hadn't been able to write a program that would automatically program the SD chips used in the controllers.

Pulling up a graphical formula package he began entering numbers. Assuming the powder was ground down to the proper micron size, it would have a settling rate of one inch per second. That meant that if it was released at a hundred feet it would take twenty minutes for it to reach the ground in calm air. Unfortunately, the air in the real world never acted like air in the laboratory, so there was really no way of knowing exactly what was going to happen.

Cutting the altitude to fifty feet meant it would reach the ground in ten minutes. The blast from the propeller and wake coming off the wings of the planes would probably push the powder down another eight to ten feet, cutting two minutes off that. Of course that didn't take into account any prevailing winds that would be blowing around Washington, or the weather.

Sitting there Mohammed wanted to scream at the uncertainty, but simply shook his head and popped up an aerial view of the Greater Washington, DC area. On the map the Capitol Building was marked with a large star. Of the thousand planes scheduled to launch, eight hundred would be aimed at this target. Each plane would fly thirty miles to its target, carrying two pounds of enriched nuclear powder, two pounds of bird flu, and a one pound charge of high explosive set to detonate on impact.

A hundred other planes were targeted at key Federal installations within the perimeter. Smaller stars sat atop the White House, Pentagon, National Security Council, NASA, Social Security Administration, US Department of Defense, National Transportation and Safety, US Postal Service, Emergency Preparedness Office and other key offices.

Large white dots marked targets for the remaining hundred planes. These targeted local facilities including the Washington DC Fire & Emergency Medical Services Department, Washington Metro Transit Commission, District of Columbia Control, Washington DC Transportation, City Wide Call Center, plus many others.

There were so many targets listed on the internet sites supporting the Washington, DC area that Mohammed found it hard to choose which to include and which to forget. In the end, he concluded that he had made enough correct choices to make it a night to remember.

The two hundred planes targeting the Federal and local facilities would be carrying the same nuclear and biological payload as the eight hundred targeting the Capitol plus an additional four pounds of explosives. This was to be the "shock and awe' portion of his attack strategy.

The attack was designed to scare the hell out of the people and overwhelm emergency services. Mohammad had carefully planned each route so that the destruction would not block any of the major evacuation routes, which were key to his plan.

Banking on the fact that the President and Vice President would be hustled out of the Capitol Building on live television shortly after the attack began, Mohammed figured it wouldn't take CNN long to spin up nonstop coverage of the event.

Knowing that most of the locals would rather hunker down in their homes than face the prospect of being trapped on the highways with their families, Mohammed had to come up with something more frightening than staying home. The idea of using nuclear material to scare the hell out of them seemed like a good bet. Once word got out that nuclear material was being sprayed on the Capital, nothing would stop them from getting in their cars and driving off onto the highways.

It was this probable human response he was looking to invoke because even with a thousand pounds of radioactive material at his disposal, Mohammed knew there was too much area to cover to see people dropping in their tracks from the exposure. Eventually people would begin to die, but it could take years for any appreciable numbers to accumulate.

Like all good battle plans, you had to leave an escape route open for the enemy, and then kill them as they raced toward the perceived safety. So while the people fought to get out of the city, and the traffic backed up and cars ran out of fuel, the bird flu would slowly settle on them like a grave blanket. When it was all over, Mohammed calculated over a million would be dead and Washington would become a ghost town.

Chapter 26
The White House Situation Room

After watching Haiwei's plane leave the ground, Petter Andersson called his brother Kettil on his cell phone. "I'll be in San Diego in two hours. What time does our plane take off?"

Holding his second Bloody Mary of the day in his left hand, Kettil looked at the clock over the bar, then back at the departing flights' schedule on his PDA. "Looks like you should change that to San Francisco. There's and a two-fifty out of there that will get us into Dulles by eleven tonight."

"See you in San Francisco." Petter said snapping his clamshell phone shut.

As he started the long walk to the ticket counter, Petter thought about his top secret job at Ericsson, and the lies he hid behind to shield Haiwei from worrying too much. On days like this it always made him feel like a heel when he told her one thing and snuck off to do something else.

He remembered how honest he had been with her when they first got married and how worried she got as he rose up the ladder and became more and more involved with secret government projects. Over the years he had told her less and less about what he really did, until it had become a kind of "don't ask don't tell" understanding between the two of them.

The hop from LAX to San Francisco took a little over an hour, and when he walked past the security area, Kettil was waiting for him.

"Beat you by ten minutes," Kettil said punching his older brother in the arm, "I've already got the tickets and checked our overnight bags."

Putting his arm around Kettil, Petter smiled. "I hope you had your wife pack mine this time. The last time we participated in a final acceptance test, the only thing I had to wear after the first day was clean underwear."

"Don't worry Petter. Britany packed your bag this time. There's so much crap in the bag I was surprised that she got the damned thing closed. Besides, we're only going to be there for a day this time."

"Thank God. I swear you got some of Dad's farmer genes in you when you were born. You don't seem to mind wearing the same clothes for two or three days."

"There's an advantage to that. Eventually the clients get tired of smelling me and sign-off on the equipment."

As they walked towards their departing terminal, Kettil handed Petter his ticket. Half an hour later they were sitting in first-class, watching the parade of coach passengers file by. After eating lunch they both pushed their seats back and dozed until they landed.

At eleven-twenty they touched down at Dulles and took a shuttle to the Airport Marriott. The next morning they were up and dressed in time to grab a quick coffee before they were picked up by two security agents in a black Suburban and whisked away to the White House for the Final Acceptance Test of the Situation Room.

Ericsson had won a large portion of the recent renovation contract and now that everything was installed, it was the Andersson brothers' job to get a signature for the final payment. Today, they would be working with representatives from the National Security Council, Homeland Security, and the White House Chief of Staff to prove that everything worked as advertised.

After a thorough security check, they got on the elevator accompanied by two agents who looked like they would rather blow their heads off than take them to the Situation Room. Petter couldn't help but smile as they rode down to the sub-basement where the Situation Room was located. He guessed that it had been built near the employee dining area so food could easily be brought in during long meetings.

Looking over at Kettil, he caught him eyeing up the recently upgraded security camera. In the Surge Room, a technician snapped a still of Kettil's face from the streaming video and fed it into the feature extraction algorithm which produced a file containing a sequence of numbered feature reference points. From there the computer quickly matched reference points to identities stored in its facial model database. Ten seconds later a name tag with Kettil's picture slid out of a laminating printer and dropped onto the desk beside Petter's.

When the doors opened, they walked into the reception area and were pleasantly surprised by the finished product. They had both been there twice before. Once when the room had been stripped down to the studs and concrete and again when the Ericsson equipment had arrived with the technicians who were going to install it.

145

Walking over to an attractive wooden cabinet, the lead agent opened the lead-lined door and grabbed two plastic airport security type trays. "Please deposit everything except your wallet in these."

Kettil put his phone, Blackberry, and keys into one of the trays and handed it back to the agent.

"Your watch and any writing implements too, please," the guard said holding the tray in front of Kettil.

"Good catch," Kettil said taking off his Bluetooth enabled wristwatch. I completely forgot about that."

"Little bit of overkill, isn't it?" Petter said dumping his belongings into the tray. "I'm pretty sure that nothing on the market will operate in the electronic dead zone we've created in here."

"We're more worried about the cameras built into everything today," the agent responded, as he closed the cabinet.

An attractive agent, wearing a CIA identification badge with Linda Longsteam printed under her picture, emerged from the Surge Room. Smiling she walked over and handed them a badge. "Please wear these while you're here and don't leave the Situation Complex."

"Which way is the door, Linda?" Kettil asked smiling.

"It's right there. Where should I have your body shipped, Kettil?" Linda asked waiting for an answer.

"Not much of a sense of humor in here today." Kettil said looking at Petter.

"Don't look at me," Petter answered, "You dug this hole yourself.

"Just kidding, Kettil. I haven't shot anyone in at least a month." Linda said. "Listen, you two sit down in the corner there by the entrance to the Surge Room. After the briefing, Petter can stay in here and I'll take Kettil into the Surge Room so he can monitor the news broadcasts.

In the main room six flat panel displays provided video output and acted as touch screen writing pads. The walls and ceiling contained microphones and speakers. Today the plush leather executive chairs that normally sat around the long rectangular conference table had been replaced with smaller chairs so that twelve people could be seated around it.

Another ring of chairs had been pushed against the walls on three sides bringing the total seating capacity to thirty. Inside the Situation Room a view of the lawn could be seen through the one-way bullet proof glass, mirrored to make it impossible for anyone outside to see what was going on inside. Continuously filtered air, adjusted for proper temperature and humidity, exchanged the air in the complex every three minutes to provide a comfortable working atmosphere.

Next to this room, information officers sat in the Surge Room, monitoring Internet traffic, news feeds, and bulletins from state and local governments for anything important enough to forward one to the National Security Adviser, Hadley Stephenson, who acts as a filter for the President, passing on concise amalgamations of information that come in from various sources.

When Marine General Keith Zimmerman walked out of the Surge Room and to the head of the table, the chatter died down.

"Welcome to the Situation Room Acceptance Test (SRAT). Today's test will help verify that all essential systems are working in preparation for the TOPOFF 4 exercise that will be held next month. SRAT is based on the first TOPOFF exercise held in 2000. The only significant difference is that we are substituting Sarin Gas for the Mustard Gas used in that exercise. SRAT will commence at 0900 hours and last until the trusted agent, standing in for President Webber, is safely inside the U.S. Strategic Command Underground Command Center at Offutt Air Force Base in Nebraska."

Pointing to the back of the room the General continued. "Linda Longsteam will handle requests for outside lines and meals."

Linda stood and looked at her clipboard. "You should all find three meal slips tucked into your notebooks. Please fill these out with your menu choices. Coffee, tea, and other beverages, along with baskets of snacks, are in the coffee area near the bathrooms."

After Linda sat down, the general continued. "The SRAT attack location is the Washington Metro Subway at the Federal Triangle Station, six-tenths of a mile to the southeast."

Technicians in the Surge Room brought up live video feeds on the six displays showing satellite views of: the Federal Triangle Station; the CIA Headquarters in Langley, Virginia; FBI Headquarters; Pentagon; the Boeing 747-200B jet on the tarmac at Andrews Air Force Base; and the 911 Emergency Complex that had been set up to receive SRAT calls.

The general walked over to the aerial view of the station and used his finger to draw a large 'X' over it. Ericsson mapping software quickly converted it into an icon complete with zoom bars and precise latitude, longitude, and altitude readings.

Stepping back he continued, "A four-square block area has been cordoned off at this location. National Guard personnel are acting as subway passengers." A picture-in-picture (PIP) popped up on the monitor showing the final makeup being applied to the soldiers inside.

On the second display another PIP popped up showing a view from inside a helicopter approaching the CIA Headquarters. "During the SRAT test we will also be certifying the new VH-71, designed to replace the President's old Sea King. This helicopter is built around the European Agusta Westland EH101 and is designed to operate on two of its three engines."

Looking towards the Surge Room and getting a thumbs-up from a technician, the General smiled. "Let's see if that's true."

As the General slid the volume control up on the panel, the technician flipped a switch and a few seconds later the alarms and flashing lights inside the cockpit announced that engine number two had shut down.

"Control, this is Marine Bravo, I have a shut down on engine number two," the pilot said in a relaxed voice. "Disengaging number two."

"Rodger, Marine Bravo. This is Control. Radar shows you three miles out. Do you want to declare an emergency?"

Looking back at the stand-in agent who apparently hadn't been briefed about the engine test, the pilot held his finger off the transmit button and began shaking the control stick back and forth. "Mayday, Mayday, We're going down. I don't know if I can hold her."

As the agent's breathing became rapid, the pilot started a rapid decent then quickly pulled up and leveled off. "Control, Marine Bravo, responds well on two engines."

Petter leaned over to Kettil. "I hope that agent packed some clean underwear."

The General, who couldn't contain a little smile, looked at the wall clock which read 8:45. "Any questions before we take a ten-minute break?"

After fielding a couple of what he considered nonsense questions, the General walked back to the Surge Room and Linda came over to Petter and Kettil.

148

"Better take a few minutes to use the bathroom before the test starts. The first few hours are going to be pretty intense," Linda said pointing towards the break area.

"I'll take your advice on that one," Petter said.

"Me too," Kettil chimed in.

When they walked into the bathroom it was empty, but by the time they were washing up it was packed. Outside they saw Linda holding two large insulated coffee cups that had their names stenciled above the large SRAT Team logo.

"Here, use these. I had them made with special lids so you can't dump your coffee into anything important," she said smiling.

"You must have been a Girl Scout," Petter said taking his cup.

Linda looked into his eyes and smiled. "I use to be, but now I guess you could say I'm more of a Boy Scout."

"Sorry, Kettil and I are one hundred percent married," Petter said blushing a little.

"Well at least ninety-nine percent." Kettil said filling his mug with coffee.

Linda laughed. "Nice to know there are at least two honest men left in the world. Come on, Kettil. I'll show you where you're sitting."

After being escorted into the Surge Room and given a seat, Kettil was introduced to Joe Doeman, who was running a Sniffer Program on local television news channels.

Although Kettil was about twenty feet away from Petter, he could still see the monitors at the far end of the main room through the door, which had been propped open. Taking a long look at the Federal Triangle Station he noticed all the other buildings surrounding it.

"Is anybody working around the station today?" He asked Joe.

"Since the news media has been advertising the test for two weeks, I'll bet only a few people showed up. If it were me, I'd just take a vacation day and avoided the circus."

At nine o'clock, the fire chief gave the signal to start the two large ventilation fans aimed up the stairs of the Federal Triangle Station terminal. A few seconds later, a Marine sergeant popped a white smoke flare and placed it on a step in front of the fan. Back in the Situation Room, Petter watched the live satellite feed of the area and saw the smoke billow out of the terminal.

Sixty seconds later, a bank of fifty cell phones in the terminal began dialing the 911 Auxiliary Call Center with pre-recorded messages. Petter watched the displays as they followed the action at key points. Inside the Auxiliary Center dispatchers, taking calls in less than thirty seconds, had pinpointed the location and began dispatching vehicles for Engine Company Two on F Street.

Inside his mobile command center, Deputy Fire Chief Smoky Watson listened to the radio. "Command one. Smoke reported at the Federal Triangle Station. Many victims report convulsions and trouble breathing. An explosion of unknown origin was also reported - advise extreme caution."

Kettil noticed that text messages began appearing on the display he was watching. "Looks like the news media is getting in early on this one," he said punching up the volume on his earpiece to listen in.

Before the renovation, anybody with a hundred dollars could have listened in on police scanners. Now that the emergency radio systems in Washington had gone digital, the old scanners were useless. Anyone listening in today would have to have one of the new five hundred dollar receivers.

Just then two more banks of cell phones activated at other stations. As dispatchers began working the problems, the main electricity to the Call Center was cut. The battery-holding system that was suppose to keep the computers and phone system working until the backup generators started failed, and the center went black. Emergency lighting snapped on and showed that the pressure of the exercise was beginning to get to the dispatchers as they began swearing and shaking their heads in disbelief.

The emergency generators came on forty seconds later, but it took five minutes before the system was completely up. After that it didn't take long for the dispatchers to locate the other call location and tag this exercise as an organized terrorist attack on the subway system.

Inside the vehicles from the F Street Fire Station rolling towards the Federal Triangle Station, another message came in. "Command One Central, be advised that two more stations have been hit. This is beginning to look like an organized attack on the subway system. Possible gas attack, HAZMAT teams are on the way. Advise waiting until they verify air quality before entering station."

By now the intercepted messages from the news media were beginning to overload the Sniffer equipment. Kettil watched nervously as he waited for the redundant text algorithms to begin reducing the text to a more manageable size. The engineers at Ericsson didn't let him down and a few seconds later the output slowed to a readable pace.

As the trucks pulled up to the station, a police officer guided them into a spot on the opposite side of the street. The crews got out and began pulling out air-packs anxious to begin rescue operation.

"Hold on guys. We've got to wait here until the air is checked. Didn't you hear the last dispatch?" Smokey said as he positioned himself between the trucks and the station.

As he tried to keep his men calm, two little girls came running around the corner and headed toward the station's entrance.

Finnigan, a probationary member of the fire house, broke ranks and ran across the street after them. "Hey, you two, don't go in there."

The girls giggled and began running faster. Once they reached the door, they disappeared inside. Finnigan followed them and soon was grabbed by two Marines. "Looks like your dead," one said while the other slapped a 'Dead Victim' sticker on his back.

"What the hell are you talking about?" Finnigan screamed, as the Marines began dragging him over to their sergeant.

"I don't expect you to like it, but this is a training exercise. And right now you are dead. If it will make you feel any better you can lie down over there next to the girls," he said pointing to the blanket beside the steps where the girls were trying their best to pretend they were dead.

"Shit," Finnigan said before turning away from the sergeant and joining them.

Outside, Smoky had managed to contain the rest of his firefighters without reminding them this simulation had been in the works for weeks. As the HAZMAT vehicles rolled up beside him he breathed a sigh of relief.

The two technicians quickly donned their protective suits and began walking toward the white smoke still curling out of the station.

"No detectable radiation," the first one radioed back.

The second technician holding a portable SAW/GC Vapor Analyzer sucked in a volume of the air and waited for the computer to make an analysis. "Keep everyone back. We've got Sarin gas here."

Inside the Situation Room, Hadley Stephenson had seen enough. "Implement Protection Order One Two Alpha" he said with a voice that demanded attention.

As agents guarding the stand-in president raced onto the stage, many people in the audience began to jump up. Fortunately, their director clicked on his wireless microphone, stood up and turned around. "Everybody relax. This is only a drill."

Four minutes later President Webber's stand-in was back in the helicopter on his way to what was soon to become Air Force Alpha. By the time he arrived, the Washington Homeland Security Threat system had been raised to Severe and the 'Alert DC' message system was activated.

It began sending text messages to: cell phones, Blackberries, PDA's, computer emails, pagers, and fax machines; computer-generated voice messages to selected phone lines; and Emergency Alert System (EAS) announcements over local radio and television stations.

To test the Transportation Department's 'Walk-out Plan', local Boy and Girl Scouts had been enlisted. As the scouts, along with leaders and parents, walked to pick-up points, they were bused to the Washington Nationals Baseball Stadium to enjoy a free concert given by Bruce Springsteen and the E Street Band.

As Air Force Alpha rose from the airport, Petter and Kettil relaxed and took a coffee break.

"It looks like we passed with flying colors," Petter said watching the dotted line trace the progress of the Boeing 747-200B jet as it headed for Offutt Air Force Base in Nebraska.

Kettil toasted his brother, raising his SRAT mug high in the air. "Now you get to come back to San Diego for a little R&R."

Chapter 27
Haiwei's Heartbreak

The flight back to Cambridge, Massachusetts, would have been hard enough if Petter had come all the way with her, but he had business in San Diego, so they boarded separate planes in Los Angeles and Haiwei flew home alone.

Monday morning Haiwei got up at six and dressed in her blue long sleeve uniform with frog buttons and mandarin collar. She went down the stairs, through the kitchen and out the back door into the exercise garden she loved so much to do her t'ai chi exercises.

She began with her warm-up breathing exercises and soon realized how stiff all the traveling had made her. Needing some extra work to relieve the tensions that had built up, Haiwei decided to perform the one hundred-eighty step long form very slowly. Thirty minutes later, her mind was calm and her body relaxed.

After eating breakfast Haiwei would have normally gone to work, but since Halley was starting her master program at MIT the first week of September she had taken off the entire month of August.

It would have been a great plan if Halley had come home with them, but now that she was staying in Jakarta for an extra week, all the work of getting her ready for school fell on her mother.

Still, shopping for clothes and picking up books was better than working, so while Haiwei was disappointed about not having Halley with her, she jumped into the task of outfitting her daughter in the latest campus fashions. Over the next week she managed to supplement her daughter's wardrobe nicely without breaking the bank and anxiously awaited Halley's return, so she could show off all the new outfits.

The following Wednesday, Haiwei answered every call that came in with a cheery "Hello," as the time for Halley to board the plane for the long flight home drew near. While she was eating lunch she began to worry and picked up the phone and dialed Petter, but only got his answering service. Figuring he was either in an early meeting or having breakfast, she hung up and sent him a text message. A minute later he responded, letting her know he would see if he could reach Halley.

An hour later, after he had tried three times to contact Halley by phone and text message, Petter dialed the desk at the Mulia Senayan hotel. After briefly making an inquiry about Halley, he asked for the assistant manager. After a short pause, he was talking to the night manager who sounded a little less than chipper, understandable since it was three in the morning in Jakarta.

"No, Mr. Andersson, Miss Halley has not checked out, but she does have a wake-up call scheduled for five-thirty. Would you like me to connect you?"

Thinking about the grueling trip Halley was about to make, Petter decided not to bother her. "Has she ordered any breakfast?"

"Nothing on the computer," the manager responded politely. "Would you like to send something up?"

"Yes, I'd like to send her up three scrambled egg whites, unbuttered rye toast with jelly and a pot of tea, a few minutes after the wake-up call."

"Yes, sir. Will that be all?"

"Yes. Thank you," Petter said disconnecting.

Then he called Haiwei back and told her everything was all right and that he'd see them both on Friday.

On the thirty-first, Haiwei rode towards Logan Airport in a limo she had hired and was dropped off half an hour before Petter was scheduled to land at four-thirty. She was carrying a small bouquet of flowers she had picked from her garden for Halley, who was due an hour after Petter landed. She made her way to the security checkpoint and waited.

She hated the fact that since the 911 attacks nobody was allowed to wait by the gate for their loved ones. Today the plane from San Diego was actually early, so she had a pleasant surprise when she spotted Petter strolling up the hallway toward her.

"Hello baby," Petter said as he scooped her up and swung her around.

"Oh, I'm so glad you're finally home. It's been so lonely in that house with no one to talk to," Haiwei said between kisses.

"Let's get a drink while we wait for Halley," Petter said leading Haiwei towards the Cheers Bar and Grill.

After giving the waitress their order, Haiwei told Petter about all the shopping she had done for Halley and the books she picked up from the college book store. After telling Haiwei his account about the new communication system installation, they figured it was time to go back to the security checkpoint and wait for Halley.

Passing the Arrival Board Petter smiled. "It looks like the plane has already arrived. We'd better hurry."

Having traveled abroad frequently they knew that Halley would have to pass through customs, so they hurried off in that direction. Peeking at the long lines of people waiting to be checked, they looked for Halley, but couldn't see her. After half an hour of waiting, Petter spotted two stewardesses carrying blue shoulder bags with the golden Singapore Airlines logo and went over to ask them how many more passengers they thought would be inside.

"I think we're the last," the taller of the two said politely smiling.

"That can't be. Our daughter was on that flight and we haven't seen her," Petter said getting a little concerned.

"Follow me and we'll check the flight manifest. Better have your wife wait here in case I'm wrong."

While Petter went with the stewardesses, Haiwei waited, still hoping that Halley would appear, but fifteen minutes later Petter ran up to her. "She never showed up for the flight."

"What do you mean?" Haiwei asked as her stomach began to knot.

"She had a reservation, but never showed up," Petter said with a worried look on his face.

Taking out his Blackberry he typed in a message asking why she had missed her plane then sent it to Halley. Then he scanned back through his emails looking through the messages and discovered that he hadn't received anything from her since he got back to California.

"When was the last time you talked to her?" he asked Haiwei.

"I haven't heard anything from her since she sent me a message that she was going sailing three days after I got back.

Petter quickly dialed the desk at the Mulia Senayan and got the same assistant manager he had spoken to on Wednesday. "Listen, this is Petter Andersson. I need to know if my daughter ever checked out of my room. Yes, room 814."

"No one has checked out, but according to our records she was scheduled to vacate the room yesterday. The cleaning staff will be going in this morning to prep it for a new guest scheduled to come in today."

As she listened, Haiwei became more and more concerned as Petter continued to talk with the manager. "Ask him if we can extend the room for another week," she said tugging on his arm.

"Listen, can I extend the room for another week?" Petter said making a face and tilting his head from side to side.

After some time the manager agreed to leave the room untouched and to extend it for another week, which Petter thought would at least give the Jakarta police a clean crime scene, if it came to that.

On the way home in the limo, Petter and Haiwei went over their options. While in Jakarta, Petter had met with George Burrows, an Ericsson technician in charge of the WCDMA/HSPA network upgrade. If push came to shove, he could call him up and have him start pushing the local police to launch an investigation. The problem was, neither of them knew what had happened to Halley and didn't want to panic just yet. But just as a precaution, he emailed Burrows a picture of Halley he had snapped with his cell phone and a brief explanation of the problem.

Haiwei's instinct was to pack some things and book the next available flight out, which made a lot of sense to Petter. The problem was that he was scheduled to be in Brazil in four days to head the negotiations team working on the next phase of the GIS mapping system Ericsson had installed there four years ago. Since he was the primary contact, it would be hard to find a replacement on such short notice.

By the time they got home it was after eight and Petter soon found out that the American Embassy closed at 4 P.M. on Friday. Since it was already Saturday in Jakarta, he would need to wait until the next morning when they opened at seven- thirty.

Next Petter called his brother Kettil in San Diego to see if Halley had called her cousin Kathy. Unfortunately, Kathy was out shopping with her mother and both had left their cell phones in the charger at home. Kettil assured Petter that he would have her call him as soon as she returned.

An hour later the phone rang and Petter answered, expecting it to be Kathy, but he heard a strange female voice on the other end after he said hello.

"Is this Petter Andersson, Mr. Petter Andersson?" the voice asked.

"Yes, this is he."

"Well this is Joy, Dr. Imad's assistant here at the Jakarta Hospital"

"Yes?" Petter said motioning to Haiwei to pick up the extension in the other room.

"I'm afraid that I have some rather bad news, Mr. Andersson and I hate giving it to you over the phone like this," Joy said pausing.

"Is it about my daughter, Halley?" Petter blurted out, when he just couldn't stand the suspense any longer.

"Yes, I'm afraid so. You see she came down with diphtheria last week and was admitted, but three days ago she took a turn for the worse."

"Is she all right?" Petter asked, as Haiwei came into the room and began hugging him.

"No. We tried everything we could, but she died two nights ago."

"Why didn't somebody call us when she was first admitted?" Petter almost screamed into the phone.

"Well honestly, we didn't know who she was. Halley was in and out of consciousness, so delirious and unresponsive to our questions that we figured she was working the streets as a low class ayam. The only way we found out she was your daughter was from a gentleman who came in with a picture. From Ericsson, a Mr. Burrows, I think," Joy said becoming more business-like.

"And you're sure it is my daughter," Petter asked softly, as the reality began to sink in.

"Yes. Positive. Mr. Burrows' picture of your daughter showed the same locket around her neck as the girl when she came in. So I'm sure, but that's only part of the problem, you see," Joy said her voice trailing off.

"What problem are you talking about? You tell me my only daughter is dead and there is some other problem I'm supposed to be worrying about."

"Well you see we would have had to do it eventually anyway, if you wanted to bring the body back home. So there is nothing to get too upset about," Joy said hoping for the best as her shoulders raised and tightened.

"What the hell are you talking about?

"Now, there's no need to yell. I'm trying to tell you. You see there was a mix-up in the morgue and your daughter was taken to the crematory and well. . . ."

"You've cremated my daughter!" Petter screamed, as Haiwei went pale and began to sob.

"I can understand your anger, Mr. Andersson. We were shocked when we found out what had happened. The director of the hospital had authorized me to offer you two options. We will happily pay for the ashes to be shipped back to your residence or pay for a round trip ticket so you can come pick them up yourself. Under the circumstances I'm afraid that is all we can offer at this point," Joy said hoping the call would be over soon.

Calming down a little, Petter thought about a thousand things at the same time. "Just a minute, let me talk with my wife."

Holding Haiwei close and petting her head Petter asked in a soft voice. "Should we have Halley's remains shipped here or do you want to go over and bring her back.

Haiwei looked up at Petter and hated him for the first time in her life. Of course she knew that it wasn't his fault that Halley had died or had been cremated, but he was never there when she needed him.

Taking a deep breath she looked him in the eye and said, "If you won't come with me. I guess I will have to go alone." Then she walked out of the room, upstairs to their bedroom and slammed the door.

Picking up the phone, Petter said. "I believe my wife will be coming over to pick up the remains. Can you have someone call her tomorrow to make the arrangements?"

By the time the call had ended, Joy had given Petter the hospital's contact information and thanked him again for his understanding. Putting the phone down, she relaxed back into the soft leather chair in Dr. Imad's office. A second later she felt Ramadan's warm strong hands messaging her neck.

"You did a wonderful job, Joy. It was important for us to get a family member to come for the container and getting the mother to come is the best of all possible outcomes. Nothing is more believable than a grieving mother when it comes to getting something through customs."

•••

Two days later, Haiwei sat alone on Halley's bed in the hotel room. She had had every intention of going to the hospital, getting Halley, and bringing her back immediately, but she felt exhausted and too drained to face that just yet. As she fell back on the bed, Haiwei caught a faint trace of Halley's fragrance lingering in the breeze she had stirred and fell asleep.

The next morning she was awakened by a knock on the door.

"Room Service, Mrs. Andersson."

Haiwei got up and looked at herself in the mirror on the way to the door. She looked as bad as she felt.

"Yes, come in," she said pulling the door opened.

"Your husband, Petter ordered this for you and I found this envelope by the door when I arrived," the waiter said handing her the envelope and placing the covered tray on a small table.

"Is there anything else I can get for you?"

"Not right now, thank you," she said walking to the door, holding it open and then locking it as the waiter disappeared down the hall.

Over coffee, Haiwei opened the envelope and found a letter from Dr. Imad inside. It began with another apology about the unfortunate circumstances surrounding the death of her daughter and ended with how much it would please the doctor and his assistant to come over and deliver Halley to her personally.

Somehow the offer seemed a little strange, but the letter pointed out how impersonally the whole transaction would be handled at the hospital. As she ate breakfast, Haiwei thought about the trip to the hospital and how she would handle riding in a cab with a box containing her daughter's remains. In the end she dialed the doctor's number and arranged for him to come over at two in the afternoon.

Haiwei spent the rest of the morning packing Halley's belongings into her two suitcases. Then she turned her attention to straightening up the room. As she methodically checked the drawers, she came across an ashtray full of change, which she thought she would leave for the cleaning staff.

As she walked over and put the ashtray on the coffee table, the change shifted, exposing something blue under the coins. It turned out to be a tiny blue Micro Media Card from Halley's Blackberry. Probably a spare, Haiwei thought, as she had no way of checking it now. So she dropped it in her purse and continued cleaning.

At exactly two, Joy arrived with Ramadan, who was introduced as Dr. Imad. As Haiwei let them in she noticed that Joy was carrying a large silk bag with some flowers sticking out of it.

"I am so sorry we have to meet like this," Dr. Imad said holding out his hand as Joy walked over and placed the bag on the coffee table.

"I appreciate you taking the time to come to me,." Haiwei said distracted by the bag she knew must contain Halley's ashes.

"Please, let's sit down. I have some things I need to go over with you," the doctor said motioning Haiwei towards a group of chairs near the windows.

As they passed the coffee table, the doctor's leg brushed against it, causing the change to rattle.

"Sorry," he said sitting down across from Haiwei.

Joy pulled another chair near the doctor and sat down, blocking Haiwei's view of the bag and began speaking.

"As I told your husband on the phone when we first talked, Halley died from diphtheria, which, as you probably know, is highly contagious."

"Since Halley had her DPT shots, I don't see how that is possible." Haiwei interrupted.

Leaning in towards her, Dr. Imad shook his head slowly. "It is quite rare, but even with booster shots every five years it sometimes happens. The tests were quite conclusive."

Joy continued. "Since diphtheria is so contagious the body must be cremated before it can be shipped out of the country. This ensures the public's safety and allows foreigners to take their loved ones home. In order for you to carry the remains on a commercial airliner we have placed the ashes in a special plastic container. When you get to America, the container will be passed through an X-ray machine at a security checkpoint and given back to you."

"Will they open it? I don't want anyone touching my daughter," Haiwei stated protectively.

"Provided the container remains sealed and the X-ray scan doesn't reveal anything unusual, there is nothing to worry about. It fact, it is against your country's laws for anyone to open the container – even if you wanted them to. Halley will be quite safe," Joy said flashing a concerned smile.

Haiwei put her head back against the chair. "We have decided to spread them on my brother-in-law's farm in New Jersey this Thanksgiving. Halley loved that place. It is where she would be happy."

"That sounds like an excellent place," Joy said, "I'm sure you will all remember her there. There are just a couple more things to go over. All the papers are attached to the container and you must not remove

160

them. There are four: The Consular Mortuary Certificate for U.S. Customs Clearance; The Certificate of Death; An Affidavit by the Funeral Director who performed the cremation; and a Transit Permit to get you out of Jakarta."

As they got up, the doctor hugged Haiwei. "Remember, it is very important not to open the container or remove the documents until you are safely home. If you do, the container will be detained."

"Yes, I understand," Haiwei said as she showed them to the door.

Hugging Joy and shaking the doctor's hand, Haiwei managed a smile before closing the door behind them. She knew that she should call Petter and tell him about the meeting, but at that moment she felt like she was a hundred years old and didn't want to do anything except sleep. So she turned off her cell phone and somehow managed to get hold of the front desk – telling them to hold her calls.

As she walked toward Halley's bed she pulled a single flower from the bag and brushed it against her nose. It smelled so sweet that it made her want to cry, but she was too tired to even do that. As Haiwei lay on the bed twirling the flower in the air, darkness closed in around her and she escaped into a peaceful sleep.

The next morning breakfast came again, and to her surprise, she ate it. Then she contacted the hotel's concierge and told him to get her on the next available flight back to Boston - before calling Petter.

As the phone began to ring, Haiwei walked over and sat on the sofa.

"Petter, I'm so sorry that I didn't call you last night, but I was just exhausted."

Petter felt like a heel and knew better than to say anything to set her off, so he didn't tell her that he had waited up all night for her call. "That's all right. I understand how you must feel. I'm really sorry you had to do this all by yourself."

"Well, somebody had to do it and you have your work and everything. I didn't want to just have her shipped home like a cabbage… Anyway, I'm going home on the next flight I can get. When do you think you will be done?"

"It looks like we'll be wrapping this up by the end of the week – so I should be home next Saturday. Did you have any trouble getting the ashes?" Petter asked, as he was being summoned back into the meeting.

"No. In fact the doctor and his assistant brought Halley – I mean her ashes over to the hotel. The only thing is I'm afraid to take the box out of the bag," she said getting up and grabbing the empty glass vase off the top of the television.

"Why don't you try now?" Petter said in a supportive voice.

"Wait I'm getting something to put the flowers in," she said cradling the phone against her ear with her shoulder and filling the vase half full in the bathroom. As she came out she placed it next to the bag and pulled the flowers out. "These flowers the doctor brought are just lovely."

Petter hoped that she would get the container out of the bag before his team came out in the hall and carried him back into the meeting. "Okay, it sounds like you're stalling now. Just take the box out while I'm still on the phone and tell me about it."

Reaching into the bag like it was filled with snakes, Haiwei quickly grabbed the box and put it down on the table. "I touched it."

"What does it look like?" Petter asked, thinking there were probably a thousand better questions he could have asked.

Haiwei reached down and picked the container up again. The whole thing couldn't weight as much as a five pound bag of sugar.

"It's curious, Petter. I keep having the most bazaar thoughts. I just compared it to a bag of sugar. Not much to look at – it's all wrapped up in brown paper with a bunch of documents attached. I don't know what I expected, but it looks pretty ordinary," she said giving it a little shake.

"I really have to get back into my meeting, Haiwei. Call me when you get back home, if you leave today. I love you," Petter said heading into his meeting.

"I love you, too," Haiwei said sitting back down on the sofa.

She shook the box again, listening closely to the sound. If she didn't know better she could have been shaking a big box of elbow macaroni. She started to laugh and went to put the container down, but dropped it against the corner of the ashtray, which sent the coins flying off in all directions.

"I'm sorry baby," she whispered, as she picked up the box and inspected it.

The only damage was a light scrape on the paper that was almost imperceptible. "I'll have to be more careful with you – won't I?" she said kissing the scar.

Then she became really frightened, as she realized how crazy she would look if somebody saw what she was doing. Luckily, the phone

162

rang. It was the concierge letting her know that there was an available seat on the flight due out at seven that night. Wasting no time, Haiwei told the girl to book the ticket and to send someone up for her bags.

Later that night she slept curled around the black silk bag in her lap as she headed back home. By the time she got to Logan Airport in Boston the sun was setting. During the trip, Haiwei had come to grips with the tragedy and had already figured out exactly where to spread Halley's ashes on the horse farm in three months.

Since there was no need to check through security, she headed for the baggage area. She was surprised to see an unfamiliar driver from the local transportation company she always used, holding a card with her name on it.

"You must be new. I haven't seen you before. Tom must be branching out. There are four bags, all blue with a red vertical stripe," she said handing him the ticket envelope with the claim tickets stapled to it.

"Fazul, Mrs. Andersson. I'll get the bags."

The driver smiled and disappeared into the crowd, waiting for the carousel to start moving. Five minutes later returned with all the bags loaded on the cart. He led Haiwei out to a van waiting at the curb.

"What happened to the limos?" Haiwei asked, as the driver opened the back and put the bags inside.

"Big wedding booked all of Tom's cars. We had to rent this one just for tonight, Mrs. Andersson. I hope you don't mind, but I picked up another passenger who's headed for Cambridge, too," Fazul said sliding the side door opened.

Before she could respond, Haiwei saw a large full-figured lady in her fifties sitting on the bench against the opposite side of the van. She was holding a small pet carrier on her lap and looked up when Haiwei started to get in.

"Hello, my name is Betty and this is Corky." The lady said tilting up the carrier a little, "we've just come back from Las Vegas, where Corky helped me win big at the craps tables."

"That sounds interesting," Haiwei said, "I didn't know they let pets into the casinos."

"Well, of course not. Corky plays with his toy dice and I write down all the numbers he turns up before I go and play. When one of his numbers comes up, I bet big and usually win," Betty said picking up the carrier and making some kissing sounds.

"Definitely something loose in that brain," Haiwei thought, as the car pulled out.

About twenty minutes later the van was getting hot and Haiwei asked the driver to turn on the air conditioning."

"Sorry, Mrs. Andersson, but the thing is all the way up now. I can put the windows down," he said pressing the buttons on the door.

An instant later the wind blasted Haiwei's hair, sending it flying in all directions. As she reached up to pull it out of her eyes the van veered quickly to the right, and the bag she had been carefully guarding slipped off her lap. For an instant she lost sight of it as it slid across the seat and disappeared into the darkness.

"Put that God damned window up and watch where you're going," she screamed at the driver.

"Now, now, he was just trying to help," Betty said handing her the black bag.

"Yes, I'm just tired. I'll be so glad to get home," Haiwei apologized, and then she cuddled the box inside the bag and was silent for the rest of the ride.

When the driver put the last bag inside her house, Haiwei slipped him a twenty dollar bill and closed the door. She made it as far as the chair in the living room and collapsed. Outside the van's tires squealed as it pulled away and turned onto Sparks Street. Haiwei made a mental note to talk to Tom about Fazul's driving habits the next time she used his service.

As the van headed down Brittle towards Rt. 16, Betty pulled off her wig and stuffed it into the large purse between her feet. Then she swung the wire gate on the pet carrier open and removed the silk bag Haiwei had been carrying. The whole charade seemed like such a bother when they could have just taken the box and dumped the cremated ashes in a ditch somewhere.

"How did I do honey? Got the bag just like I said I would." That dumb shit doesn't have a clue."

As Fazul watched in the rearview mirror, she began opening the bag to see what was inside. "Put that thing on the seat and get up here."

"What the hell is so important about this thing anyway?" Betty asked as she moved up to the front passenger seat.

164

Fazul reached inside his jacket pocket and pulled out a thick envelope and handed it to her. "This is for all your hard work."

As Betty concentrated on counting her money, Fazul pushed a twenty-two caliber pistol behind her ear and pulled the trigger twice. "You did great, baby."

Chapter 28
Occoquan Incubator

Once he was on the interstate, Fazul set the cruise control two miles per hour below the speed limit and stayed in the right lane as he headed south. At one in the morning he sailed under the Easy Pass monitors and onto the New Jersey Turnpike. By this time Dead Betty, as he had come to call her, was beginning to get a little ripe. Originally he had planned on dumping her in Baltimore on his way to Occoquan, but she was getting to be more than he could stand. So he zeroed in on Atlantic City.

Fazul had been to Atlantic City several times and thought of it as a microcosm of America. In its heyday people had come there to vacation and walk on the boardwalk because it was bright and clean and new. But since its heyday the glitter had turned to grime and all but the poorest vacationers had gone elsewhere. The casinos had been able to restart the city's heart and more tourists headed back to be entertained by the street musicians and shop owners, but behind the glitter the city festered.

It was towards that Atlantic City Fazul was heading. He had been born and raised in the seedy back streets of Iraq, so he knew how they worked. To him they weren't scary, but business as usual. Watching pimps beating their ladies and drug dealers stuffing $100 bills into their socks as they plied their trade provided free entertainment to those watching from the shadows.

And as he turned off the Atlantic City Expressway onto Arctic, headed towards the projects a block south of the Absecon Inlet, he was about to provide some entertainment of his own. Approaching Maine Avenue he reached over and unbuckled Betty's seatbelt and opened the door a crack. Sitting back down, Fazul stepped on the accelerator and turned the wheel sharply to the left as he entered the turn. Dead Betty exited the van head first and made a loud cracking sound as she hit the pavement and did a flip in the air before landing on the sand. Driving west on Maine, Fazul snapped the wheel to the right for a second and the passenger door slammed shut.

Now that he was alone and didn't have to worry about getting pulled over with a dead girl sitting in his van, he relaxed, rolled down the windows, turned up the CD and headed back to the strip to use the bathroom and clean up. An hour later he pulled the van into a service station and told the attendant to fill it up.

As he crossed the new section of the drawbridge, the rising sun sparkled in the water as it danced along towards the nation's capital. Half an hour later, he turned off I-95 S towards Occoquan and gassed up again on Gordon Boulevard. After two days with very little sleep, Fazul pulled to a stop in the alley at the end of Commerce Street and shut the engine off. A minute later the cremation container was in the freezer compartment of his refrigerator and he was asleep on the red antique leather couch he used for a bed.

Fazul had picked Occoquan for his base of operations for several reasons. First, it was nine miles south of the Beltway and just one mile off I-95; second, it sat across the street from the Occoquan River, which offered unimpeded access to the Inland Waterway and Atlantic Ocean; and third, it was a sleepy little town that enjoyed being overlooked.

Another advantage was the fact that what little business Occoquan did support catered to the antiquing and handmade jewelry crowd, so it wasn't unusual to see FedEx, UPS, DHL or US Postal Service trucks making their daily deliveries and pickups. He especially liked this three story building, because vehicles could park on Mill Street and use the first floor entrance, or drive down Commerce Street and back right up to his back door.

What he didn't like was the fact that in all probability he would be dead before his birthday next spring. It wasn't something that he dwelt on or that even crossed his mind much these days, but it was inevitable. Frankly, he was surprised that he hadn't been arrested and carted off to Guantanamo already. But coming to grips with death had given him the freedom to face life, and he had vowed long ago to enjoy what time he had left.

By the time Fazul woke up, it was three in the afternoon and he had consciously erased all memories of the past forty-eight hours except for the fact that he had four pounds of an unnamed strain of Bird Flu derived from N5N1 sitting in his freezer. Normally, that would have sent a chill through him, but he knew that it was relatively safe compared to the next shipment scheduled to be delivered the following spring.

After setting up the coffee maker, he took a long hot shower and dressed for his evening meeting with his boss. The rest of the afternoon

167

was spent installing the wiring harnesses into six more plastic control modules.

Fazul had just finished packing and labeling the last box when the UPS driver knocked on the back door and walked in. It was a routine they were both used to and a minute later the load of 8x8x16-inch boxes was in the truck and headed towards fellow Jihadists scattered around Virginia and Maryland.

Fazul arrived at the restaurant after a two block walk. Ihmad was already sitting at a corner table by the back window, watching the fishing boats. As Fazul sat down, Ihmad handed him a copy of page six of the Atlantic County edition of The Press.

"I thought you were going to dump that bitch in Baltimore," Ihmad said barely able to keep from screaming.

Since there didn't seem to be any advantage to lying, Fazul counter attacked. "I didn't see you offering to drive to Cambridge, and besides, by the time I got there, something foul bubbled out of her every time I hit a bump in the road. It still smells like a sewage treatment plant inside. I want a new van."

Figuring there was little else he could do, Ihmad shrugged his shoulders and handed him a drink, secretly wondering if this hadn't been Fazul's plan all along.

"To the revolution," he said quietly, as they raised their glasses together.

After ordering, Ihmad got down to the business at hand. "How many units have you shipped to date?"

"So far thirty-six controller units and forty-eight of the Wi-Fi enabled PDAs have been shipped."

"Do you still think you are on target to have everything delivered on time?" Ihmad asked as the waitress delivered their food.

Using his fork for punctuation, Fazul began explaining the problems he saw with the plan from the very beginning. "From my standpoint it's the easiest job in the world right now, but as we get closer to the attack the risk increases greatly. If one of the recipients gets caught now, there will be nothing suspicious about the materials the authorities will find in their possession. That will all change when the nuclear material arrives next spring. It will need to be shipped out first and stored in their homes for nine months. It is easily detected and traceable directly back to me. So our plan depends on a thousand families living a simple life, staying

168

out of trouble and deciding not to collect the rewards that are on our heads."

Ihmad smiled. "I agree the plan can unravel at any point. Its beauty comes from the fact that Americans never think that far ahead. Hell, they're ready to pull out of a war they've been winning for the past year just because they are tired of fighting."

Fazul agreed with Ihmad's last point, but still wanted to vent. "I guess the part that bothers me the most is the fact that all the bird flu must be shipped out at the beginning of January to ensure its potency. How the hell am I going to ship out a thousand boxes without the delivery company getting suspicious?"

"By that time I don't think it will matter, but you can split them up among the four or five largest carriers over a week or two. That should reduce your exposure. Besides, once that's done you can beat it out of town and disappear," Fazul managed a weak smile, but knew in his heart that the chances of getting away after his part was completed were very slim.

When they parted outside the restaurant, Ihmad handed him a bag of candy. "This should be enough for you to last for another month. There will be a new van parked behind your building tomorrow morning with the keys under the driver's mat. Treat it well, as it will be the last one you get for free."

Walking back to his building, Fazul wondered how many more times they would meet before the whole thing came apart. Climbing the slate steps up from Mill Street to the back of the building, his legs felt exceptionally heavy. Once inside he walked over to the kitchen table and dumped the contents of the bag out.

Under the candy three bundles of bills were banded together in hundred, fifty and twenty dollar denominations. This month there was a bonus stack of prepaid gift cards that totaled an extra $5,000 for returning alive with the bird flu. Fazul knew that if he had been killed, other team members were ready to step in and get the box of ashes and they probably wouldn't have taken the time to set up a simple switch operation.

Chapter 29
The Trial of Ning Wang

Ning was nervous as he drove west toward the model airplane club in Tai Tong. True to his word Ali had provided all the equipment and raw materials Ning had requested, but not a single dollar of cash. Over the last three weeks Jin had been working double shifts at the Lucky Dragon, but the bills continued to accumulate. Ning knew that this was his one chance to break out of poverty and enjoy a better life, so he had worked day and night during that time to perfect the model. The only problem was that he had never had the opportunity to see if it would really fly.

Early on, he had decided that the plane's design should be based on the type used by short take-off and landing aircraft he had read about. After several days of searching on the internet, Ning had pieced together something he thought might actually be able to lift the 5½-pound payload that the design required.

The wings of course were the key. The final design consisted of three parts: a leading edge wing slat, which funneled air up and over the main wing on take-off; a thick cross-section wing to provide lift; and full span ailerons, which acted as flaps and provided additional lift.

One problem with the leading edge slats is that they increased drag when the aircraft reached level flight unless they are pulled back against the wing. Ning had devised a simple spring apparatus to push the slats out until the airplane leveled out and the pressure against the leading edge corresponded to twenty-five mph.

Knowing it would be disastrous if the slates didn't retract uniformly, Ning had placed the wing assembly on top of the plane and in effect had created a single wing design. The wing also utilized a winglet to add more lift and reduce tip vortices to a minimum.

As Ning pulled in, Ali moved out of the way and ended up beside the open driver's side window.

"Glad you got here a little early, Ning; I had to wave-off a lot of drivers to keep this space for you."

Ning thanked him, walked around to the back of the van and opened the double doors.

"The model is ready, I put it together according to your instructions and hopefully we will see it fly today," Ning said as he began pulling the sections from the van.

A few moments later, Ning led the way to the take-off area carrying the fuselage and his accessory box, while Ali carried the dissembled wings. When Ning found a spot he liked, he put the box down and gently set the fuselage on the ground.

"Now, let's see if everything fits together," Ning said pulling out the blank navigation module.

Ali looked around at the small groups focused on their own planes and reluctantly handed Ning a control module he had just received from Fazul in Virginia. "Here's the test module. Make sure the USB connector lines up correctly."

Ning lined up the square indentations molded into the module with the mounting bracket he had built inside the fuselage and pushed it gently into place until he heard the click of the locking clips. Then he reached for the set of three weights.

"Use these weights," Ali said pulling a set he had weighed himself out of his jacket pocket, "not that I don't trust you, but you understand I must certify this test for Mr. Din."

Although Ning didn't like the insinuation that he might have shaved some weight off the weights, he had brought, he didn't say anything, as Ali's weights seemed to be proper.

"Do you have the PDA that will control the flight?" Ning asked.

Again Ali looked around and surveyed the area before pulling it out of his pocket and handing it to Ning.

Ning looked at the PDA and was a little puzzled. "Am I supposed to turn this on before I put the rest of the plane together or wait until it is time to launch it?"

"It is designed to wait five minutes before the program starts so you do what you think is best," Ali said shrugging his shoulders.

Ning knew he could assemble the plane in less than a minute, but decided to postpone turning the computer on until later. So he plugged in the USB connection attached to the servo motors used to control the plane and slid the PDA into its slot in the navigation module. Next, he filled the one liter fuel tank and pushed it up into position from the underside of the fuselage until it clicked into place, forming a smooth surface on the rear half of the plane. Then Ning squeezed a little clear ball pump until he saw the fuel had reached the carburetor.

"Okay, give me the wing assemblies," Ning said reaching out his hand to Ali.

"The wings are designed to go together before securing them to the plane," Ning said holding up the two wing-halves and sliding the square wing supports into the receiving channel until they joined together, forming a single wing.

Ning secured the wing to the top of the fuselage with four large plastic screws. A few seconds after that, the five-minute countdown began on the PDA computer's display that was clearly visible though the clear plastic canopy in front of the wing.

"There. That's all there is to it. The five steps can be done in less than a minute with a little practice: place the control modules inside the plane; add the PDA computer; add the weights; snap in the fuel tank and prime the lines; assemble the wings and mount them to the fuselage," Ning said connecting his electric starter motor to the small motorcycle battery inside the accessory box.

Ning could tell Ali was impressed with the easy assembly, but he knew all would be for nothing if the plane refused to get off the ground.

As the PDA flashed down from ten seconds, Ning mated the starter motor to the cone in front of the propeller and waited. Then the program came to life and began testing each servo. As they watched, each control surface was moved through its range of motion until they had all been tested and set back to their neutral position.

When the Start Engine command flashed on the display, Ning hit the power switch on the starter motor and began to turn the engine over. It took a little longer than he would have liked, but eventually the engine fired and began running on its own.

Ning smiled and removed the starter motor. Then he held the plane as the computer ran the engine up to full throttle and back down to an idle. A moment later a message flashed on the display - "Point the plane toward the end of the runway."

Ning hurried out to the middle of the take off strip and lined the plane up. He stood there holding the tail until the launch timer reached zero and the engine powered up.

It was the longest five seconds in Ning's life, but in the end the model plane lifted off and began lumbering into the sky toward the east.

172

When the model was two hundred feet above the ground it began to level off and the slats retracted back against the wing. A minute later it turned west and buzzed over Ning's head. Then it banked left and disappeared in the sky to the south.

"What do we do now?" Ning asked.

"We wait," Ali said looking at his watch, "let's get some lunch."

"What are we waiting for?" Ning asked, as he packed up his box and began following Ali back to the van.

"I have someone in Dangan, Guandong who will tell us if the plane makes it that far. If he sees your plane, you will get the contract. If not, my business with you is completed," Ali said lighting up a cigarette.

Sipping tea at a small table by the snack bar, the two waited for the call that would determine Ning's future. Fifty-six minutes later it came. Ning was to die a rich man.

Chapter 30
Treasure Hunt

Stewart loved Thursdays because it was the night that Cindy was out with her girlfriends. The only bad part was that when she returned, he had to listen to her tell him about everything she had done while they were apart. So if he had to listen to her accounts of how great the wine tasting party was or how the movie had made her cry three times, he was going to make the most of the next three hours of scavenging on the web worthwhile. Tonight he had been especially attentive while talking with his wife Cindy until her cell phone began playing the theme from Jersey Girl.

From past experience, Stewart knew Debby was on the other end. She always called when she was two minutes away so Cindy could get downstairs before the girls pulled into the No Parking zone in front of the apartment. Stewart kissed her goodbye and patted her on the bottom playfully as she ran to meet her friends.

Once that was over, he turned off the murder mystery that had been playing on the television, picked up his half empty Corona Light and headed towards his computer. Over the past month he had spliced together enough ten-second porno clips to create two one-hour movies. The problem was they didn't amuse him anymore. So tonight, he was going to do what he really enjoyed: hunting for porn.

Originally, he had thought about deleting both movies before starting his third masterpiece; but in the end he kept the second because it still contained a few scenes that might be useful. What he liked best about making his own movies was that he could tailor them as he saw fit. Searching for hours he would eventually come across the perfect smile on the perfect face talking in the perfect voice doing the things that he could never get his wife to do.

He didn't know where the thousands of girls came from or if they really enjoyed appearing on the hundreds of provider websites that were used by millions of smaller companies to make billions of dollars. Logically, it seemed impossible that there could be so many girls willing to give it up for a few dollars. But tonight, as he began searching, he pushed that thought out of his head and figured that as long as they were here for free, he was using them to satisfy his fantasies.

Like most people who weren't too computer savvy, Stewart had contacted the local cable provider for his internet service and let the installer place the wireless equipment where he thought it would produce the best coverage. So like millions of other customers the only indication that Stewart had a wireless connection on his media enhanced desktop was the tiny antenna sticking up behind it.

In the closet down the hall, the cable modem and wireless base station sat together blinking sporadically. As Steward issued requests from his keyboard, files were downloaded. The LED that lit during transmission normally flickered sporadically, but since the ping-bot virus arrived, it flickered every second. The funny thing was, the equipment could be sitting right in front of a computer scientist and it would have still gone unnoticed, because everyone had stopped paying any attention to them a long time ago.

Everyone that is, except Ahmed, Saif, and Mohammed, who were conducting the first test of the Sym-Bot Navigation System in Washington, DC that evening. The principle behind the system was simple. Each of the two hundred thousand wireless base stations that had been activated was sending out a message, basically "My name is Stewart Beckman" in the form of Stewart's sixteen digit IP address. Unlike names, IP addresses are unique.

The PDA sitting in Fazul's test plane had a list of all the IP addresses and the locations where they lived (Stewart Beckman, 38° 54' 17.77 North, 77° 01' 45.58 West, Elevation 84 Feet), or in layman's terms, 1301 Massachusetts Ave NW. It also had a map and a program to help it find its way from one milestone to the next. This meant the plane could be blindly dropped onto the electronic grid that Mohammed was creating, and the navigation system would fly to the target by itself.

Tonight the test plane was going to fly from the junction of Piney Branch Road NW and Park Road NW to Fazul's Occoquan Workshop. The twenty-mile distance was well within the specs of the actual attack planes and allowed more fuel to be added to compensate for the increased pressure caused by the addition of a complex muffler that nearly erased any engine noise. It was so quiet, in fact, that Ahmed almost reached down to spin the propeller again after the engine started.

Holding the plane by placing his legs on either side of the tail assembly, Saif waited patiently as Ahmed walked away from the apartment turnaround and out onto the Park Road Bridge. When he signaled that no cars were coming, Saif grabbed the tail and stepped back. He pointed the plane down the middle of the bridge and together they watched it take off into the west. A quick email to Mohammed from a coffee shop down the street and their job was done.

Sitting in his room at the Hotel Mulia, Mohammed could only wait for another email from Fazul confirming the results of the test. He wished there was some way to watch the plane, but figured if it crashed along the way there was a good chance the incendiary charge it carried for self-destruction would start a fire that would be newsworthy.

Before the plane left the ground, it had already received seven location pings and began turning left as it climbed away from the bridge. Passing over Pierce Mill Road and Rosemont it confirmed its heading and climbed as the terrain rose ahead of it until it leveled off. For about a mile it lost all communications, but the obstacle avoidance sensors built into the bottom of the navigation module didn't sense any danger, so it just kept flying.

Picking up some more pings as it approached Cathedral Avenue, it climbed another fifty feet. At Connecticut Avenue the sensors picked up a heat source straight ahead and the plane slowed, tilted up and climbed slowly up and over the building like a helicopter.

As the signal strength increased, it kept climbing until the signals began to fade away. Then it leveled off and began flying normally. It continued picking its way through the city canyons until it came to Canal Road NW, where it paralleled the Francis Scott Key Bridge. Since it was dark and the plane was painted flat black, the only thing anybody looking in that direction would see was a shadow blocking out the building lights on the other side. It was flying too slowly and silently to attract anyone's attention.

Half an hour later, it sailed over Mill Street in Occoquan and landed in the turnaround by the water treatment plant where Fazul was waiting. After carrying it back to his workshop, he phoned Ahmed and told him to pass the word on to Mohammed that the maiden flight had been a success.

Chapter 31
Roommates

As Sarah returned to her car with the last box from her apartment, she wondered if she would regret her decision to move in with Ty. That thought disappeared quickly when she heard the front door bang as he ran to catch up with her.

"I hope you're cool with this set up, after giving up your lease and everything," he said grabbing the box and waiting for her to open the Miata's trunk.

When the box was in the trunk, he closed it and turned around. Sarah put her arms around his waist and smiled. "What do you think?"

"Baby, all I know is that you make me feel wonderful whenever I see you and now I will see you all the time," he said leaning back against the car and giving her a kiss.

Sarah had had her eye on Ty from the first day they met at the Internet Monitoring Complex at Foggy Bottom.

He had graduated from the Naval Academy at Annapolis, attended Top Gun Training at Falloon Naval Air Station near Reno, Nevada, and was completely full of himself. Besides all that he was smart, good looking, ambitious and seemed as comfortable addressing five hundred students at the university as he did talking to her when they were alone.

While Ty was worldly, Sarah was just the opposite. She had started to develop earlier than all of her friends and looked eighteen by the time she was in junior high. Because she was attractive she had received a lot of unwanted attention all through high school, but she ignored it to focus on academics as a way of escape.

When Sarah began her undergraduate work, she dated a few times, but still she found the pressures of dating too much to handle and buried herself in her college work. Now, at twenty-eight, she had earned the right to be called doctor and probably would have remained buried in the basement complex for the rest of her life if Ty hadn't arrived on the scene.

One thing she loved about him was that he was interested in some of the same things she enjoyed: computers, the internet, and security protocols. The other thing she liked was the way he made her feel as he coaxed her to do things that she never would have imagined – like flying and sky diving.

Sarah still thought about the weekend he had taken her out for her first jump. She was scared when he finally convinced her to go and didn't sleep much the night before her first tandem jump.

Ty had picked her up at six in the morning for the hour-and-a-half drive to the air field southwest of Fredericksburg. During the car ride down I-95 she cuddled up beside him and enjoyed the music blasting from the radio.

When he pulled into the parking lot at the airport, she sat up. "I can do this, right?" she asked as she sat up in her seat.

"Easy as falling off a bridge," he said using his right hand to demonstrate.

After paying for her first jump and signing her life away on the release forms, Ty took her to the student manifest desk and picked up the training syllabus, logbook, and USPA A-License Proficiency Card. He took her back to the dressing area and handed her a jumpsuit that he had picked up for her the week before.

"You don't want to look like a newbie when class starts," he said getting into his own.

Sarah liked the way the suit fitted and loved the purple and white design, since purple had been her favorite color for as long as she could remember.

"I'll see you after class," Ty said then walked her back to class and disappeared.

Four hours later he reappeared with messy hair and a smile a mile wide. "Hope you were paying attention, I got you booked on the first flight for a tandem jump with an old buddy of mine."

Sarah frowned. "I thought I'd be jumping with you."

"Afraid not. Doctors don't operate on their wives and jumpmasters don't strap their friends into the forward harness on the first jump. Don't worry. Matt's been doing this for over twenty years and has only broken a couple of bones," Ty said winking at her.

"Only a couple?" Sarah asked poking him in the ribs and making him spill some of his coffee.

"Don't worry, Sarah. I promise not to break any today," Matt said as he walked over and shook her hand.

Five minutes later they were piled in the back of a pickup truck, along with five other first-time fliers and instructors, headed toward the twin turbo-prop sitting on the tarmac. Once inside, Sarah was surprised at how small the interior was as she duck-walked toward the cabin behind Matt.

Once the newbies were seated, the regulars loaded onboard. "What's the hula-hoop for?" Sarah asked Ty, who was sitting across from her.

"They're practicing for a competition next month. The guy holds the hoop and the four girls fly through it. Nothing much to it after some practice," he said as the plane leveled off and slowed down.

Sarah's heart started racing and her mouth got dry as the people closest to the door simply waddled up to the door and disappeared. Then she felt Matt snapping their harnesses together and tugging on them to make sure they were tight.

"Okay, Sarah, keep your head down and your body bent over so you don't bang my head on the overhead," Matt said helping her get to her feet.

As they moved toward the door, Ty inched ahead of them. By the time it was their turn to jump, he had positioned himself outside the plane with one foot on the step and his right hanging on to a handle above the door.

"Okay, Sarah, now cross your arms across your chest and don't grab on to anything," Matt said. "I'm going to count to three and then we're going."

"Don't open your mouth until your chute opens," Ty yelled as he stuck his head back inside the plane for a second.

When Matt started counting, he began rocking his body back and forth, to build up to the final leap into air. Sarah had never felt as helpless in her life as she looked down toward the ground three miles below.

"Three," Matt screamed and catapulted her out into nothingness.

For the first few seconds it felt like she was diving off the high platform at the college pool, but as her speed increased a pressure began building against her body. Ten seconds later she was falling at terminal velocity and it felt like she was lying on a soft mattress. Then she remembered her training and arched her body back and extended her arms and legs. When she looked up from the ground that had been hypnotizing her, Ty was there floating a few feet away waving at her.

Sarah was so scared she couldn't wave back. She opened her mouth to say sorry, but the wind instantly dried it out and she snapped it shut. Ty saw the panic in her eyes and slowly drifted back about fifty feet and flipped over on his back. She didn't know why that relaxed her, but it did and she slowly waved with her left hand.

While she watched Ty pretending that he couldn't get back around on his belly, Matt reached down and tapped on her altimeter. That scared the hell out of her because she had completely forgotten he was still attached.

"Dumb," she thought as she mentally skimmed down the checklist they had gone over in class at least ten times.

By the time the altimeter had spun down to six thousand feet she was ready and reached down with her right hand and pulled the plastic T-handle that opened the chute. Suddenly there was a loud pop and the harness cut into her groin.

"Damn it," she screamed as it suddenly became quiet as they slowed.

Matt laughed. "I usually save that for when it doesn't open."

"Sorry, I didn't expect it to stop us that fast," Sarah said apologetically.

"That's okay. Stand on the top of my feet so I can adjust the attachments a little," Matt said holding his feet out so she could see them better.

"Just don't drop me," Sarah laughed back at him.

"Not now. The hard part is over. When we land keep your feet up so I don't trip over them and I think we'll try a stand-up landing," he said as he loosened the straps just a bit.

"Where did Ty go?" she asked, as they drifted slowly toward a big circle beside the runway.

"I guess he'd be the one landing in the middle of the circle with the 'LOVE U' chute," Matt said with a chuckle.

When they landed directly on the **X**, Matt unbuckled the harnesses and waved to Ty. "I still got closer than you did – greenhorn."

"Yea, but I've got class," Ty shouted back as he ran to Sarah's side.

"Well what did you think?" Ty asked Sarah as she began gathering up her chute.

"I don't know. I think we better do it a couple of more times before I answer."

As she returned to the present, Sarah was pretty sure she wasn't going to regret moving in with Ty.

Chapter 32
Great Balls of Fire

When the FedEx truck rolled up at ten in the morning Fazul was ready with the next six control units. However he was a little surprised when the driver rolled his cart through the back door.

"Where do you want these bowling balls?" the driver asked.

"Just put them against the wall over there, Scott," Fazul said pointing to a place beside the couch.

"Now that the summer's over, I thought it was time to start pushing something for the indoor crowd," Fazul said.

"You couldn't find anything lighter? The freight on these is going to kill you," Scott said loading the boxed controller units onto the hand truck.

"Well that's not my problem, I'm just the middleman. Besides, nobody ever thinks about the shipping and handling when they order things. These are limited edition balls; only a thousand are being made. I already have orders for the whole lot," Fazul said.

"You know I'm in a winter league myself. Don't suppose you could let me buy one of these, could you?" Scott said thinking they must be pretty hot if Fazul already had preorders for the whole lot.

"Why don't you take one, Scott, and let me know now you like it. These are extra samples they sent me for final approval," Fazul said walking over and grabbing one of the boxes.

"Are you sure you want to give me one of these?" Scott asked taking the box.

"Don't worry about it. Just be sure to have the holes drilled around the company's logo. After all, you wouldn't want to spoil the psychedelic artwork." Fazul said rearranging the controller boxes so the bowling ball would be on the bottom of the stack.

"Thanks a lot, Fazul. I really appreciate it. If there's anything I can do for you, just say the word," Scott said shaking Fazul's hand.

"You're welcome, Scott. Just keep up the good work and get me through the Christmas season. That'll be enough," Fazul responded.

Fazul unpacked one of the balls and put it on the postal scale. It weighed in at exactly fifteen pounds, as expected. A tape measure, along with some simple math, proved it was eight and a half inches in diameter. Next he checked the etched logo and found that although it had been cut a little deeper than expected, it wouldn't attract anyone's attention. All in all it was a perfectly normal bowling ball.

Pulling out the top drawer of his desk, Fazul retrieved a funny looking screwdriver, which had a tip shaped like a branding iron and two three-by-one inch round rubber rings. After throwing the rings on the top of his desk, he lined the business end of the screwdriver up with the capital letter of the second word in the Logo and pushed it in until he heard a slight click.

Placing one hand on each side of the ball he unscrewed it until he had half in each hand. Then he put each half in one of rings and adjusted them until they both were level. A round cavity that had been machined out was visible in the center of each half.

Fazul then walked to a metal cabinet and retrieved a plastic replica of the spreader unit that would eventually be filled with nuclear power; a used Geiger counter he had picked up at a flea market south of Richmond; and two old watches with radium dials he had bought from one of the local antique dealers in town.

Setting the Geiger counter on the table, he unscrewed the top of the plastic spreader and dropped the two watches inside and screwed the top back on. Next he placed the spreader unit into one of the cutouts and turned on the Geiger counter and held it six inches above the spreader unit.

The dial registered eight hundred fifty thousand counts per minute. When he turned the volume up, the sound of a thunderstorm falling on a tin roof filled the room.

Now it was time to see if the lead and boron mixed in with the plastic the ball was made from actually worked as advertised. As soon as he picked up the other half and began lowering it into place the reading on the meter began to drop and the steady buzz began to break up into a stream of audible clicks.

When he lined up the threads and started screwing the ball back together, the needle dropped to near zero, as the Geiger counter began to register normal background radiation readings.

Fazul smiled and grabbed the Geiger counter. Walking around the room, first away from and then towards the ball the reading didn't change at all. Now, all he had to do was to wait for Abd to deliver the goods.

While Fazul's day was going marvelously, Scott was beginning to sense a problem.

He couldn't believe that Fazul had actually given him the ball after he all but begged for it. Taking gifts from customers was one of the big no-no's that had been drilled into each driver from the first day they started working at FedEx. If Fazul called up and complained, Scott would be in big trouble, not that he thought it would happen, but you never know.

Beside that nagging thought, Scott was getting anxious about how he was going to get the box off his truck when he got back to the depot. All he had to do was get caught by his supervisor trying to carry out a box addressed to someone else. Then a call came in that answered his prayers.

"Scott, I need a pick up at Fort Myers. Do you want to grab it before you come in?" his friend Eugene the dispatcher, asked.

"Only if I can stop by the Bowling Center. I've got to check up on the league schedule to see who we're playing against next week," Scott replied.

"Just between you and me, I'm so hot nobody's going to beat us this year," Eugene answered.

Scott laughed. "That's what you say every year."

"Well, one of these years it's going to be true. Now, get over to the quartermaster's office and see what they've got," Eugene said.

After picking up the package, Scott headed for the bowling center. Before he got out of the truck, he peeled the shipping label off the box then carried it inside to the shop.

"Hey Larry, can you drill this ball for me by Saturday?" he said placing he box on the counter.

Larry opened the box and took the ball out. "She's a beauty, Scott. Never saw one like this. Let me take a look in the computer to see what I've got. Not too much before then. You want the same holes as last time?"

"Yea, but can you make the middle finger hole a little deeper? I keep touching bottom," Scott said handing Larry his credit card.

Running the card, Larry smiled. "You know, if you bought one of our balls the drilling would be free."

"I know, but I got a great deal on this one, so it's worth it," Scott said taking his card back. "See you Saturday."

Three days later, Scott picked up his ball when the alley opened and grabbed a lane before all the kids showed up at nine. He hated to admit it, but they drove him crazy with all their yelling and screaming. "Must be getting old," he thought.

A minute later, he had set up the computer score keeper and was ready. Sliding his fingers into the ball for the first time put a smile on his face, as his fingers didn't bottom out. In fact, he could have sworn that the holes actually got bigger toward the bottom.

Then he lined up and threw a perfect hook into the pocket for a strike.

After two more strikes, Larry came wondering over to see how he liked the ball. "Not bad Scott, just nine more and we'll snap your picture for the alley's Hall of Fame."

"Stop it. You're going to jinx me," Scott said grabbing the ball and lining up for another throw.

By the time he had racked up six strikes in a row a few of the regulars had wondered over to watch. Five minutes later, Scott had bowled his first perfect game and bowed to the crowd who was applauding.

"Better see how long this will last," Scott said pressing the 'New Game' button on the control panel.

When he was six strikes into his second game bowling on all the other lanes had stopped as everyone in the building cheered him on.

"I guess you like that new ball a lot by now," Larry interjected as Scott held his hands over the blower unit to dry them off.

"Yeah, I just might keep this one," he shouted back over the roar of applause from the crowd.

A few minutes later, Scott threw his twenty-fourth strike and went down in the record books at the bowling center as the best or luckiest bowler of the past five years.

Sitting for his picture on a chair placed under the alley's logo, Scott proudly held his new ball in his lap and smiled bigger than he ever had in his life.

Chapter 33
Leg Three

Up until this point of the race, the seas had been relatively calm and the winds predictable. All that changed on the second day out of Melbourne, Australia. Mother Nature threw a fresh gale into the mix, with forty knot winds beating the waters of the Tasman Sea into thunderous blue-green mountains and dark frothy valleys.

The crew of the Saudi II had little choice and soon had reeled in the sails and deployed a large sea anchor to keep the boat headed into the wind. After nearly two days of the unwelcome rollercoaster ride, the waters calmed and the race resumed.

Abd was below deck checking out the boat's electronics when Captain Ibrahim climbed down the stairs carrying a clipboard. "How's everything going?"

"Not too bad sir. We lost our main communications antenna and one of the GPS units, but the backups are working and all the cameras are online," Abd said pointing to the array of monitors built into the navigation console.

"How about the keel-wing?" the Captain asked, as he leaned toward the displays.

Abd flipped the switches that brought up the four underwater cameras, showing the keel-wing operating normally. "It looks none the worse for wear."

"Good," Ibrahim said as he handed Abd the clipboard. "Here's a list of items we need to have waiting when we get to Lambton Harbor in Wellington."

"I'll send it out right away," Abd said.

After typing the list of replacement items into the computer, Abd attached it along with a progress report to an email and sent it to the support team waiting in Wellington, New Zealand.

Figuring nobody would be bothering him for awhile, he isolated the satellite phone from the computer's master log and dialed Abdullah. "Is this Joe's Pizza? I want to know if you deliver to Occoquan?"

"Yes we deliver, but we'll be closing in about five minutes," Abdullah replied over his disposable cell phone.

Knowing that meant the cell phone was about to run out of minutes or batteries, Abd continued quickly. "We will be arriving in Rio next month and want to know if you will still be open for business."

"Yes the new ovens will be installed by then. Please drop in and try our new Russian Delight." As the phone began to beep, Abdullah twisted it in two and threw the pieces in a trashcan as he walked out of the Botanical Garden and down the block towards the large detached house he had rented.

Entering though the basement, Abdullah bolted the door and adjusted the window blinds. Behind him a black cloth strung on metal wire partitioned the room in half. Behind the cloth the sounds of electric motors and air fizzing to the surface of aquarium tanks could be heard. Ducking through a slit in the fabric, Abdullah was bathed in the bright blue light streaming out of four fifty-five gallon drums. Circulation hoses from each metal drum ran to an electric chiller, equipped with canister filters, and an air pump pushed against the wall under the sink.

Peering inside the closest one, Abdullah watched the Cichlidos and Killifish swimming around amid the bubbles swirling up from the air stones sitting on the bottom next to an emergency weight pod.

The workers at the stone quarry had done a beautiful job building these spare pods. Aside from the extra fifty pounds, they were indistinguishable from the ones cutting through the Tasman Sea in the keel-wing of the Saudi II. Inside the pod two hundred fully functional nuclear spreader units waited to be delivered.

Grabbing a small wire fishnet from a nail, he skimmed a dead fish off the surface and dumped it into to an old coffee can on a bench behind him. Pulling on a string he pulled out the aquarium thermometer.

"Seventy-nine degrees. That's good, my little beauties."

After skimming off a few more dead fish and checking the temperature of the other three drums, Abdullah went up the stairs to the kitchen. After washing and drying his hands, he pulled a large calendar off the wall and sat down at the table.

He marked off the days as he talked to himself. "Three more days to Wellington, two for re-supply, twenty-two or so for the trip here, and we'll be free men in less than a month."

Suddenly Fahid jumped into his mind. "Where the hell is that lazy monkey?" he said out loud.

They had only one rule the whole time they had been living in the house, which was that only one of them could be gone at a time. Now it appeared that Fahid had gone out too. The first place Abdullah looked was the living room where he had left him putting a new coat of paint on the walls. An opened paint can was there along with a couple of rollers, but no Fahid. A muffled noise upstairs caught Abdullah's attention and he went to investigate.

As he turned the knob and started pushing on the bedroom door something wedged against the bottom. Looking through the crack, Abdullah saw a pair of white bib-overalls on the floor and Fahid's naked butt thrusting wildly into something under him on the bed. By the size and shape of the legs propped up against Fahid's thighs, Abdullah assumed he had lured one of the local prostitutes into the house. His first instinct was to bust through the door and throw the bitch out, but it had been a long two months guarding the pods, so Abdullah closed the door and went back downstairs.

He was cleaning the paint off the rollers in the kitchen sink when his landlord, Humberto, opened the front door and walked in. A few seconds later, Humberto's son, Miguel, came in, dragging an old five gallon bucket of paint with small holes cut in the lid. As he moved, water squirted out of a hole every now and then, which was quickly licked up by the family's pet cat, Gato.

"Good afternoon, Abdullah. Little Miguel has some more fish for your tanks and I have come looking for Morela. I sent her over here an hour ago to collect the rent, but she has not come home. Have you seen her?"

He was pretty sure she was up in the bedroom working out with Fahid, but knew that it would probably be best not to mention that to her father right now. "Sorry I just got home myself. I'm sure she's just taking her time coming home. You know how teenagers are."

In an effort to stall Humberto, Abdullah reached for his wallet. "Listen Humberto. Remember when I told you we didn't know exactly when we would be leaving?"

"Yes sir. I remember that very well," Humberto replied, looking a little dejected.

"Well, it looks like next month will be our last. So here's the five hundred for next month and an extra five for the short notice," Abdullah said fanning out ten one hundred dollar bills.

"I'm going to miss the two of you. You've been very good tenants. I think little Miguel will miss you too. Won't you, Miguel?" Humberto said looking down and patting his son on the head.

"Yes, Papa, but I will miss the $10 for the buckets of fish even more," Miguel said laughing.

"That's what I like, an honest boy," Abdullah said holding out a brand new ten dollar bill. Go down and put them in the tank for me and there's another ten in it for you."

Giggling at the prospect of doubling his pay, Miguel dragged the bucket over to the door and began sliding it down to the basement one step at a time. After he had gotten about halfway down, Gato disappeared down the steps too.

Since lifting the bucket was out of the question, Miguel left it on the floor and pried the top off. The fish inside began darting around so fast that they sounded like they would blast right through the plastic bucket.

Miguel knew this was not good so he quickly grabbed the coffee can from the table, dumped the dead fish on the floor, and began using it to put the fish in the large drums. This is what Gato had been waiting for and he batted the pile with his paw, chasing the one that moved the fastest across the floor.

By the time Miguel had all the fish in the drums, Gato had eaten all the dead fish and lay on his side purring.

"What's the matter, little Gato? Don't you want any more?" Miguel said looking in the plastic bucket at the one he had missed.

Grabbing it by the tail, Miguel held it over Gato's head to make the cat jump high in the air. At first the cat just laid there looking up at the fish, but when it began wiggling he sprang up and snatched it from Miguel's hand.

When he returned to the kitchen, his father and Abdullah were sitting at the table drinking beer. "Okay. They are in the tanks," he said holding out his hand.

"That's a good boy," Abdullah said pulling a ten out of his shirt pocket and handing it to Miguel. "Get yourself a soda out of the refrigerator."

"Get me one too," Morella said walking into the kitchen.

"What have you been doing for the last hour?" her father asked.

Taking a bottle of soda from her brother, Morella smiled back at him. "Well when I first came over I helped Fahid paint the living room.

Then we went upstairs to see what colors I thought would go best with the new curtains Mommy made."

Abdullah thought she sounded pretty convincing, but wanted to see if Humberto was buying the whole act.

"Okay. But the next time I send you someplace you'd better come back a lot quicker, understand?" her father said shaking his finger at her.

"Yes Father, I will. Did you get the rent?" Morela asked coyly.

"Yes I did your job for you. Let's get home for dinner before your mother starts hollering at me, too."

When they had left, Fahid came into the kitchen. "Wow, that was close."

Abdullah could only shake his head. "It was bad enough when you started screwing around with his daughter at night, but now every time I turn around you're at it. See if you can keep from getting caught for the next three weeks. Please."

Fahid smiled. "So, you have a date now?"

"Twenty-seven miserable days and we'll be out of here. Do you think you can keep it in your pants until then?" Abdullah said getting a couple more beers out of the refrigerator and giving one to Fahid.

While he did think he could, Fahid decided that he probably wouldn't. "Don't worry about me. I can be like a camel in the desert."

"I'm not sure what that has to do with anything. Once we get the pods loaded you can do whatever you want, just use your head now."

189

Chapter 34
Port Elizabeth

Standing with fellow troopers McFadden and Flenard on the deck of the Coast Guard Cutter Bertholf, Sanchez looked like he was ready to kick some serious ass. His first two months on the Homeland Security Department's Container Monitoring Task Force had been pretty boring, but last weekend they began the first of four boarding exercises.

During the first exercise, Sanchez's team had gotten their asses kicked by a team of Transportation Security agents who were posing as terrorists guarding the target container. Today they were ready to redeem themselves and get a little revenge in the bargain.

The whole reason the HSD had dumped two million dollars into the exercise was to find cracks in the methods and procedures presently being used to guard Port Elizabeth in New Jersey.

As they waited by the rail, Sanchez looked back east and smiled. He had always loved the ocean and riding aboard the first Legend Class cutter built for homeland security made him proud.

The skyline of New York had disappeared an hour ago and now the only thing that caught his eye was the band of greenish water from the Gulf Stream that they had just entered.

"Twenty minutes until intercept," announced the ship's hailing system. It quickly brought him back to reality.

Taking the paintball pistol out of its holster, Sanchez pointed it down toward the water fifty feet out from the ship and emptied eight shots into the water. He watched the eight little pools of red turn pink as they merged together before the wake hit the spot and erased his artwork.

After reloading the pistol, he slid it back inside the canvas holster strapped to his assault coveralls. "Listen, I don't want to wait until the next Saturday. Things can always change. Those TS agents are here now so let's make them dance today."

"I'm with you, TL," McFadden barked back.

Flenard just patted his weapons and smiled.

Steaming toward the container, Sanchez was surprised at how much bigger it was than the one boarded last week. A minute ago it had been a tiny dot on the horizon. Now they were still half a mile away and it was the size of a house.

"Two minutes until intercept. Boarding parties stand in at their assigned positions," announced the speakers on all decks and echoed across the water.

"I'm glad they know we're coming. It looks like they could run right over us and still make it to Port Elizabeth on time," McFadden remarked as they headed to their station.

Fortunately, the container ship was fully loaded and riding low in the water. If it had been empty they never could have boarded it through the opened doors on its port side. The scenario they were acting out today was centered on the Container Security Initiative or CSI as they called it. The container ship had come from Malaysia, one of the twenty foreign ports that had agreed to participate with the United States since the Initiative began shortly after the 911 attacks. Together, those twenty foreign ports were the debarkation points for seventy percent of the all the cargo that entered America by ship.

Today, Sanchez's team was searching for a high-risk container that had been unintentionally mislabeled and passed through regular screening prior to being loaded aboard.

The day before Sanchez left Port Elizabeth, he had been included in a high level meeting where the organizers of the exercise reviewed the information not given to the rest of the participants. Container 060606 was reported to be mislabeled as it was carrying medical equipment containing radioactive material. To make the exercise as realistic as possible, all the teams had attended special safety class and were required to wear film badge dosimeters during the drill.

Once on board the container ship, each team had a specific assignment. While one team checked the ship's manifests, others reviewed radio logs and interviewed the crew. Sanchez's job was to locate the container, check it for radiation, and label it as requiring special handling.

As he led his team down the first flight of stairs, they donned their protective headgear and pulled out their pistols. Each man had been given different colored paintballs to use so observers could easily tell who shot whom. A few minutes later they reached the first deck that offered access to the cargo hold.

"What do you think?" McFadden asked quietly. "Should we start here or go to the bottom and work our way up?"

Sanchez thought about it for a couple of seconds before moving toward the watertight door. "You all have your repelling gear, right?"

As McFadden and Flenard slipped off their backpacks and pulled out their equipment, Sanchez walked over to the sound powered phone and dialed up the bridge. "Let me talk to the manifest coordinator. . . ." After a slight pause he continued, "Have you located the container on the loading diagram?"

Sanchez scribbled some notes on the palm of his hand with a pen as he listened. "Okay, thanks," he said hanging up the phone.

"It seems like we're in luck today. The container is on the lower level, but it's accessible from a catwalk about thirty feet on the other side of this door."

As he got into his climbing harness, Sanchez looked up at the bright light behind a wire cage over the watertight door. "We've got to get rid of the light before we do anything."

McFadden swung the cage away from the light, but quickly drew his hand back when he tried to unscrew the stubborn bulb and burnt his fingers. "Damn it," he said blowing on his fingers.

"Out of the way, amateur," Flenard said turning his pistol around and holding it by the barrel.

A second later the glass crashed to the deck and the filament burned out, leaving them in darkness.

"Hope nobody sees that until we're out of here," Sanchez commented as he un-dogged the watertight door and swung it open.

Duck walking a few steps out on the catwalk, Sanchez looked around and began to realize just how big this ship was. Despite the rows of lights trailing off into the distance, the hold was a mass of black and gray shadows.

"How the hell are we going to tell where those TS Agents are in this?" Flenard asked kneeling down on the hard metal.

Sanchez looked around then pulled a pair of night vision binoculars he had picked up at Shack Electronics the day before. "I don't think they can hide from this," he said scanning around the suspect container six decks below.

"There they are," he whispered, pointing downward. After passing his little toy around, everybody had located the agents.

McFadden spotted a couple of portable cameras set up to capture all the action for the debriefing following the exercise. "Sanchez, did you spot the cameras?" he said passing the binocular back to him.

Taking another look, Sanchez smiled. "I think we should split up. McFadden, you and Flenard repel down behind them. I'll go down to the bottom and make my way over to the container."

As he walked back towards the door Sanchez knew he was breaking protocol, but he knew if you wanted to win you had to play by your own rules. "Give me five minutes and then zip down behind them. When they hear me coming they won't be looking for you two," he whispered, closing the door as he left.

Watching the seconds tick away as they waited to drop over the side of the catwalk, McFadden and Flenard both reached down and snapped off the safety on their pistols. When Sanchez opened the door below and walked into the cargo hold shining a huge battery powered spotlight he'd picked up along the way, they both chuckled.

Sanchez stood there, silhouetted in the doorway, probing around with the bright beam of light until his teammates landed silently behind the agents. When they were down and unhooked from their ropes, he switched off the spotlight and moved quickly into the shadows. Moving along in the shadows, he could hear at least one of the TS agents working his way towards him. Thinking quickly, Sanchez tied a piece of cord to the spotlight and switched it on again. Then he scrambled up on top of the container he had been standing beside.

Just before the agent rounded the corner, Sanchez raised the light five feet off the floor and began moving it towards the end of the container.

"Shit!" The agent managed to get out before firing off a volley of paintballs at the blinding light.

From Sanchez's position, it seemed like McFadden and Flenard started firing the same time he did. Seconds later, all the TS agents were taken down.

At the postmortem an hour later, the three troopers were commended for defeating the terrorists and achieving their goal of securing the container. When the meeting ended, Sanchez led McFadden and Flenard down to the parking lot and offered to buy them a beer, but they took a rain-check and promised to celebrate together after the last exercise next weekend.

Dumping his gear in the trunk, Sanchez noticed he had forgotten to turn in his dosimeter. Since he didn't even know if it was real, he decided to turn it in after the final exercise next weekend.

Chapter 35
Leg Four

The layover in Wellington, New Zealand was only going to last for two days. No inter-harbor race, none of Sheik Saud's extravagant parties, only restocking and repairs before the sixty-seven hundred mile leg of the race began. The leg from here to Rio de Janeiro was the longest and most isolated part of the journey and Abd felt relaxed for the first time since they had sailed out of Vigo.

After taking a look at the keel-wing one last time, Abd wandered up on deck and looked around at all the activity. For the past day he had heard the rest of the crew running up and down the stairs and across the deck carrying provisions. Taking his time installing the new communications antenna and GPS unit had eaten up the first day. This morning every time someone came looking for him, he had been hunched over the navigation consol pretending to make final adjustments until they got tired and left.

Now with only four hours until the race started again he was beginning to get the feeling that he should take advantage of the land while it was there. Once they pulled away, he wouldn't have the opportunity for another three weeks.

It didn't take him long to find a bar along the docks. Before he finished his first drink, he had an attractive lady sitting on each side of him. If the girls in Melbourne had been friendly, then their cousins here in Wellington were desperate. Not wanting to cause a scene, Abd tried to politely tell them to buzz off, but the more he insisted the more they pressed.

Eventually he broke down, pulled them close and whispered, "If you two want to party then go get us a room."

"Well, ducky, what are we going to pay for it with, our good looks?" they responded together.

"Here's a hundred. That should buy us something," Abd said pulling a bill off the wad he pulled out of his jacket pocket.

Grabbing the bill, the girls rushed out of the bar and returned a few minutes later, giggling. They each grabbed an arm and soon had him outside.

Steering Abd towards an alley beside the bar the taller girl smiled. "Let's take a shortcut over to the hotel."

Before Abd could protest, they had dragged him halfway down the alley where their two boyfriends were waiting.

"Okay, Lovey, let's have the money," the tall girl's boyfriend said pulling a knife out of his pocket.

Most normal men who found themselves in a situation like this would have gladly handed over their money and figured they were lucky enough when they escaped with their life. The problem was that Abd wasn't anything like a normal man.

He had killed a Russian soldier when he was eight for slapping his sister. His total had been increasing ever since, so a couple of thugs in the middle of a deserted alley didn't even raise his heartbeat. "I think I'll be kind to you today and let you walk out of here on your own two feet."

"Are you crazy or what?" asked the biggest man.

"Probably, but it's a once in a lifetime offer that others would have prayed for," Abd said not moving an inch.

What happened next can best be explained as a contest of sheer willpower as Abd focused on the leader. Thinking he wasn't paying any attention to her, the leader's girlfriend pulled a straight razor from her purse and flipped it silently open with her thumb.

"Last chance, boys and girls," Abd said moving his right foot slightly forward. "What's it going to be?"

Seeing that his girlfriend was about to strike, the leader raised his hand and yelled. "Julie! Stop!"

But it was too late. As the girl raised the razor high above her head and charged forward, Abd spun and crossed his arms together, forming a cross block aimed at the girl's elbow. A split second later the razor flew out of her hand and her elbow snapped like a dry twig.

"Sorry, Julie, looks like you lose," Abd said. Smiling, he pulled his right hand back and thrust his elbow into her chin. When she settled to the ground, she looked like a bloody jack-o-lantern.

"Now, I didn't have to do that last part, but I wanted to show you that I'm not afraid to really hurt you. So for the last time are you going to leave or not?"

Julie's boyfriend was visibly shaken and ran to her side. "You son of a bitch, she's dead."

Abd reached down and placed his fingers on her carotid artery, keeping an eye on the others the whole time. "Nope, she's not dead yet, but if you don't get her to the hospital soon, she will be."

"Shit. How am I going to explain this to a doctor?" the guy asked with tears beginning to roll down his cheeks.

Abd pulled out his wad of bills and peeled off four hundred-dollar bills. "Here's another hundred a piece for the entertainment. Now get out of here and forget you ever saw me or I'll come back and finish what you started."

Turning away from the unhappy little group, Abd walked out of the alley and back to the Saudi II, happier than he had been in months. Half an hour later the Saudi II was lined up waiting to start leg four of the Ocean Race.

Chapter 36
Practice Makes Perfect

Ahmed and Saif had been driving around for an hour and still hadn't decided where to launch the test plane. The first two flights had been short, only a couple of miles away from Occoquan, but this time they had been told to launch the specially equipped model northeast of the Capital.

"I'm getting tired of all this driving. Let's pull off at the next exit and launch the damn thing," Saif said pointing to the Greenbelt Road sign ahead.

Ahmed checked his mirrors and pulled over into the right lane. "I hate this. Why do we have to keep risking our necks all the time?"

Three right turns later they found themselves in the Greenway Center. Since it was a little past nine at night the parking lots around the office buildings were practically empty.

"You know there are probably a dozen security cameras in this complex," Ahmed said nervously looking around as he pulled into a parking spot on the west end facing the Capital Beltway.

"What's the difference? There's no good place to launch this thing. Let's just do it," Saif said getting out of the van.

A minute later, the plane was on the blacktop and Saif was pulling the thick leather prop-guard glove onto his right hand. The plane was one of the models Ning Wang had designed. It was equipped with the standard navigation module plus extra fuel, a self-destruct incendiary charge, a fantastic muffler, and a small video camera that recorded views directly down and in front of the plane. The pre-programmed chip inside was targeted to land the plane at the end of Mill Street in Occoquan, where Fazul would be waiting for it to arrive.

Saif switched on the camera and PDA then waited a few seconds to see if the computer would pick up any beacon signals before firing up the engine.

"It's nice to know there are porn addicts everywhere," he chuckled flipping the prop around.

The plane started on the second spin and was remarkably quiet, thanks to the muffler that reduced the engine noise to practically nothing. Saif pointed the plane down the parking lot and released it. A few seconds later it was airborne and climbed steadily up and over trees planted along the perimeter of the complex. By the time Saif threw the leather glove into the van and closed the back door, it had disappeared into the blackness overhead.

Besides having a built-in compass, the navigation unit inside the plane was equipped with sensors that could detect heat, light, and altitude. Mohammed had based the design of the navigation system on one NASA used in the space shuttles. All the data in the system ran through four duplicated programs that crunched the numbers. If they didn't agree, majority ruled.

Since the plane was designed to fly at thirty mph, the computers had plenty of time to make decisions. In the event the PDA couldn't pick up a signal, the navigation unit relied on its compass and obstacle avoidance algorithms until communications were reestablished.

If something went wrong, the plane was set to self-destruct either on impact or two hours after the computer was turned on. Once Fazul knew where the plane was released, he could scan the papers the next day for any suspicious fires. If a fire started anywhere within a mile of the flight path, he would try and determine if the incendiary charge was responsible.

After leaving the Greenway Center, the plane headed southwest, flying over an expanse of woodlands paralleling the Baltimore-Washington Parkway until it picked up a signal from Crest Park Drive. From there to 54th and Spring Lane, little chirps guided it along steadily. When it began flying down the middle of the Anacostia River the signals became intermittent, but settled again as the plane approached 41st Avenue. Flying straight towards Occoquan, the plane used various preprogrammed maneuvers to avoid buildings and adjust for changes in the altitude of the landscape.

Ahmed and Saif had no way of knowing that they had picked the perfect place to launch the plane. But as it flew along silently, its flight path bisected the Hart and Dirksen Senate Office Buildings and came within twenty-five feet of the Capitol dome as it headed towards the Potomac.

The signals faded at Water Street and a sudden tailwind accelerated the plane towards the opposite shore. Normally, the navigation unit would have been able to calculate the air speed by comparing signals from the ground, but since none were available it was relying solely on its obstacle avoidance systems as it sped across the water.

The plane neared the shore and the sensors began picking up a tall housing complex on Crystal Drive in Arlington. At the same time, signals from the wireless base stations were reestablished. Since the obstacle avoidance program took precedence over navigation, the computer processed the information from the heat and light sensors.

If a computer could panic, this one did, as the added speed made the building look twice as big as it really was. Shuffling through its bag of tricks the computer settled on the slow vertical climb routine that turned the plane into a lumbering helicopter. The program called for more power and the plane pulled vertical and climbed up the building. The added power and reduce airflow across the muffler caused it to glow cherry red.

The altitude sensor that normally measured the distance to the ground was now being used to keep the plane locked ten feet from the side of the building. As it continued to climb, it passed a balcony, veering out then back in as the computer compensated for the protrusion.

Inside a small apartment on the twelfth floor, Velma Frazer sat cuddled up on her couch reading another murder mystery. The small television she used to block out the street noise was tuned to her favorite channel and playing quietly, until a commercial came on and jumped the volume up a couple of notches.

Grabbing the remote, she clicked the mute button and mumbled something under her breath that would have gotten her children's mouths washed out with soap when they were growing up with her in Missouri. Looking up at the television with disgust, Velma froze as she watched a dark figure float up on the other side of the sliding glass doors. The figure looked in at her and seemed to smile out of the corner of its mouth. A few seconds later it was gone.

Normally she would have just written it off as another delusion of old age, but there was a big difference between thinking she heard her dead husband talking to her and the thing she had just seen.

A minute later the plane cleared the top of the building and continued on to Occoquan where Fazul was waiting.

Back inside the apartment, Velma's mind was racing as she searched for some kind of reference, finally settling on Jesus. Picking up a pencil and pad, she began sketching. Five minutes later she had a reasonable figure of a man with outstretched arms framed in the window. His head

200

was to the right and a big cherry red smile looked westward. Since she didn't have anything to color the lips, she drew little lightning bolts coming out of his mouth.

After a restless night trying to get the vision out of her head, Velma walked over to the computer and scanned the picture. Half an hour later, she emailed her story about Jesus' visit to the National Inquire.

Nobody was more surprised than Velma, when a reporter knocked on her door three days later. After signing a release form and posing with the drawing for the photographer, Velma was presented with a check for $250.

Two weeks later, she made the cover of the weekly magazine. It showed Velma holding up the drawing she made. The caption "Jesus visits Washington, DC" in bold print. Readers were directed to the story on page five.

When Ihmad tossed a copy to Fazul at their next meeting, it was obvious to them that she had seen the plane.

Fortunately for Velma, neither of them thought anyone else would make the connection.

Chapter 37
Christ the Redeemer

As they came across the finish line in Rio de Janeiro, everyone including Abd was up on deck waving to the people in the other boats that had come out to welcome them. Since nobody had made any inquires about the incident in the alley, Abd figured he was safe, but had taken advantage of the three weeks at sea to grow a beard.

Knowing they would be in port for the next two weeks, Abd blended in with the other racers and spent his time enjoying the pleasures of Rio. Eventually, Abdullah contacted him and they decided the best time to switch the pods would be during the big sendoff party that Sheik Saud had arranged the night before the race started again.

The night of the big party, Abd had volunteered to stay aboard the Saudi II so that the rest of the crew could enjoy the festivities. At the prearranged time a pontoon party boat pulled up alongside the Saudi II. Soon Abdullah and Fahid had it secured to the railing and Abd helped them climb aboard.

"Glad you are punctual," Abd, said leading them down to the navigation station.

"So this is where you've spent the past six months. I thought it would be a lot bigger," Abdullah said sitting in one of the chairs.

"We do what we must do," Abd said switching on the underwater lights and bringing up the keel-wing on four monitors. "Are you ready?"

"As ready as we'll ever be," Fahid said leaning over Abd's shoulder.

"Okay, here we go," Abd said raising the red plastic cover and exposing ten eject buttons illuminated with green.

When he pushed the one labeled "Four," the button illumination changed to red and a slight shudder ran through the Saudi II. On the monitor the pod shot out of the keel-wing toward the bottom where it kicked up some sand when it landed. In quick succession, he pressed five, six, and seven – each sending a shudder through the boat.

"Now it's your turn," Abd said leaning back in his chair.

"Our part will take a lot longer than that," Fahid said turning toward the stairs.

After returning to their party boat, Abdullah threw two weighted winch lines into the water between the pontoons and began feeding out rope until it went slack and he knew they were on the bottom.

"You stay here Abdullah, and I'll attach them to the pods," Fahid said slipping into his scuba gear.

"I thought we were going to do this together?" Abdullah replied.

"Yes, I know that's what we said on the way over, but I think it will go faster if I strap the pods and you pull them up," Fahid said before jumping into the water.

"Sure. Fine idea," Abdullah said to himself.

Abd, who was watching the monitors, saw Fahid appear, pulling a rope behind him. In less than a minute he had it attached to one of the pods and gave it two quick tugs. As it started to drag away, he began working on the second pod. Soon that one was being pulled away with Fahid holding on for a free ride as he slid out of view.

A few minutes later he was back for the other two. In less than fifteen minutes the four old pods were on the party boat, along with Abdullah and Fahid.

"Let's just dump the hot ones overboard and then you and I can position them into place," Fahid suggested.

Together they dumped the four replacement pods into the water. While Abdullah got into his gear, Fahid maneuvered a metal box containing the flotation bladders they were going to use to move the replacement pods into the keel-wing. "Let's hope this part goes as well as retrieving the lead ones did," Abdullah said pushing the box into the water.

Ten minutes later, Abd watched the monitor as Abdullah and Fahid sailed into view, each holding onto an electric scooter. A bladder, partially filled with air, counterbalanced the weight of the radioactive pod that trailed behind on a rope. When the pod was positioned under the keel-wing, Abdullah pulled a lever and the pod dropped to the bottom, a few fathoms below.

The two divers slid another bladder that looked like an inner tube, around the pod and Abdullah began filling it with air from his tank. A minute later the pod began slowly rising off the bottom. When the pod was positioned under the keel-wing, Fahid inflated another bladder under it. As that bladder took the weight, the pod began sliding into place. Working as a team, Abdullah and Fahid worked to release the

203

donut and float the pod up into the keel-wing. Twenty seconds later, Abd heard a click and the illuminated number four button turned green again.

An hour later Abdullah and Fahid had installed three of the pods and were working on the fourth when it got stuck about halfway into its chamber. Not knowing what to do, Fahid decided to release the air in the balloon and see if the pod would come out. It didn't. He tried to wiggle it. Nothing happened. He kicked at it, but again nothing happened.

Now that he had taken all his anger out on the pod, Fahid started going over calculations in his head. The pod weighed two hundred fifty pounds. With the fifty-pound compression spring, that brought the total insertion force to three hundred pounds. The other pods had locked into place when the nine cubic foot balloon was about half full. Which all made sense, figuring sea water weighs sixty-four and a half pounds per cubic foot.

Since the pod had lodged in a manner that it was not willing to release, Fahid had to figure a way to get it to go in. He motioned to Abdullah to get another bladder and a sling from the box. Soon he had the sling under the pod and a balloon on either side of the keel-wing. As they began filling the two bladders, the pod began slowly inching forward until something let loose and it shot into place with a thud. When they released the air and pulled the sling away from the keel-wing a long piece of curled up lead was laying on the canvas. Fahid showed it to Abdullah and then held it up in his hand towards the cameras.

They spent the next fifteen minutes gathering their equipment and headed back to the party boat.

Abd was waiting for them when they broke the surface. "What happened on that last pod?"

"She's got a fat ass," Abdullah said as he climbed back aboard the boat.

"Seriously, I need a little more than that," Abd said angrily.

Fahid climbed up on deck and held out the coil of lead. "It must have been scraping on a weld or something. It peeled off an eighth of an inch of cladding."

"I'm not worried about that. I'm worried that the damn thing won't come out again." Abd said tossing the lead over the side.

"If you want you can try popping it out now. We can put it back again." Abdullah said.

Abd looked at his watch and figured it would be less than an hour before the crew started coming back from the party. "No. Let's just leave it alone and hope for the best. There's always New York if it doesn't work in Baltimore."

"Okay, your choice," Abdullah said as he started untying the party boat from the Saudi II. "At least Fahid and I can get out of here. The rest is up to you."

Abd jumped back onboard the Saudi II and watched them disappear across the harbor.

The next day the next leg of the ocean race started. Abdullah and Fahid were among the crowd of onlookers that had gone up to the Peak of Corcovado Mountain to watch the boats sail away. Standing next to the stone railing under the outstretched arms of Christ the Redeemer they were glad their part of the operation was over. Now all they had to do was figure out what they were going to do with all the extra money they had before they returned home.

Chapter 38
Old Baltimore

After eighteen days and nearly five thousand nautical miles, it looked like the Hollywood's crew was going to win the Rio de Janeiro to Baltimore leg. As the sun disappeared below the horizon, captain Ibrahim on the Saudi II switched on the running lights illuminating the instruments centered between the twin steering pedestals.

"Fourteen hours," he muttered under his breath. "Ally, take over here."

Going below, Ibrahim found Abd sitting at the navigation console. "What do we have between here and Baltimore?"

"Looks like it's going to be a quiet night. Steady winds and three to four foot seas," Abd said without looking around.

"Any sign of the Hollywood?" Ibrahim asked unfolding a chair next to Abd.

"Last time I got a GPS update, she was thirty miles ahead of us," Abd said bringing up the report on one of the monitors.

After a little mental calculation, Ibrahim smiled. "Okay, let's reconfigure the keel-wing."

Abd switched on the underwater lights and cameras before reaching for the slider bar on the console. "If we hit something it's all over," he said looking at Ibrahim.

"No guts, no glory," the captain fired back.

Abd pushed the control forward and the keel-wing transformed into hydrofoil, which slowly began raising the boat out of the water. A few seconds later the keel-wing was the only thing still in the water.

"Smooth as a baby's bottom," Ibrahim said as the boat became rock steady and the speed increased by five miles an hour. "Six hours of this and we'll have a chance."

After Ibrahim went topside, Abd sat glued to the displays. He had hoped the captain would never resort to this tactic, but now there was nothing he could do except pray that nothing bigger than a feeder fish lay in their path.

Back on deck, the captain took the wheel from Ally. "Get some sleep, come back and relieve me at three."

"Giving them the slip are we, Captain?" Ally joked.

"This time could be the last," Ibrahim replied. "Two first place finishes makes it worth the risk," Ibrahim said with a chuckle.

When he was alone, Ibrahim switched off the lights on top of the mast and dimmed down the instrument lighting. Humming an old nautical tune, he began scanning the horizon for the Hollywood.

At two in the morning the captain reckoned they were even; and by the time Ally returned, the Saudi II had pulled ahead another five miles. Whistling a little tune, Ibrahim walked back down the steps to the navigation console. "Keep her in the air for another hour then let her down gently."

At four in the morning, Abd pulled back the hydrofoil control and the hull of the Saudi II gently slipped back into the water. After one last look at the keel-wing, Abd turned off the underwater cameras and lights. The last few hours had been exhausting and now all he wanted to do was sleep. Pulling a blanket out of an overhead bin, Abd wrapped it around his shoulders and dropped to the floor. As he drifted off, he thought about how happy Sheik Saud would be with another win under his belt.

As soon as the Sheik had announced that he was entering the race, the press began portraying him as an eccentric old fool. One reporter even tagged him the Saudi version of Jed Clampett from the Beverly Hillbillies. Many lesser men would have taken it personally and gotten mad, but the Sheik simply laughed it off. He had expected nothing less when he started. A man with a vast fortune and no knowledge of sailing was bound to be ridiculed.

Like a consummate politician, the Sheik kept accepting requests for interviews and talking about his dream to bring water to the desert through desalination. Even the late night talk show hosts got on the bandwagon throwing out a zinger once or twice a week as the Saudi II's construction continued.

All the ribbing quieted down when the Saudi II won the second leg of the competition between Cape Town and Melbourne. It was the first leg where the keel-wing had been used as a hydrofoil and Abd had stayed glued to the monitors each time the hull lifted out of the water, helplessly scanning the clear water ahead for obstacles.

The week-long party Sheik Saud threw in Melbourne must have cost a million dollars. Even Abd enjoyed the wine, women, and song, since there was nothing in the keel-wing except lead pods. Today was much different and even as he dozed, Abd could feel the tension building.

As Captain Ibrahim watched the twin engine cigarette boat screaming across the open ocean towards them, he pushed the intercom button to the navigation station. "Abd, wake up! Sheik Saud's coming out to rendezvous before we start up the channel."

"I'll be up," Abd responded sleepily.

Climbing back up into his chair at the navigation console, Abd's thoughts returned to the present. Smiling, he wondered how quickly all that good press would turn to hate if word leaked out that Sheik Saud's precious sailboat was carrying four pods of nuclear material.

Of course, the Sheik had never known anything about the terrorists' plans for America. His sole purpose was to build goodwill. Abd did think it was ironic that most of the 911 terrorists had come from Saudi Arabia, but then it didn't matter where you were born when the recruiters started working on you. One day you were the apple of your mother's eye and the next you were poking her eye out with a stick - as the hate they instilled in you began to boil.

Before leaving the navigation station, Abd picked up a small signaling device and set the four pods holding the nuclear material on remote release.

By the time he climbed the steps and walked into the open air, the cigarette boat had circled the Saudi II and was pulling up alongside, easily matching the sailboat's sixteen knots. As the two boats ran along inches apart, two crew members held on to the rigging and reached out for the Sheik. Seconds later he was set gently on the deck and the cigarette boat peeled off and began heading back to shore.

Moving like a drunken old man, Sheik Saud made his way back to the navigation stations and smiled at Ibrahim and Abd. "Congratulations gentlemen, looks like our secret weapon has won another leg."

"You have Abd to thank for that," Ibrahim said putting his arm around Abd.

"Yes, I was a little skeptical when he came up with the idea, but it looks like the four years at Cal Tech weren't wasted."

"No better place than America to get a good education," Abd said chuckling out loud.

Half an hour later, the twin expansions of the Bay Bridge came into view. News helicopters filled the air, each, jockeying to get a good angle as they focused their cameras on the Saudi II. Hundreds of private boats lined the water near the banks and, as the Saudi II neared the finish line, a loud cheer began filling the air. When it crossed under the bridge a loud cannon fired, marking the end of leg five for the Saudi II.

As the crew reeled in the sails and the helmsman started the diesel, Abd scanned the water ahead for a place to release the canisters. A few minutes later as the Saudi II approached Gibson Island, a huge power boat raced across their bow, creating a two foot wake. When the wake hit the Saudi II, Abd pushed the remote and felt three little shivers run up his feet from the deck.

Abd looked around to see if anyone else had noticed anything, but everyone was either busy stowing gear or waving to the crowds. So Abd took advantage of the situation and ducked back below deck. Halfway to the navigation station he saw a single red led flashing under the pod control cover. Flipping on the underwater cameras he could see that four, five, and six had been jettisoned, but number seven hadn't budged. Now the only thing he could do was reset the panel and call Ihmad.

Grabbing a disposable cell phone, Abd dialed Ihmad. "We've got a problem. Only three of the pods dropped. About two hundred yards off the lower tip of Gibson Island. . . I'll get back as soon as I can. . . Yes, I'll be at the party."

Sitting inside the large white tent, Sheik Saud had erected over the Harbor Amphitheater for his wine and cheese party, Abd looked at his watch and pouted. All along, his plan had been to drop the pods and disappear in Baltimore, but now that was impossible. Fortunately, a team of local security guards had been hired to guard the entrance – keeping everyone without a security badge away from the dignitaries and crew who were partying inside.

"Some more wine?" a pretty waitress asked.

"Yes please," Abd said holding up his glass, "only an hour to go and you'll be free."

The girl laughed a little. "I wish this would go on all night. It's not often we get to work with such interesting guests. It must be really exciting to race one of those sailboats."

Now it was Abd's turn to laugh. "I guess. If you don't mind eating dehydrated food and having saltwater sprayed in your face, twenty-four hours a day."

"Well before I came over from the Renaissance, I saw the videos playing in the banquet room while we were setting up for dinner. You all look like you're having such a great time. I'd do anything to be able to take a year off and sail around the world," the waitress said pivoting slightly back and forth on her heels. "Maybe I'll see you at the hotel."

"Don't believe a word that old scoundrel says," Ihmad said as he strolled over and held out an empty glass.

The waitress quickly poured Ihmad's wine and left the two terrorists staring at each other.

"How did you get in here?" Abd whispered.

"I just waited near the tent until someone came out and I could snap a picture. Once I had that, it only took me twenty minutes to zoom in on their badge, print and laminate my own. What do you think?" He asked holding the badge up for Abd to examine.

Abd took the badge and held it up to his. "Very nice."

"Truth be told, I could have probably gotten in here with something I dashed off with colored pens and some plastic wrap, but I didn't want to take any chances," Ihmad said taking back his badge.

"We've already picked up the three pods you dropped. I've been studying the design of the keel-wing and it looks like we can place a small plastic charge above number seven before we slide the other three replacement pods back inside. I'll have the divers wire it up to the release mechanism so it fires when you send the normal signal," Ihmad said finishing his wine.

Abd drew in a slow breath and smiled. "Picking up the last one in New York is going to be a lot trickier than the last three."

"That's my problem, not yours. Just try to drop it somewhere along the Jersey shore, near the city." Ihmad said handing Abd his empty glass. "Good luck with that waitress."

As Abd watched Ihmad walk toward the exit, he saw him stop and say something to the girl that had poured their wine. As he reached the exit, he dropped his badge in a trash container and disappeared.

Later that night as Abd sat in the formal banquet room finishing his salad, the waitress slid between Captain Ibrahim and Abd. "Are you finished with that, sir?"

"Why don't you call me Al," Abd said handing her the empty bowl.

"Nice to meet you, Al. My name is Lisa. Is there anything you need right now?"

"No, but I was thinking that you might like to come join me for the inter-harbor race later in the week. It's not much compared to sailing around the world, but I think you'd enjoy it," Abd said.

"Come on, you're making fun of me now. There's no way you can get me on that boat of yours," Lisa said blushing a little.

Turing toward Ibrahim, Abd waited for him to finish chewing. "Captain, this is Lisa."

"Pleasure to meet you, Lisa," the captain said clearing his throat.

"I'd like to bring her aboard for the inter-harbor race this Wednesday," Abd asked, trying not to laugh.

"Not a problem, everyone's entitled to bring a friend aboard during the competition. Besides how could I say no, when you're responsible for our win today. Looking forward to seeing you on Wednesday, Lisa," the captain said.

"Looks like dreams do come true." Abd said discreetly slipping her his spare room key card. "Maybe we can get together later to make arrangements."

Chapter 39
Tickling the Tiger's Tail

Sitting on the couch by the back door of his office, Fazul waited for Ihmad to wheel in the first load of lead bricks from the truck parked behind the building. The one-by-four-by-eight inch interlocking bricks weighed thirteen pounds each and were curved in to form a ring around the pod already sitting on the hydraulic jack in the middle of the twenty-four inch square lead plate on the floor beside the workbench.

"Damn, these things are heavy," Ihmad said dragging the hand truck up over the doorsill.

"Sure you don't want to stay and help me unload the first bunch of dispersal units?" Fazul asked, taking another draw on his cigarette.

"I think I'll wait until you practice on the first few layers. Then if you still have all your fingers, maybe I'll stop by and watch one night when I don't have anything better to do," Ihmad said rolling the bricks over by the pod. "But I will help you build your little Castle."

Fazul put his cigarette out in the ashtray on the coffee table and joined Ihmad. Working together they soon had the first ring of bricks completed.

"That's perfect," Fazul said as he surveyed the spacing, "we've got about an inch all the way around."

Taking the remaining six bricks off the hand truck, Ihmad looked up at Fazul. "You get the next load."

Over the next half hour they continued building up courses of lead bricks. When the last layer was completed, the silver enclosure was slightly higher that the top of the workbench.

"Is that enough or do you want to add another layer?" Ihmad asked.

Fazul took a yardstick off the workbench and laid it across the little silo they had built. Picking up a ruler, he measured down four inches to the top of the pod. "I think its okay there. Let's try putting the roof on our little Castle."

Ihmad reached up and swung the electric chain-winch that attached to the ceiling over to the workbench. He connected it to the eyehook built into another lead plate that matched the base. After raising the plate a few inches in the air, he swung the arm that the winch was attached to over the Castle and gently lowered it onto the bricks.

"I think we have a winner," Fazul said stepping back and admiring their work.

"If you're happy, I'm happy," Ihmad said, "Let me bring in your personal protection gear. Then I'm out of here."

After wheeling in a large box containing respirators, face shields, leaded lab aprons and gloves, Ihmad hugged Fazul. "Good luck my brother. Hopefully, you will not glow in the dark the next time we meet."

Walking Ihmad to the door, Fazul glanced at the clock, which read two AM. "Watch your speed on the way out. These Occoquan cops love stopping cars after midnight."

"Don't worry about me. Just take care of yourself," Ihmad said climbing into the cab of the truck, "I'll see you next week."

As Fazul watched Ihmad drive away, he envied him and wished he could leave and forget the whole thing. As it was, he was sitting in Occoquan with two hundred-fifty pounds of highly enriched uranium and four pounds of dehydrated H5N1 bird flu. His filing cabinets held the address of all the co-conspirators that he and Ning Wang were mailing models and control units to. Tonight he felt like he was the primary target while everyone else in the operation was scattering to the winds. And he was scared.

For the next hour he worked slowly, separating eighteen bowling balls into four rows of nine half-spheres. After unscrewing each ball, he placed the two halves into large rubber rings that stabilized them on the floor with the flat sides containing the circular dispersal cavities facing up. When he finished setting the last half-sphere into its ring he grabbed a beer from the refrigerator and lit another cigarette before collapsing on the couch.

Stalling for time, Fazul reached down and flipped on the Geiger counter and turned up the volume. The random clicks it registered a few weeks ago when he was experimenting with the watches had been replaced with a steady more persistent tempo caused by the radioactive decay inside the pod twenty feet away. As he sat there, he wondered what was going to happen when he finally cut the top off the pod.

His plan tonight was to load and pack eighteen bowling balls in the shortest amount of time possible. The problem was that cutting the top off the pod was going to take some extra time. Even with all the equipment he had to work with, Fazul calculated it was going to take at least ten minutes to load the balls and screw them back together.

As he took the last swallow of beer, he knew it was time to start, but found himself wandering over to the window and watching the outgoing tide suck the water in the river out to sea. The full moon sparkled in the dark water and seemed to beckon him to follow.

Finally, he went to the closet and pulled out a yellow jumpsuit and pulled it over the clothes he had been wearing. Then he put on the leaded lab apron, respirator, and face shield and gloves; before pressing the switch that raised the slab of lead covering the top of his Castle.

When the slab had risen a foot, he released the button and reached for a very large pipe cutter he had constructed to slice through the side of the pod. Adjusting the tension with one hand, Fazul started pulling the device around the pod until the circular blade broke through the shell. Immediately, the clicking from the Geiger counter doubled. One more turn and the top could be removed.

After putting the cutter back on his workbench, Fazul removed the top of the pod and sat it on the workbench. As he did, the clicks turned into a low growl. Picking up a threaded hook, he quickly inserted it into the center of the dimpled plastic container and removed the eighteen dispersal units, arranged like eggs in a carton with uniform separation. Now the Geiger counter's growl turned into a scream that echoed through the office. If he had had the time he would have turned the volume down, but extra time was the one thing he didn't have.

Keeping his chest pointed toward the plutonium, Fazul backed around the bowling balls until he was standing between the two center rows. Bending down he placed the plastic container on the floor and loaded the first two balls. Pushing the container ahead of him he worked his way back toward the Castle until all eighteen units had been inserted into the ball's secret cavities.

After leaning the empty plastic container against the wall, he lowered the lead slab back on top of the Castle. Quickly moving down the balls, he sat the top half of each ball into place. As he did the scream from the Geiger counter dropped an octave every time a dispersal unit was covered. Working his way back up the two lines of balls, he screwed them tightly together, reducing the output from the speaker each time, until only random clicks were heard, as he finished.

Glancing at the clock, he realized that it had taken him fifteen minutes to complete the operation so far, but he still wasn't finished. Fazul picked up the dimpled plastic container and quickly carried it down the front steps and out the door. Running as fast as he could, he picked his way thought the moonlit darkness and along the docks that led out into the river. Then he spun around and let the empty container go. Hopefully, the strong current would pull it away from the dock and down river by morning.

Hurrying back inside his workshop, Fazul undressed and took a long shower before spending the rest of the night packing and addressing the boxes so they would be waiting for Scott when he arrived for his morning pick-up.

Chapter 40
The Big Apple

Sitting at the navigation console as the Saudi II cut through the evening darkness, Abd couldn't shake the feeling that he was heading to his doom. The GPS showed the sailboat was twenty miles off the Jersey shore and currently running third as the fleet headed north toward the mouth of the Hudson River.

While they were still an hour away from the finish line at Liberty Island, Abd busied himself studying the depth charts. His first inclination was to dump the pod when the captain made his turn north, up the Hudson. Since they were arriving at the end of an incoming tide, the divers would have about thirty minutes to retrieve the pod in relatively still water.

The daily tidal flow between Sandy Hook and Rockaway Point of 57 billion gallons of water created urgency in the pods recovery process. That meant the pod had to be found quickly before it was covered with sand or swept out to sea. The latter posed the greatest danger; it increased the possibility of the pod getting caught in the nets of fishing trawlers crisscrossing the area with dragnets. If that happened, it wouldn't take the authorities long to figure out that someone was planning a serious attack on the United States.

As Abd sat at the navigation console, he overlaid the standard depth chart with a map that showed the wrecks scattered along the bottom that were well known to the local divers. Taking everything into consideration, he decided that a site designated U2 was ideal. It was about a mile out, halfway between the tip of the Earle Naval Weapons Station piers and the northern tip of Sandy Hook. According to the map, the remains of an old barge sat level with the bottom twenty-six feet below the surface.

To Abd, it looked like that area was somewhat protected from the current and shallow enough to give the divers more bottom time than they would have in the Hudson. Now, all he had to do was convince captain Ibrahim to take the Saudi II there.

If this hadn't been the shortest leg of the race, he doubted that Ibrahim would listen to anything he had to say. But the Saudi II was built for the long haul, not a trip across town. They had already slipped to third place and now the Ericsson boat, a quarter of a mile behind them, was threatening to cut their point score for the leg even more.

Watching the storm that had seen them off in Baltimore beginning to merge with another system coming in from Pennsylvania, Abd had an idea and punched the intercom. "Captain, take a look at the monitor. I've laid out a course that would bring us west of Sandy Hook, just in time to catch the storm headed for New York."

Studying the line, Ibrahim's eyes narrowed. "Are you out of your mind? That will take us miles out of the way."

"You've got to trust me on this one, captain. If we hit it right, we should ride up the Hudson like we're flying," Abd shot back.

Looking back, Ibrahim saw the boat behind them slowly gaining ground. The captain shrugged his shoulders, "What the hell? At this rate were likely to come in dead last. Give it your best shot."

"You won't be sorry, Captain, I promise," Abd said plotting the course to the first waypoint over the Rickseckers wreck. "Just follow my line. I'll keep making adjustment from the console as the storm approaches."

As the Saudi II headed toward an Engine Wreck scattered on the bottom under sixty-six feet of water, Abd looked at the aft camera monitor and watched the Ericsson lean over and head west.

Just to be on the safe side, Abd turned on the underwater lights and cameras, but only water showed on the monitors. When the GPS told him they were over the wreck, he pressed the intercom. "Okay Captain, bring her around to a heading of two hundred and forty-six degrees."

The captain didn't respond, but Abd felt the ship answer as Ibrahim spun the wheel. Directly ahead lay the wreckage of the U.S.S. Turner, which exploded in 1944 --while anchored-- killing 138 sailors. As they approached the wreck, the depth gauge showed fifty-five feet.

"Steady as she goes," Abd said into the intercom.

"It looks like that storm is going to beat us," Ibrahim responded.

"Not from down here, just follow the line," Abd cajoled.

A few minutes later they were approaching the remains of an inverted keel sticking slightly out of the bottom at thirty-eight feet.

"Okay Captain; bring her to three hundred and ten degrees." Abd said watching glimpses of the bottom barely visible on the monitors.

Abd watched the ocean's bottom roll by as the Saudi II inched closer to the bottom as they sailed over the Bronx Queen. "Cut her back to two hundred forty-seven degrees."

"How's the depth?" the Captain asked.

"There's still plenty of water. I'm showing twenty feet below the keel," Abd replied.

Abd knew that the U2 site had a depth of twenty-six feet, which still gave the boat a margin of ten feet. His concern was the constantly shifting sand along the northern tip of Sandy Hook that they were about to parallel.

As they reached the tip, Abd watched the bottom slowly rising beneath the boat. Checking the chart against their present position, he realized that the bottom was moving up faster than he anticipated.

With nothing else to do, Abd reached for the hydrofoil control and nudged it back until the boat was a foot higher in the water. "What the hell are you doing down there?" Ibrahim yelled into the intercom.

"Just increasing our safety margin a bit," Abd answered.

As the bottom of the keel-wing began kicking up sand along the bottom, Abd raised the boat another six inches.

"If you do that again, I'm going to come down there and kick your ass overboard," the Captain screamed, so loudly that his voice echoed down the steps. "If someone snaps a picture of us completely out of the water, we'll be disqualified."

Fortunately for both of them, the bottom began dropping away as they cleared the wandering sandbar that the currents shuffled along the bottom.

When Ibrahim spun the wheel and pointed the Saudi II up the Hudson, Abd punched the eject button on pod number seven. He was pleasantly surprised to see it slip out of the keel-wing amid a cloud of bubbles created by the small explosive charge that finally dislodged the stubborn cylinder.

Abd quickly picked up his disposable cell phone and dialed Sheikh who had left Sandy Hook an hour ago. "You guys have to pick up your tickets to the U2 concert at Madison Square Garden."

"Okay, Daddy," Sheikh responded.

As the bottom began dropping away, Abd reached up and put his hand on the hydrofoil control to lower the boat back into the water. Just then the storm hit and the sailboat accelerated to thirty-five knots.

"Leave her up until we hit the Verrazano-Narrows Bridge," Ibrahim said over the intercom.

Back at the George Washington School of Engineering, the seventeen word conversation was targeted as possibly subversive, since it was conducted between two prepaid cell phones. After the call was converted, processed and discarded as useless drivel by ECHELON, the disk sector that stored the call was erased as the computer impartially queued up another call to analyze.

A wave hit the side of the Chris Craft Roamer just as Sheikh was folding the phone closed. The impact knocked the phone out of his hand. Holding the wheel with one hand, he reached down through the water sloshing on the deck and grabbed it. By the time he raised the device back to eye level the light dimmed and the smell of something burning inside caught his attention.

"That's one," Sheikh said looking at Hasan and Ayman dressed in their wetsuits. He tossed the useless phone into the water.

Suddenly, a giant wave loomed ahead of the boat and Sheikh gunned the engines. The Roamer tilted up and crawled up the wave until it leveled off near the top. As the bow tilted down, the props hit the air and the twin five hundred horsepower engines screamed as they spun up.

When the boat landed, water exploded all around them. The automatic bilge pump that had been running since they left Sandy Hook couldn't keep up anymore. Moments later, the high water bilge pump fired up and the alarm began blasting.

"Cut that damn thing off," Sheikh screamed over the thunder echoing across the water. "We should be there in another minute or two. You two get ready to jump."

Hasan and Ayman held on to the side and inched their way back towards the tanks that were resting in a rack next to the swimming ladder. Cracking the main valve, they sucked on the mouthpieces to make sure everything was ready. Earlier they had both agreed that it would be safer to jump overboard holding the tanks and put them on underwater. That way they wouldn't have to worry about dropping them or slipping and banging them against the boat.

The high waves and the ridiculous angles the boat twisted through made it impossible for the GPS to lock onto the satellite constellation chirping away in space. So Sheikh had to rely on the intermittent readings from the radar and depth finder as the boat lopped forward. Fortunately, the three terrorists had spent the past year diving the wrecks in the area, as they practiced for attacks that had always been called off at the last minute. During that time, Sheikh had learned to read the bottom like the palm of his hand, and he wasn't about to let the storm cheat them out of their first real mission.

Spotting a familiar shape on the bottom, he pulled back on the throttles and the boat slowed and began pitching more violently. "Okay, here we are."

Ayman and Hasan grabbed the tanks and cradled them in their arm as they rolled off the side of the boat. Immediately, they were in a much more peaceful world and soon had the tanks strapped to their backs and their flashlights on. Heading toward the bottom, they saw that Sheikh had dropped them directly over the wreck. Hovering just above the bottom, they looked around, but couldn't see the pod.

Ayman unzipped a pocket on his wetsuit and pulled out a little tracking device. Turning it on, he slowly pivoted around through 360°, waiting for it to locate the transmitter. After another try he gave up and put it away. Now their only option was to head off in the direction of the Saudi II and hope they found the pod before their air ran out.

Twenty minutes later, they were about to give up when Hasan spotted a fresh track in the sand. Following it they soon discovered the pod rolling back and forth in a little depression on the bottom. On closer inspection, they saw part of the ejection spring protruding from the end where the charge had been set.

It didn't take long for them to strap a girdle around the cylinder and attach one end of a long rope to it. Ayman tugged on it as hard as he could to be sure it wasn't going to come undone. He activated a self-inflating balloon attached to the other end and the rope shot to the surface.

Circling the area in the boat, Sheikh spotted the balloon as the wind and waves drove it north. Pushing the throttles forward, he chased after it. On the bottom Ayman and Hasan watched the rope play out. As it did, it formed several coils that playfully danced around the divers. One of the large coils formed a loop over Ayman's head and then slowly descended as Sheikh, on the Roamer above, snagged the balloon with a gaff and tied the rope to the aft rail, just as another large wave hit the boat.

Below in the darkness, Hasan's flashlight was knocked from his hand as the rope zipped into a straight line between the pod and the boat above. He scrambled after it as something bounced off his shoulder. Grabbing the light and twisting around toward the pod he saw Ayman's headless body standing on the bottom with two streams of red blood pumping out of the severed neck. When he realized what had happened, he convulsed and just managed to pull his mouthpiece out before he vomited.

Minutes later Hasan pulled himself up the swimming ladder and flopped down on the deck gasping for air.

"What the hell is the matter with you?" Sheikh asked.

"Ayman is dead!" Hasan managed to wheeze out, as he fought to catch his breath.

"Dead? What do you mean?" Sheikh asked kneeling down beside his friend.

"The rope cut his head off," Hasan said as Sheikh helped him to his feet.

"That's two," Sheikh said. "Help me get that pod on deck so we can get out of here."

"What are we going to do about him?" Hasan asked as the two men began pulling the rope in.

"Nothing much we can do about him how. The best thing to do is just leave him where he is and concentrate on getting this thing back to Occoquan," Sheikh said.

On a calm day it would have been hard for two men to pull the 250 pound pod to the surface, but tonight it was nearly impossible. Eventually, they came up with the idea of looping the rope around the rail and letting the boat do most of the work as it rose and fell with the waves. When the pod surfaced, they waited for the swim platform to dip below the water, and then pulled hard and the cylinder rolled onto the wood. Now all they had to do was get it from the platform to the main deck.

Sheikh climbed down onto the swim platform and together they moved the pod up and over the back of the boat, letting it crash to the deck. The cylinder hit top down, compressing the broken ejection spring. When the pod bounced back off the deck, the spring expanded and shot out of the pod, flipping a half turn before hitting Hasan's right palm.

Looking at the metal protruding from the back of his hand, Hasan instinctively grabbed the spring and pulled it out of his flesh. "Let's get out of here before something else happens," he screamed, sticking the injured hand into his left armpit and squeezing it between his arm and side.

"That's Three!" Sheikh shouted to the sky.

By the time the storm passed and the moon broke through the clouds, Hasan's hand was bandaged and the pod was loaded into their van.

"Let's get a room around here tonight." Hasan said crushing a cigarette under his shoe, "I'm too tired to drive to Occoquan tonight.

Chapter 41
NJTP

Trooper Sanchez had been patrolling the New Jersey Turnpike for the past four years. During that time he had covered its entire 122 mile length, but usually stayed closer to his hometown of Perth Amboy. Mondays were hard enough, but today he was especially tired from working over the weekend with his team on the Homeland Security Department's Container Inspection Initiative at Port Elizabeth, New Jersey.

Now that it was almost over, he wondered if the DHS had really learned anything important or were just going through the motions. The exercise must have cost a couple of million, and Sanchez hadn't seen much in the way of improvements come out of the recommendations. Outside of getting to ride along with the Coast Guard as they boarded container ships, checked paperwork and scanned for nuclear and biological material, it had been a pretty boring experience.

He was really glad that it would be over after next weekend. His wife's parents were coming to spend Columbus Day with their grandchildren.

"Well, what the hell, I can't change it now," he said out loud.

Spotting a Mercedes-Benz ML550 coming up on his left in the HOV lane, he watched the driver pass. "No passengers," he said switching on his lights and pulling in behind the car.

This was Sanchez's favorite summons because it was pretty cut and dried. Judges liked to make examples out of anyone who clogged up the HOV lanes without the proper number of passengers. Pulling behind the 550, Sanchez turned on the LED strobes in his light bar and punched the license registration into his mobile data terminal. As he followed the vehicle back across to the right shoulder, the plates came back clean.

Sanchez grabbed his hat and was about to exit his cruiser when he saw the driver's door pop open. He quickly grabbed the mic and punched the PA button "Do not exit your vehicle."

As the door continued to swing open, Sanchez's pulse began to rise as the perceived threat triggered a shot of adrenalin into his system. "Stay inside your vehicle," he said more firmly.

A second later the door slammed shut, but Sanchez was still primed to fight. Drawing on his training, he began the slow breathing exercise he had been taught at the academy. Four seconds in, hold for four, out for four. After a couple of cycles, he felt his heart begin returning to its normal rhythm.

"That's better," he said to himself.

Exiting his cruiser, Sanchez checked the traffic, unsnapped the safety strap on his holster and walked to the 550, ready to draw his weapon. Checking inside he saw two small children strapped into their booster seats in the back and relaxed a bit.

Standing back a little behind the driver, who was a female in her late twenties, Sanchez motioned for her to roll down her window.

She shook her head and said something he couldn't understand because of the loud traffic noise created by the steady stream of traffic behind him. Reaching down slowly for the handle the woman nodded her head and made a gesture indicating that the window didn't work. "Okay if I open the door?"

Sanchez nodded and she slowly opened the door. "Sorry officer, but the damn window doesn't work. What did I do wrong?"

"To tell you the truth, I thought you were driving alone in the HOV lane, but I see you have your kids with you," Sanchez answered in a matter of fact tone.

"Yeah, they need to figure out a way to indicate that somehow. But since the windows don't even work on this thing, I think it will be a few years until that happens."

"Sorry for the inconvenience," Sanchez said smiling.

"Don't worry about it. I hate driving this tank, but my husband insists that it's the only way to protect me and the kids."

"He might have something there," Sanchez said as he turned around and returned to his cruiser.

He watched the woman pull safely back into traffic and decided it was time to grab a cup of coffee at the Joyce Kilmer Service Area, so he called in to the dispatch center and got the okay.

After a quick trip to the restroom and a cup at the counter, he had relaxed and was ready to roll again. Picking up a container to go, he was walking back out across the parking lot when he saw a twelve passenger van slowly moving down the exit ramp toward him. It slowed to a stop and parked diagonally across two spaces a lane over from his cruiser.

Sanchez walked towards the van, placing the coffee on the hood of his cruiser on the way. By the time he got to the van the driver was outside.

"What's the problem?" he asked the driver, who was leaning against the fender.

Sheikh looked at Hasan sitting inside the van, and then back to Sanchez. "My friend had a little fishing accident last night and I'm trying to get him home so his wife can patch him up. We stopped up the road for breakfast and he's been complaining ever since. I told him to pull in here to use the bathroom and that I'd drive the rest of the trip."

"Do you two have identification?" Sanchez asked politely.

Sheikh pulled out his New York driver's license and handed it to the trooper. Then he reached into the van and waited for Hasan to pull out his wallet. "Here's his, too."

"You two stay here while I run these." Sanchez said. Then he walked back to his cruiser and got inside. After the computer verified the licenses and identified the van as a rental unit from Virginia, Sanchez was inclined to let them continue on their trip.

Just to be on the safe side he started his engine and pulled around the lot so he would be able to line them up on the dashboard camera connected to his patrol video system. After stopping, he walked back to the men and handed them back their licenses.

"Okay here you go, but from now on park between the lines," he said addressing Sheikh.

"No problem officer. I don't want anyone to scratch the paint. You know how finicky those rental agencies are," Sheikh responded. "Say, do you have a first aid kit in your car? We still have a long drive in front of us."

Thinking it might be a good idea to get a look at the wound under the passenger's bandages, Sanchez smiled. "I've got a kit, but you'll have to change the bandage yourself."

"Not a problem," Sheikh said waiting for the trooper to retrieve the kit from his trunk.

Sanchez returned with the duty bag he used on the practice exercises and pulled out his first aid kit. "Here you go."

"Thanks man. This guy's got no insurance."

225

As Hasan sat on the edge of the seat with his feet on the blacktop, Sheikh grabbed a plastic zip-lock bag out of the kit and handed it to him. "Here's something for you to hold on to while I operate."

When Sheikh cut through the bandages and pulled the dressing off, Sanchez took a good look at the wound. The first thing he noticed was that it definitely wasn't made by a gun.

"Gaff got him?" Sanchez asked.

"Yeah, the blues were running like crazy after the storm last night - caught his hand, when I was pulling a giant into the boat. I got a mess in the back. You want some?" Sheikh responded.

"Not today. Besides I never really liked them. Too oily," Sanchez said.

"My wife smears them with mayonnaise and wraps them in aluminum foil, makes them taste a lot better," Sheikh said putting the last strip of tape on the new bandage.

Without thinking about what he was doing, Sheikh sealed the plastic bag and stuffed it into the bag along with the first aid kit. "Thanks, man that should help it heal a lot faster."

"Can I go to the bathroom now?" Hasan asked with a painful look on his face.

"Sure buddy," Sheikh answered handing the bag back to the trooper. "Is it all right if we go now?"

"Sure, just practice your parking," Sanchez said.

Knowing that chance had favored them, Sheikh patted Hasan on the back and the two of them headed toward the bathroom without looking back.

Chapter 42
Irrepressible Youth

Since his family had escaped while Saddam was still in power, it was hard for fifteen-year-old Yahiye to remember much about his early life in Iraq. The only thing he remembered for sure was the fact that he never went hungry growing up in Latifiya, south of Baghdad. So the constant ranting of his father, pointing out the terrible destruction and atrocities perpetrated against the people in his homeland fell on deaf ears.

Besides, Yahiye liked living here in America and was especially excited when he started his sophomore year of high school. Last year he had managed to get on the school's bowling team as a substitute. Now a year older, he felt that he had a good chance of becoming one of the regulars.

His biggest problem was the fact that his father didn't like him hanging around with Americans and had refused to buy him the equipment he needed to fit in comfortably. The only thing that saved him from being ridiculed was the fact that he was a great bowler.

Yahiye was so excited when he sneaked into his father's closet and found an opened box with a brand new bowling ball inside. For weeks after its discovery, he had waited for his father to give it to him, but that still hadn't happened. Because his family didn't celebrate any of the regular holidays enjoyed by his friends, Yahiye figured that he would finally get it on his birthday a week before Thanksgiving.

So like most teenagers, he started bragging to his friends on the team that he was getting a new ball. But when he came to school on Monday, his friend Larry was surprised to see how dejected he looked.

"What's the matter, Yahiye? Didn't you get the bowling ball?" Larry said walking up next to his locker.

"I basically didn't get anything. Not even a piece of candy. I hate my parents."

Larry kicked the locker in front of him. "That sucks. I thought you told me you found a new ball in your dad's closet?"

"I did. In fact, I checked it again yesterday and it was still there. I don't understand what's going on," Yahiye said as he grabbed his books and the two boys headed for class.

"If you can sneak it out of the house, I can get my friend David to drill it for you over at Greenbriar's," Larry bragged.

"My father will kill me if I take it. You don't understand what a bastard he is," Yahiye said with a scowl.

Larry stopped and turned Yahiye around so he could look him in the face. "Listen, nobody else in your house is ever going to use that ball. Just get David to drill it for you. Then you can use it when we bowl and sneak it back after the game."

Early the next morning, Larry's mother pulled into the driveway and he jumped out of the car and ran up to Yahiye's house.

Yahiye's mother, Amina, answered the door. "Hello Larry. What are you doing here?"

"I lent Yahiye a book yesterday, and then remembered that I need it for my first class today. Is he in his room?" Larry said.

"Yes, he's upstairs," Amina said pointing.

Larry ran up to Yahiye's room and took the wadded up newspaper out of his backpack. "Where's the ball?"

Yahiye dropped to the floor beside his bed and slid the box out. Without saying a word the two boys stuffed it into the backpack and raced down the stairs towards the front door. "Bye, Mom, see you tonight," Yahiye said waving as the two boys disappeared out the door.

Once they were buckled up in the backseat of the car, Larry pulled two handheld video games out of the netting in front of him. For the remainder of the ride, the two boys were oblivious to everything except who was winning.

"Okay, you two, time to get out and learn something," Larry's mother said pulling to a stop in front of the school.

"Thanks, Mom," Larry replied as he shut off his unit and stuffed it back into the netting.

"Thanks, Mrs. Davis," Yahiye said climbing out of the car.

"Goodbye, I'll pick you two up after practice. Just give me a call when you're done."

"Thanks Mom," Larry said again adjusting the straps that were cutting into his shoulders.

When school was finally over, Larry and Yahiye climbed onto a bus with the rest of the bowling team and were dropped off at Greenbriar's. As they passed the driver, the boys showed their parent-pick-up permission slips.

Inside the bowling alley they headed for the equipment shop. Larry spotted his friend talking with a man wearing a bright red bowling shirt at the cash register. The boys walked up slowly and waited for a lull in the conversation.

"What's up, Larry?" David asked after a minute.

Larry pulled the ball out of his backpack and sat it on the counter. "My buddy, Yahiye, needs his ball drilled."

"Wow, that's really a coincidence. Scott here has a ball exactly like that."

"You get that from Occoquan Imports?" Scott asked, running his hand over the ball.

"Yea, I guess," Yahiye replied.

"Hope you have the same good luck with yours as I did with mine," Scott said picking the ball up, "I bowled back to back three hundreds the first day I got mine."

"Nobody can do that," Larry interrupted.

"Wrong," David said. "Look up on the wall over the snack bar. Scott's up there, pretty as you please."

"Well, I've got to run, David. Good luck with your bowling there, kid." Scott said putting the ball back on the counter, "be careful with that one, feels like it's all of sixteen pounds."

"Thanks, Mr. Scott," Yahiye said holding out his hand, "never shook the hand of someone that bowled a three hundred game."

"Two, if you don't mind,' Scott said shaking Yahiye's hand. "See you around."

After Scott left, David took down the sizing apparatus and soon had Yahiye's measurements written down on a piece of paper. "You two stay here and let me know if somebody comes in, while I go in the back and drill," David said.

In the back room, David installed three bits in the drilling machine and set the angles. Starting the machine, he whispered a little prayer and began pushing the drills toward the plastic. Drilling balls was at the top of his least favorite things to do, because once you started it was almost impossible to fix a mistake.

As the drills bit through the plastic little blooms of smoke began rising from the holes. "That's funny, never saw that before," he said backing the bits out.

Looking inside he saw the holes were only an inch deep and wondered what was causing the bits to heat up so much. After waiting a minute he began drilling again, pressing gently on the feed arm in an attempt to keep them from overheating. But after another inch the smoke appeared again. "Shit," he yelled, letting the bits cool for another minute.

On the third attempt the bits finally reached their intended depth and he shut the machine off. Looking inside with a small flashlight he saw some shiny powder at the bottom of the middle finger hole. Since his fingers were too big to fit into the holes, David picked up a pencil and pressed the eraser against the powder.

Pulling it out, he sniffed at the eraser then touched his tongue to the rubber. "Doesn't smell like plastic," he said reaching for some repair glue in one of the cabinets.

Ten minutes later he emerged with the ball and waited for Yahiye to test the holes. "How does it feel?"

"A lot better than a rental," Yahiye said. "Why is it so hot?"

"Must be made out of something new. It took three tries to drill it out. It'll cool down in a few minutes. You sure it's okay?" David asked hoping he hadn't screwed it up.

"Yea thanks, David. I really appreciate it," Yahiye said with a big smile.

As Larry ran to join their team, Yahiye stopped by the rental desk and got a pair of shoes. Looking up at the picture of Scott, he wondered if he would ever be able to bowl a perfect game.

During the first game, Yahiye struggled to get used to the new ball, which seemed slippery going down the lane. By the time practice was over, he had settled into a modified helicopter hook and managed to bowl a respectable one seventy-eight.

"See you tomorrow at school," Larry said as his mother pulled into Yahiye's driveway. "Don't forget to bring my backpack."

"Don't worry; I'll give it to you tomorrow morning." Yahiye said getting out and waving as the car backed out of the driveway.

With each step towards the front door, Yahiye's heart pounded faster as his guilt about the ball grew. Taking the emergency key from under an ornamental cement frog, he slid it into the lock and quietly unlocked the door and went inside.

From the smells coming from the kitchen he could tell his mother had pushed dinner back waiting for him to return. Peeking around the corner Yahiye could see his father reading the paper at the kitchen table while his mother put the finishing touches on a large bowl of salad.

Tiptoeing up the stairs, Yahiye made it to his bedroom and slid the backpack under the bed, just as his little sister Tigris pushed the door open. "What are you doing up here? I thought you were bowling."

"Guess I fell asleep. Let's go eat," Yahiye said getting up and rubbing his eyes.

Chapter 43
Damaged Goods

Fazul was walking back to his workshop from the post office on Mill Street when the van Sheikh was driving zoomed past him in the early twilight. As it turned south on Ellicott, a block away, Fazul picked up his pace. By the time he climbed the steps and walked around to the back, Sheikh was sitting on a dilapidated old bench with his feet propped up on a wooden cable spool that served as a table.

"I thought you were going to be here early this morning," Fazul said sitting down beside him.

"It's lucky we got here at all after last night," Sheikh said lighting up a cigarette, "Ayman is dead and Hasan's hand is all cut up. Worse yet, the top of the pod got punched open."

"How bad is the pod?" Fazul asked.

"Doesn't look too bad, but that's your department, not mine. After you check the pod, I want you to take a look at my brother. He may need some medical attention," Sheikh said offering Fazul a cigarette.

As Sheikh filled Fazul in on the details, Hasan woke up and got out of the van. "Mind if I sleep on the couch? I'm bushed."

"No, go ahead. There's a bucket of fried chicken in the refrigerator. Feel free to help yourself," Fazul said.

After Hasan went inside and closed the door, Fazul turned to Sheikh. "What the hell is the matter with him?"

"That's why I want you to check him out. He's been acting strange ever since we picked up the pod," Sheikh answered.

After talking for another half hour, the setting sun had completely disappeared from the sky. "Stay here while I get the Geiger counter," Fazul said rising.

Sitting there alone in the darkness, Sheikh could hear Fazul walking toward the far end of the room. He was just about to light up another cigarette when the lights from a slow moving vehicle began illuminating the embankment that led to the back of the shops along Mill Street. Before it got to the cul-de-sac where he was sitting, it turned into another driveway and the lights went out. Just as he was about to relax, it sounded like something was knocked over in the workshop behind him.

A few seconds later, Fazul appeared in the doorway adjusting the controls on the Geiger counter. He walked slowly around the van twice taking readings then walked back to the bench and sat down. "We got two big problems. First, Hasan's hand is hotter than a baked potato. On top of that the hole in the pod is positioned to point directly at the front passenger seat."

"So, he's going to die?" Sheikh asked.

"I'm telling you that even with the best possible care, it's doubtful that he'd live for more than a week or two. The problem is, we can't even take him to a walk-in medical office. As soon as they took an X-ray, they'd know radiation was involved and call the police or FBI," Fazul said.

"So you're telling me he's screwed?" Sheikh asked starting to get up.

Fazul reached up and pulled him back down. "No! I'm trying to tell you, that's why I just shot him."

Sheikh's mouth dropped open, "You son of a bitch," he said reaching for Fazul's throat with both hands.

Fazul thrust his arms up inside Sheikh's then brought them around in circles trapping Sheikh's wrists in his armpits. "Listen to me. He was already a dead man. I shot him; it was quick and clean. We've got bigger things to worry about. If this place is discovered before the attack everything we worked for will mean nothing."

Sheikh struggled to free himself, "Bastard!"

"Think of all the people who willingly gave up their lives to get this stuff here. I just couldn't take the chance. Think about it," Fazul said slowly relaxing his hold.

There was nothing more Sheikh wanted to do at that moment than squeeze the life out of Fazul, but in his heart he knew he was right. He also knew that if they managed to pull off the attack, he would make killing Fazul his top priority. "Okay, what's the second problem?"

"The second problem is that you're going to have to take that pod to Ihmad," Fazul said standing up, while keeping a wary eye on Sheikh.

"Why can't I just leave it here?" Sheikh asked.

"I can only handle one pod at a time and I'm already working on the first one," Fazul replied.

"What about the radiation?" Sheikh asked, in an urgent tone.

233

"First I need to see how bad the damage is, but I'm pretty sure we can seal it up so it won't cause any more problems," Fazul said walking toward the van.

Opening the side door, he peered in. Seeing that the hole in the top was only about a half inch in diameter, he smiled. "No problem, I can have that fixed in five minutes. After that, I want you to take it directly to Ihmad. Once he has it, you two figure out what you want to do with Hasan's body. Just remember that it must never be found."

After applying a lead patch to the top of the pod, Fazul helped Sheikh move Hasan's body into the van. "Sorry about your brother, but there was nothing else I could do."

"You're still a bastard, Sheikh said starting the engine, "you'd better hope we don't run into each other after this is over."

Walking back inside, Fazul knew he had done the right thing. He also knew that he had turned Sheikh against him and wondered how that would play out over the next five months.

Picking up his cell phone he dialed Ihmad. The call went directly to voicemail, so he left a message. "I fixed the leak in the fish tank. It should be arriving shortly. I want you to test it out and be sure it's okay. Can we meet for lunch tomorrow?"

Right now all Fazul wanted to do was get some sleep, but he knew he had to get another shipment of balls ready for the morning pickup. Deciding he would work better after a couple of cups of coffee, Fazul when to the kitchen area and set up the pot. While it was brewing, he dumped two spoons of sugar into a clean cup and went to the refrigerator for some milk.

When he opened the door, he was shocked to see the box of dehydrated bird flu sitting next to the chicken. "Lucky I found that," he said putting it back in the freezer compartment.

As he waited for the coffee maker to finish its last set of belches, he wondered if Hasan was reaching out from the grave, trying to get even.

The next morning, eighteen boxes sat stacked against the wall when Scott walked through the back door with his hand truck. "Morning Fazul, see you got some more work for me."

"Yea, I'll probably be shipping them out till Christmas. Then the whole craze will die out, like usual," Fazul said looking up from his desk.

"You know what's crazy. I just saw a kid at the alley with one of these balls the other day. I remembered you said they were a limited edition, so I thought it was a little strange that someone else in the area had one so quickly," Scott said piling the boxes on the hand truck.

"I'm sure he doesn't have one of mine. Must have been something that looked similar," Fazul said getting up and walking over.

"No, it looked just like the one you gave me and it must have been brand new, because the kid was getting it drilled out. Hope he doesn't bowl a three hundred like me and get his picture in the paper, too," Scott said tightening a strap around the top row of boxes.

Suddenly, Fazul felt like a mouse that ran down a hole and discovered he was inside a snake. "You never told me you bowled a perfect game. Where did that happen?"

"It was at Greenbriar's over in Fort Myers. You probably didn't know it, but I'm ex-army. Anyway, the first time I tried the ball you gave me, I bowled back-to-back three hundred games. Got a picture of me on the wall with the ball on my lap and everything," Scott said puffing out his chest.

"Guess you didn't catch the boy's name you saw with the ball, did you?" Fazul asked.

"Not really, something like, Yes-he, can't really remember. He was there practicing with his team for the big regional competition coming up this weekend. Are you going to have anything ready for this afternoon's pickup?" Scott asked, backing toward the door.

"Not today. See you tomorrow, if nothing comes my way," Fazul said closing the door.

Fazul was frantic. So far he'd only shipped out one hundred and sixty-two balls and some kid had already gotten his hands on one. Ihmad wasn't going to be happy when he found out about this.

●●●

While he sipped his tea at the Waterfront Inn, Fazul was beginning to get nervous. It was already a quarter to one and still no sign of Ihmad. If he missed this meeting it would be the first time he hadn't shown up when requested.

"It doesn't look like your friend is coming today," his waitress said startling him. "Do you want to order?"

235

"That might be a good idea. Let me have the scrod with steamed vegetables and a house salad with vinegar," Fazul said. "And bring me another tea."

"Right away," the waitress said as she finished writing the order down.

When he had finished lunch, Fazul paid the bill with one of his pre-paid debit cards and walked back to his workshop.

As he approached the back door he heard the shower running. Unlocking the door quietly and peeking inside. He said, "Ihmad, is that you?"

"Who else do you think would be in here taking a shower, the CIA?" Ihmad barked back.

Fazul relaxed. "You want some coffee?"

"No, I want some scotch," Ihmad yelled back. "Leave it on the kitchen table."

A few minutes later, Ihmad walked out of the kitchen carrying his glass with a towel wrapped around his waist. "I haven't done that much digging in years. Nobody's ever going to find that body."

Pulling some pants from a bag on the couch and holding them up Ihmad smiled. "I love Goodwill. Where else can you buy a hundred dollar pair of pants for five bucks? Let me get dressed."

Fazul shook his head and laughed as Ihmad grabbed the bag and walked back towards the kitchen. "You're the only person I know who has a million dollars socked away that would even think of walking into a Goodwill store."

"So, who's smarter?" Ihmad shouted back closing the bathroom door behind him.

Fully dressed, Ihmad returned and poured himself another glass of scotch. "So why did you want me to stop by today?"

"Originally I wanted to talk to you about Sheikh, but now something more important has come up," Fazul said not knowing where to start, "before I began shipping out the loaded balls, I gave an empty one to the FedEx guy – who takes it to an alley and bowls two three hundred games with it. Now his picture is hanging on the wall and some local paper even ran a story about him."

Fazul could tell by the way Ihmad's jaw was tightening that he wasn't happy, but figured he better get the whole story out before the verbal barrage started. "To make matters worse, he tells me there's a kid at the alley that has one too."

Surprisingly, Ihmad didn't say a thing. He just took another sip of scotch and sat down. After a minute of digesting what he had just heard, he finally spoke. "I guess one of our conspirators has a son walking around with one too many hands."

"That might work back home, but that's not going to solve our problem here. I did find out the kid's supposed to be at Greenbriar's Alley in Fort Myers this weekend. The FedEx guy thinks the kid's name is Yes-he or something like that."

"Let me see the list of people you shipped balls to," Ihmad said.

Fazul walked to his desk and returned with a clipboard, handing it to Ihmad. "The ones with X's have been shipped. They're not in any kind of order."

Ihmad scanned through the pages until he found the name he had been searching for. "Looks like little Yahiye needs some special attention. Guess I'll have to take up bowling."

"How the hell did you pick the kid's name out from that list?" Fazul asked dumfounded.

"Don't forget, it took me a year to find the thousand people on this list. I know every detail about every family member and most of their pet's names. I can tell you where they were born, why they want to help us, and what buttons to press if they start to have a change of heart." Ihmad said. "That's my job and I'm damned good at it. Now you take care of yours and everything will be all right."

"Don't worry about my part of the operation. I know exactly what I need to do," Fazul said glad that he wasn't the focus of Ihmad's wrath.

"Give me one of those empty balls and let me get out of here," Ihmad said.

Chapter 44
The Final Exercise

Sanchez had barely made it to the Coast Guard Cutter Bertholf in time to participate in the last Container Monitoring Task Force Exercise. As he ran down the passageway toward the briefing room, his duty bag kept banging against his leg. By the time he entered the room, he was out of breath and headed for the only empty chair in the front row.

"Well, nice of you to join us today, Trooper Sanchez. Did you forget when we were leaving?" the Transportation Security Agent in charge of today's exercise asked. "I hate to put you on the spot, but the Coast Guard would like you to return the film badge dosimeter, if you still have it?"

Rummaging through his duty bag, Sanchez found the badge and held it up. "Got it right here. Sorry, I guess I got a little carried away with the celebration after we kicked your ass last week," Sanchez said turning around and giving his teammates the thumbs up signal.

Waiting for the laughter to die down, the agent walked over and took the film badge from Sanchez and handed him a new one that the technician had ready.

"The badge I'm passing around now shows the results of having been exposed to radiation. As you can see, it is dark grey in the center where we placed a small radioactive sample for a few seconds." Handing Sanchez's badge to a technician standing beside his portable darkroom, he continued. "When we develop Trooper Sanchez's badge, you will see that it is clear, meaning it has not been in close proximity to radioactive material."

Fifteen seconds later, the technician pulled the developed film out and looked somewhat perplexed. "Sir, I think something must be wrong. This badge is entirely black."

"Okay, Sanchez. I'm getting pretty tired of your foolishness now. What did you do to the badge? Put it in a microwave or something?" the agent said taking the film and holding it up to the light.

"No, sir, it's been in my bag since last weekend."

"All right, Witterman, get out the Geiger counter and prove to everyone that Sanchez isn't a terrorist," the agent said taking Sanchez's bag and placing it on the table.

As soon as the device was turned on, it began emitting a high click rate, which turned into a low growl as the detector moved closer to the bag.

"I'm getting very bored with your shit, Sanchez," the agent said watching the technician open the bag and dump its contents on the table.

Grabbing a set of long forceps, Witterman began separating the contents until he located the source of the radiation. "Got it, sir," he said grabbing the plastic zip-lock bag of bloody bandages and holding it up next to the detector.

"Oh shit," Sanchez said as he flashed back to the van at the Joyce Kilmer Service Area.

After explaining how the bandages got into his bag, Sanchez found himself being airlifted off the cutter back to Port Elizabeth, the zip-lock bag and its contents locked in a heavy metal box in the cargo hold. Ten minutes later, the helicopter bumped down at the far end of the parking lot where his boss, Harris, was waiting to drive him back to his cruiser.

"I went over the computer tapes before I got here and found the vehicle identification query you made on the van. What else do we have to work with?" Harris asked with a serious look on his face.

Sanchez closed his eyes for a second. "A couple of guys in the van said, they'd been fishing for blues, when one of them got gaffed. They even asked me if I wanted some to take home. But wait, I've got it on video."

"That's what I wanted to hear," Harris said smiling for the first time Sanchez could remember.

After watching the tape twice, Harris got out. "Take that evidence over to the DNA Lab. They've already been notified that you're on the way. Make sure they check you out after they go over your car. Book a motel if you don't feel like driving back tonight."

On the way over to the lab, Sanchez thought about his encounter with the men. If Harris hadn't been so good natured about the whole thing, he probably would have started beating himself up over the incident. Now he just wanted to be sure he was all right and hadn't carried anything home with him.

After three hours at the lab and hand scrubbings to get rid of the contamination from rummaging around inside the bag earlier, he was given a clean bill of health. Walking out to his cruiser, Sanchez could feel himself start to shake, as he thought about what would have happened if he had carried the contamination home. That's when he decided he would take Harris' offer and spend the night alone before facing his family again.

When he woke up at five-thirty the next morning, he felt much better. After checking out of the motel, he drove home looking forward to a long shower and a well deserved sick day that he had decided to take before falling asleep.

All that changed when he turned the corner onto his street and headed for home. Before he got very close, he saw the news vans parked along the curb and knew he wasn't going to get much rest today.

"How does it feel to have been so close to two terrorists on the FBI's most wanted list?" a cute female reporter asked shoving her microphone into his face.

"Less threatening than finding all of you camped outside my house," he said pushing through the crowd.

"We understand that you may have discovered they were carrying nuclear material. Did they say anything that would lead you to believe they were in the process of making a dirty bomb?" a tall man asked.

"I don't know where you get your information from, but I can tell you they only appeared to be interested in fishing for blues when I talked with them," Sanchez said as he pulled the storm door opened and disappeared inside.

"Honey, what the hell is happening?" his wife, Kim, asked. "It's been a mad house here since late last night."

"Sorry, if I had known there was going to be a circus here, I'd have come home last night. I just wanted to unwind before I told you the story," Sanchez said hugging her.

As they embraced, their five year old daughter, Sandy, squeezed between them. "Are you all right, Daddy?"

"Yes Pumpkin, I'm all right. Doctors looked me over from head to toe and said I would live to be a hundred," Sanchez said as tears began to trickle down his face.

Chapter 45
Josh's Big Win

Since they moved to Lake Delta, Amy hadn't managed to keep herself very busy. The first few weeks she was rearranging the few items she had brought with her from Silver Spring finally giving up and dragging them out to the garage. When she tried to think back to the house swap, everything blurred together. Amy ran around opening bank accounts, buying Josh and Samantha new clothes for school and getting them registered.

If it hadn't been for Kim and Jill knocking on her door to see if she wanted to join the home owners association, she probably would have sat in the house enjoying her solitude. But they had and it didn't take long before the three of them began hanging out and gossiping over tea at each other's houses most mornings.

Kim's husband, Brian, worked as a speech therapist at the School for the Deaf, which was pretty much an eight-to-five job. When she met him for the first time, Amy could see why Kim loved him so much, with his great physique and quiet unassuming personality.

Jill's husband, George, on the other hand, worked at the Griffiss Business and Technology Park and didn't have regular hours. Amy suspected that as a kid he suffered from ADHD, because he was still hyperactive and a bit impulsive. What finally won her over to him was his great sense of humor and twinkling blue eyes.

The research center was tucked into one corner of what had been Griffiss Air Force base before it was decommissioned back in the late 90's. Recently the runways had been recertified and a large portion of the base had become the Oneida County Airport, which was part of the reason Duke had come up so often to visit them.

Amy always looked forward to Duke's visits. Then one day while she was chatting with her friends, Jill brought up the fact that there was going to be a model airplane competition at the Technology Park on Veteran's Day. When Amy reluctantly told them that Josh was going to be piloting one of the planes, her friends insisted all their families would go cheer him on.

The following night, George brought home a stack of front row tickets to the competition and Amy found herself cornered into smiling and pretending that it was something she wouldn't miss for the world.

The Friday before the competition, Duke and Ty had flown up and rented a large passenger van at the airport. By the time they arrived it was nine at night.

"Hi, baby, we brought you a bushel of crabs," Duke said nodding back at Ty holding a large wooden basket. "I thought maybe we could have your friends over tomorrow night for a little party."

"As long as you two promise to clean up the mess," she said hugging her father, "let me get a towel before you go running through the house with them."

After the crabs were safely tucked away in the garage, Duke and Ty went up to see what Josh was doing in the lab. When they got there, he had the three jets lined up in a triangle formation on the floor. The lead plane was sitting up on blocks about a foot higher than the others.

When Josh heard them coming he flipped up his VR goggles and smiled. "Hi, Pop-Pop. Come here and take a look at this."

"You two put on your goggles and tell me what you think about this idea," Josh said.

"I've replaced the gun reticle with ones designed to help you two line up on me when we're flying in formation," Josh said waiting for them to get their goggles on.

When Duke's eyes adjusted, he saw a dime-size circle over the right wingtip. "Looks like I'm on the right."

"Then I must be on the left," Ty said bending over and touching the left wingtip with his hand."

"The idea is to keep those circles lined up when we do our formation routines. That way it should look a lot better than it did last week," Josh said laughing a little.

"Yeah, Ty was a little sloppy," Duke said slipping off his goggles.

"Me. You were flying like a greenhorn, you old coot," Ty responded.

Then they all started laughing and planning their strategy for Tuesday's event.

The night before the race the weatherman had predicted a light dusting of snow, but Tuesday dawned bright and clear with a slight breeze and warmer than usual temperatures. As she cooked breakfast, Amy resigned herself to the fact that there was no graceful way of getting out of attending the competition.

After breakfast, Duke supervised loading the models and equipment into the van. When the other two families pulled into the driveway, everyone, including Amy was ready to go.

When they arrived at the airport, a respectable crowd was already assembled along the quarter square mile area bounded by Brooks Road, Bomber Drive, a strip of yellow tape and Donaldson Road, where a makeshift gate had been built out of yellow police tape. After dropping Amy and Samantha off with friends, Duke continued on to the pit area to begin prepping the planes.

As they approached the security checkpoint, the three families were screened the same way they would have been inside the terminal.

"Sorry ladies, we just need to check your bags. Are you carrying any containers filled with liquids?" one of the security guards asked with a smile.

A couple of minutes later they continued toward the other spectators, minus four containers of bottled water and two juice boxes their girls had been drinking when they walked up.

"I guess it will never end," Amy said angrily.

"They're just trying to keep everyone safe," Kim said waving back at the guards.

"How the hell does making us throw away our water keep anyone safe?" Amy asked in a disgusted voice.

"It must make sense to somebody," Jill said spotting her husband sitting in front of the chain link fence. "There they are."

As Amy sat down between her two friends, Samantha climbed up into her lap and pointed at Josh. "There's Josh, he's going to win today, Mommy."

"What makes you think that?" Amy asked.

"Cause he's been working on those planes for weeks," Samantha said. "Besides Daddy was the best and Josh is going to be just like him."

Amy felt a shiver go through her as she held back a tear and couldn't think of anything she wanted to say.

"What's the matter?" Jill asked. "You look like you're going to cry."

"Just thinking about Mark," Amy said. "He'd be so proud of Josh."

After a local singer belted out the National Anthem and three high school bands put on a parade, the announcer took over the microphone and wound the crowd up for the start of the competition.

"Welcome to the Veteran's Day Radio Controlled Model Airplane Competition. I would like for the Veterans in attendance to stand as we show our appreciation for their sacrifices."

That brought about half of the crowd to their feet as the others began clapping and whistling as loud as they could. "And how about the competitors who promise to put on one heck of a show today," the announcer yelled.

Another wave of applause swept through the crowd as the first team fired up the engines on their bi-planes. Once the planes were idling, the team members picked up their controllers and walked to the starting line. Standing there with their individual frequency flags flapping in the light breeze at the end of the controller's extended antenna, they waited for the announcer.

"Each team has three minutes to perform their routines. They will be graded on the maneuvers registered earlier with the judges who will award points based on difficulty, execution, and flow. Teams will be shooting for a perfect score of 300. Let's see which one gets the closest," the announcer said then began the final countdown, waiting for a thumbs-up signal as he went down his checklist. "The clock is ready. The judges are ready. The team is ready. So, let's start the competition."

As the lead bi-plane rolled toward the starting line with its two companions close behind, the pilots adjusted their throttles smoothly. Picking up speed, the nose wheels lifted off the ground just as they crossed the starting line and they were airborne. After gaining altitude, the planes began a synchronized slow roll that held together until they tried to reverse it and one of the planes began drifting away from the formation. After recovering, the planes lined up for a Split S, rolling a half turn and then simultaneously executing an inside loop to turn around and stay within the competition area. As they continued to perform they seemed to get a little better. Except for the bobble, the team did well and landed within the prescribed time limit.

"Let's have a hand for the first team up today," the announcer said. "And here come the scores 80, 70, and 85, for a combined score of 235. Not too shabby."

As the competition continued, the top score kept increasing until it stood at 280.

"Not much wiggle room," Duke said as they watched the team ahead of them finishing up their performance.

244

"Maybe we shouldn't have volunteered to go last," Josh said looking a little apprehensive.

"That might work in debates, but the other teams already have their scores. We're going to have to be really good to place today," Duke said looking down at Josh. "Really good!"

"Well, let's give'um hell then," Josh said determined to win.

As the planes landed, the announcer picked up the microphone. "Okay that wraps up the propeller planes today. That last team scored three sets of 90 for a total of 270. Let's give them a hand for a great demonstration."

When Josh led his team out to start their planes, the announcer picked up the tempo. "I think we may have saved the best for last today, ladies and gentlemen. The last team flying today is lead by twelve year old, Josh Baker. Today, Josh will be flying with Tyrone Turpin from the Department of Homeland Security and Josh's grandfather Duke Ransom. As you may already know, Duke is a former Vietnam era Navy pilot who became an ace flying Phantoms during that conflict. Today Josh's team will be flying Ajax's newest Phantom jet modeled after the plane that Duke made famous."

When their planes were fired up, Josh walked to the starting line and waited for his grandfather and Ty to pull down their VR Goggles. "You two ready?" Josh whispered.

"Ready, Captain," Duke said smiling broadly as he waited for Josh to start powering up his plane.

"Let's get 'um, tiger," Ty said laughing a little.

When Josh saw the timer give the announcer the final thumbs up, he began slowly accelerating towards the starting line. Once all the planes were in motion Duke and Ty lined up on their respective wingtips; and as Josh's plane crossed the starting line, they became glued into position.

Josh began his sequence with the Immelman, flying straight and level then pulling up one-half loop followed by a one-half roll that had the jets flying straight and level in the opposite direction.

When the planes reached the middle of the field, Josh pulled his plane up into a quarter loop, cutting back on the power to perform a Hammerhead stall. Once his plane fell through the next 180°, he applied power and recovered flying back in the opposite direction again.

245

Completing an Inside Loop that covered the entire field, Josh then put two half-Cuban Eights together as the planes flew one way and then the other. This was followed by two Split S maneuvers and an Inverted Circle around the entire area.

"Okay guys, lose the goggles," Josh yelled over his shoulder. "It's time to dance."

With the crowd roaring from the stands, the three planes glided low and slow towards the middle of the field. When they were lined up twenty feet apart the planes pulled up and sat motionless in the air. Then they arced up and played leapfrog in front of the bleachers. Many of the people in the crowd jumped to their feet and clapped wildly.

"Okay, time for the big ending," Duke said as the planes again lined up motionless in front of the grandstands.

Josh applied a little power and raised his plane forty feet in the air. Then Duke and Ty began slowly circling their planes around his – keeping the tails pointed toward the ground the whole time.

By now everyone was up and clapping as the three planes picked up speed then flared smoothly and executed three perfect landings.

"That's the best flying I've ever seen!" the announcer screamed into the microphone. "The judges seem to agree and have awarded Josh's team a perfect score of three hundred."

Later when the three top teams received their trophies, Amy stood and clapped the loudest as Josh accepted the first place award.

Chapter 46
Getting Ahead

Robin Tremble never liked the ocean very much. So she was less than excited when she drew an assignment to report on the new Terrapin Excluder developed at the Wetlands Institute in New Jersey. Still, she pasted a smile on her face, as her cameraman, Woody, framed her in a shot that would show the crab trap coming up behind her when it broke the surface.

Holding a cabled microphone, Robin waited for her que on the deck of the Merry Weather, a commercial crabbing boat out of Red Bank. "What you are about to see is a new device designed to save 15,000 turtles that drown annually when they are attracted to the bait placed inside the crab pots along the Jersey Shore."

When the red marker, ten feet above the pot, moved into view, Woody signaled Robin to point at the trap. Turning and looking for the yellow plastic rectangle, Robin's attention was drawn to a large bloated fish that the crabs were paying special attention to. A second before she realized what was happening, Woody dropped down. Trying to keep her in frame, he zoomed in on the back of a human head.

The instant her mind finally latched onto what she was looking at, Robin began screaming like a first-grade girl who had just had a frog thrust into her face. Then the trap swung down onto the deck and the head broke away from the dozens of blue claws that had carried it to the surface. As the faceless head rolled across the deck, it brushed against her leg. Robin vomited into the stiff breeze and melted to the deck in unconsciousness.

By the time the 6 o'clock news aired, the tape had been edited and the text loaded into the teleprompter. The news anchor lead off with a quick list of national and international bullet items, then began the lead-in for the local news.

"We advise viewer discretion for our lead story. The contents may not be appropriate for small children. A severed head was discovered by the crew of the Merry Weather, a commercial crabbing boat, off Red Bank early this morning." Having three kids of his own, Matt Meredith knew that it takes longer than ten seconds to get kids to do anything, but he had at least satisfied the FCC requirement.

247

"What you are about to see is actual footage shot by our news team, on the boat when the grim discovery was made." The clip rolled, as Matt continued. "As you can see the crab trap is being pulled to the surface by an electric winch. When it comes out of the water it will be swung over and dropped on the deck."

On the video, it wasn't easy to see what was hanging off the side of the net because the station director had insisted on putting a smudge dot over the head. Still as the camera zoomed in, dozens of sparkling blue crab claws could be seen holding something in place. Fortunately for Robin the clip ended with the crab trap still swinging in the air over her head.

Inside the New Jersey Police Forensic Lab, Dr. Summer Covey smiled as she got up to fill her coffee cup again. She had already viewed the original tape several times and knew the general public wasn't ready to view the remains she was about to examine in the autopsy room down the hall.

Entering the examination room, Summer took a sip of coffee before setting the cup down on her desk and removing a plastic apron from a hook on the wall.

Her lab assistant, Robert met her half way to the examination table at the other end of the room and pulled a latex glove from the box he was carrying. "Let me help you with the gloves, Dr. Covey."

"That's what I like about you, Robert always willing to go the extra mile to make my life easier," she said as she held out her hands.

"Better get busy with that head you X-rayed earlier. It's all over the news. You can bet the State Police aren't going to wait long on this one," Summer said pulling the stool out from under the stainless steel examination table.

As Robert walked back from the cooler with the head wrapped in cloth, Dr. Covey began humming a little tune that helped her relax. "We might as well weigh it first," Summer said pointing to the organ scales hanging over the end of the table.

Robert placed the head on the scale. "Just shy of five pounds," he said waiting for Dr. Covey's instructions.

"Crabs must have gotten more of the brain than I thought," Summer said.

"I'll hold it, while you cut the top of the cranium off with the Stryker," just give me a minute to figure out how to get a good hold on the damn thing.

Normally, Robert would have used a scalpel to make a crescent shaped incision from the back of the right ear to the crown of the head and then back to a point behind the left ear. Since the crabs had already eaten away the face down to the bone, he simply worked his fingers under what was left of the scalp and pulled it down over the back of the head.

After thinking about the best way to hold the head, Summer pulled her face shield down and slid two fingers into the empty eye sockets and placed her other hand under the neck stump. As she steadied the head, Robert turned on the vibrating Stryker saw and made a circular cut around the equator of the cranium. When the cut was finished, he picked up a metal hammer with a hook at the end of the handle and began prying the skull cap off. Even with half the brain gone, there was still a slight sucking sound as the bone broke free.

Since the spinal cord was severed at the C-3 vertebrae, Robert slipped his hand under the brain and pulled gently. A moment later the cord broke free and slid out of the cranium.

"Weigh that and then take a couple samples before you string it up in the jar of formalin," Summer said getting up to take a look at the X-rays.

Looking at a prominent supraorbital ridge, occipital protuberance, and square mandible, she confirmed what the square back hair cut had suggested all along; the victim was a male.

Using the closure of the endocranial and epiphyseal plates, she estimated the age of the victim to be between thirty and forty.

Now that she had determined the sex and age of the victim, she was ready to begin searching for the cause of death.

"Robert, set up the diagnostic imager, so I can take a look at the neck," Summer said draining the last bit of coffee from her cup.

Sitting down on the stool again, she began moving the miniature camera over the tissue. Zooming in on the C-3 vertebrae, Summer noticed some tiny strands of yellow nylon embedded in the bone. "Looks like this guy got tangled in some kind of rope. Hand me a collection kit, please."

"What do you think, drowning or strangulation?" Robert asked as he handed her the kit.

"It's hard to say. There's not much left to look at," Dr. Covey said as she finished teasing two long pieces of the rope fiber loose from the bone, "I want you to collect as many samples as you can. Then send the samples to the DNA lab for analysis. If the body doesn't turn up, we're going to have to rely on SDIS and CODIS to figure out who this guy is. Better give the skull to Obeck so he can cast the teeth and examine the fillings. It looks like they are made of gold, probably foreign. Nobody here can afford that anymore."

Normally, the news stories surrounding the head would have died out after a few days, but once the media latched onto it, they refused to let it go. Dr. Covey had worked at the lab for the past four years and had never met the Governor when he breezed through the facility during the annual inspection. She was surprised to get a call from his personal assistant a week after her initial examination, asking what was taking so long to identify the victim.

By the time she hung up the phone, Dr. Covey had been told in no uncertain terms that the Governor wanted fast action on this case because it was topical and fit in with his "Get Tough on Crime" philosophy. His assistant also hinted at the fact the Governor was a big fan of "CSI" and "48 Hours" on television and believed any crime could be solved once the police had recovered a body. At that point, Summer wanted to remind the assistant that they had only received a half eaten head, but decided it wouldn't do any good to point out the obvious.

So, like a dutiful child, Summer spent the rest of the day checking that everything was moving through the various labs and would be ready for Wednesday's upload to the FBI's Combined DNA Index System.

In the United States, the FBI is responsible for funding and operating CODIS, and the New Jersey Lab is one of only four regional mitochondrial DNA labs. So Dr. Covey had the advantage of knowing who owed her favors and which ones to call in to get the results the Governor expected.

Dr. Covey had worked at the lab since it opened and she knew the federal and state governments had spent millions setting up the facility. As a seasoned professional, she wasn't naive enough to think identifying the victim was going to do more than give the Governor

250

another bullet-point to use in his pre-election campaigning. Still, it was the first time anyone from the Governor's office had contacted her. Despite all her skepticism, she still felt a pressure to perform. That feeling had gotten her through Harvard Medical and the grueling internship at Johns Hopkins before she finally settled down in forensics. It was the place where she functioned best.

All together the state's 140,000 record index and the 3 million national records gave her a shot at identification if the victim had ever been convicted of a crime. Still, that was a long shot. If nothing was matched in those systems, she could search through the FBI's National Crime Information Center's records from the Canadian Government and INTERPOL, which held an additional five million records.

By the end of the week, Summer had the Y-DNA and mtDNA cross matching results, which traced the victim's family tree back to the Middle East. Once that fact was established, she knew the Department of Homeland Security would be keeping a close eye on any additional data fed into the system that matched the head.

Besides that, nothing of interest popped up on the 8 million records in the DNA computers, so she forwarded the DNA results to the Facial Reconstruction Unit and dove into other cases that had been piling up.

The following Wednesday afternoon, Summer had finished cutting a Y-shaped incision in the trunk of a twenty-four year old woman who had been beaten to death by her live-in boyfriend. Halfway through the process of peeling the skin, muscle, and soft tissue off the chest wall Summer's boss walked in, carrying a printout.

"Looks like the Governor owes you one now," he said setting the paper next to the dead girl's head.

"What are you talking about?" Summer asked.

"Got a match on the head you were working on last week," he said smelling the air. "Think they're serving lamb chops for lunch today?"

"I'll give you a lamb chop over the head in a minute, if you don't stop asking that every time you come in here while I'm peeling someone apart," Summer said letting the skin fold back against the body and picking up the paper. "I remember seeing something about these two brothers on the news over the weekend. Didn't a trooper stop them or something?"

"Yep, we had the trooper in here last Friday night for a little decontamination work. Nothing serious, a couple of scrubs with the brush and he was clean," her boss said. "Can't imagine how he feels talking with two guys on the Most Wanted list and not recognizing them."

"Guess he had a better chance than we did," Summer said. "Wonder if I'll get invited to the Governor's Ball this year?"

"If we're still around after the bomb goes off, I guess," her boss answered.

"What bomb?" Summer asked with a look of concern on her face.

"The one they're making with the radioactive material they found on one of the terrorists," her boss said tracing a big mushroom in the air with his fingers. "Nobody's saying much about it, but I've heard the rumors that someone in the area is making a dirty bomb."

"If that's true, I want a raise, so I can buy some more good wine to drink before I die." Summer said.

"I'd be happy to bring some by, if you like," her boss said smiling.

"I don't think you can authorize a raise high enough to make that dream come true," she said turning back to the body.

"Can't blame an old bachelor for trying," he responded. "What with the end of the world coming and everything."

Chapter 47
Out with the Old

Abdullah and Fahid, dressed in yellow rain gear and rubber boots, methodically worked their way through the rooms on the second floor, dousing everything with kerosene from five gallon plastic containers. Meeting in the hallway, they each stabbed the bottom of their container with a knife and set them hanging over the first step, then walked down ahead of the cascading liquid to the first floor.

On the main floor, they each grabbed another container and began covering the rugs, furniture, and floors in two semi-circular paths that met in the kitchen. Punching holes in these containers they walked downstairs into the basement.

"I'm going to miss this place," Abdullah said surveying the room which had been emptied of any evidence that it had once held the nuclear pods.

"Not as much as I will," Fahid said smiling. "That little Morela was crazy in bed."

While Fahid got out of his rain gear, Abdullah picked up the last container of kerosene and began pouring it on the pillows they had brought down from the bedrooms earlier. Walking over to the steps, Fahid reached up to a timer he had installed, "When to you want this thing to go up in smoke?"

"The plane leaves at nine, so set it for three hours. Maybe we'll be able to see it when we take off," Abdullah said as he dribbled a line of kerosene from the ring of pillows over to the steps.

•••

"Tell you what I'm going to do, Miguel. Tonight after supper, I'm going to take Gato down to the Veterinarian Clinic and see if they can fix him up," Humberto said stuffing another forkful of poached fish into his mouth.

"Can I come, Papa?" Miguel asked perking up a little.

"Not this time. It's going to be late by the time I get back and I want you in bed like usual," his father said. "When you two are finished put Gato in that old leather bag we use to take him in for shots. "Don't forget to put a towel in the bottom. I don't want him throwing up on the leather," Humberto said getting up and walking out to the porch to have a cigar.

Ten minutes later, the children pushed the screen door open and Miguel handed his father the leather bag. "He looks so sick, Papa. I'm worried that I'll never see him again."

"Don't you worry; I'm sure that nice veterinarian at the clinic will know what to do," Humberto said closing the bag and standing up.

Humberto got to the clinic just before it closed and slipped in as the receptionist walked to the door with the last pet owner to lock the door.

When Humberto opened the bag and she saw the sick cat, she smiled a little and wrinkled up her brow. "Don't worry, Dr. Carolina will be right with you."

A few moments later, the pretty veterinarian came in and took the clipboard Humberto was filling out. After scanning down the General Information form, she looked at him. "What seems to be the problem with little Gato here?"

"He's been throwing up a lot and doesn't seem to want to eat anything," Humberto said.

Taking the bag from Humberto, Dr. Carolina walked to the first examination room and put it down on the stainless steel table. After looking in the lethargic cat's eyes and ears, she grabbed a rectal thermometer. "This usually gets a strong reaction," Carolina said moving the cat's tail out of the way and inserting the instrument.

Outside of making a faint attempt to look around to see what was happening, Gato seemed unconcerned.

"Pretty high temperature," Carolina said as she pushed open the cat's mouth, "how old is Gato?"

"Three or four," Humberto answered.

"That seems a little strange. Half of his teeth are gone," Carolina said pushing gently against the only remaining canine with a tongue depressor, "he looks like he's a lot older than that."

Just as the vet was about to withdraw the tongue depressor a tooth popped out and rattled across the metal table. "That's not good," she said picking up the tooth and looking at it closely.

Watching the cat, Humberto began to get a little scared. "What the hell is the matter with him? He didn't even notice his tooth came out."

"I'm not sure. The only thing I can do is take an X-ray and keep him here night. Tomorrow, when my assistant comes in, we can do some blood work. But to tell you the truth, Gato may not be alive by then," she said waiting to see if Humberto just wanted to put the animal to sleep.

"Should I stay here while you take the picture?" Humberto asked.

"That will be fine," Carolina said pulling the business end of the wall mounted X-ray machine towards the table. "You can help me, if you want to."

"What do you want me to do?" he asked.

"Let me get a film cartridge from the other room," Carolina said leaving for a moment.

While she was gone, Humberto looked down at Gato and remembered all the fun Miguel and his sister Morela had playing with the cat. Humberto had been indifferent to the cat since he initially brought it home to keep the mice out. Now as he looked at the sick animal on the table, all he wanted to do was walk out of the office and forget all about the dumb thing.

"Okay, pick up Gato so I can get this under him," Carolina said when she returned.

Humberto hesitated for a few seconds before finally picking the cat up in his arms. "You're sure he doesn't have anything contagious?"

"Not really," Carolina replied taking the cat from him and positioning Gato on top of the 14 X 17-inch paper cartridge. "Go stand over by the door while I take the picture."

When Humberto was in place, Carolina picked up the electric trigger and backed toward him, watching the spiraled cord to be sure it didn't catch on anything. Pressing the button caused a slight buzzing sound that lasted for a second.

"That's all there is to it," she said snapping the trigger back in place and waiting for Humberto to pick up the cat again.

Realizing it must be getting late, Humberto glanced at his watch. "How much longer is this going to take?"

"We're all done for now. Let me put this in the developer and grab a cage from the back," Carolina said disappearing again.

A moment later, she returned carrying a brown plastic cage, which she placed on the examination table. "Put him in here and then I'll walk you to the door. You can come back tomorrow, we open at nine."

After locking the clinic's door and turning out the office lights, Carolina walked back to the lab and took the plastic film out of the developer. Walking to the sink to rinse off the chemicals she stopped and held it up to the light.

"Guess I'll have to do that one again," she said looking at the film, which was completely black.

When the second slide came out of the developer the same way, Carolina was puzzled. Taking the next cartridge out, she ran it through the developer to make sure the films hadn't somehow been contaminated. When that one came out clear, she knew something was terribly wrong.

Acting on a hunch, she grabbed another unexposed cartridge and headed back to the examination room. Pulling Gato out of his cage, she placed him on the paper cartridge and watched the wall clock. Thirty seconds later, she put him back in the cage and walked back into the lab. This time, the X-ray film showed the smudgy outline of a cat.

By the time Humberto got back to his house it was quarter to nine and his wife, Catalina was alone in the living room watching television. "What did the vet say about Gato?" she asked, turning the volume down with the remote.

"She's not sure what the problem is. Said he might not make it till morning," Humberto said sitting down beside her. "Should we get another cat if Gato dies?"

"Let's wait and see what the children want to do before we jump into anything," Catalina replied. "Better go kiss the kids goodnight."

Miguel was still awake when Humberto walked in to his bedroom and sat down on his son's bed. "How is Gato?" Miguel asked sleepily.

"The vet said she would not be able to tell until they do some blood work in the morning," Humberto answered smoothing back his son's hair. "If something bad happens to your cat, do you want to get another one?"

"Nothing's going to happen to Gato," Miguel said pulling the covers up over his face so his father couldn't see the tears in his eyes.

"Of course not," Humberto said kissing Miguel on the forehead. "Tomorrow we'll both go over and see how Gato's doing. Sleep tight."

Humberto was feeling really sad when he left Miguel's room and walked down the hall to say goodnight to Morela. But the feeling left immediately, when he opened the door and saw that her bed was empty. After checking the bathroom, he raced back down to the living room to his wife.

256

"Where is Morela?" He asked excitedly.

"Isn't she upstairs?" Catalina asked calmly.

"If she was upstairs, I wouldn't be down here asking you where she is," Humberto responded angrily.

Together they ran upstairs shouting her name. By the time they reached the second floor, Miguel was standing outside his room. "What's all the yelling about?" he asked.

"Do you know where your sister is?" Humberto asked.

"I think she was talking to her new boyfriend, Fahid on her cell phone. Then I heard her sneak out again," Miguel said like it was no big deal.

"What do you mean her boyfriend? Catalina shouted.

"The two of you must be blind as bats. The two of them have been sneaking off together since she first met him," Miguel answered his mother, like she was dumb as dirt.

A block away, Morela was talking on her cell phone as she approached the rental property. "I told you a hundred times, I don't want to get an abortion. I love you and I want to get married and live together forever."

Standing in line to board his plane, Fahid knew he only had a few minutes before he would have to shut off this phone. "I do want to marry you. You are the most beautiful girl in the world, but Abdullah and I need to fly to a meeting about our fish exporting business. I left some money in the upstairs dresser in my room."

"When will you be back?" Morela asked unlocking the front door and walking inside.

"We'll be back in a week. You sure nobody knows about the baby?" Fahid asked looking at his watch.

"You're the only person I've told so far," Morela answered as she became aware of the aroma of kerosene. "What did you do to make the house smell so funny?

"We set off some bug spray canisters. The cabinets in the kitchen were full of cockroaches. Smells terrible, doesn't it?" Fahid said. "Listen, I got you an engagement ring. I hid it in the bedroom, so you'd have to look around for it."

"Like a treasure hunt?" Morela squealed as she ran up the stairs to the bedroom. "What kind of ring is it? Is it in a box or what?"

"It's all wrapped up in a gold paper. Call me back when you find it. I love you," Fahid said hanging up and handing his ticket to the agent.

"She's got to be the dumbest girl you've ever met," Abdullah said buckling his seatbelt.

"They're all dumb when they're in love," Fahid said looking at his watch and seeing it was one minute till nine.

Back inside the rental house, Morela found the clip of money in the top drawer of the dresser right away and began pulling the other drawers open quickly as she searched for the gold box.

In the basement, the timer clicked and four wires wrapped around holiday sparklers stuck into the ceiling began to glow red. A few seconds later the fist sparkler ignited, sending a shower of sparks onto the damp pillows, which slowly caught fire.

As Humberto turned the corner and ran up the street towards his rental property, he could see a light on in the upstairs bedroom. About half a block away he saw Morela moving up and down, as she continued searching the dresser.

"I'm going to kill that bastard Fahid when I get my hands around his neck," her father thought, as he pushed himself to run faster.

Inside the house the fire had reached the kitchen. It had been no mistake that Fahid had chosen to use kerosene. He wanted incineration, not an explosion, and the kerosene was doing exactly what he expected, as it spread through the living room and up the stairs toward the second floor.

By that time the cellar was an inferno and the first floor was fully engulfed. Outside, the only thing Humberto could do was scream for Morela, as he watched the glass in the windows begin to explode from the heat.

By the time Morela shifted her focus from the ring to the smoke that was pouring into the room and across the ceiling, it was too late for her to escape. Lying down on the floor gave her just enough time to press the speed dial key on her phone, which she used to call Fahid.

"I love you more than anything, Fahid," she said beginning to feel the heat build in the room.

"I love you too, baby. Did you find the ring yet?" Fahid asked, as the plane taxied down the tarmac.

Chapter 48
Picking up a Split

When the manager of the Greenbriar arrived at six on Saturday morning, Ihmad was sleeping in his car. By the time he realized the sound he heard was a car door slamming shut, the manager was halfway to the door.

"Wait a minute," Ihmad yelled, getting out of the car and running to catch him.

Reaching the door the manager stuck his key into the lock and opened the glass door.

"Hey, Tony," Ihmad yelled closing the distance. "Wait a minute."

"Can't," Tony said. "Wait here, until I turn the alarm off."

A minute later, Tony returned. "What can I do for you?"

"I was in here last night and David gave me this employment form to fill out. He said you guys were going to be busy today and that if I came over early you might hire me," Ihmad said trying to look like he needed the job.

"Ever worked at an alley before?" the manager inquired.

"A little, when I was a lot younger, but you never forget how to collect money and spray shoes," Ihmad answered.

"Normally, you'd have to work a day or two for nothing so I could see how you worked out, but today is going to be insane. How much are you expecting to make?" Tony said.

"Tell you what, feed me a couple of meals and give me a fifty. If you like what you see, we can talk about the job tomorrow," Ihmad said.

"Okay, what's your name?" Tony asked.

"Just call me Fayez – like the candy, but with an F."

"Okay, Fezz, you got yourself a deal," Tony said leading him inside. "You know how to check the pin setters?"

"All I really did was check for jammed or missing pins," Ihmad said.

"That's a start. I'll turn the lights on at the desk," Tony said walking away.

"I'll be right back. Got to get my gym bag from the car so I can change into something more comfortable," Ihmad said running towards the doors, "be back in a second."

When Ihmad came back, Tony had disappeared inside his office behind the main desk. "Where should I put my bag?"

Flipping a switch, Tony pointed out the door. "There's an employee break room at the back of the pro-shop. Throw your stuff in one of the lockers over there. Then get busy checking the pinsetter. The mob will be here at nine."

Passing the snack bar, Ihmad looked up at the picture of Scott holding his flaming ball and smiled as he continued to the pro-shop he had visited the night before.

The break room consisted of a couple of tables in the corner of the large room. Besides a refrigerator, sink, coffee machine and microwave, the majority of the area was used as a warehouse to store equipment and supplies. After setting up the coffee machine, Ihmad changed into a gray jumpsuit and was slipping on a pair of new shoes when he heard some thumping coming out of the vertical baler built into the rear wall of the building.

Cocking his head to hear better, Ihmad walked over to the machine and knelt down beside the collection bin. "Good news David, I got the job," Ihmad said. "Thanks for letting me help you close up last night."

As Ihmad closed the metal door and locked it into place, the thumping got louder. He reached up to press the start button, just as Tony walked in. "If there's one thing I can't resist, it a hot cup of fresh coffee."

"Best stuff in the world," Ihmad said pressing the button.

As the hydraulic cylinder mashed the cardboard, Ihmad reached his hands up over his head and made a loud yawning sound to be sure Tony couldn't hear David's desperate screams.

"Sounds like you're ready for some," Tony said reaching for another ceramic mug. "Guess I'll have to paint your name on one of these."

"Better wait until you see if you like my work first," Ihmad said. "How about showing me how to get to the pinsetters?"

By the time Ihmad inspected the machinery and cycled each pinsetter, the first school bus pulled into the parking lot. Half an hour later the place was packed and the noise level had risen to the point where the building sounded like a busy bee hive.

Working behind the counter, Ihmad was kept busy running back and forth grabbing shoes for the grade school teams. Every time he returned to the desk he searched the crowd for Yahiye, but so far he hadn't been able to spot him. Then as suddenly as the mad rush had started it was over, as the coordinator grabbed the wireless microphone and began welcoming the various schools and coaches.

"I need to take a break," Ihmad said as he turned and walked toward the bathrooms.

When Ihmad was far enough away from the desk that he didn't have to be worried about being called back, he slowed his pace and began seriously searching for Yahiye. Before he found him, Ihmad heard a voice he recognized calling his name. Turning around, he saw Yahiye's father Salim, walking in his direction.

"Ihmad, what are you doing here?" Salim asked.

"Cleaning up the mess your son Yahiye has gotten us into," Ihmad said bluntly.

"Whatever are you talking about? Yahiye is a good boy. He would never do anything without my knowledge," Salim said defensively.

Ihmad put his arm around Salim's shoulder and turned him towards the snack bar. "Does anything in that second picture look familiar?" he said pointing to Scott's picture.

"Have you gone crazy? I've never seen that man before," Salim said taking a step away from Ihmad.

"Do you recognize the bowling ball he is holding?" Ihmad said stepping back towards Salim.

"What's so special about that ball?" Salim asked as his mind raced to make a connection.

"Did you receive the three boxes that were sent to you?" Ihmad asked.

"Yes. They're safely tucked away in my closet at home. But I thought we were not to talk of this in public? Has something changed?" Salim said.

Ihmad could tell by the expression on Salim's face that he still didn't know what he was talking about. "Then you're telling me you never opened the boxes?"

"Or course not. What was the use? According to what you told me, it should only take a few minutes to assemble the parts at the proper time," Salim said realizing that whatever his son had done was probably going to be paid back with the family's blood.

"Okay, take me to Yahiye," Ihmad said.

261

As they walked toward the lane Yahiye's team was using, Salim saw the ball in his hand and realized that his son must have stolen it from his closet. "That little shit," Salim said stepping off to confront his son.

"Wait," Ihmad said holding Salim. "Let him finish."

As the two men watched, the captain of the rival team picked up twenty nine in the tenth frame putting his team ahead by twenty-two points. Yahiye, who was bowling last on his team, got up and grabbed his orange and red flame ball - positioning his left foot behind the middle diamond. As he stepped forward and released the ball, someone on the other team coughed loudly.

"Is cheating the only way you guys can win?" Larry shouted at the captain.

"Better watch your mouth or I'll knock it into next week," the captain shouted back.

The pins exploded, as the ball smashed head on into the number one pin. When the pinsetter finished cleaning up the mess, Yahiye was looking at a seven ten split.

"Don't let that scare you, Yahiye. Send those losers home with their tails tucked between their legs," Larry yelled.

Without acknowledging the confrontation that was building behind him, Yahiye lined up again and sent the ball straight down the alley a quarter of an inch away from the gutter. When it hit the ten pin the ball dropped into the gutter and sent the pin flying straight across into number seven.

"That's the way," Larry and his team shouted, as they realized they were going to win the match. "We only need six to beat them."

Without hesitation, Yahiye walked back to the return rack and waited for his ball to pop up. To add insult to injury, he bowled a strike on his last ball and was in the middle of getting congratulation pats on the back when the opposition captain strolled over towards him.

Without saying a word, the captain picked up Yahiye's ball and threw it diagonally across the alleys as hard as he could. It landed two alleys away on the lane separator with a loud cracking sound. Flying into the air again a silvery powder sprayed out of the ball as it continued bouncing across three more lanes.

While everyone was watching the spectacle unfolding between the two teams, Ihmad grabbed an empty bowling bag and shoved it into

Salim's chest. "You have one minute to grab that ball and get it out of here. Do you understand?"

"Yes," Salim shouted back. "What about my son?"

"I'll take care of Yahiye. On the way home you've got to get rid of that ball. The longer you have it the more likely you are to die from the radiation. Drop it in a river or lake. "When you get home, take your clothes off and put them in a plastic garbage bag. Then take a half a dozen showers before you get dressed again. I'll bring Yahiye to your house tonight."

"Go tell him to come with me. Get the ball and disappear."

A minute later Salim had retrieved the ball and was heading out the front door and Yahiye was standing in front of Ihmad looking very scared.

"Come with me," Ihmad said sternly.

Without a word, he led him back to the employee's break room and threw him into a chair. "What you tell me in the next minute will decide the fate of your entire family. Do you understand?" Ihmad shouted.

"Yes, Mr. Ihmad." Yahiye said as tears started running down his cheeks, "I didn't mean to do anything wrong. I was just borrowing the ball so the kids wouldn't keep laughing at me. I wasn't going to keep it."

"Did your father ever tell you what we do to people who steal back home?" Ihmad asked.

"They get their hand chopped off," Yahiye answered as his lower lip began to quiver.

"Well today, I'm going to let you keep your hand," Ihmad said.

"Yes," Yahiye said smiling a little.

As the two were talking, Tony came running into the room. "There's some metal powder on twenty-two that's spreading all over the place. Grab the shop-vac over there. I'll get the..."

Before he finished the sentence, Ihmad pulled out a 9-mm automatic and shot him twice in the chest and once in the head. "Sorry Tony, I quit."

"Yahiye come with me," Ihmad said to the boy who was still holding his hands over his ears.

But the boy was frozen.

"I said, come with me," Ihmad repeated grabbing the boy around the waist and lifting him off the floor.

Running out the front door, Ihmad lowered Yahiye to the ground and began pulling him around the side of the building towards the parking lot in front of the building. Racing towards the car, Ihmad unlocked the doors with his remote, scooped up the boy and tossed him into the passenger seat.

"Now it's your turn to do something," Ihmad said handing him a second remote. "Press the panic button."

When Yahiye hesitated, Ihmad pulled out his gun and pointed it at the boy. "I said press the god damn panic button."

A second later, twenty feet of primacord split the gas main running along the back wall of the building. Ten seconds later two incendiary devices touched off the gas and the back third of the building collapsed.

Safely inside the car, Yahiye couldn't believe his eyes as he watched the windows explode sending a shower of broken glass into the air.

"Larry!" Yahiye screamed, as he watched his best friend scramble out of the smoking building.

"Guess your friend was born under a lucky star," Ihmad said starting the car.

Half an hour later, Ihmad walked back into his apartment and flipped on CNN. Shots from a dozen angles showed the building still burning as dozens of fire fighters poured water on the blaze and rescue workers loaded injured students and teachers into ambulances.

"See what can happen when you steal something," Ihmad said as he picked up the phone to tell Salim his son was alive and well.

Chapter 49
Overlap

After the Greenbriar incident, the Department of Homeland Security's top priority became figuring out how nuclear material from CERN had ended up at the bowling alley and how much was loose in America.

Early on, they discovered the radioactive material blowing around northwest Iraq had the same nuclear fingerprint as the stuff found at Greenbriar. Reexamining and piecing together information from the NRO spy satellites, Predator flyover, and SEAL recon, they decided it was time to deliver their findings to the President.

"Mr. President, I would like to present some of the background material before I go into the main points of the presentation," Dr. Cornelius said pausing to see if the Joint Chiefs were going to object. "The nuclear material we are dealing with undoubtedly came from CERN's experimental Plutonium Production Reactor, to which the United States contributes 25 million dollars a year."

"You mean we funded the material those 300 school students were exposed to?" the President said a little exasperated.

Dr. Cornelius cleared his throat. "Unfortunately, that is true, but it is because of that funding the Swiss have been so eager to work with us. So at this point, I would say it's a double edged sword. The big problem is that after careful examination of records all the plutonium from the PPR can be accounted for."

"How is that possible?" President Webber asked.

"Someone is lying, Mr. President." Cornelius stated.

"Duh-h-h, you think?" the Army Chief of Staff, William Walls, said.

Dr. Cornelius smiled. "Yeah. We're pretty sure we nailed that one," he said waiting for the snickering to die down. "Outside of sending inspection teams to every reactor in operation, there's no way to be sure what core materials are inside. However, a few possibilities come to mind. The first place terrorists would go looking for nuclear material is Russia. Ever since the Soviet Union dissolved, record keeping is all but non-existent. To make matters worse, they were still in the process of removing 500 tons of highly enriched uranium and 50 tons of plutonium from their weapons arsenal when the split occurred."

"Something we've already paid them $200 million to complete, Mr. President," the chair of the Congressional Oversight Committee said flipping though a binder to verify the number.

"Quite true," the doctor confirmed.

"But, you said the plutonium came from CERN," President Webber said.

"Yes, Mr. President. What I'm suggesting is that someone inside Russia may have acted as a broker for some kind of deal," Cornelius said.

"How would that work?" the President asked.

"Let's say, I'm a party interested in building a new reactor, like a developing country or a large university, investigating the advantages of plutonium powered electrical generation. Since I have all the official licenses and approvals required, I look around for some inexpensive plutonium and discover the people working on the PPR project in Switzerland are practically giving the stuff away. I write a check and buy enough to start. Then in the middle of the night, some guy from Russia calls with a swap offer. Says he's playing 'Let's Make A Deal'. An even swap of plutonium plus a huge pile of cash or a two for one deal with free shipping," Dr. Cornelius said pausing.

"You're talking like you're trading baseball cards," the chief of the Joint Chiefs interjected.

"It's getting closer to that every year," Cornelius countered. "Just for the sake of argument, let's pretend that happened. Now the terrorists have nuclear material from a neutral country, some place we're not going to bomb into oblivion, like we tried in Iraq. The terrorists know we'll figure out where the stuff came from, so they protect their homeland while they get ready to strike in America."

"Does the CIA have anything to say about that hypothesis?" President Webber asked.

"Not a peep out of the Russians, officially, sir. But there are rumors circulating about new money being pumped into the Ukrainian National Space Agency. It seems someone is interested in keeping their Sea Launch Complex up and running. Had a couple of hits from our facial identification boys in Mexico City on two terrorists slipping in, but they could never track them down. Might have been they're dealing drugs," General David Mulch responded.

Realizing he might have left something important out, Mulch continued. "Sorry, sir. INTERPOL passed us a piece of interesting Intel on a cat in Rio that died from radiation poisoning. Local authorities disposed of the carcass before we could get our hands on it. The old man that brought it into the vet's office is mourning the loss of his only daughter. So he only talked with our agent for a few minutes."

"How about our intermediaries in the State Department?" Webber asked Secretary of State Claire Cozen.

"Putin is too busy pushing his agenda to become Czar of the United Russian Party to worry about our problems. Besides, he enjoys sitting on top of his wells and watching us twist in the wind as the price of oil continues to climb. If he knows anything, you can bet he won't be telling us," Dr. Cozen answered.

President Webber leaned back in his chair and looked at the ceiling for a second. "Okay Dr. Cornelius; go on."

"From the reconnaissance data, it looks like the material was at the quarry in Iraq for about two months. In all probability, the material came out in a twenty-ton truck," Dr. Cornelius said showing some video of the truck along with the calculations used to determine the figures he was about to expound upon. "Reviewing data on the number of people in the truck, the amount of fuel, depth of tire tracks and degree of sway when cornering, we estimate about two to three thousand pounds of material were transported. Of course, that weight would include the weight of the shielding."

"What can they make with that much plutonium?" the President asked.

"Kind of depends on the purity and how clever they are. Critical mass for Pu-139 is ten kilograms or about twenty-two pounds, which is a sphere about four inches in diameter. So, if it is pure, they could create about a hundred self-sustaining reactions."

Bringing up some pictures of the Godiva device, Dr. Cornelius continued. "Here's a before picture of a piece of some nuclear material set up in a lab back in 1954. The apparatus was being used to investigate the effects of neutron reflection. Here's the same device after the material went super-critical."

"Looks like somebody put a cherry bomb in the thing," one of the analysts commented.

"Yes, not very dramatic, I'm afraid." Cornelius said. "The most spectacular thing reported by the scientists was a bright flash of blue light and some warming of skin."

"So what's the worst case scenario?" The President asked.

"There are two possibilities. First, that they will make eight to ten low-tech bombs, say twenty kilotons each. If they set them up in an overlapping circular pattern with a four mile radius between ground zero points, the resulting fire storm would wipe out a hundred-square-mile area - Washington, DC, for example," Dr. Cornelius said.

"Seems like more destruction than the two hundred kiloton blast would produce," the President said.

"On an empty piece of dirt, that would be true. But we're talking about a city filled with things that burn. Can you imagine the amount of gasoline alone that is sitting around in service stations and vehicles? Then there's the natural gas, jet fuel, tar, rubber, trees, lumber. The list goes on and on," Cornelius said waving his arms around.

"Okay, I get it. What's the second possibility?" President Webber asked.

"Mixing it with dirt and driving dump trucks along the highways would be insidious. Or they could start mailing the stuff out in envelopes like the anthrax incident. Maybe they'll just dump it in subway systems. The point is, there are a million ways to deliver the stuff once you have possession. Thus, the question: do you go for the big bang or the mass hysteria produced by a prolonged psychological campaign?" Cornelius concluded.

President Webber clasped his hands together and rested his chin on top of the two index fingers he extended. "I want the Chairman from the Joint Chiefs to answer my next question. If you had the material, what would you do with it?"

"I'd stick it right up Saddam Hussein's ass, Sir." Admiral Lance Cahill responded without thinking about it.

The President smiled. "Don't think that's an option, Admiral Cahill."

"Sorry Sir. That just kind of slipped out. If it was up to me, I would pick a handful of cities and touch off a bomb every week or two. That way, nobody would know how many I had or when they would stop. Probably hit Los Angeles first, during the Academy Awards next February. That way I'd have a great worldwide audience and the people on the west coast wouldn't feel exempt any more. You know, CNN would have a logo and lead in music up in fifteen minutes after the first bomb when off," Admiral Cahill said almost smiling.

"The FBI has been awfully quiet," President Webber stated in a plaintive tone. "Anything to add to the mix?"

"Unusually high activity on the web. ECHELON keeps issuing alerts, but nothing that hit the wall has stuck so far," Bert Quiver said.

"So what I'm hearing is, we're going to get nuked and nobody has any idea of who has the bombs or when they will strike?" the President said standing up. "I want you to get your god-damned asses working twenty-four-seven until you can come up with a little more than that."

With that, he whirled and strode out of the room with his staffers rushing to catch up with him. The President was not a happy camper.

Chapter 50
Amplification

When Ty wasn't handling emergencies stirred up by the ECHELON computer, he was romancing Sarah. He had even taken her along a couple of times when he practiced flying his jet model. But both of them got a little bored flying the thing around in circles.

Ty was putting his model in mothballs when Sarah came home for lunch while he was dismantling the wings. "Why are you taking your plane apart?" she asked.

"I don't know. Guess the novelty has worn off," Ty said.

"It is pretty boring flying it the way it works now. It would be a lot more fun if you let me yank out that stupid line of sight control system and install a satellite phone board in it," she said getting the mayonnaise out of the refrigerator to make some sandwiches.

"Sorry?" Ty said with a dumbfounded look on his face.

"Yeah, back in the day when I was taking some APT courses, I worked one of the first satellite phone systems. The project was really cool. It used LEO satellites that circled the globe every 70 or 90 minutes. The project went bust because the volume of subscribers never got above the breakeven point. I still have a couple of boxes of parts back at work," Sarah said carrying the sandwiches over to the kitchen table.

"I didn't know you worked on stuff like that," Ty said.

"It's not very exciting now. You see CNN using them all the time now. Back then it was state-of-the-art," she said, "just too damned expensive. Still costs about $10 a minute to use one of them."

"Guess I better stick with what I have now," Ty said carrying over two glasses of iced tea.

"Not a problem, if you want to switch. I still have a pile of $5,000 vouchers," Sarah said pouring a few chips on her plate.

"They can't be any good now," Ty said laughing a little.

"Sure they're good," Sarah said. "They're part of the deal that the buyout company made to get their hands on all the satellites and equipment for five cents on the dollar."

A week later, Sarah and Ty had converted the plane over to satellite control and even added intercom capabilities to the VR Glasses, so Ty could talk over the phone while he was flying.

For the initial flight, Ty took the reconfigured model to a park where he was familiar with the terrain. Tilting the VR glasses up over one eye, so he could get used to the delay introduced by the satellite he pushed the throttle forward. It took about a second between the time the plane moved and when he saw the motion in his glasses.

After flying around in a large circle, he relaxed and pulled the glasses down level. Now things heated up. The last thing he wanted to do was crash the plane, so he decided to try to land it on a long level area. Straightening the plane out so it was flying straight towards him, Ty eased the power back and watched the ground come up slowly as the plane got closer to him. Killing the engine, he heard the plane touch down to his left, while the video showed it was still a couple of inches off the ground. Lifting the goggles quickly, he watched the plane roll to a stop ten feet to his right.

Starting the plane up again, he made the plane fly a half circle, then pointed it in the direction of his apartment. After a few minutes of standing there looking like an idiot, he got tired and sat down on the grass. Ten minutes later he saw his apartment coming up and the plane wasn't going to have enough fuel to get back to the park.

"Shit," he said cutting back on the power and circling around to look for a place to land.

After ruling out landing in the parking lot or alley, the only thing that looked promising was the roof. "This isn't going to be easy," he thought.

Landing on the roof had pluses and minuses. On the plus side was the fact that there weren't any cars driving around or kids playing that could run over it or take it home as a souvenir. Another big plus was the fact that the roof was flat and about two hundred feet long.

The biggest minus was the one-second delay. If he flew in for a normal landing, he'd need to drop down quickly after clearing the brick facade that rose four feet above the roof on all sides. He doubted that he could land the plane there, even if he was standing on the roof watching it without the glasses.

Recalling how Charlie had stood the plane on its tail during the demonstration, Ty decided that was the only choice he had. Coming in slow, he pulled the plane up, cut back on the power and switched the plane's camera to a rear view. Watching the loose stones on top of the tar roof blow around he knew he was too close, so he goosed up the power a little and waited for the plane to respond.

Playing with the controls, Ty eventually had the plane hovering about ten feet above the roof. Easing the power back slowly he waited until he figured the plane was about two feet above the roof and cut the engine.

Turning into the driveway of his apartment complex, he was relieved to see that there were no police cars or fire trucks parked in front of his building. Pulling into his parking spot, he reached for his cell phone.

"Duke, I've got a problem," Ty said getting out of his car and leaning against the side.

"Didn't mess things up with Sarah, did you?" Duke asked.

"No, it's nothing to do with Sarah. Got a lot to tell you, but right now I need help getting my plane off the roof of my apartment building," Ty said.

"How the hell..." Duke began.

"Forget about that for now. Can you help me get the thing down?" Ty interrupted.

"Doesn't somebody there have a key to the roof?" Duke asked.

"The last thing I want to do is ask the manager for a key to the roof, so I can get my jet model down," Ty respond angrily.

"Okay. Okay, just a thought. Let me call Tom up. I'll get back to you," Duke said laughing.

"Okay, I'll be in the apartment, call my house phone," Ty said. "And thanks."

A few minutes later, Duke called back. "It looks like we're in luck. Come over to my house about nine and I'll take you for the ride of your life," Duke said.

"Okay, I'll bring a six pack." Ty said.

"Better make it a case," Duke responded. "Maybe two."

At nine, Ty pulled up to Duke's and rang the bell. Duke answered the door wearing his leather flight jacket. "If you don't have to take a leak, we've got to get going."

"I'm fine," Ty said a little confused. "Where are we going?"

"SOF is conducting a special training operation tonight and we're going along for the ride," Duke said walking towards Ty's Corvette.

Half an hour later, they were climbing aboard a specially equipped helicopter the SEAL team was using to practice urban warfare. A pod of

272

speakers above the main rotor blasted out inverted sound wave patterns that nullified the blade vortex interaction, the high speed impulsive noise and another thirty harmonics making it the quietest helicopter in the world.

Twenty minutes after taking off, Tom slipped through the maze of canvas partitions and sat down across from Duke and Ty. "We're going to be over your building in a minute. Have you ever handled a zip-line decent, Tyrone?"

"Are you crazy or what? I'm not zipping anywhere," Ty shouted back.

After the laughter from the SEAL team died down, Tom smiled. "Guess I'll have to do it then. Give me the keys to your apartment."

"You are the craziest bunch of guys in the world," Ty said fishing around in his pocket for the keys.

"Hoo-YAH," echoed through the chopper.

"You two can watch on the monitor," Tom said switching on an LCD display behind him and disappearing the way he had come.

"The guy's nuts," Ty said.

"Hoo-YAH," echoed through the chopper again.

"Better quit while you're ahead," Duke said laughing.

Suddenly the forward motion of the helicopter stopped and Ty could tell it was descending by the popping in his ears. When the chopper was about eighty feet above the building, they saw the rope drop to the roof. A second later, Tom slid into view as he rode the rope down using his Swiss seat harness. By the time his feet hit the roof and he unhooked, the other two SEALS were on their way down.

As the last man down retrieved the plane, Tom and the other SEAL attached claps to the brick façade, dropped some rope and slid over the side. When they each got a hand on the plane, they slid down in unison.

Once Tom was on the ground, he raced into the building with the model as his companion climbed back up to the roof. Two minutes later, Tom climbed back up and rejoined his team. Stepping onto the bottom rung of a rope ladder dangling down from the helicopter, Tom was lifted off the roof.

"You've got to do something about that dog of yours, Ty," Tom said coming around the partition a minute later.

"Damn thing nearly licked me to death."

"I thought she was a better judge of character," Duke said.

"They all go crazy for a man in a uniform," Ty said laughing.

When the mission was over an hour later, the men retired to a parking lot behind one of their favorite hangouts and polished off the two cases of beer Ty bought. Figuring they definitely needed more to drink, the team headed inside to relax and see if any quail had shown up looking for a good time.

"You coming in, Tom?" one of them yelled as they headed for the back door.

"I'll be right there," Tom said.

When the last SEAL walked through the door, Tom turned back to Duke and Ty. "Officially, you guys were never with us tonight. So if you go home and you're arrested for murder, don't expect to use us as an alibi. Understand?"

"What the hell are you talking about?" Duke said. "Ty and I have been here drinking for the past three hours. Right, Ty?"

"Absolutely! Virgin Mary's on the Rocks all night," Ty said holding back a laugh.

"Okay, now that that's over, how the hell did your plane end up on the roof?" Tom asked.

"Great story behind that! You know the models we got from Ajax?" Ty asked.

"Sure saw you fly one a few weeks ago," Tom said.

"The thing got pretty boring after awhile. So I asked myself why the novelty had worn off quickly. Then it came to me the freaking thing is so fast that you can only fly it for a minute before it's time to turn around and fly back before it gets out of range," Ty explained.

"Okay, what does that have to do with it landing on the roof of your apartment building?" Tom asked, again.

"Long story short - Sarah helped me hook it up to a satellite radio so I could fly it wherever I wanted to. No limits. The problem is if you fly it past the point of no return, you have to land someplace else," Ty said finally getting his point across.

Duke smiled and nodded his head. "So you were flying around and knew you couldn't get back. Decided to land on the roof of your apartment building. How the hell did you manage to land a jet model on a two hundred foot roof?"

"Remember the demo the guy's at Ajax put on for us?" Ty asked triumphantly.

"Sure. They flew the hell out of the plane that day," Duke responded.

"Well I just pulled the plane up into a vertical position and danced it along on its tail until it was a foot or two above the roof and then cut the power. Thing's made of carbon fibers, one quarter the weight and ten times the strength of steel," Ty said with a big grin on his face, "I want to retro-fit the planes you and Josh have, next time we go up to Delta Lake. That way we can fly the planes anywhere we want."

"That sounds like it would be a lot of fun," Duke said. Too bad, the things will only stay in the air for half an hour at full speed."

"I thought about that after I got home today," Ty said.

Then he and Duke said, "External Fuel Tanks," at the same time.

"I've got to hand it to your girlfriend, Ty. I think you have a winner there," Duke said. "Let's go celebrate."

Ty looked at his watch and shook his head. "Can't do it tonight, I've got an early meeting tomorrow. If Tom can take you home, I'll buy next time."

"Not a problem," Tom said. "I wanted to talk to Duke alone anyway."

When Ty drove away, Tom and Duke went into the bar and had a couple of beers with the team. After an hour of watching the youngest member of the team convince a sweet young thing at the bar to sneak out the back door with him, they decided they'd had enough entertainment and said goodnight.

As Tom started driving toward Duke's place, he reached over and turned the radio off. "Duke, how long have we known each other?"

"Ten, twelve years. Why?" Duke replied.

"Something I've wanted to talk to you about for the last couple of months," Tom said.

"I've heard that line before. Just do me a favor and skip all the crap about not telling anyone else. We've already been there and done that a hundred times before," Duke said.

"Yeah, guess if I can't trust you, I might as well quit looking. Anyway, a couple of months ago there was a SEAL recon mission in Iraq near Dubardan. Place was so hot they had to use rovers to scout the inside because of the radiation. The only thing inside was some grinding equipment and a bunch of dead workers," Tom said waiting for a reaction.

"So the Bush-man was right all along? They do have WMD capability," Duke said turning his back slightly to the door so he could watch the expression on Tom's face.

"Well if they did, it's gone now," Tom replied, looking at Duke for a second.

"If it took that long to find the stuff, how do you know somebody just didn't move it to another hidey-hole?" Duke asked.

"Intel finally pieced together enough to track it as far as Kuwait, and then it went cold. But there's more. A couple of days after the recon, a small team of Seabees went in to bury what was left and tripped a wire. Now the stuff is in the talcum powder they call sand over there," Tom answered.

"Come on, you're pulling my leg now. The President would have been all over the television bragging about being right, five minutes after they found the stuff," Duke said trying to rationalize why the story couldn't be true.

"Normally, but this time someone got to him before he could put his foot in his mouth, like he did on the Lincoln with the Mission Accomplished banner. Besides, by now, the stuff is so diluted, you could roll around in a tub of it all day and still live to be a hundred," Tom took a breath and pointed his finger at Duke.

"Think about the repercussions if it became public knowledge though. All the parents would be marching on Washington to get their kids out of the radioactive desert and half of the Joint Chiefs would be ready to attack Zurich. It's a no-win situation. So somebody with some brains stapled his mouth shut."

Duke reached over and gently took control of the steering with his left hand until Tom realized he had started drifting into another lane and started concentrating on driving again.

Chapter 51
Splitting Hairs

Ask an average American to describe an Iraqi terrorist and you'd walk away with the idea that they're all dumb as stumps, but that certainly wasn't the case when you reached Mohammed's level.

As the oldest son in a wealthy family, Mohammed enjoyed the good life in one of the richest countries in the Arab world before the Iran-Iraq War began. As a ten year old, the thing he liked most was attending school. With his quick mind and keen intellect, Mohammed was at the top of his class.

During that eight-year war, Mohammed's outlook changed as much as his homeland. Like most children, he was shaped by his environment and drawings of horses and sailboats turned to soldiers, tanks, and bullets flying through the air.

Halfway through his junior year of college, Iraq invaded Kuwait. The smack of reality the Gulf War inflicted on his psyche profoundly changed him for the worse. As a young adult living and studying abroad, his new focus was on learning the history, science, and philosophy required to destroy America.

With the DHS hell-bent on tracking down the nuclear material discovered on the New Jersey Turnpike and at Greenbriar's in Fort Myers, Virginia, Mohammed needed to do something to slow them down.

Recalling the work of George Miller, he decided the best way to do that was to give them more problems to solve. As his classroom experiments confirmed, the more problems you have to think about the slower you become. Hopefully, he could put the intelligence community into overload and they wouldn't be able to effectively concentrate on anything.

"Magic Seven" was the number he was shooting for, because that was the number Miller had confirmed in his research. The problem was Mohammed didn't really know what the DHS was currently working on and what they considered a crisis. But in the end he decided three more problems would be enough to push them over the edge.

There's an old saying that goes, "To a hammer everything looks like a nail." Mohammed naturally decided the best thing to start with was a Denial of Service attack on Washington. This would also give Fazul an opportunity to fly his prototype model around Washington and confirm the grid didn't depend on anything except the electricity running to the wireless transmitters. Besides, it was time to kick the Computer Emergency Readiness Team in the pants and tear them away from the hot cider and cinnamon donuts they spent the night wolfing down on Halloween.

Mohammed laughed when he opened the directory he had created back in 2004, remembering the havoc his MyDoom worm had caused on the web. At the time, the SCO Group and Microsoft had each offered a quarter of a million dollars for him. Now with the $10 million the American government had on his head, he thought the first two offers were a little low.

According to government figures, that worm had cost the world $39 billion and it had only run for twenty-four hours before the built-in timer shut it off. Today the net was a lot bigger and he was a lot smarter. After setting the start timer for 6 AM on October 31, Mohammed removed the stop timer, just to kick it up a notch.

He had first gotten the idea for his virus from studying DNA and how four nucleotides (A, T, G, and C) automatically fit together in a preset order. While the sixty-four program parts he created were no match for the three billion base pairs that make up the human genome, they were every bit as elegant.

The whole idea of his virus was for each tiny program to sneak into a computer, without being detected, and start making copies of itself that were included in outgoing emails.

While that was going on, each little program would be crawling around inside the computer looking for other parts of the puzzle that had arrived. When they met up they would combine and wait for other parts to arrive, the whole time still sending out copies of themselves.

Once all the numerous pieces were hooked together, the program was ready to take over. When the time came, Mohammed's program grabbed control of the CPU and dedicated itself to sending out as many emails as possible to the contacts stored in its email contact file. The beauty of the program was that once it started the only way to stop the emails was to disconnect it from the Internet. Turning the computer off just put the program to sleep. When it was powered back up, or the reboot routine finished, it simply began sending out emails again.

The only way to really get rid of the virus was to bring the computer up in a single user mode and either reformat or swap out the main drive. If the system administrators had religiously followed a backup protocol and tried to reload the disk, chances were the 64 pieces would reconnect and take over the machine again.

After Mohammed finished coding all the pieces, he launched the Task Manager on an isolated test computer and began loading in emails that each contained one of the 64 building blocks of his master program. As each email was received, the CPU usage jumped to four percent then settled back to the two percent it reported when nothing besides the operating system was running.

As the pieces began looking around inside the computer for each other, nothing unusual showed up on the graph, but a sharp twenty percent spike indicated that the final piece had been found and the program was ready. Still nothing to worry about as the transit time was less than a second. When the timer rang and woke the program up, the CPU jumped to two hundred percent and the Task Manager's windows froze. Mohammed smiled, knowing that the machines two CPUs were fully occupied sending out emails to /dev/null.

Now that the coding and testing phase was over, Mohammed had to install the virus in a single computer to get the whole thing started. So he loaded his creation into a USB flash drive and headed out to the Research Center to pay Dr. Ramadan a visit.

When he walked into the doctor's office unannounced, Ramadan had a flinch response that caused him to suck in a breath of air and his heart to begin beating a little faster.

"Well, I wasn't expecting to see you today," Ramadan managed as he got up to greet Mohammed.

"Yes, it's been awhile. How are things going on your end?" Mohammed asked as he looked around the office.

"Everything on my end is set. We've completed the clean up and are back to plain old everyday research. Nobody would ever suspect the bird flu came from here," Dr. Ramadan said.

"That's good to hear. You never know where the CIA will show up. I wouldn't want anything to happen to you. We've been together much too long." Mohammed said thinking about Halley more than usual. "I was hoping that you'd buy lunch before I left."

"Not a problem, my old friend." Ramadan said picking up the phone and making some arrangements. "It should be laid out in the dining room by the time we arrive. Just let me go to the bathroom before we leave."

"Okay. Do you mind if I check my email, while you're gone?" Mohammed said.

"Don't be so formal. You know you can do anything you want when you're here," Ramadan said walking out of the office.

By the time the doctor returned, Mohammed had uploaded the virus into half a dozen of the Research Center's computers and returned to his chair.

"Okay, all ready, my friend," Dr. Ramadan said poking his head back inside his office.

"Can't wait," Mohammed smiled.

Chapter 52
Lighter than Air

Mohammed was amused the first few days he watched CNN's 24-hour coverage of his virus attack, but after almost a month of watching the same old thing, he was getting bored. Since every other story highlighted the efforts of the United States Computer Emergency Response Team, he figured it wouldn't be long before they busted through the front doors of the Research Center and seized Dr. Ramadan's equipment.

If there was one thing Mohamed didn't trust, it was people and his next two bogus attacks depended heavily on the seven million Muslims living in America.

Together, the two plans required an individual investment of about six dollars. Rather small sums of money when you considered both were capable of crippling the United States for a few days. Their beauty lay in their simplicity and the fact that most of the parts were freely available in any fast food restaurant.

To get things rolling, Mohammed sent a box of a thousand twelve-inch aluminum foil sheets with a colorful Thanksgiving turkey printed on one side to each of the 1,200 mosques in America. A single sheet of instructions, that could be reproduced locally, accompanied each box.

The instruction sheet resembled a typical fifth-grade science worksheet with a list of the items and simple drawings that showed how to assemble the parts into the finished products. The items listed on the sheet consisted of: two twelve-inch plastic straws; two pieces of light-weight aluminum foil; one helium filled balloon; one packet of artificial sweetener; one Holiday Card (Christmas, Hanukkah, Kwanzaa, etc.); one postage stamp; and some adhesive tape.

Since people were less dependable than computers in Mohammed's world, he had little faith that either of his new ideas would do much harm to America, but he had done his part.

•••

Kettil and his family usually left for Jorgen's farm the weekend before Thanksgiving, but an emergency cropped up at Ericsson that looked like it might keep them in San Diego this year. But after pulling several all-nighters, Jorgen had solved late Wednesday afternoon and was headed towards the elevators when his PDA beeped. His first inclination was to just keep going, but since Jay was a friend as well as his boss, he turned around and headed back toward Jay's office.

"Hey, Kettil, I just wanted to thank you for pulling another one out of the fire for the team. After talking with Barbie, I upgraded your tickets and contacted limo services at both ends. Hope it helps get you to your family celebration before all the turkey is gone. Thanks again," Jay said handing him a printout of conformation numbers.

"Thanks, Jay. I really appreciate it. I'll have Barbie put a couple extra cookies in your Christmas basket this year," Kettil said smiling.

"Right, you say the same thing every year and I've never gotten a single extra cookie. Get out of here and grab some shuteye before the driver arrives," Jay said shaking his hand and patting him on the back.

Kettil took Jay's advice and jumped into bed after giving Barbie some suggestions on what to pack for him. The last thing he remembered saying was, "And make sure Kathy wears something warm. The weatherman says it's going to be a cold one this year."

By the time nine-thirty rolled around, all the bags were packed and sitting by the front door. When the doorbell rang, Barbie checked the security monitor, but before she reached the speaker button Kathy raced to the door and opened it. "Glad you got here a little early," She said. "Mom! Dad! The limo's here!"

"Great," Kettil said racing down the steps and grabbing two of the bags, "let me give you a hand."

"No need for that, Mr. Andersson," commented the driver.

"I know, but I need to make room for my sister-in-law's pumpkin pie."

"Must be a good cook," the driver said grabbing a couple of bags and walking out to the car with Kettil.

"Been married a long time?" the driver asked, to pass the time.

"Seems like forever. I have dreams about going to kindergarten with the lady," Kettil said picking up the last bag and setting the alarm.

"Out here, if you've only been married once you're classified as a saint. Sounds like you're one in a million, Mr. Andersson," the driver said heading out to the car with Barbie and Kathy walking behind him.

"A million what is the question," Kettil mumbled under his breath as he checked the lock and pulled the door closed.

When they got to the airport, the driver piled the bags up at the curbside check-in station. "Have a great Thanksgiving."

"You too," **Kettil said slipping** the driver two twenties.

"That's **already been taken care** of by your company," the driver said eyeing the **money**.

"Don't **worry, I won't tell** anyone if you don't," Kettil said slipping the money **into the driver's hand**, "thanks for getting us here in plenty of time to catch the plane."

After waiting **in line for ten** minutes the bags were banded and the tickets printed. **Putting his arms** around his two ladies, they headed off to the screening area.

"I thought **this place** would be empty by ten," Kathy said.

"One of the two busiest travel days of the year," Barbie said hoping Kettil caught the touch of her voice.

Half an hour later, the doors were pulled shut and the jet lumbered into the air towards Atlanta, four hours away. The women each had a glass of wine and talked for a few minutes before drifting off to sleep. Kettil on the other hand was wide awake, so he punched up a movie in the display on his seat and soon was oblivious to his surroundings. The movie was long over and Kettil fast asleep when the plane started its descent into Atlanta at 5 a.m.

"Please restore your trays and seats to their full upright position and check your seatbelts prior to landing," drifted into Kettil's jet black universe.

Looking over and smiling at what sleeping in a reclined position can do to a lady's hairdo, Kettil nudged Barbie. "You want to get breakfast when we land? There's about an hour layover."

"I need tea, desperately," Barbie moaned.

After a short makeover in the ladies' bathroom, they just had time for a chai tea before getting on the plane bound for Newark.

"Next time your boss screws with our vacation, tell him I'm coming over and kicking him square in the ass," Barbie said settling down into her window seat.

"I'm not sure that will help, but I'll pass the message on to Jay when we get home," Kettil said chuckling, "by the way, you need to put a few extra cookies in his basket this year."

"Look, we go through this every year. Everyone gets a dozen. The place I buy them from charges five dollars apiece for the damn things," Barbie said in full whine mode.

"No really, you need to add half a dozen this year. It cost him six grand to exchange the tickets and hire the limos. He did everything possible to help me out," Kettil said a little too loudly.

Barbie hadn't heard Kettil use that tone with her in a long time, but she knew an order when she heard it. "Okay, but tell him not to expect this every year," she said turning toward the window and closing her eyes.

"How about you Kathy? You ready to fight with Dad too?" Kettil asked, tossing a blanket across the aisle.

"No Daddy, I just want to get there and make sure Hunter and the twins are all right. In the beginning it seemed like a good idea to come out and get a little rest, but I've sure been missing them," Kathy said sadly.

"First time is always the hardest. I remember putting my hand on your back while you were sleeping, just to be sure you were still breathing. But you don't have anything to worry about. If Hunter has a problem, his mother or Aunt Janet will bail him out," Kettil said reassuringly.

"I know you're right, but I just want to get there and give each of them a hug, Dad."

"It's not going to be easy this year, Pumpkin. Have you thought about what you're going to say on Saturday when they spread Halley's ashes?" Kettil asked, softly.

"I really don't know. I've written down a hundred things, but none of them seem appropriate. It's been such a long time since she died, you'd think I'd be over it by now," Kathy said with tears beginning to swell up in her eyes.

Kettil reached across the aisle and held his daughter's hand. "It's never easy to saying goodbye to someone you love. I know you'll do fine when the time comes."

"Excuse me sir. I need to get by," the stewardess said politely.

"Sorry," Kathy said turning away from Kettil and pulling the blanket up around her shoulders, "I love you Daddy."

"I love you, too," Kettil whispered back, squeezing her hand.

At eight o'clock, as the plane crossed the North Carolina–Virginia border, 4 million helium filled balloons were released in the Eastern Standard Time Zone. Attached to the string of each balloon was a little square box made of drinking straws and aluminum foil.

Alternating sides of the box panels showed pictures of President George Webber and a colorful turkey with the inscription "Turkeys Can Too Fly..." under both.

The smaller boxes were attached to rubber balloons, which meant they would slowly climb to 30,000 feet before exploding. The larger aluminum boxes were attached to balloons made of Mylar plastic. These balloons had a much shorter life expectancy, springing a slow leak at 6,000 feet and settling back to earth.

Since they were put together by grade school students who were told to vary the sizes, no two were exactly alike, which suited their designer perfectly.

Unfortunately, for Kettil and the thousands of other airline passengers, the little boxes were exactly the right size to bounce back short and long distance radar signals. That began fogging up the readouts, when they reached a few hundred feet.

Before anyone actually figured out what was going on, an executive order was issued through the FAA to ground all planes immediately. So Kettil and his family found themselves landing at Philadelphia International Airport instead of Newark.

Sitting inside his hotel room in Jakarta, Mohammed watched CNN impatiently until they spun up the story about a minute after the order went out. "Yes!" he exclaimed, standing up and clapping his hands.

Now America had another problem to deal with besides the nuclear material and the internet virus.

Chapter 53
Ashes to Ashes

Instead of arguing about how many points to give each other on the football games after breakfast, like they did other years, all the men and kids were gathered around Jorgen's television in the living room watching CNN coverage of the balloon attack. When a second barrage of balloons floated up from the Central Time Zone at eight a.m. local time, President Webber ordered the grounding of all commercial aircraft until further notice.

On a normal day that would have been a serious blow to America, but on Thanksgiving it was catastrophic. And CNN was there following each heartbreaking story of families stranded far from home, many without the resources available to survive more than a couple of days before their money ran out. Of course, everyone knew it was a terrorists attack, but couldn't figure out who the terrorists were or how they had organized such a clever plan.

When the first radar reflector drifted down from the sky, a local teenager snapped a couple of digital pictures of it and sent it in via the 'I Report' website. Two minutes after CNN received the photos, the graphics department snapped together a logo and added a lead-in stinger and waited for the commercial break to end.

A 'Breaking News' banner scrolled across the screen bottom on Jorgen's television "CNN has just received photos of one of the balloons sent in by an I-Reporter in Crystal Lake, New Jersey," a voice said as a photo of a ruptured plastic "Happy Birthday" balloon flashed up on the screen. "Not much of a Happy Birthday for America," the male reporter said.

"Certainly not," his female counterpart interjected. "Today is as far from happy as you can get."

"I think Kettil would be able to argue that point," Petter said.

"Think you're right on that point," Jorgen said looking around for one of his sons, "Jason, how about getting me another cup of coffee? And put a little more milk in it this time. Thanks."

"Oh, Dad," Jason said jumping up and grabbing his father's cup. "Anybody else?"

"I'll take some too," Petter said holding his cup out.

On the television the picture of the colorful turkey popped up looking very festive.

"I didn't think turkeys could fly," Jorgen's youngest daughter, Jeannie said looking up at her father.

"They can't," Jorgen confirmed.

"Not any more than good old George W can," Petter responded, when the next photo came up on the screen. "But he certainly was a turkey."

"Who's the President of the United States?" Jorgen shouted.

"George Webber, God help us," all the Andersson children replied at once.

"I kind of like that one," Jorgen said laughing.

"Now we're switching over to Brenda Todd-Snodgrass, who's with Professor Glen Hollingsworth at Princeton's Applied Physics Laboratory," the news anchor said.

"Yes, Larry. I'm here with Professor Hollingsworth. Professor what can you tell us after looking at the photos of the recovered balloon?"

"Well, the perspective doesn't allow for accurate analysis, but having bought a balloon very similar to the one in the picture for my ten year old niece, I'd say the aluminum reflectors it's attached to are about a foot square," the professor said taking another look at the picture.

"And what's significant about that?" Brenda asked.

The professor looked up as if she had just asked him why rain falls to the ground. "Perfectly obvious, isn't it? The L-Band radar used to insure proper spacing in the air traffic corridors between airports operates at one to two gigahertz." Seeing a blank look on the reporter's face he continued. "That makes the wave length six to twelve inches."

Brenda's brain churned away at full speed. "So what you are saying is that reflector is perfect for bouncing back radar used to control aircraft?"

The professor lowered his expectations significantly and began again. "You are correct. There are two different types of radar used to control aircraft, L-Band for long distances and S-Band for short distances. The reflector in the picture looks like it was designed to reflect the L-Band radar. Since S-Band was also knocked out, there must be other balloons carrying smaller cubes."

The light dimly flickered in Brenda's eyes before it went out and she returned control back to the anchor at CNN.

Jorgen's focus shifted back to the family room and he immediately realized that he still didn't have his coffee and that Jeannie had crawled up into his lap. "Jason, coffee!" he yelled towards the kitchen.

"Daddy, is it bad to tell a secret?" Jeannie asked quietly.

"Depends, Pumpkin. What kind of secret is it?"

"It's about the balloon in the picture," Jeannie said pulling her dad's arm down around her.

"What about it?" Jorgen asked, deciding that he wasn't going to be getting his coffee any time soon.

"Two of the girls in ballet were talking about letting balloons go today for some kind of celebration," Jennie said. "One of them even showed the aluminum turkey, like the one on TV."

"Are you sure?" Jorgen asked. "I've seen a lot of turkeys around town that look like the one on the television"

Jennie turned around on her father's lap so she could look at him. "How many had Turkey's Can Too Fly printed on them?"

"Well then, I better look into it, Sweetie," Jorgen said. "Let Daddy go get his coffee."

"Okay, but I'm not in trouble, am I?" Jennie asked, with a troubled look on her face.

"No way, you're my best girl aren't you?"

"I hope so," Jennie said smiling again.

"Okay then, let me get my coffee," Jorgen said as he got up and put her back in the chair.

"It looks like we're going to have to get our own coffee, Petter," Jorgen said motioning for his brother to come with him.

As they walked to the kitchen, he told Petter what Jeannie had told him.

"Better at least call the police," Petter said.

When they walked into the kitchen, Janette was on the phone and the other ladies were each busy slicing up vegetables.

"Great!... Yes, terrible isn't it... How'd you manage that... Okay, see you all then," Janet said hanging up the phone in the kitchen, "thank God, they'll be here in an hour. Kettil's taking a cab from Philadelphia. That's going to cost him plenty," Janet announced, before returning to her cooking.

"If I know Kettil, it's his boss who will be picking up the tab on that one," Petter said relieved that his brother wasn't stuck in one of the airports profiled on the news.

"That's a load off my mind," Haiwei said looking up from the bowl of potatoes she was peeling. "Kathy will be here in time for Halley's ceremony. Somehow I think those two are still connected."

Picking up the phone, Jorgen dialed the non-emergency number for the Freehold Township police. "Yes, I thought it might be a good idea to call in and report what my daughter said about the balloons. Yes. Yes. Okay. Thanks."

Jorgen turned to Petter with a surprised look on his face. "It seems half the kids in town know somebody that launched a balloon this morning, some kind of celebration ceremony."

"That's really strange," Petter said scratching his head.

When Kettil's family arrived, Kathy ran to Haiwei, giving her a big squeeze and bursting into tears. "I really miss Halley," she managed to get out between sobs.

"Yes we all miss her, but she's up there smiling down on us. So don't be sad. Besides, Hunter is waiting for you in the family room. Don't want to wait too long to rescue him from the twins."

"I know he's been taking good care of them," Kathy said scampering out of the room, "but I'd better check, just to make sure."

After giving up hope that any of the football games were actually going to be played, the three brothers left Kathy and Hunter cuddling on the couch and retreated to the basement.

"Whoever orchestrated that balloon attack was a genius." Kettil said feeling his shirt pocket absentmindedly for a pack of cigarettes, "First it was box cutters, now balloons. What the hell are they going to come up with next?"

Watching his brother, Petter smiled. "I thought you said you had quit smoking."

"Give me a break, will you," Kettil said. "It's just dumb luck that we even got here. If Jay hadn't changed the tickets, I'd be stuck in Chicago, along with ten thousand other passengers, all trying to find a non-existent room."

"Okay. Take it easy. I think we better sneak out and get your nicotine levels back up a notch or two," Petter said making a face at Jorgen, "Sorry."

"You two go enjoy yourselves. I'm going to see how the girls are doing with the dips and chips. They've got to have something ready to munch on by now."

"Grab some pretzels, if you can. We'll be out by my car," Petter said heading out the back door, "what's really bothering you? I thought you were addicted to adrenalin."

"Don't get me wrong, I love to put myself in situations that carry some kind of risk, like skiing down black diamond trails and parasailing, but it's getting so you don't know where these guys are coming from. Hell the next thing you know, they'll be jumping out of cereal boxes with razor blades," Kettil said lighting up his first cigarette of the day.

"It is getting kind of spooky. Kind of like those white rats in the lab that get random shocks. Poor bastards go crazy after awhile," Petter said. "You've got to learn to relax a little. Besides think of all the nifty things the government will be asking us to build for them. Next year's bonus could float into the six figure range."

"Money's not going to do us much good if this keeps up. Pretty soon it'll cost a hundred bucks just to fill our gas tanks. If Webber has his way, half of the freaking grain is going to be turned into alcohol, which means food prices will spiral out of control. And everyone, but him, knows there's not enough power in alcohol to muster up a healthy fart. Where is it all going to end?" Kettil said looking up at the balloons floating across the sky.

"I don't know, but one thing's for sure, it not going to be boring."

By four o'clock the turkeys were sliced up and dropped into the aluminum warming trays next to the mashed potatoes, and everyone was called to the main table for the blessing.

"Bless us, O Lord, for these thy gifts, which we are about to share through Christ our Lord. And bless Halley who was taken from us. Grant her peace in your loving kindness. Also, bless and protect all the people stranded in the airports and help them to remember that through you all things are possible. We ask this in Jesus' name. Amen," Janet said.

After the customary Amen from the kids, they bounded off toward the food like little rabbits.

"Take it easy, I promise there's more than enough for everybody," Janet yelled to no avail.

By the time the last adults had fixed their plate, the older kids were lining up for seconds. An hour and a half later even Kettil couldn't force down another bite.

"Looks like a good time to walk some of this off," Petter said winking at Haiwei. "Why don't we all mosey up to the hill and say goodbye to Halley, before we start in on the dessert."

"If that's all right with everyone, I'll get the box," Haiwei said standing up.

A few minutes later she and Petter appeared at the back door and began walking towards a small hill ringed with Tiki torches where the rest of the family had assembled. Walking slowly up a path with the box of Halley's ashes in her hands, Haiwei smiled when she saw the lake on the other side.

"I don't want to make this a morbid occasion," Haiwei said. "But you'll have to excuse me if I start to cry. The tears aren't for the loss of Halley, as much as they are joyful remembrances of the happy pictures of her playing here as a child."

Motioning for Kathy to join her, she continued. "I still remember all the times Halley and Kathy swam in that lake and them sitting bareback on horses, trying not to slip off when the horses bent down to take a drink."

As she paused to take gather her thoughts, a line of flashing police cars escorting two mobile labs from the CDC pulled into the driveway and paused next to the farmhouse. An officer got out of the lead car then jumped back inside and the caravan proceeded to the hill.

"This is a police emergency. Please remain calm. Stay where you are and wait for the technicians."

Jorgen looked at Haiwei, then down at Jeannie. "Is there anything you forgot to tell me?"

"No Daddy. Honest," Jeannie said pushing closer to her father.

When the technicians dressed in hazmat suits, started walking up the hill without the police, everyone knew that something serious was happening.

"Which one of you is Haiwei Andersson?" one of the suited figures asked.

"I am," Haiwei said stepping forward.

"Hello, I'm Dr. Albright from the CDC. Do you recognize the man in this photo?" Dr. Albright asked, holding a flashlight on the picture.

"Yes. That's Dr. Imad. From Jakarta." Haiwei said taking the photo in her hand, "he's the one that brought Halley's ashes to me in the hotel."

"And these two?" Albright asked.

"That's that stupid lady with the dog. So that must be the driver that picked me up at the airport, when I got back," Haiwei said with a puzzled look on her face.

"The man in the first picture is really Ramadan. Dr. Ramadan. He ran a biological research center south of Jakarta. And we have every reason to believe that the box you are holding contains an extremely virulent form of the H5N1 bird flu. May I please have the box?"

"Are you going to take it away?" Haiwei asked, still unable to believe what was going on.

"It depends on what we find when it's tested. If it's not dangerous, I promise to bring it right back to you," Dr. Albright said holding out her hands.

Nobody said a word until Albright and the box disappeared inside the truck. Then Petter spoke. "What the hell is going on?

"I haven't got a clue," Haiwei said with a blank look on her face.

Jeannie pulled on Jorgen's coat sleeve. "Is this about the balloons, Daddy?"

"No baby. It's not about the balloons. Try not to worry about it," Jorgen said.

"Why do they have Halley's box?" Jeannie asked.

"They just want to be sure she's really in there. You know like a magic trick. Remember how good she was at playing hide and seek?"

"Sure, Dad. She was the best. Is she playing a trick on us again?" Jeannie asked, looking up at her father with innocent eyes.

"We'll just have to wait and see, baby. We'll just have to wait."

Inside the lab, Dr. Albright put the box into an isolation chamber then raised the protective lead shield and switched on the X-ray machine. Watching the contents carefully, she rotated the box and watched what looked like normal ashes tumble around inside.

"Don't know what that proves, but it looks pretty normal," she said to the tech who had accompanied her up the hill.

Drilling a small hole in the center she extracted some powder and dropped it into a mass-spectrograph. "Graph looks normal too."

Finally, Dr. Albright retrieved another sample, hydrated it, and dropped it into the strip-test she had developed for the sample from the Research Center. "Negative. Damn. Looks like Haiwei had the ashes from a cremated body all right. What the hell happened to the rest of the virus?"

Before the trailer door opened, the police cars turned off their flashing lights and started to pull away.

"That looks like a good sign," Petter said.

Then the lab door opened and Dr. Albright carried the box back up the hill and handed it back to Haiwei. "Sorry for all the fuss. But I really thought you had been tricked into bringing back something that could have killed half the planet. Sorry for the interruption."

Chapter 54
Dust to Dust

Ironically, Mohammed's final diversionary attack made its first appearance in Jackson, New Jersey, where trace amounts of anthrax had shown up during the Amerithrax mail attacks in 2001-02. The cleanup of government buildings was estimated to be $2 billion, but big business had spent ten times that amount instituting security procedures to protect themselves and their employees. Knowing that the United States Postal Service was still a bit touchy about powder in the mail, Mohammed figured it would be a good button to push as he worked to draw attention away from Fazul's work in Occoquan.

•••

Seeing the technicians called in to fix the broken zip code scanner were still tinkering with the unit, Postmaster Reed Meadows came over to have a look at their progress. "How long is it going to take the two of you to get that thing back together?"

"Another ten minutes," Ed said looking up.

"Hey Reed, sorter three just went down," one of the other workers yelled, as the machine became quiet. "It's jammed good this time."

After walking over, Ed opened the case and tugged on an envelope that was wedged into one of the tracks. There was a tearing sound followed by a little puff of white smoke that followed the envelope out of the machine towards his face. Before he realized what was happening, he sucked some of the powder into his mouth.

"What the hell," he said as he began coughing.

"You all right, boss?" the other tech asked, patting him on the back a couple of times.

Catching his breath, Ed began laughing. "Sweetener," he said reaching into the envelope and pulling out a torn packet, "I've been using this stuff for the past ten years. Still leaves a bitter taste in my mouth."

Reed grabbed the envelope and looked at the address. "It looks like someone wishes President Webber would lose a few pounds next year."

•••

As far as Mohammed was concerned, the holiday mail campaign had been the easiest to pull off. Originally, he had thought he would have to hack into a couple thousand blogs and stir up some interest in bugging

294

the President, but after talking up the idea of smaller government is better government, the college crowd picked up the ball and began running with it. Once the anti-war groups joined the parade, Mohammed let go of the reigns.

As Christmas approached, the nightly news programs began graphing the extraordinary amount of mail received at the White House. Even though most of it was being held at regional sorting offices, it was still clogging up the system and slowing mail delivery on an average of four to five business days.

The post office wasn't alone in trying to keep up with the demand. Since all the government agencies were still in the process of trying to track down the nuclear material, bird flu, and culprit behind the internet debacle, every agent had been required to pull double shifts since mid-September. Those agents with enough time to retire put in their papers, while agents who weren't fully vested just up and quit.

To help stem the tide of departing agents, the government instituted an incentive program, promising large bonuses and years added to employee's net credited service for anyone that stayed an extra year. But attrition was still setting new records.

Another program began actively recruiting college students receiving their diplomas at the end of the fall semester. But despite all their enticements the ranks in the intelligence community were dwindling. This fact didn't escape the President or the reporters at CNN, who seemed bent on seeing how high they could raise the stress levels in America.

In Jakarta, Mohammed smiled as he watched the reports in his room with Ramadan. "This is going better than I ever dreamed. The Americans are wound up tighter than a drum."

"That's easy for you to say," Ramadan replied, as he relaxed on the couch. "You didn't have to give up anything. Ten years of research was destroyed when you incinerated my lab."

"Stop whining, you should be happy you finally made the breakthrough you've been working on for all these years."

Ramadan smirked. "Still the CDC has been playing with that sample for weeks now. What if they discover some kind of cure?"

Mohammed looked Ramadan directly in the eye. "Then you should worry, because they already know that who created it."

Chapter 55
Empty Shell

It took six weeks, but the Computer Emergency Readiness Team finally traced the first occurrence of the computer virus back to the lab near Jakarta. After a little political arm-twisting, a team of agents and scientist from the United States was reluctantly allowed to accompany the local authorities when they raided the complex.

The American team consisted of: Castanet from the CIA; Creedmoor and Johnson from CERT, and Dr. Madelyn Albright. Of the four, only Albright had insisted on coming because one of the things mentioned in the center's charter was the study variants that led to the 1918 pandemic. Since Albright had done her doctoral paper on the pandemic, she wanted to know if Dr. Ramadan had discovered anything new.

As for the other three, Castanet didn't ask questions, merely going where he was sent and hoping he'd still be alive to collect his pension ten years from now when he retired. Creedmoor and Johnson, on the other hand, wouldn't have been here at all, except for their constant bragging about how good they were. So, partly to get rid of them for a couple of weeks, and mostly to see if they were really as good as they claimed to be, their boss didn't hesitate when asked who he wanted to send.

At 6 a.m., as a small caravan of vehicles made their way up the road towards the main gate, tension built inside the truck carrying the American team.

"First time you two have been on an investigative team?" Castanet asked Johnson.

"Certainly not, we've been on dozens. Just never thought we'd get a crack at catching the author of MyDoom," Creedmoor said tapping out the beat to a tune on his IPod.

"Guy's kind of a legend. This time he's going down as the only hacker who actually brought the entire Internet down. Ghosts from that last virus will be popping up for years," Johnson said in awe of the whole situation. "It's just that we usually walk into an office building with a couple of cops, not half the freaking army."

"Well when you play with the big boys, things get a little dicey. They did give you two Kevlar to wear, didn't they?" Castanet said looking out the window to conceal his smile.

The convoy rounded the last turn and slowed to a stop at the main gate. Castanet watched through the windshield as the captain in charge of the operation got out of his car and walked inside the small guard shack. A minute later he returned, raised the barricade manually, and climbed back inside his car.

"That looks a little strange," Castanet said reaching inside his jacket and grabbing his automatic.

"What the hell are you going to do with that?" Creedmoor shouted, ripping his earphones out and sticking his head out the side of the truck to see what was going on.

"No guards," Castanet said racking a round, "I never like the unexpected."

When the vehicles stopped in front of the main building, Castanet jumped out. "Wake the lady up and stay in here for awhile. I'll be right back."

A minute later he was standing alongside the captain, "What do you think?" Castanet asked.

"Might as well go in," the captain said pulling the door handle.

As the door swung open, a thin cloud of white powder and smoke drifted out of the building.

"Poison gas," the captain screamed, turning to run away.

"Not likely," Castanet said crouching down to get a better look inside, "it smells too metallic. Better get somebody here with some ventilation equipment."

By noon, the air in the main building had been replaced and the investigative team was allowed inside. The first thing they noticed was that the inside of the building was completely empty.

"Looks like the inside of a crematorium," Dr. Albright said examining a small piece of metal she pried off the cement floor, "from the looks of things, I'd say the whole place was bathed in oxygen before it was touched off."

A technician ran over to the group holding a couple of printouts. "Environmental-bots show the same thing in all the sub-levels, but it will take a day or two before we can get you down there. This place is huge."

"Think you can round up four air-packs?" Castanet asked. "From the pictures, it doesn't look like anything could have lived through this inferno."

"I'll see what I can do, but remember, if you get hurt down there no one's coming to drag you out," the tech said.

"Understood," Castanet said waiting for the technician to leave," I think we should get down as soon as possible, don't you, Dr. Albright?"

"I agree. You never want to be the second person to a scavenger hunt."

An hour later, Castanet led the others down through a white haze to sub-level one. "You two computer whizzes keep track of where we are on the blueprints. And remember, we only have another hour of air. Who's keeping track of that?"

"I am," Johnson said shining a flashlight on his watch, "this kind of reminds me of spelunking in Pennsylvania when I was a kid."

"Figures you'd be down in some hole, chasing creepy-crawlers around," Creedmoor said tripping over a piece of metal sticking out of the floor.

Going through the opening where electronically-controlled doors once stood, Castanet spotted part of a hinge that still clung to the cement. "Looks like some bits survived."

"Follow the ginger bread," Dr. Albright said.

After looking around the first sub-level they located steps leading down to the lower floor and began finding equipment they could actually recognize.

"Not so bad down here," Creedmoor said brushing white ash off the top of a rack of servers, "if there's another level, I might even find a computer that's not char-broiled."

"According to the blueprints this is the bottom," Johnson said shining his flashlight over the diagram.

"Don't believe everything you read, kid", Castanet said shining his light though a crack in one of the walls, "how's that for beginner's luck, Doctor."

"It a cinch nobody would have found it without the smoke. Now the question is how are we going to get inside?" Madelyn opened her backpack and fishing around inside.

Knowing the good doctor wouldn't have plunged into her bag without a good reason, Castanet stood there to see what she was up to.

"What do you think? Left, right, or slider?" Albright asked, tracing the outline of smoke streaming into the room.

"Crapshoot from what I can see," Castanet replied.

"Sixty-eight percent of doors open to the right." Creedmoor announced.

Castanet smiled. "The kid says 'right'."

"Hope he's correct. I've only got one bottle of this stuff," she said sliding three paper-thin pieces of wet brownish plastic into the line on the wall, "time to get out of here and let Mother Nature do her work."

The group moved around the corner and Johnson checked his watch. "Down to forty-five minutes."

"That's cutting it pretty close. How fast do you think we can get out of here?" Castanet asked.

"We're lab rats. If we can't get out of here in ten minutes we don't belong in the gene pool," Creedmoor shouted and pounded the wall with his fist.

A split-second later, the concoction exploded, followed by a loud thud. "Sounds like Mother's done," Albright said walking back around the corner.

Creedmoor found an electric panel and started flipping switches, like a madman. Seconds later the hum from an exhaust fan could be heard and smoke began disappearing into ceiling vents. As the room cleared a fully functional bio-lab appeared before them. Clicking the last few switches turned on the computers and emergency lighting.

"Not bad, for a geek," Castanet said taking it all in.

While Creedmoor and Johnson started downloading the drives into the specially built memory sticks, Castanet followed Albright around as she poked her nose into every drawer and storage bin.

"Nothing here is worth all the trouble that went into building this place," the doctor said sounding a little disappointed.

"Can't be true, Doc. Nobody dumps money into a lab like this, just for show," Castanet said jumping up on a table and pushing on the ceiling tiles, which didn't budge.

Jumping back down, Castanet continued his search for something unusual, but wasn't having much luck.

Johnson, busy downloading another computer, suddenly stopped when he found a bunch of files that someone had saved two days ago. "Hey doc, over here."

"Find something interesting?" she said walking over.

This system has more security on it than the CIA's flying saucer."

When he heard that, Creedmoor came running. "Let me see that."

"Before you start fiddling with that, how'd you find out about our saucer?" Castanet asked.

"What?" Johnson asked, just before being poked in the ribs by his buddy.

"He's pulling your leg. Say, that's interesting," Creedmoor said pointing to a diagram of a cryogenic freezer that should have been standing in the corner at the far end of the room, "let me sit down for a second."

As Creedmoor typed away trying to break into the freezer's control program, Johnson ran to the corner and bent down to examine the floor. "Something was here. There are four little circles where the thing sat."

"Yes! Creedmoor shouted when he finally gained access.

Fortunately for Johnson, Castanet was close enough to pull him out of the way when the ceiling opened up and the freezer unit was lowered quickly to the floor by two massive hydraulic arms.

"That thing must weigh a ton," Johnson said realizing how close he had come to being squashed like a bug, "thanks, man!"

Inside the unit, a small crystal vial containing a few grams of white powder sat suspended in bubbling liquid hydrogen. Dr. Albright walked over and studied the apparatus for a few seconds. "Now this looks like what I came for," she said opening the unit and pulling the transportation unit out of the freezer.

"You sure you want to do that?" Castanet asked, backing up a little.

"I'm pretty sure. We've got similar units back at the lab in Atlanta. These things usually have a shelf-life of about six hours," the doctor said slipping the unit into a special compartment in her bag, "now all you have to do is get me past the guards with this thing."

"Were you two ever on the track team?" Castanet asked Creedmoor and Johnson.

The geniuses both looked up at the same time with a puzzled look on their faces. "What?" they both responded at the same time.

"If you weren't, you probably aren't going to be in the gene pool much longer," Castanet said pointing at a bright red digital clock that had just popped up on the computer's master display.

Before anyone could say a thing, warning blasts from loud speakers began keeping time with the clock as it counted down from ten minutes towards zero.

"Okay, boys and girls, it's time to leave," Castanet screamed over the din.

Nine minutes later the investigative team raced out the front doors of the research center screaming "Go, go, go."

Initially everyone outside was taken by surprise, as they watched the four maniacs jump into their truck and peel away. A few seconds later, a dull thud shook the ground and everyone got the idea that leaving was probably not such a bad idea.

As everyone scrambled to a vehicle, the rumblings got closer and louder. Unfortunately, the last truck was backing up to turn around when the last blast blew the entire front of the building into the air, burying the vehicle and its occupants under tons of rubble.

Chapter 56
The Infamous Level Five

Standing in front of the robotic isolation chamber on Level Four at the CDC Laboratory in Atlanta, Dr. Albright manipulated the robotic arms and removed the crystal vial from the liquid nitrogen. Securing the vial in an insulated rack, Madelyn snapped off the tip and withdrew a small sample before sliding the rack back into the cryogenic freezer. Examining the powder under an optical microscope and seeing nothing especially noteworthy, she re-hydrated the sample and prepared the Standard and Quick tests for H5N1.

Dr. Albright hoped the sample would test positive for H5N1, so she could move to the Level Three protocol and get out of the positive pressure suit that had always made her a little claustrophobic. Still, protocol demanded that all unknown material must start here until classified and experience had taught her it was better to be safe than sorry.

She wasn't sure if it was the way the sample had been hidden away in Jakarta or her post-doctorate work on the 1918 Spanish Flu pandemic, but the sample definitely had her spooked. While she waited the thirty minutes for the Quick Test results, she scanned though the computer files on the virus.

Everyone in her field knew that over the past 400 years there had been twelve pandemic outbreaks, and that there were two minor outbreaks for every major one. The last major outbreak was the Spanish flu in 1918. Since then two minor outbreaks had occurred: the Asian flu (H2N2) in 1957 that killed one-and-a-half million people; and the Hong Kong flu (H3N2) in 1968 that killed a million.

The Spanish flu of 1918 (H1N1) with a Case Fatality Rate of twenty percent and the Clinical Attack Rate of twenty-five percent, for every 100 people on the planet the Spanish flu killed five. Back then the world population was a measly one point six billion which meant that 80 million died from the disease. Holding everything else constant and adjusting for today's population, approaching seven billion, and three hundred fifty million would die.

The trouble was that everything had changed because of international air travel, the virus that took six weeks to spread from the United States to Europe and Africa in 1918, and three weeks to spread

302

from Hong Kong to the United Kingdom, would spread from the United States to Europe in a matter of hours.

Normally, there were three waves of flu related deaths. The initial wave would produce death rates only slightly above those normally attributed to the annual flu strains that swept the world. Five times as many people would die when the second wave hit. And the third wave would kill about twice as many as the first. With the period between waves lasting from three to nine months, there would be just enough time to manufacture a vaccine using conventional chicken embryo techniques under optimal conditions.

If the vaccine was developed and the United States obtained its usual ninety million doses, the President would have to decide which ninety million Americans would receive the shots. But in a bidding war with the world, exactly how many doses the United States would get was uncertain.

Thirty minutes later, the timer went off and Madelyn checked the results, which were negative. "Damn. Okay, my little chickadee, what are you?"

After preparing a slide for the optical microscope and finding nothing unusual, Dr. Albright began the arduous task of separating and coating a sample of the virus with platinum to make the transparent biological material visible under the electron microscope. Initial shadowing with enhanced computer overlay showed a virus with a five-fold axis with a five-pointed star abstractly visible on the computer display.

Knowing that it would take weeks to run enough tests to know what potential was locked inside the virus, Dr. Albright pressed the intercom. "Clatter, if you're there, I need four pairs of animals loaded into the exposure chamber," she said flipping on the monitor.

"Yes, Dr. Albright."

"Let me have chicks, piglets, ferrets, and chimpanzees," she said watching Clatter get up from his chair and walk toward the nursery interlock.

"Okay. Do you have any preferences on the age of the ferrets and chimpanzees?" Clatter asked,

"Not really," Albright answered.

"This is going to take awhile. I'll buzz you when they're set up," Clatter said.

303

After entering the air lock, Clatter scrubbed in much like he was going to perform surgery and climbed into a sterile jumpsuit before entering the animal housing complex. Like most research centers, the CDC had spent millions insuring that the animals were healthy and hadn't been exposed to anything that would produce antibodies in their blood. Outside the monotony of living in isolation, the animals enjoyed an idyllic life until their number came up and they were selected as the subject for an experiment.

With no more guilt than a farmer selecting a couple of chickens for dinner, Clatter walked down the rows of animal containers selecting the animals Dr. Albright had requested. He knew that once Albright had satisfied her intellectual curiosity, the animals would be frozen and shipped off to be incinerated, but he had stopped worrying about that long ago.

The intercom buzzed. "The animals are ready, Dr. Albright."

"Thanks, Clatter."

"Commencing the first exposure test at zero-two-thirty," Madelyn said checking the video equipment to be sure everything was running correctly.

Introducing a small amount of atomized virus into the chamber, she watched the animals for few minutes. Seeing no change in their behavior, Madelyn followed the decontamination steps and went to her office.

Protocol demanded that she notify the World Health Organization, but Madelyn still had a few hours of wiggle room before that became mandatory. Kicking off her shoes, she reclined on her leather sofa and drifted off to sleep dreaming about the prominence that discovering a new virus would bring.

"Dr. Albright. Dr. Albright," her personal assistant, Reed said over the office intercom.

Oblivious, Madelyn continued to sleep. As the gentle knocking on the door grew more persistent, Madelyn stirred. "Yes. What is it?"

Cracking the door and peeking in, Reed said, "You have a meeting at two. I can call and reschedule it, if you like."

"What are you talking about?" Madelyn said sitting up and rubbing her eyes.

"You have a meeting in half an hour. Do you want me to reschedule?" Reed asked.

Looking at the wall clock, Madelyn reached up with both hands and ran her fingers through her hair. "Tell them I'll be there. And get me some coffee."

After Reed left, Madelyn went to her desk and brought up the cameras in the exposure chamber and saw the animals had survived the night and were behaving normally. "Curious," she said.

•••

Two weeks later, the animals were still alive and tests confirmed that the virus had not produced any measurable antibodies. On the other hand, tests on human cells indicated that the virus thrived in human tissues, but Dr. Albright still was a long way off from discovering anything that could be published in a scientific journal.

"The only way to really know how virulent the virus is would be to test in on a human subject," Dr. Albright said at the Wednesday staff meeting.

"So basically what you're saying is that we have to kill some human beings to prove this stuff is dangerous?" her boss, Randy asked.

"Sounds ludicrous, I know, but what the hell am I supposed to do?" Albright countered.

"We might be able to get a volunteer from a hospice or somebody on death row," another researcher offered.

"What about it, Goldstein? Is that something that would pass legal?" Randy asked the attorney in attendance.

"It's been done before, but from what I'm hearing Albright doesn't even know what she's been playing with down on Level Four," Goldstein answered, cautiously.

"I didn't ask you to verify her science. Can you get us a volunteer or not?" Randy asked.

"I can, but they're going to be almost dead when you get them anyway. Is that going to do you any good?" Goldstein asked, feeling like he was being painted into a corner.

Randy smiled. "Let's start with that and then figure out where we can get some healthy specimens."

•••

After a lot of false leads, Goldstein finally located a promising applicant withering away in a urine-drenched nursing home for the indigent. As the nurse led him down the hall toward the woman's room,

305

he took shallow breaths through his mouth to avoid sucking the pungent odor into his nose.

"Mrs. Bleckley, there is a gentleman to see you," the nurse said loudly as they entered a small room with a bed shoved against each wall and a small wooden table with some rickety chairs squeezed in between.

"Yes, yes," an old lady said spinning around in her wheelchair, "you don't have to shout at me. It's those other three who can't hear worth a damn. Now get out of here and leave us alone."

After the nurse left, Mrs. Bleckley rolled over to the door and stuck her head out to make sure the pesky nurse had really left. "Good riddance to bad rubbish," she said maneuvering back toward the desk in the center of the room, "pull up a chair and make yourself comfortable."

"So Mr. Goldstein, what do I have to do to get out of this place?" the old lady asked, with a note of desperation in her voice.

"Well, as the bulletin you responded to stated, the CDC is looking for a few volunteers who are, ah, well," Goldstein said looking for the right word.

"Ready to kick the bucket," Mrs. Bleckley chuckled.

"No. Well, maybe. And I'm here to see if you're willing to participate in an experiment we're doing with a new virus," Goldstein managed to get out.

"It's going to kill me, is it?" The old lady asked, smiling.

"Maybe, but we're hoping that it won't come to that," Goldstein lied.

"If it ain't going to kill me, you can get your ass right out of here," Mrs. Bleckley said pounding her fist on the table.

"You want to die?" Goldstein asked with surprise.

"How long have you been in this place?" Mrs. Bleckley asked.

"Ten minutes. Why?"

"I've been here for eight and a half years, ever since my three ungrateful kids sold my house out from under me when I was eighty and squandered my savings on doodads and thingamabobs. After the first few weeks, I couldn't remember what clean air smelled like. Forgot what real food even looks like. You get me out of here and get the stink blown off me for a week and I'll do whatever you want. Just bury me in a clean box with a rose in my hand and I'll tell Jesus you did well by old Mrs. Bleckley."

•••

306

By the time the lawyers were done wrangling paper, and Mrs. Bleckley was transported to Atlanta, she had enjoyed ten delightful days of freedom accompanied by her nurse/chaperone Christine Windsock.

"Today's the big day," Christine said as they finished eating breakfast in their room at the Executive Hotel, "still want to go through with it?"

"A deal is a deal," Mrs. Bleckley said scraping up the last bit of eggs Benedict with her fork, "every day has been like Christmas since I got out of that stinking hole. I only hope my children get put in a place like that when their time comes around. Freaking assholes!"

Christine couldn't help but laugh at the direct nature of the old lady she'd bonded with the first day they met. "I'm sure they'll get what they deserve. Anyway, I want to be sure that you know you can back out right up until they give you the virus. But once that happens, there's no turning back. You understand that right?"

"Sure I understand, but I'm not going back to that hellhole, no matter what. Sound like an ex-con, don't I. You'll never take me alive, you dirty coppers," the old lady said pretending to shoot a pistol around in the air, "don't you worry over me, Christine, I know you're trying to help me, but everything is going to work out for the best."

"Guess we better get down to the car then," Christine said getting up.

Mrs. Bleckley wiggled into her new coat and smiled as she saw herself in the full length mirror they passed on the way out of the suite they had been staying in. "Not too bad for an old lady."

"You look marvelous, darling," Christine said holding the door for her.

"Thank you, my dear," Mrs. Bleckley said as she headed for the elevators.

During the ride to the CDC, the old lady looked out the window and smiled as she took in everything the city had to offer. When the car turned into the complex and headed down the ramp to the underground parking lot, she waved out the back window and said, "Bye, bye blue skies, bye, bye."

Half an hour later, as she was changing into a hospital gown, Mrs. Bleckley reached into her pocket and pulled out a heart-shaped pendant on a metal chain and handed it to Christine. "I want you to have this. It's the only thing my children didn't take away from me. Just make sure I get the rose in my coffin and it's yours."

307

Turing the clear stone around in her hand, Christine figured it to be about five carats worth of cubic zirconium dangling on cheap stainless steel chain. "You really don't have to give me anything, Mrs. Bleckley. I'm not supposed to take gifts and this, well it looks like it's worth a lot."

"Nonsense, girl it's just a trinket I picked up when I was about your age. Besides, no one will ever know it's not real the way it sparkles. Kind of reminds me of the glacier ice we used to cool our cocktails with back in the day," Mrs. Bleckley said tossing her week-old clothes in a trash can by the door.

"Well, okay, but don't tell anybody," Christine said slipping the necklace into her pocket, "better get you on the gurney and down to the lab for all the tests."

A couple of hours later, Christine watched two lab technicians wheel Mrs. Bleckley into the exposure chamber. "I feel like a pincushion, Christine. Don't forget my rose when this is over," the old lady said over the intercom.

"Are you sure you want to go through with this?" It's still not too late to change your mind," Christine asked, ignoring the sighs from the handful of scientists behind her.

"A deal is a deal," Mrs. Bleckley reiterated.

Dr. Albright pushed the mute button and put her hand on Christine's shoulder, spinning her around. "Okay, you whiny little bitch, you did your advocate thing, now get out of here and let me do my job."

Prying Albright's finger off the mute button, Christine looked over her shoulder at Mrs. Bleckley and smiled. "I won't forget the rose. Good luck," she said as a tear ran down her cheek.

Intentionally bumping into Dr. Albright as she headed toward the door, Christine whispered, "If you ever touch me again, I'll break your fucking neck."

"Well then, let's get on with it," Dr. Albright said a little more flustered than usual.

Twisting her head to relieve a sudden tension in her neck sent her long hair whipping around her shoulders, as she walked to the control panel under the large glass window separating the two rooms.

"Mrs. Bleckley, this is Dr. Albright. Everything is ready. I've released the lock on the atomizer. All you have to do is press the red button on the end of the wand and we can begin the experiment."

"Like this?" the feisty old lady said picking up the control wand and pressing the red button down.

Dr. Albright looked at the infrared monitor and watched a cool blue cloud of virus float into the room, then smiled. "Excellent."

"Kind of anticlimactic, if you ask me," Mrs. Bleckley said. "Mind if I take a nap now?"

"Not a problem. Would you like us to give you something to help you get off?" Dr. Albright asked.

"Nope, I've been napping for years. Wake me up if anything exciting happens."

A few minutes later, the monitoring devices reported the old lady was sleeping peacefully, despite the fact that she was completely wired into an array of sensors monitoring every aspect of her physiology.

Over the next twelve hours every reading remained within normal limits and the researchers began entertaining the idea that the virus wasn't an airborne variety. Then an alarm sounded.

"Probably nothing," the technician at the control panel said adjusting the controls on the temperature monitor, "the old lady just turned over on her side."

Dr. Albright ran to the window. "Mrs. Bleckley, are you all right?"

"Tarnation, can't you just let me be?" the old lady asked, as she flopped over on her back again.

Now three more alarms sounded as the blood gases, pulse and pressure gauges all zeroed out. Flipping through the various camera angles the technician spotted the problem. "The connector's popped loose."

"Shit," Dr. Albright screamed. "Mrs. Bleckley, can you see the connector with all the wires beside the bed?"

"I see it, but I ain't touching it. Electricity scares the dickens out of me. I think it would be better for me if you came in and fixed it."

Albright pounded her fist on the four-inch plastic window. "Bleckley, just reach over and squeeze the plastic together. Nothing bad will happen."

"Well, let's see what I can manage," the old lady said reaching out and tugging on the cords."

"No, not like that," Dr. Albright screamed, as Mrs. Bleckley begin tugging wildly on the cords and new alarms began blasting inside the observation room.

309

Thirty minutes later. Dr. Albright and two technicians in positive airflow suits entered the exposure room through an airlock, which automatically closed behind them.

"Did you bring me my Danish and coffee?" the old lady asked Dr. Albright, as the technicians reconnected the wires and calibrated the equipment.

"Of course, Mrs. Bleckley. Apple Danish and coffee with milk and sweetener - just like you requested," Dr. Albright said opening the waterproof container that had protected the food during the chemical shower in the airlock.

Spotting a couple of broken connectors a technician turned to Dr. Albright. "It's going to take awhile to put this room back together."

"Sorry," Mrs. Bleckley said smiling like an impish child "but I told you electricity scares me."

Dr. Albright looked through the window at the wall clock in the observation room. "I've got to get to a meeting. You two get this stuff back online."

After passing through the airlock and scrubbing her suit in the chemical shower again, Dr. Albright walked into the changing room and quickly slipped into her business attire. Arriving ten minutes late, she glanced at the quarterly budget meeting agenda and realized she would be stuck here for the rest of the day. So she sent a text message to the second shift supervisor requesting that he oversee the repairs to the equipment and to notify her if Mrs. Bleckley's condition changed during the night.

•••

The next morning Dr. Albright slumped onto a barstool in her kitchen and turned on a small television while she waited for the coffee to finish brewing. As the commercial ended she was surprised to see an aerial view of the CDC complex flash up on the screen.

"Officials at the CDC's new $214 million research lab in building eighteen aren't saying what diseases workers might have been exposed to last night when a lighting strike knocked out power to BSL-2 through BSL-4, causing the loss of negative air pressure. The director of the complex has asked non-essential personnel to stay home until contacted by their supervisors." The reporter voiceover continued, but Dr. Albright was already out the door and in her car speeding toward the facility when he finished.

After frantically trying to contact someone at the facility, Dr. Albright finally gave up and arrived to find the parking lot nearly empty. As she passed though security she smiled at the guard. "Where is everybody?"

"Probably all home polishing up their resumes, after last night," the guard said shrugging his shoulders, "all the bigwigs were here from ten till two in the morning, when the power came back on. There are supposed to be back at six this morning. Why are you here so early?"

Dr. Albright smiled. "There may be a couple of empty rungs higher up on the ladder, after this." She then hurried to her office.

Once inside, she raced to her desk and tried to bring up the cameras in the exposure room on Level Four, but everything was dead. Since there wasn't anything she could do until the meeting, she went to the break room and started a fresh pot of coffee. When it was finished, Dr. Albright filled her cup and went to the executive boardroom and waited for the others to arrive.

She was dosing when the first director arrived. "Good morning, Dr. Albright. I wasn't expecting to see you here today."

"Yes, so I gathered, but I have a team down on Level Four and I can't get any of the monitors in my office working down there," Dr. Albright said as she woke up.

"Not good," the director said. "All the computers dumped last night, so we had no way of knowing who was still in the building. I'm guessing that half of the circuit breakers in the building tripped. The only reason we decided to come back today was that everything from Level-One up never lost power. What was your team working on?"

"I picked up a new strain of the N5H1 virus near Jakarta last month. We were doing an airborne trial on a human volunteer," Dr. Albright responded.

"How many people were down there?" the director asked, concern growing on his face.

"It's hard to say. When I went to the quarterly budget meeting at four, we were in the middle of a shift change. At that time there were two technicians working on equipment in the exposure room. "Level Five," as the techs call it when we're working with humans. Since the storm didn't hit till ten, I'm guessing that would put five to six people in the observation room, plus the test subject."

311

By seven, all the directors had arrived and been apprised of the situation. When Goldstein arrived and provided copies of the approved requisition and release form with Mrs. Bleckley's notarized signature, Dr. Albright began pressuring them to allow her to accompany the restoration team. In the end they relented and approved the request.

If her positive pressure suit had made Dr. Albright claustrophobic, the emergency re-breather she wore on the way down to Level Two pushed her to the edge of a full blown panic attack. "How can you stand these things, Chuck?"

"Pretty easy when you think about the alternative, Doc," the team leader said as he led them down the stairwell, "the chemical re-breather keeps out airborne particulates without using electricity, which allows the batteries to be used exclusively for the P-N Junction Coolers."

"Are you serious? This thing is hot as hell," Dr. Albright responded.

"If you think you're hot now, try turning the cooler off," another team member said over the radio.

"I'll take your word for it," Dr. Albright responded.

As the team made its way to the electrical room on Level Two, Dr. Albright was reminded of the incinerated building near Jakarta. The only difference was that the thick white smoke had been replaced by the eerie red glow from the emergency lighting units on the verge of crapping out altogether. Through her helmet, the lab air was clear, but Dr. Albright knew that nobody was really sure if any biological agents had escaped during the twelve hours the electricity had been off.

When the main circuit breakers were reset, the florescent lights in the suspended ceiling flickered on. As the team left the electrical room, computers and automated laboratory equipment began powering-up, filling the level with strange sounds punctuated with an occasional crash as unattended glassware was knocked to the floor by robotic transport mechanisms and partially filled centrifuges vibrated off tables.

After a systematic search of the space, the only thing the restoration team had found was a couple of unsealed collection containers, some broken glass, and laboratory coats discarded by the scientists as they exited the level.

Level Three presented a few more problems, as double-door access labs had automatically sealed, trapping a few workers inside. By the looks of the place, researchers had either disregarded protocol by breaking through doors designed to contain contaminates or settled back and waited for the restoration team to arrive.

"Looks like a cozy couple," Chuck said as he and Dr. Albright stood outside one of the labs. Inside an attractive female lab assistant was sleeping comfortably in the arms of a much older man, on a bed fashioned out of seat cushions and lab coats.

Dr. Albright knocked on the glass. "Are you two okay?"

"We're fine," the older man said in a low voice. "How long before we can get out of here?"

"It's going to be a few more hours before we're sure there's nothing loose on the level," Chuck said.

"We'll be here," the man said settling his head back down.

When all the staff members on the level had been located and identified, the Restoration Team began making its way down the steps to Level Four.

After entering the electrical utility room and getting the power flowing again, Dr. Albright led them through the changing room to the first hermetically sealed door. "The thing won't open," she said giving up on the electronic lock and trying the manual override.

"Have a look at it, Eric," the team leader said as he rebooted the computer that controlled the closed-circuit camera system.

When the monitor came up, he swallowed hard before panning around the exposure room. "Eric! Stop!" Chuck shouted. "Dr. Albright, you better have a look at this before we do anything." Chuck said stepping back and turning away from the monitor, as his mouth went dry with fear.

Since she thought Chuck was just getting out of her way, Dr. Albright wasn't prepared for the spectacle displayed on the monitor.
Inside the Exposure Room, everyone appeared to be dead. As Albright zoomed-in on Mrs. Bleckley, it became apparent that the old lady had suffocated in her own fluids.

After examining each of the other seven bodies, Dr. Albright looked up. "Whatever that stuff is, it's airborne and batting a thousand."

"Then why aren't the animals all dead too?" Chuck asked.

Dr. Albright panned up to the cages along the far wall and paused. "It must be unique to humans."

"Lucky us," Chuck said wondering how he was ever going to clean up this mess.

Chapter 57
Come into My Parlor

Now that Sarah was living with Ty, Duke was alone more than he liked. Against his better judgment, he had been thinking about accepting Amy's offer to come up and move in with her and the kids. After getting a market analysis done on his house in Silver Spring, he figured he would have plenty of money to buy his own place on the lake, if living together was too much of a strain.

Now, with two days to go before he flew up with Ty and Sarah to celebrate Christmas, 'Lake Delta Style', and Duke had pretty much made up his mind to make the move. However, that idea was put on the back burner when he received a letter from his old Vietnam commander of his who had gone into politics.

After reading the letter, he realized that the only difference between politicians and the 'love-you-long-time' girls in Vietnam was that politicians were less honest. On the surface Senator John Cannonbaum's invitation to attend President George Webber's State of the Union Address seemed too outlandish to be true. But to play along with the game, Duke dialed the Senator's number.

"Hello, this is Duke Ransom. I'd like to speak with the Senator, if possible." Duke said expecting to be given the Washington runaround, and he was immediately placed on hold.

"Oh, yes, Mr. Ransom, John said, you might be calling. My name is Mary-Jo, and I'm the Senator's personal secretary. The senator is on the floor now. The mortgage bailout bill is coming up for a vote. He did want me to find out if you would be attending the State of the Union Address on January 28; that's a Wednesday." Mary-Jo finely concluded.

Duke was flabbergasted. "How did my name get on the list?"

Mary-Jo laughed a little. "Yes, I know it must be a shock, coming out of the blue, it's mostly politics, like everything else in town. The President wants a representative from each of the services from Korea through Iraq standing there, so he can acknowledge the sacrifices average Americans have made to protect our freedom. Senator Cannonbaum submitted your name and your number came up. Guess in a way you won the lottery. Of course, you passed the required

314

background check and military profile criteria, or you wouldn't have received the Senator's letter. Can I mark you as a Yes?"

"I wouldn't miss it for a million dollars," Duke said without thinking.

"Okay, then you'll receive more information early in January." Mary-Jo said.

After hanging up the phone, Duke called Ty and was pleasantly surprised when he agreed to come over later that night for a couple of beers.

•••

Ty knocked then let himself in, carrying a six-pack of beer in one hand and a bag of pretzels in the other. "Congratulations, you old fart. I never thought you'd be sitting in the gallery on national television, next month. Your grandkids are going to have something to write about in school this year."

"Yeah, I guess so," Duke said a little dejected, "but you can bet that Cannonbaum got pretty far down his list before coming up with my name."

"I think you're selling yourself short. You've got more salad on your uniform that most of the Chiefs of Staff. That's got to count for something," Ty said.

Duke reached for a beer. "Maybe I'm just getting cynical in my old age, but the guy hasn't contacted me in a year and now he's inviting me to the biggest event in Washington. But it makes me wonder."

Ty sat down, opened the pretzels, offering some to Duke. "Well, if you don't want to go, call him and tell him you changed your mind."

"No, I said I'd be there and I will, besides the exposure might help me with the Phantom endorsement."

"Well, then, don't complain if you're both in bed together," Ty said laughing.

"The Senator is definitely not my type, But, you're right, can't complain if we're both using each other. Guess I'm just as bad as he is. Besides, I hear there's a great after-party, so there's a double payoff in it for me. Did you get a plane so the three of us can fly up for Christmas?" Duke said motioning for some more pretzels.

"I got the Bonanza 36 this time. It should get us there without any problems. Are you still planning on flying your Phantom model up?" Ty asked.

"If you're sure that new belly tank will give it the range."

Ty winked and pointed his index finger at Duke. "I had mine up last week for almost two hours, most of it at full throttle. That's about four hundred miles. It's only three hundred to Lake Delta, so you shouldn't have any problem. Besides, I want to try the re-fueling collar to see how that works."

"Next thing you'll be telling me is you're planning on building an R/C Tanker," Duke said laughing.

"You know, Sarah was talking about that yesterday. She's not much for aerial combat, but thought it would be interesting to play around and see how much weight she could get into the air. Every time I think I know everything about her, she comes up with something new."

•••

Cruising along at 6,500 feet, Duke had been flying his Phantom model next to the Bonanza for an hour. "You know, I kind of like flying without the glasses up here; easier on the eyes. Besides, when I catch the pressure wave off the wing, the thing pretty much flies itself."

"Now that we're pretty much in the middle of nowhere, I'd like to try the refueling collar," Sarah said looking down at the terrain ahead.

Flipping the glasses down from the top of his head, Duke performed a vertical loop, ending up 1,000 feet behind the Bonanza and lined up on the collar. "With the exception of all the plastic tubing taped to the wing, this looks pretty realistic," Duke said tweaking the joysticks on the control panel.

Pressing a button activated a servo that rotated the Phantom's refueling nozzle into position. "Damn, that looks authentic," Duke said smiling.

After a little maneuvering around, Duke connected with the collar and a small LED next to the nozzle turned yellow. "There you go, as pretty as you please."

Sarah manually pumped fuel through the tubing and into the jet. "Let me know when the LED turns green."

"Stop," Duke said.

"Okay, now for the tricky part," Sarah said looking at the clear plastic bottle of fuel to see how much went into the jet, "when you press the refueling button again, it will disconnect the jet and stow the nozzle. So throttle down a little and remember the thing is two pounds heavier now."

316

Duke followed Sarah's instructions and disconnected. An instant later, the Phantom was engulfed in a ball of fire as the engine ignited some excess fuel leaking from the collar. A second later the fireball was gone.

"Shit," Duke said as he and Sarah began to laugh, "looks like I might need a new set of decals."

•••

"How did you get a week off?" Amy asked Ty when the three of them strolled though the front door.

"I quit," Ty laughed. "This is my girlfriend, Sarah."

"Sarah, you sure you want to hang around with a man who would just up and quit his job?" Amy said giving her a girly hug.

"They already hired him back - with a bonus! Besides, he's my soul mate. I love him just the way he is. Thanks for letting me come up. Your house is beautiful."

"Better give her the grand tour, Sarah," Duke said looking down at Josh, "that way the guys can sneak in a game of pool. Somebody told me he can actually sink a few every now and then."

"I can beat both of you, with one hand tied behind my back," Josh said running towards the steps.

By the time there were half way through their first game, Josh was giving his grandfather a run for his money. "Uncle Ty, are you going to do the set- up for my plane too?" he said sinking another ball.

"If that's what you want. Makes it look a little funky, but it sure extends the range. On a good day you'd be able to fly all the way down to Silver Spring," Ty said.

"Better put the refueling collar on, too, while you're at it," Duke said watching his chances of winning this game dwindle.

Josh looked up from the table. "You guys have a tanker now."

Ty smiled. "Not yet, but we tried the prototype collar out while we were flying here. Sarah's building the tanker back where we work in Ashburn."

"That would be great. That way we could all meet up and have dog fights and stuff," Josh said as he prepared to sink another ball.

317

Chapter 58
Reconstituted Juice

Fazul's plan had always been to load the H5N1 atomizers, ship them out, and leave Occoquan before the attack started. Since the Greenbriar incident, every government agency in the area was tracking down bits of information that would eventually lead them to his workshop in Occoquan. The only thing that had saved him, so far, was the fact that none of the shipping companies shared their computer data. If they had, it would have been an easy matter to figure out; he had 1,000 special customers living on a ring 30 miles from the Capitol Building, in Washington, DC.

Now that it was time for him to reconstitute the H5N1 virus and complete the final step for the attack, he was more scared than he had ever been since first coming to Occoquan. Busying himself organizing the atomizer units and Bio-Hazard bags around his workbench, Fazul hummed a little tune to keep the panic under control. Rolling the second 55-gallon drum of nutrient into place, he surveyed his workspace and couldn't think of anything else to do before suiting-up.

Fiddling around with Plutonium never really bothered Fazul, because he had learned to rely on Geiger counters to monitor the source and strength of the radiation. Handling H5N1 on the other hand, required blind faith in procedures he had never used. After reading everything he could get his hands on about the way the CDC handled bird flu, Fazul decided that a micron filtered air mask and gloves weren't going to give him piece of mind. So, he searched the internet and ended up shelling out a hefty two thousand dollars for a bright yellow, Level-A HAZMAT suit. Adding an optional remote compressor, and a hundred feet of hose, the total was almost $3,000 in all.

"Money well spent," Fazul thought, pulling the last bit of slack out of the orange air hose connected to the compressor outside. He then sealed the bottom of the window shut with duct tape. Now every major opening in the room had been sealed.

Because the air coming into the suit was too cold to be comfortable, Fazul put on a pair of insulated coveralls and matching jacket. The extra layer of clothing made getting into the yellow HAZMAT suit a little more difficult, but at least Fazul wouldn't freeze his butt off. After zipping up the suit and sealing the overlying flap into place, he reached

318

down and picked up the air hose and walked over to the freezer. Opening the top door, he took out the box of N5H1 virus out of the freezer and returned to the workbench.

There were many ways he could have re-hydrate the powder, but Fazul decided it would be best to add the powder to the liquid, so it could easily be pumped into the empty atomizer tanks. That way, the concentrations would be uniform and less powder would become airborne. In order to watch the levels in the drums, Fazul had constructed clear plastic covers that could be sealed with the standard ring that came with the original metal tops. He also added an electric paint stirrer to each lid, which insured the powder didn't settle to the bottom of the liquid while he worked.

Positioning the lids so the stirring paddles could be used, he switched them on and waited for the liquid to begin swirling around. When the center of the liquid dropped and formed a vortex, he carefully poured half of the dehydrated H5N1 virus into each drum and sealed the plastic tops shut.

"No turning back now," Fazul said setting a cheap kitchen timer for five minutes and waiting.

When the bell went off, he turned the motors down and waited a minute for the rotation to slow. Dropping the inlet tube from an electric pump into a small hole in the first drum, Fazul slid the output tubing into the first atomizer unit and stepped on a foot controller. A few seconds later, liquid began filling the reservoir. When the liquid was near the top, Fazul took his foot off the controller and watched. The liquid flowing out of the tube stopped immediately.

Screwing the top on, he reached for the Bio-bag and slid the loaded atomizer inside, sealing the end. "One down, 999 to go," he said placing the bag on a rinsing rack he had fashioned out of welded wire.

Five hours later, Fazul dropped the last loaded atomizer onto the top of the fourth wire container, which now held 250 units. Standing up, he stretched to ease the pain that had built up in his back during the filling operation. After working out the kinks, he opened a box of twelve aerosol disinfectant bombs and popped the lids off the first two cans and pushed the continuous spray locks into place against the nozzles. Trailing two clouds of white mist behind him, He placed the cans strategically at the far end of the workshop and returned for two more.

When he was finished, the workshop was filled with a cloud of thick white disinfectant.

When the cloud finally settled, he repeated the process again. This time, making sure the plastic shipping bags received an extra thick dose as he moved them around with his arm. An hour later, he released another barrage and felt his way to the shower where he turned on the water and scrubbed the outside of his HAZMAT suit. Figuring that nothing could have survived the disinfectant, Fazul walked out the back door of his workshop and turned off the compressor.

Fazul unzipped the suit and climbed out, being careful not to touch the outer covering with his hands. Getting a large plastic leaf bag out of his van, he used two sticks to stuff the suit inside. He tied the bag to the hatch handle on the back of the van and drove down the street to a trash dumpster near a construction site, where he disposed of the bag.

Half an hour later, Fazul emerged from the bathroom of a local fast-food restaurant, wearing a new set of clothes he had brought with him when he first arrived. Two 'Big Breakfast Meals' later, he felt much better.

When he returned to his workshop, Fazul held his breath, opened the door and walked inside. As he disappeared, a white cloud poured out of the opening and mixed with the morning mist coming off the canal, becoming invisible. As he scurried around inside opening windows, new plumes of disinfectant wafted up the outside of the building and disappeared in the mist. After making three trips inside, Fazul climbed back into his warm van and fell asleep.

By the time the sun rose at 7:18, the building had aired out. An hour later, the engine in the van stopped. As the temperature inside dropped, Fazul became restless, until the cold finally woke him.

Cursing his stupidity, Fazul climbed out of the van and kicked the door shut with his foot. As he entered the workshop and closed the door behind him, he noticed that a layer of ice had formed over the remains of yesterday's coffee pot. To remedy that problem, he opened a new can of coffee, rinsed out the pot and soon had the coffee machine brewing the first pot of the day.

He had barely finished stuffing the first 200 bio-bags into padded shipping envelopes, when the first delivery truck parked behind the building. When the driver came through the back door he turned his head, sniffing the air. "What's that god-awful smell?"

Fazul laughed, "I thought it was about time to get all the roaches out of the place. Maybe I went a little overboard."

"From the smell, I don't think you'll ever have a problem again. Is this it?" the driver asked, picking up the first of six mailing trays. "What the hell is in these? Feel kind of heavy."

"Just some dishwashing soap samples a client wanted to send out. And you don't have to worry; this is a one-time contract. Once that's done I'm taking a little vacation," Fazul said watching the driver for any signs that he thought something unusual was going on.

As he came in to pick up the last tray, the driver paused. "You know, I wouldn't mind a cup of coffee before I head out."

"No problem. The only thing is I had to remove all the dishes and food before I set off the bombs last night. Do you have something in the truck you could use?" Fazul said walking toward the sink.

"Sure. Let me get my mug," the driver said disappearing for a moment.

When he came back, Fazul filled his mug with coffee. "Hope you like it black."

"That's the only way I take it. Thanks," the driver said taking a sip, "tastes a little weird, is this a new blend?"

"Just something I picked up at the store. Sure you can handle it?" Fazul responded, thinking it might be a good idea for him to skip the coffee this morning.

As the day wore on, other shipping trucks pulled up behind the workshop and picked up more mailing trays. By the time Scott walked in at four in the afternoon, only a couple hundred envelopes remained. "It looks like business is booming again. What are you shipping out today?"

"Little samples of a new liquid soap that's going on the market in a few weeks," Fazul said taking a small envelope out of his desk drawer. "Here's that little extra I promised you when the holiday shopping season was over."

"You know, we're not supposed to take anything from our customers, Fazul"

"Don't be ridiculous, this is just between you and me. Use it to take your wife out for a nice dinner," Fazul said stuffing the envelope into Scott's shirt pocket.

Chapter 59
Last One Out

Fazul's plan to leave the next day hit a brick wall when the Department of Homeland Security raised the local Threat Level to Red. By eight the next morning, checkpoints began popping up all around Washington and continued to grow in number. By the time the day rolled around for President Webber's State of the Union Address, it was impossible to drive more than a few miles before being stopped and asked for identification. Even getting out of Occoquan was iffy, with checkpoints on Gordon Boulevard at the entrances to interstate 95.

Since Fazul's last mission was to launch three planes before leaving the workshop, he was in a quandary. Basically, he had only two choices. His first option was to simply load the planes into his van, drive around front, and launch them from Mill Street. The more he thought about it, the better the idea seemed. The only problem was, he would still be trapped in Occoquan when the main attack started.

His second option was to drive to McLean, Virginia, where a car had been left for him with fake identification that would get him to his safe-house in Shillington, Pennsylvania. Driving to McLean seemed impossible with all the checkpoints, but if he did make it, it would be a cinch to launch the planes and make a clean getaway.

Looking at the clock creeping up on three in the afternoon, he knew he had to make a move soon or he'd probably die where he was standing. Stalling for time, he ripped the cover off another pack of paper, pulled out the staple, and taped them to the road flare he was holding. If he did leave, he wanted to be sure there was nothing left of the building that could be traced back to him or his superiors.

Satisfied that the matches would ignite the flare, he picked up a spool of thin copper wire and wrapped it around the match heads, pulling them over the strike zone in the end of the flare. As he worked he heard a large truck pull up by the back door and stop. When the engine cutoff he heard one door open then slam shut. Before the footsteps reached the wooden porch, Fazul slid his hand into his pants pocket and wrapped his fingers around the butt of his revolver. Despite years of confrontation, his heart began beating faster as adrenalin surged into his system.

"Mind if I come in?" Scott asked, as he opened the door slowly.

Fazul relaxed. "Not at all, good to see you. Would you like a beer?"

Scott sat down on the couch, "I'd love one."

Walking to the refrigerator, Fazul grabbed two beers and returned to the couch where Scott was watching the television. CNN was doing a piece on the military buildup in preparation for the President's State of the Union address. During the past few days, the Army had positioned Avenger Air Defense Missile Systems mounted on Humvees at strategic locations.

As pictures of the equipment flashed on the screen, the reporter began. "Tonight marks the first time since September 11 that the Homeland security alert status has been raised to red in the Washington area."

"Not too surprising, since we've been getting a terrorist's attack every month lately," his counterpart added.

"Customs Service aircraft have been in the sky all day working in conjunction with the Air National Guard to keep air traffic away. I'm pretty sure nothing is coming in here tonight," the anchor concluded.

"It looks like Washington is locked up tighter than a drum," Scott said taking a beer.

Fazul smiled, "Hopefully everything will go as planned and tomorrow we'll all wake up smiling."

"Just one quick beer and I'm out of here, I'm already running late. The whole reason I stopped by today was to give you back the money you slipped me last week. If I had known how much was in this envelope, I never would have taken it in the first place," Scott said standing up and reaching into his shirt pocket.

"Don't be ridiculous, I told you I was going to take care of you after the holidays. Just keep the money and buy something nice for your wife," Fazul said pushing it back into Scott's pocket, "here's to a better year."

"I'll drink to that," Scott said tapping his bottle of beer against Fazul's and tilting his head back to take a swallow.

Seeing the angle was perfect, Fazul pulled out his pistol, placed it in the crease under Scott's left ear and pulled the trigger twice. By the time the lead stopped ricocheting around inside his skull, Scott's brain was jelly. For a few seconds, his face froze and he resembled a mannequin staring straight ahead with glassy eyes. Eventually, his legs buckled and he crumpled to the floor in slow motion, like a fighter going down for the count.

Fazul smiled as he put the pistol back in his pocket. "Sorry buddy, just trying to cover my ass," he said reaching into Scott's jacket pocket. Once he had the truck keys, he threw a blanket over the body and went outside to have a smoke and to see if anyone had noticed the noise. After his second cigarette, he figured it was safe to start moving the models into the FedEx truck. According to the news reports he had been watching, it was one of a dozen or so vehicles that got a free pass through the checkpoints.

Now that the fates had smiled down on him, Fazul didn't waste any time dumping kerosene around the workshop. He made sure to put a little extra on Scott, as he made his way to the back door. Then he flipped the switch by the back door that started the electric timer he had connected the flare to and locked the door. A few moments later, as he drove west on Gordon Boulevard, Fazul switched his cell phone to the television mode and tuned in CNN. Slowing at the checkpoint, he was waved through and turned onto the northbound ramp to Interstate 95.

An hour later, he turned onto the 495 beltway that, for over sixty miles, completely encircled the Nation's capital, and headed west toward McLean, Virginia. He turned the volume down on his cell phone and tuned in a radio station near Occoquan. A short while later he smiled when the disk jockey reported a large fire had broken out on the west end of Mill Street.

After twenty-five minutes of driving, Fazul turned onto Rt. 123 then onto Great Falls Street, eventually stopping at the south end of Wasp Lane. Pulling into one of the parking spaces, he saw the car Ihmad had left for him. When he was satisfied that it would get him well into Pennsylvania by the time the attack started, he removed the three models from the back of the truck. A few minutes later, he started the first one, pointed it southeast, and let it go.

Moving to the second plane, Fazul was about to engage the electric motor when he heard footsteps behind him.

"What'cha doing Mister?" a young boy asked, as his taller companion put his hand on his shoulder to keep him from getting any closer.

Startled, Fazul turned his head and smiled. "I'm just playing with my airplanes."

"That doesn't even make sense. It's already dark, Mister," the boy said with a puzzled look on his face, "why would you launch those expensive planes when you can't even see them?"

"Guess you've got me there, kid," Fazul said pulling out his pistol.

"Do you want me to shoot you both here or would you rather get into the back of the truck and hope someone finds you alive?"

The older boy started to run, but was hit in the leg and fell to the ground screaming, "Last chance to get into the truck."

"Okay. Okay. We'll get in the truck. Stop shooting," the younger boy screamed, as he ran to his friend's side.

After locking the two inside the truck, Fazul launched the last two planes, and jumped into the car. Speeding up Wasp Lane, he pressed the Panic button on the truck's electronic key he had kept and watched the lights begin to flash on the FedEx truck as he turned the corner.

Chapter 60
The Kickoff

Mohammed had spent his whole life fighting one sect or another. In the beginning it was hand to hand, but as the years went by and he moved up the ladder he had become more of an executive. Now he commanded thousands around the world, anxious to do his bidding. Like all great leaders, Mohammed had listened to many advisors, extracting the best from each. Over the past three years there hadn't been a moment when he had taken his eyes off the pieces he placed on his chessboard. Now that the sun had dawned, it was time to prepare for his Jihad on the United States before his guests arrived.

After bathing, Mohammed applied oil to his body and dressed in a new silk robe. As he stood looking at himself in the mirror, there was a knock at the door. Walking through the living room, he flipped on the half dozen flat-screen televisions before opening the door.

Two large food carts rolled into the room and the hotel staff quickly set up a food and beverage area next to the balcony door. "Will there be anything else?" the food services manager asked.

"That will do for now," Mohammed said ushering him out.

An hour later, Dr. Ramadan arrived, followed quickly by Abdullah and Fahid. As they began picking over the fresh fruit, Mohammed tuned in various news channels and adjusted the volume, using the remote control devices he had piled on a small table next to his chair. CNN's live pre-address coverage flashed across the screen in Jakarta, a full twelve hours ahead of Washington.

"We interrupt our pre-address coverage to bring you breaking news. A fire in one of the busiest hospitals in the Capital has erupted at George Washington University Hospital on 23rd Street Northwest, just blocks from the White House," news anchor Andrew Barrelman stated in formal tones, then paused, waiting for the director to feed him the name of the local reporter racing to the scene.

"Andrew, it's going to take a minute. Narrate the streaming video coming in," the director said waiting for the technician at the Master Control panel to bring it up.

The image on Mohammed's screen changed perspective to that of a helicopter flying towards the hospital. As it got closer, it was easy to see three small hot spots had already burned through the roof exposing the floor below. As the fire spread, windows began exploding as smoke billowed from the seventh floor. On the street below, white safety strips outlining the firefighters glowed in the spotlight from the helicopter as it swept the area, giving the impression that skeletons were racing through the streets setting up equipment.

"We're cutting to Amber Gristly, who's just arrived on site in one of our mobile news truck. Amber, are you there?" Andrew said.

After a slight pause, the cameraman pulled Amber into focus, centered in the main entrance of the hospital across the street. "Yes, John. And I can tell you that this is going to be a night from hell for all the patients presently being evacuated from the hospital."

"Congratulations, Mohammed," Dr. Ramadan said smiling and raising his cup of coffee, "looks like Fazul got in his final lick."

Mohammed smiled back. "Now we just have to hope that Webber doesn't get cold feet and beat it out of town."

"After all his rhetoric about staying in Iraq until the bitter end, he would look like a coward if he left because of a small fire. My money says he'll stay," Dr. Ramadan said. "What do you think, Fahid?"

"Like a frog in slowly warming water, I think they are all too stupid to jump out before it's too late. In ten minutes, CNN will forget all about the fire. And so will all the President's men," Fahid said with a sneer.

Chapter 61
Chop Chop

Before coming to America, Salih had enjoyed an easy life back in Saudi Arabia. So it wasn't his fault that he had never learned to do the simple things most Americans took for granted. Sitting on a folded blanket in the middle of his two-car garage looking at the instructions for assembling the parts surrounding him made him feel stupid. He remembered how he had once offered his neighbor $20 to change a flat tire and the curious looks the man had given him when he simply handed over the keys and waited.

He had already parked his car outside by the curb, opened the hood and connected the electric starting motor to the car's battery. So, once he got this thing together, he was sure he could get it into the air. Deciding to start with something simple, he pulled the box containing the bowling ball close and removed the ball. After some struggling, he found a grip that worked and unscrewed it into two pieces. The plastic spreader unit inside gave off a warm heat so he tucked it inside his folded legs, before dropping the pieces of the ball back into the box.

Following the instructions carefully, he retrieved the molded plastic designed to hold all the parts in place. Since each part had a unique shape it was impossible to make a mistake. Within five minutes Salih had all the parts inserted. When he had plugged all the color coded electrical connections together he fitted the assembly into the body of the plane.

Connecting the fuel bottle to the engine was a snap. But connecting the plastic control rods to the servo-motors was a little trickier. After a couple of failed attempts he managed to snap the last one into place, pulling on it to be sure it wouldn't come apart.

Since he had forgotten to get a screwdriver for the wing he got up and walked to the workbench that had come with the house and fetched a flat bladed beauty that fit the wing screws perfectly. By the time he got the wing secured he was feeling like a genius. But that quickly faded when he looked though the windshield and discovered he had forgotten to turn the computer on.

A couple of minutes later, Salih walked over and pushed the button that opened the garage door. After taking a look around, he picked up the model and walked out, setting the model down in front of the car by the starter motor. At exactly 8:30, the red controller light turned yellow and began flashing. Inside the model, the computer began running its preflight diagnostics activating servos that opened and closed the fuel valve, ran the control surfaces through their full range of motion, making last minute trim adjustments, checked the on/off valve controlled the H5N1 atomizer, and checked the connections to the block of explosive and Plutonium spreader unit.

When the light switched to a steady green, Salih picked up the electric starter motor and slipped the rubber cup over the cone in front of the propeller and pressed the ON button with his thumb. For a few seconds the engine turned, but didn't start. Just as he was about to stop and get a better grip on the plane, the engine started. Salih hadn't expected the noise to be so loud and fell back, dropping the starter motor and losing his grip on the model at the same time.

Fortunately for Salih, the engine-start program had been set to idle the engine for fifteen seconds to allow it to heat up and to give the person launching it time to get it pointed in the proper direction. After regaining some of his composure, Salih got up, unhooked the starter motor from the car, and closed the hood.

Now he was standing there in a quiet neighborhood, with a large model airplane that sounded like a dirt bike sitting at his feet. Through his panic he remembered something about pointing the plane down the street, so he bent down and adjusted the angle. Suddenly the engine revved up and he began losing his grip.

Instinctively grabbing at the plane, his hand slipped past the wing and the propeller severed his index and middle fingers. Watching everything in slow-motion, he saw the plane moving away while his fingers spun in the air. As the plane became airborne, his scream separated from the roar of the model engine and could be heard echoing throughout the neighborhood.

After picking up his fingers, Salih ran inside the house to the kitchen, pulled open a door, and grabbed two towels to wrap around his hand. To protect his family, he had sent them shopping. Now he was on his own. Remembering the medical shows he had watched, he ran to the refrigerator and pulled out the automatic ice container. After dropping his fingers into a large sandwich bag, he filled it with ice before zipping it shut.

As the scenery around him began changing from color to black and white, he bent over and took a couple of deep breaths before running back through the garage and getting into his car. Driving down the street toward the local hospital, he cursed his stupidity as the pain in his hand began radiating up his arm.

Chapter 62
Duke's Gridlock

Duke blasted his horn one more time before reaching for his cell phone. First he dialed Ty's phone, but got a fast busy, which he knew meant that all the circuits were in use. Shrugging his shoulders, he tried Senator Cannonbaum's office and got Mary-Jo on the other end.

"Mary-Jo, this is Duke Ransom. I don't know what's going on, but I'm stuck in traffic and have a feeling that I may not make the President's Address."

"Where are you now?" Mary-Jo asked, picking up a second phone and dialing the Secret Service.

"I'm headed south on Twenty-nine about halfway between Kansas and New Hampshire, but the traffic is just crawling along thanks to all the freaking checkpoints Webber has set up," Duke said blasting the horn again.

"Calm down, Mr. Ransom. I'll have a couple of the boys come rescue you. Just stay on Twenty-nine," Mary-Jo said.

With nothing else to do but wait, Duke dialed Amy's number in Lake Delta. "Hey, Amy, don't say anything to the kids, but I might not make it in time for Josh and Samantha to see me on television tonight."

"Sorry to hear that. What's happening down there?" Amy asked, strolling over to the picture window and looking out at the moon reflecting off the water.

"Webber's got the Capital locked up tighter than a drum. Checkpoints everywhere you look. So far I've been on the road for over an hour and I'm still only halfway there," Duke replied.

"Take it easy, Daddy, or you'll blow a gasket. Have you called Cannonbaum?" Amy offered.

"Yes. Got his assistant who promised to send some help, but I don't see how anybody's going to get here in time," Duke said glancing up at some flashing lights in his rearview mirror, "if things change, I'll give you a call."

A minute later, a line of police cars screamed down the center lane, cutting a wake through the gridlock behind him. After they passed, a black Hummer pulled up alongside. "Duke Ransom?" the agent in the passenger seat yelled.

"That's me," Duke yelled back.

"Understand you have a date with the President tonight. Follow us," the agent said as the Hummer pulled away.

Duke didn't have to be asked twice. He stepped on the gas and was soon cruising past hundreds of less fortunate commuters. Looking up at his review mirror again, he saw another black Hummer had pulled in behind.

The lead vehicle didn't slow as it turned into the long driveway that led to the security gate near the White House. Duke was shocked when the gate raised and the three vehicles drove past the security guards. When the truck ahead of him stopped, the two agents who had rescued him ran back towards him. "Okay, now for the formalities. Get out and spread 'um."

After being patted down, Duke watched the agents give his truck an equally thorough inspection. When an agent popped open the fiberglass bed cover and saw the two models inside. "Build these yourself?"

"Just a little hobby. Reminds me of the good old days when you knew who the enemy was," Duke countered.

"I got my kid one, about half the size of these. Seems like the only thing he's interested in. Can't complain though, it's still better than having him sit around on his butt playing video games," the agent said closing the back, "ever had a tour of the Situation Room?"

Duke smiled. "I can't say that I have."

"Then today's your lucky day. I've got to pick up a couple of guys before we head over to the Capitol."

"I thought that place was off limits?" Duke said with a puzzled look on his face.

"We ran you through the system months ago. If you hadn't come out squeaky clean, you would never have been invited to the party. Beside, with your Navy experience and guest appearances at the War College, your butt is clean enough to eat off of," the agent said turning towards the White House.

Chapter 63
State of the Union

As interested Americans began loading up TV tables with snacks and beverages beside their favorite chairs in anticipation of the President's Address, a thousand model airplanes were airborne. Flying loud and low, they began to attract attention immediately, which is exactly what they had been built to do. Roughly eighty percent were headed for the Capitol Building thirty miles from their launch points. The ones that made it that far had been programmed to fly in a half mile circle until they ran out of gas and crashed. The other twenty percent had specific targets and depending on the target, had been individually configured to do the maximum amount of damage.

None of the planes had any defenses, but their wood and plastic construction made them invisible to radar and their flat black paint made it hard for anyone searching the skies for the source of the noise to see them. If ECHELON hadn't gone into brain-lock from all the foreign chatter coming in, it would have easily figured out an attack on the Capitol was imminent and notified the proper government agencies. As it was, 911 Emergency call centers in Virginia and Maryland began receiving increased call volumes that were initially marked as pranks.

Initially, it seemed comical that so many people were calling in to report loud motorcycles and UFO sightings. But as the volume grew, the supervisors began seeing lines form on the maps that traced the callers' locations. Though they couldn't put their finger on the reason, each had a sinking feeling that something ominous was unfolding. A couple even called in to the Department of Homeland Security and got the runaround when they couldn't come up with anything more substantial than a gut feeling that something was wrong.

Inside the Capitol Building, President George Webber sat in a small waiting room, thinking about his last seven years in office. During that time terrorists had attacked America three more times. Like his predecessor, he had vowed to hunt down the persons responsible and bring them to justice, but he was no closer to knowing who he was chasing than President Bush had been after starting the whole thing.

He felt he was in a no-win situation and was sure reporters were picking him apart as he began thumbing through the speech he had spent all day yesterday rehearsing. He knew it was time to go when the photographer he had selected for tonight's event knocked lightly and cracked the door. "Mr. President, they're waiting."

"I'll be out directly." The President waited for the door to close.

Off-camera, two CNN anchors looked at the clock and shrugged their shoulders at each other. "Looks like the Secretary of the Interior drew the short straw tonight," James Beluga said stalling for time.

Co-anchor Shaw Jamison didn't miss a beat. "Well, someone in the chain of succession has to guard the football, in case something goes wrong in there."

"After everything that's happened over the past four months, he might feel like the luckiest man in Washington," James continued.

When the doors to the House Chamber opened and the event photographer emerged, James and Shaw paused. Following him, the Majority Floor Services Chief and House Sergeant of Arms marched into the chamber with red and blue ties adorning otherwise identical suits.

After pausing to allow the hundreds gathered to quiet, the Services Chief cleared his throat. "Madam Speaker."

Quickly, the Sergeant of Arms followed, prepared to announce the President, using his most Senatorial voice, a bass that seemed to rumble through the House Chambers, stilling every whisper with its resonance. "The President of the United States!"

As thunderous applause exploded, George Webber took a deep breath and walked into the room. On the circular path to the podium he signed a program, ducked past an old friend intent on hugging him, and air-smooched the wife of a Senator. As the applause continued, he passed seven of the nine justices of the Supreme Court and the Joint Chiefs of the Armed Forces. Continuing on, he shook hands and made his way to the podium, where he handed copies of his speech to the Vice-President and the Speaker of the House.

When the loud and sustained applause died down, the Speaker cleared her throat and began to speak in a loud voice. "I have the high privilege and distinct honor of presenting to you the President of the United States." Once again, the Chamber's audience rose as if propelled by a tremendous force, and the room again thundered into a cataclysmic explosion of applause."

In Alexandria, Virginia, a real explosion on the ninth floor of the George Washington Masonic National Memorial blasted though the floor into the Knights Templar Chapel below. Automatic sprinklers popped open and an automatic alarm signaled the local fire department which was already responding to an emergency at the recently opened control tower for the drawbridge on the Capital Beltway.

This was followed by fireballs at the homes of all of the President's Cabinet Members. At the home of the Secretary of the Interior, the signal from the President's Emergency Satchel stopped transmitting when what was left of the roof collapsed through the building. In quick succession, specially designed model planes targeted large vehicles at major intersections along the Beltway, effectively sealing off all escape routes leading out of Washington, DC.

Pilots in military planes patrolling the skies over Washington immediately saw the pattern of destruction and radioed the information in to their superiors. As the information made its way up the chain of command, crews manning the mobile missile positions were given the order to shoot to kill, and the Department of Homeland Security flew into high gear.

When the lead agent in the White House Situation Room got the report, he immediately flashed a message to the Secret Service agent in charge of the security detail for protecting, and guarding, the President: Get him back to the White House. He then ordered the two jets designated for the President and Vice-president into emergency standby, and got the helicopters in the air that would ferry the President to the airport.

Back inside the Capitol Building, George Webber had left the podium and walked over to the men and women he had handpicked to honor tonight. Using the remote microphone he carried, he addressed the attendees. "I'd like to break from protocol tonight and personally shake the hands of the men and women standing here tonight. They were invited to represent the various branches of America's Armed Forces that have protected us from threats to democracy since our beginnings. Commander Duke Ransom," he said holding out his hand..."

As he shook Duke's hand, beepers began going off at the front of the chamber where the Joint Chiefs sat. For a second silence filled the House Chamber, then a few Secret Service agents touched their earpieces then sprang into action, grabbing the President. While the world watched in horror, George Webber disappeared into a cloud of black suits. Instinctively, the President grabbed Duke's arm, trying to keep his balance. Deciding time was of the essence; the agents grabbed the two men as a single unit and headed for the door. By the time they reached it, the Vice-President was well ahead of them as the agents raced to the bulletproof limousines waiting outside. As soon as Duke and the President were inside, the driver mashed the accelerator to the floor and raced after the Vice-president's vehicle.

"What the hell is going on?" Webber screamed.

"It's an attack - probably terrorists. They've sealed off the entire Beltway. The helicopter is on the way to get you and the Vice-president out of here," the driver screamed. "Now buckle up and hang on, Sir."

"God damn it, I should have nuked Iraq when this whole thing started," Webber screamed at the top of his lungs.

"Looks like that would have been an excellent idea," Duke agreed. "Look at all those fires out there."

For the first time since he'd been thrown into the car, President Webber looked out the window. "Holy shit! How long did all this take?"

Figuring the question was directed at him, the driver responded. "It seemed to happen all at once. But reports of all kinds of strange things have been trickling in for the past hour or so, Sir."

As the limo raced up the White House driveway, the agent looked into the rearview mirror. "Mr. President, what are we going to do with him?"

The President smiled, "Shoot him, of course." Then remembering the Secret Service never had much of a sense of humor corrected himself.

"No, just kidding! It looks like he's in the mix for now. Duke Ransom, right?"

As they got out of the limo and raced for the front door, Duke stopped and looked up as three planes flew overhead. "Models, Sir," he yelled, trying to catch up again. "Wait."

After bounding up the steps and getting inside, he saw that the agent was leading Webber down the hall to the rear of the building. "Stop," Duke yelled.

The agent paused for a second and looked over his shoulder. "I've got to get him on that helicopter."

If Duke wasn't so out of shape, he would have tried to catch up with them and keep the President inside the building. In a last ditch effort, he grabbed a piece of marble statuary and threw it to the floor. "God damn it. Stop!"

Somehow that got George Webber's attention and he stopped dead in his tracks. "You realize of course that destroying a national treasure could get you put away for life,"

"Mr. President, you have to get out of here. The Vice-President is already in the chopper. Let's go," the agent pleaded.

As the agent tightened his grip, President Webber gave him a stern look the agent understood immediately. "In a minute, now get your hands off me," Webber said waiting to be released, "but first I want to listen to what this man has to say. Is that all right with you?" His voice was not pleasant, but vividly angry.

The agent, torn between two conflicting orders, was seriously toying with the idea of simply taking the President's earlier advice and blowing Duke to kingdom come. As he watched the President walking back toward Duke, his hand began unconsciously moving to his shoulder holster.

Suddenly, an explosion behind the White House lit the interior with a bright orange flash. A second later one of the rotors from the helicopter crashed through the wall in the room adjacent to the hallway, destroying everything in its path. The agent's flinch response pulled his arms up to cover his face, as the shock wave from the exploding fuel tanks ripped through the back of the building.

A moment later the agent came to and saw the mangled chopper burning through a large hole that had been blasted open behind him. Running to the President, he was relieved to see he was still alive. "New plan, Mr. President. Let's get down to the Situation Room."

After helping the President to his feet, the agent tapped Duke with his shoe. "You okay?"

Duke shook his head to get the plaster out of his ears and got up. "Now what?"

"Follow us," the agent screamed to compensate for his temporary loss of hearing.

Chapter 64
The Half-time Show

Mohammed was all smiles as he watched CNN replay President Webber being forcibly removed from the House Chamber. Since that was all the network had to work with, the terrorists had no way of knowing how well their plan was proceeding.

Dr. Ramadan patted him on the back. "All this looks very encouraging."

Mohammed took a long breath. "Yes, but we still don't know enough to be sure. CNN has to have reporters out investigating what's going on. Why aren't they showing anything besides Webber being whisked away?"

Abdullah threw his cell phone across the room. "Something big must be going on; I can't get through to anyone. All the circuits are busy."

Fahid walked over, retrieved the phone and returned it to his friend. "Take it easy Abdullah. That can only be good news. Have you tried to reach anybody on the west coast?"

Abdullah grabbed the phone. "They don't know any more than we do."

"We interrupt this broadcast to take you to our Atlanta offices for an important message," a faceless voice said.

"Shut up, you two," Mohammed said holding his hand up.

As the screen when black the voice continued. "For the past hour our reporters in the field have been gathering information and video that had just now been formatted into a loose timeline of events in Washington."

The screen came to life and showed Lou Kelly and Robin Dolby at a desk shuffling through papers.

Lou began. "Apparently Washington, DC has been under attack since about 8 p.m. tonight. It appears all the attacks are being carried out by specially built model airplanes. Here's a clip of one found in a park about half an hour ago.

The shaky video of a couple of young teenage boys carrying one of the attack drones appeared on the television. A pleasant female voice narrated the action. "As you can see the plane has about a five-foot wingspan. Here, let me take that for a second; and it weighs about eight or ten pounds. Put it down there so I can get a shot through the

338

windshield. There appears to be a handheld computer or PDA inside controlling the thing, but that's all I can see without ripping it apart."

As the reporter turned her satellite phone around, her face became visible. "This is Lesley Snodgrass reporting from Park View Community Playground..."

Seeing their chance to get away with the plane, the boys picked it up and began running toward the street. Lesley whipped her phone around just in time to catch the boys running up the steps to their row house. As the camera zoomed in to display the house number, an explosion blasted all the windows in the house out over Princeton Place Northwest. Lesley dropped her videophone as she dove for the ground.

Mohammed nearly giggled he was so happy. "Now that's why everyone in the world loves CNN. They tell it like it is."

Robin Dobbs's face came back into view. "That was a shocker, Lou. I hope Leslie is okay."

"If you think that's strange wait until you see our next story," Lou began, as another video was pulled up and started playing on the screen.

This time, it was a multi-car pileup at the junction of Interstates 270 and 495 that flashed on the screen. Amid the burning wreckage, blood-curdling screams could be heard as victims trapped in their vehicles were slowly incinerated. Those lucky enough to have escaped wandered around in a daze waiting for help that would never come.

"That's so horrendous, I can't even comment on it. But I can tell you this scene is being repeated at every major intersection around the Beltway tonight," Lou said as the next video rolled.

"Here, one of our reporters has tracked down a mobile lab from the CDC," Lou said waiting for the audio to cut in.

"Patrick Gasman here, talking with Justin Daily. Justin, what can you tell us about what's going on tonight?"

The young technician invited the reporter to follow him into the lab where he sat down amid a mass of electronics. "Looks like some of these planes are carrying plutonium, but I can't imagine they could lift anything heavy enough to be a bomb. Seems more likely they're dropping it in a spray or powder form."

Flipping a couple of switches he brought up a graph on the computer monitor. "See, this is way above normal background levels. But it's not consistent. It seems to be heavy in some spots and non-existent in others.

Patrick interrupted, "Is it lethal?"

"It depends on the size. If whoever made this was clever enough to grind it down to three microns, it could lodge in your lungs and kill you slowly over a year or two. If it's bigger, you could probably wash it off in the shower and live to be a hundred."

"When will you know what size it is?" Patrick asked.

"Got to get it to the lab where we can look at it under the electron microscope to be sure. That wouldn't take long if the traffic wasn't backed up. Truth is, I can't say right now," Justin answered, reaching up and removing a long filter from a vacuum pump that had been collecting air samples from outside.

"Better leave now, I have to check out the latest bio-hazard readings. Wouldn't want you to get contaminated," Justin said reaching over and holding the door open.

CNN cut back to Robin in the studio. "It looks like mom was right. Cleanliness is next to Godliness, at least for the foreseeable future."

As Mohammed continued to watch, his expectations of success grew. "Now it all depends on whether the President made it out of Washington or not. What are our chances now Doctor?"

Dr. Ramadan got up and walked to the window. "It's still too close to call. We don't know what the CDC's been doing with the samples or what they will advise the President to do. Hell, we don't even know if he's still alive."

CNN cut back to Lou in Atlanta. "News is just coming in about an explosion directly behind the White House. Initial reports indicate that a helicopter waiting to take the President and Vice-president to the airport has just blown up. A CNN News Truck has been dispatched and is expected to arrive shortly."

At the news, Mohammed jumped up and looked at Ramadan. "That does it."

Chapter 65
Arcade Games

Duke had to laugh as he watched the Secret Service running around the Situation Room trying to figure out how to get the President to what would become Air Force One when he arrived. In calmer times, he would have been stopped long before he got close to the elevator, but tonight no one paid any attention to the old Navy veteran, as they tried to figure out how to get the President out of harm's way. When the elevator stopped on the first floor and the doors opened, he half expected to be tackled to the ground, but only got a polite salute from the two Marines standing at attention outside.

"Carry on," Duke said as he walked calmly back the way they had come in earlier. He noticed the helicopter fire was extinguished and some plywood had been nailed up, sealing out the night air.

When he reached his truck, he opened the cab and exchanged his officer's hat for a baseball cap equipped with a self-contained LED flashlight in the bill. Now that he could see what he was doing, he moved around to the back, opened the fiberglass cover and lowered the tailgate.

A moment later he slipped on his VR-Glasses and turned them on. "This is Duke. Is anybody on-line?

"Pop-pop, are you okay?" Josh asked excitedly.

"Sure I am. What say we kick a little ass before this thing is over," Duke said pulling his glasses down his nose so he could see enough to pull Josh's jet to the tailgate.

"Don't think you're hogging all the fun, you old fart," Ty chimed in.

"I was hoping you'd climb out of that hole you live in long enough to get some air," Duke said topping off the tank in Josh's plane and flipping on the power. "Can you see anything now, Josh?"

A few seconds later the computer in one of the Low Earth Orbit satellites allocated a video channel and established a communications link between Josh's plane and his VR-glasses, "Ready to go, Pop-Pop."

"Okay, give me a minute to get your plane set up. Once you're up, circle around till I get up there."

"Josh, I'm about two minutes out. Look for me when you get airborne," Ty said pressing the throttle on his controller, "Sarah's still down in the complex fiddling with her Tanker."

"Looks like a great night for a turkey shoot to me," Duke said watching Josh's jet take off down the side of the White House.

"Hey, Ty, what the hell is going on?" Duke asked, as he powered up his jet and backed up a few feet to get away from the hot exhaust.

"Nobody knows. The only thing I can tell you for sure is ECHELON's having a meltdown. You can already see that model planes are exploding all over the place," Ty said waving his wings so Josh could spot him coming in from the west.

"I guess it's a good thing these satellite phones never caught on or we'd be locked out like everyone else," Duke said positioning his plane in between the other two.

"Now that we're up here, what are we supposed to do?" Josh asked, as he switched through the planes various vision modes.

"I'm not sure; anyone have any bright ideas?" Duke said feeling a little stupid, "I guess it would have been a good idea to keep these things loaded with bullets."

"If nobody has a better idea, let's try burning one out of the air with the exhaust," Ty offered.

"Okay, you pick it out," Duke said pulling back on his throttle, "Josh and I will hang back for awhile."

Watching from above as dozens of black shadows circled the White House, they watched Ty's plane slowly descend into the swarm, like a lion picking its prey. Once the decision was made, the jet swooped down quickly until only a few yards separated the two planes. Then using the techniques that had won them the First Place ribbon, Ty pulled back on the throttle and pitched the nose up slightly as the jet sailed slowly over the wooden model, setting it on fire.

Switching to the rear view, Ty was about to congratulate himself when the plane's high explosives ignited and began burning like a magnesium flare, lighting up the White House lawn. Pushing the throttle full forward, Ty almost collided with another plane before pulling up into a climbing spin. "Guess those babies are loaded for bear," he said a little shaken.

"Must be C-4," Duke said watching the explosive burn out well above the ground, "from the looks of it, they're self-cleaning."

A few minutes later, Josh scorched another one. Not to be outdone, Duke lined up on two that were flying side-by-side and lit them both up.

"You two are going to have to do better than one at a time or we will be here all night," he said laughing.

As they continued to burn the ghost planes out of the sky, they attracted the attention of a CNN News Van that had come to investigate the bright fireworks arcing around the White House. Climbing out, the cameraman stuck his camera through the bars of the security fence and zoomed in on Duke sitting comfortably on the tailgate of his truck operating his remote controller.

"What's he up to?" the reporter asked, watching the live-feed monitor inside the van.

"Looks like he's having the time of his life, doing something," the cameraman said panning up as another arc of flame lit up the front lawn, "son of a bitch, he's toasting them!"

As another shadow burst into flames behind him, the reporter watched the camera swing around and focus on Josh's silver jet. "Either they're faster than lightning or there's more than one avenger up there."

"I'm switching the feed to Atlanta," the reporter said leaning inside the van, "back up so I can get in the shot."

"This is Berry Short, outside the White House, where a lone Naval Officer is doing the impossible, single handedly, clearing the sky of terrorists' assault aircraft. A remarkable feat, when you realize that the millions of dollars worth of defensive weapons moved into the area haven't been able to detect, let alone destroy, the black harbingers of death."

Back in Atlanta, CNN technicians weren't doing any better than the Secret Service at figuring out what was going on. Currently, retired military strategists had been brought in to discuss the way the President was manhandled at the Capitol as he was physically dragged out of the building.

"I would have thought the Congressmen and military would have behaved much more professionally, but as the tape revealed, they seem to have immediately reverted back into survival mode the instant President Webber was removed," an intellectual looking gentlemen said shaking his head in disgust.

"Quite right. I have a feeling heads will roll when this is over and voters get a chance to react," an equally pompous strategist agreed.

The producer punched his microphone button, "Does anybody have anything remotely interesting coming in?"

343

"I've got something from a van in front of the White House," a tech announced over the party-line they were all hooked to.

"Get it queued up. I'm falling asleep listening to these guys," the producer said switching to the anchor's channel, "I'm dumping this shit. Get ready to jump on a live feed from outside the White House, some local staffer named Berry Short."

A second later, the video of Duke came streaming in over the strategists, who were cut off in mid-sentence. "Sorry about that," the anchor said, "but we got a reporter outside the White House. What do you have for us, Berry?"

"Believe it or not, there's a Naval Officer sitting nonchalantly on the back of a pickup truck. The man seems oblivious to the events unfolding here tonight as he watches what now appear to be model airplanes loaded with some kind of incendiary devices zeroing in on the White House. Take a look over my shoulder."

As the cameraman began zooming in on Duke, a wooden model ran out of gas above the White House and began gliding directly at the van. By the time it was halfway across the front lawn, Ty spotted the shadow floating toward the two men. Coming in fast, he toasted the model and pulled up as it burst into flames, burning out 50 feet from the fence.

"Much as I hate CNN, I don't think we want to cut your fifteen minutes of fame short," Ty said circling around and buzzing Duke.

Duke stood up and waved at the reporter. "Might be the best story he ever gets to cover."

The cameraman hadn't seen the plane coming, but he sure felt the heat on his head and looked up just as the flame went out.

In her house on Lake Delta, Amy stood up when she saw her father on the television. "Josh, your grandfather is on the news. Come down here."

"I know Mom. I'm helping him and Ty fight off those other models."

Amy ran up the stairs and found Josh at the controls of his jet model while his sister sat by his side watching a monitor showing the view from her brother's plane. "How are you doing that?"

"Satellite phones," Josh answered, like everyone in the world had two or three. "Ty's girlfriend hooked us up."

Samantha gave her mother a quick glance. "It's not like he does this every day."

344

"Maybe you better come downstairs with me. I'm not sure I want you watching all the violence." Amy said holding out her hand.

"Can't I stay up here? You said they're showing the same stuff on the news," Samantha pleaded.

"Okay, but if I yell for you, you better get downstairs quick or I'll tan your bottom, young lady."

Samantha snuggled against Josh, "Thanks Mom."

Chapter 66
H5N1 or What?

After the CNN news team left, technician Justin Stone dissected the event in his mind. Under the circumstances he had done well and mentally gave himself a thumbs-up for his performance. "Guess that's my fifteen minutes of fame," he said to the night air as he watched the little pockets of fire in the distance from the opened door of the mobile lab. Behind him, the timer on the automatic bio-hazard analyzer buzzed which meant the easy part of his job was finished.

Sitting down, he punched up the results on the computer monitor and breathed a sigh of relief when the results came back negative. Before beginning the rest of the tests that had to be done manually he pressed the transmit button on the emergency radio. "CDC-Atlanta, this is ML-27. Initial slab results are negative. I'm starting the individual labs now."

"ML-27, CDC-Atlanta, I'll pass your results on."

Justin reached up and grabbed a plastic bag labeled Anthrax and put it on the table next to the marble cutting board he was using to slice sections off the end of the filter from the vacuum unit. In one clean motion, he sliced off a section and dropped it into the bag, making sure the blade of the scalpel didn't cut the plastic. After pressing the triple seals back together, he squeezed the bag hard, rupturing the internal reservoirs of reagents. Fifteen seconds later the liquid in the bag remained clear. On the computer he pulled down the menu list for Anthrax and selected Negative.

He performed similar tests for smallpox, salmonella, and tularemia, which all produced negative results. But when he did the test for H5N1 the liquid in the bag turned a bright red.

"CDC Atlanta, ML-27."

"CDC Atlanta."

"ML-27. Test for H5N1 is positive."

As the radio remained silent, Justin began to get concerned. "CDC Atlanta. This is ML-27."

"Sorry, ML-27. I want to get Dr. Albright up here so she can talk with you personally. That will take a couple of minutes."

"CDC Atlanta, ML-27 standing by."

Figuring it might be a good time to impress his boss, Justin ran the test Dr. Albright had developed for the new H5N2 strain she discovered in Indonesia. The results were less spectacular as the liquid turn slightly pink.

"ML-27, CDC-Atlanta, this is Dr. Albright. What have you got for me?"

"Dr. Albright. I've gotten a positive on H5N1. The test for H5N2 resulted in a liquid that is slightly pink in color."

"Justin, put the bags on the scanner and send me a picture - Over," Dr. Albright said with a puzzled look on her face.

When the picture came through, one bag looked bright red and the other one seemed clear. "Justin, I can't see any color at all in the second bag."

"It's very pale, kind of like when you test a swimming pool and hold it up to the light," Justin said as he began to realize he had at least been exposed to H5N1, "what should I do, Dr. Albright?"

Sensing he was about to go ballistic, Albright thought for a moment. "ML-27 - CDC Atlanta. Take it easy, Justin. You know the H5N1 is only twenty percent lethal, which means you have an eighty percent chance of surviving without any treatment. Besides, if your shots are up to date and you've been taking your pills, I don't think you have anything to worry about."

Justin wasn't sure if he believed her, but decided to accept her evaluation of the situation at face value. "Okay Dr. Albright I should be okay then. Everything is up-to-date and I always take my pills."

"Glad to hear that, Justin. Keep testing and let me know if anything else shows up."

"Thanks, Dr. Albright - Ml-27- Out."

Back at the CDC, Dr. Albright turned to the dispatcher. "Contact another unit on a secure link and have them repeat the tests for the avian flu." Then she got up and ran out of the room.

Racing to her lab she quickly performed the same two tests Justin had done and got the same results. Now she wasn't sure if the virus had mutated or the test she developed was unreliable. Over the next half hour, she methodically thawed a sliver of Mrs. Bleckley's flesh and dropped the tissue into a test bag. Ten seconds later the liquid turned slightly pink and she ran back to the communications room.

"Can you get me through to the President?" she asked the operator.

Chapter 67
Ill Tidings

Inside the White House Situation Room, the Joint Chiefs of Staff huddled together, debating who had launched the attack and why nobody seemed to be able to stop it.

"I wouldn't say nobody was doing anything about them," Agent Jones interjected, as he came back into the room.

General Wes Jerome scowled, "Quiet. I want to hear what the agent has to say. After all, if somebody has come up with a way to attack planes that radar can't find – I want to hear about it."

The agent pointed up at the ceiling. "Duke Ransom, retired Navy, is outside right now keeping them away from the White House. By the looks of it he's doing a good job, too. I watched him burn one that tried to get in here a minute ago out of the air. He says he's getting help from his grandson somewhere in upstate New York and a friend over in Foggy Bottom."

"That's a bunch of horseshit. Communications is locked up tighter than my ass during a rectal exam. What's the old fart using?" Jerome yelled sarcastically, "Black Magic?"

"He got a real slick model jet. Comes in over the little buggers and torches them. Go see for yourself, if you don't believe me," Jones replied. "But there is a problem. Duke says he's only got enough fuel to keep fighting for another twenty minutes."

Pointing at the feed from CNN that had just popped up on one of the monitors, Admiral Ray Derry smiled at the Army Chief of Staff. "It looks like the Navy's saved your asses again, boys."

Moving to the monitor, the Joint Chiefs watched as the cameraman outside focused on a flat black plane coming in from the east. As it passed over the camera toward the White House, a miniature Phantom came up from behind, tilted skyward and set it on fire. As the fire ball headed toward the front of the building, the Joint Chiefs began raising their shoulders unconsciously, as it got closer. At the last second it burnt out like a roman candle and they relaxed.

"It looks like we've got another candidate for the Medal of Honor," Admiral Derry said proudly.

While they continued to watch the monitor, the cameraman caught three Phantom models racing along the treetops in formation.

348

"Hate to break up the party," Secretary of Defense Bert Tensor said coming out of the Surge Room with President Webber, "but it's time to review our options."

While everyone found a seat around the conference table, Bonnie Froggatt circled the table distributing a two-page status report she had been piecing together over the last hour.

Bonnie stood by waiting until they were all seated. "The bullet points at the top of the first page were put together by my team and represent information that has been verified by two or more sources. The remainder of the document offers various response protocols offered as talking points."

The President looked around the table at each man to see if anyone was going to make a play for attention. When they didn't, he looked up at Bonnie and smiled. "Please continue."

"At approximately 8:45 tonight, Washington was attacked by what can best be described as sophisticated model airplanes. The Beltway has been effectively sealed off leaving everyone inside trapped. This seems to have been accomplished with a fleet of small planes." Clicking a remote, she continued." As you can see in the video clip, the planes have a wingspan of about five feet. The reporter in the video estimated the weight to be about nine pounds."

As everyone watched, the video shot through the plane's windshield showed two boys carrying the model into their house followed by the explosion. Leaving the video in loop mode, Bonnie began playing a shot of Duke igniting a model and the resulting fireball.

"ATF and FBI analysis of the videos indicates each plane is carrying about two pounds of plastic explosive similar to C-4, but with a shorter burn duration. If it was actually C-4 and burning, it would detonate on impact," Bonnie said like she was teaching a class of tenth graders.

Bringing up a magnified frame of the bottom of a model on the third monitor, she continued, "You will notice a small opening on the bottom of the fuselage. We believe this is some type of spreader for the Plutonium that has been picked up by stationary air quality monitoring stations and CDC mobile labs operating in the greater Washington area."

General Jerome's mouth dropped open. "God damn it! Next you'll be telling us miniature paratroopers are jumping out with guns ablaze."

Everyone at the table chuckled nervously, as the Secretary of Defense held up his hand. "You haven't heard the best part yet," he motioned to Bonnie, "Go ahead and finish."

"Two of CDC's mobile labs have reported positive hits on H5N1 avian bird flu." Clicking the remote control again, Bonnie brought up a map of Washington. "As you can see, the nuclear and biological readings form an abstract pinwheel. This is due to the circular wind pattern currently in effect over the area. Unfortunately, a high pressure system from the south is scheduled to hit in less than an hour. Contamination will spread up the east coast to Maine by this time tomorrow."

President Webber sat quietly, waiting for someone to speak, but a heavy silence fell on the room. "Okay gentlemen, let's hear some suggestions."

"Looks to me like we're pretty much screwed," Jerome said looking to his comrades for help.

Before anyone could offer a suggestion on what to do next, Bonnie hurried into the room. "A Dr. Albright from the CDC in Atlanta is on the phone, says it's an emergency." When she saw the President nod, she activated the speaker phone in the middle of the table.

"Hello. This is Dr. Albright from the CDC. Can you hear me?"

"Yes, Dr. Albright. This is President Webber. I'm here in the Situation Room with the Secretary of Defense and the Joint Chiefs. What do you have to offer?"

Now in a much quieter voice, Dr. Albright began. "I don't pretend to know what's going on up there, but before you do anything, I need you to listen to me."

The President couldn't help but laugh. "Actually, Dr. Albright, there doesn't seem to be very much we are able to do. My best hope is that the planes will eventually run out of gas and we'll be able to go out and assess the damage."

"It's too late for that, Mr. President. I've been getting reports from our mobile labs that a new variety of avian flu had been released on the Capital," Dr. Albright said.

President Webber smirked. "Yes, I've been briefed on all the various types of biological agents terrorists might use. As I recall, that one seems more likely to wipe out the chickens in China than to kill us."

"That probably is true for the H5N1 variety. That virus has a tough times making the jump to humans. But recently, I discovered a lab in Indonesia that seems to have reconstructed the Spanish Flu that killed twenty percent of the people who became exposed. However, tests have led us to believe this new virus is a variant of both viruses. The problem is this new virus seems to be one hundred percent lethal to humans," Dr. Albright said waiting to see what reaction that was going to invoke.

President Webber couldn't believe what he was hearing. His first reaction was that of disbelief. "You're telling me you have tested this new virus on humans?"

Dr. Albright figured that wasn't going to slip by. "To make a long story short. Yes, we had a human volunteer. Some things got out of hand and everyone that was exposed died. But right now that's not important. Have you seen the weather report lately?"

"Yes, a cold front is coming in. Will that help?" the President asked.

"Maybe, if it was going down to zero, but it's not. It's going to blow up the east coast, spreading the virus all the way to Canada. The only chance we have to stop it is to burn it up," Dr. Albright said.

"We're already doing a good job of that," General Jerome said, "haven't you been watching the news?"

Figuring she didn't have anything to lose, Dr. Albright tried to calm down. "You're not paying attention to what I said. You'd have to burn it up. All of it! At least everything inside the Beltway, probably need to go out another ten miles to be sure you get it all." Her voice rose perceptibly. "You, your family, your staff, their families, the landmarks, and most of the 6 million people living in the greater Washington area!" Dr. Albright screamed into the phone, "do you understand?"

Everyone in the room sat in shocked silence. Finally, the President spoke. "Dr. Albright, does anyone else besides your staff know about this flu?"

Dr. Albright tried to regain her composure. "The day after the accident, I sent samples to the World Health Organization, and to labs in England for verification. By now, they will have confirmed our findings."

"Thank you, Dr. Albright, for getting my attention," President Webber said turning off the phone.

He had long ago given up being remembered fondly as one of America's best presidents. In fact, at various points in his administration he would have gladly settled for being forgotten all together. But now he was being forced to make a decision that would ensure he would be remembered as the most ungodly President of all time, and he didn't like it a bit.

Worse yet, he had every reason to suspect that once he gave the order to launch, nobody would be willing to carry it out. And from what he remembered of Dr. Cornelius' lecture, success would depend on one hundred percent of the thousands of people in the chain of command complying with the order he knew he must give. "Bonnie, how much time do we have until the wind shifts?"

"Forty-five minutes, give or take," she answered, like somebody had asked how long before dinner.

"See if you can track down Dr. Cornelius," the President requested.

Standing up, he smiled. "Okay, gentlemen, time to roll up our collective sleeves and get the show on the road."

Chapter 68
Bone Dry

After scorching his tenth plane, Ty headed in for a landing near Duke's truck. "Look out old man, I don't want to toast your toes."

Duke flipped his glasses up and saw Ty's jet rolling toward him on the grass. "What are you doing down here?"

"Filler her up and check the tires, please," Ty said as his plane bounced over the grass and stopped a few feet behind the truck.

"Okay, but I've only got enough for one tank then we're SOL," Duke said setting his Phantom into a three-degree turn and putting the controller on the tailgate, "Josh, keep an eye on my plane for me."

"Don't worry about that. I've got you covered, Pop-pop."

Duke grabbed the last bottle of fuel from the truck and began filling the tank. "I was hoping Sarah would make it up here."

"Sorry, Duke. I had to break into the maintenance shop and mix up some fuel," Sarah said. "I'm on my way, but this thing is overloaded and flying like a Christmas goose."

•••

Inside the Surge Room, technicians worked frantically to establish communications with the key players. "Averaging the wind speed and estimating the launch points and time interval, it looks like we're going to have to incinerate about 360 square miles," Dr. Cornelius said over a military link that had been set up in his home.

Turning to the display, the President looked at the size of the area slowly increasing, as it covered central VA and continued moving north. "Who's in the hot seat?"

"Since it would take the Tridents based in Bangor, Washington, too long to reach us in time, I'm counting them out," the Secretary of Defense said as he punched away at his laptop, "our only chance is to use the boats based in Kings Bay, Georgia. Of those, two are in overhaul and six are deployed on station, leaving the USS Maryland (SSBN-738) and the USS Wyoming (SSBN-742) coming back from patrol. Both carry twenty-four missiles, each fitted with eight warheads."

Dr. Cornelius interrupted. "Wait a minute while I verify some numbers." The doctor punched some numbers into his calculator and studied the result for but a moment. "Yes, that might just do it.

Together the boats can deliver 384 warheads. That gives us one 475-kiloton blast per square mile over a circular target area eighteen miles in diameter. Normally, that wouldn't be enough power to destroy everything, but because of the firestorm effect I spoke of before, it should be enough to get the job done."

"Can you clarify that a little?" President Webber asked, feeling like he was a hundred years old. "You're telling me that two Trident subs can't destroy Washington, DC?"

Dr. Cornelius paused then began speaking like it was the first day the new freshman class entered his lecture hall. "Well after the dust settled, there wouldn't be much of Washington left, but we're talking about killing a virus, not people. And to be honest I'd put a dollar on the fact that some people would survive such an attack. Of course, it would be dumb luck, standing in exactly the right place when the bombs when off so shockwaves canceled out or building shadows protected them. It happened in Hiroshima and it would happen here."

"I've got the captains and weapons officers of the Maryland and Wyoming standing by, Mr. President," Bonnie said poking her head into the Situation Room.

Dr. Cornelius' voice became softer, "But that was before the material was in place for the fire storm. Today, we have covered most of Washington with asphalt roads and tar roofs. Vinyl siding covers our homes and plastic is in everything from the cars we drive to the cups that hold our coffee. Six million automobiles carry an average of ten gallons of gasoline, one gallon of oil, and four rubber tires. Propane cylinders in gas grills adorn every backyard." Feeling he was going a little overboard, he paused. "In other words we're already surrounded by enough flammable material to incinerate us. All we need is a high temperature trigger."

The President got up slowly and walked over to the Defense Secretary, "What's the status?"

"Sir, the REACT system has retargeted all 48 missiles. The boats are hovering and the captains are standing by for your order."

"I can't believe that blowing a hole in two states and the District of Columbia is better than quarantining and treating people who become infected", the President said. "How can I give an order like that?"

The Secretary of Defense put his hand on President Webber's back. "The results from the CDC in Atlanta have been duplicated in two other labs. Whatever they whipped up in Jakarta is a nightmare. If it gets out, the entire population of the World is at risk," he said leading the President toward the bank of monitors, "hell, if CNN breaks that story, England and France will hit us right before China and Russia take out the entire east coast. You've got to give the order now."

Looking up at the map, the President reached into his pocket. The plastic card handed to him that morning by a courier from the National Security Agency felt like it weighed ten pounds. "Okay, give me the football."

"Yes sir, Mr. President," the Armed Commissioned Officer said hurrying to the table with the 40-pound briefcase.

He placed it on the table and spun the dials on two separate small combination locks. When they opened, the Naval Officer pulled up the lid.

The President reached into his inner pocket and removed a small cream-colored envelope. It bore no markings. He looked around the room, feeling the panic in everyone's mind as he tore it open and removed a single sheet of paper. He looked at the series of numbers and letters that comprised today's codes which allowed him to call for a nuclear strike anywhere in the world. At this point, what he was about to do weighed immeasurably on his mind. This was reflected in the eyes of everyone there. No President in history had taken this final step. No President wanted to be the one to go down in history as the person who set off nuclear weapons, especially within his own country. His legacy was about to be sealed for all eternity.

"I always hoped I'd never have to use this on our enemies. Now it turns out I'm destined to unleash a nuclear bloodbath on America," he said sliding the card in and running his index fingers over the electronic readers.

"Tell the networks I'll be ready in one minute," President Webber said as a technician adjusted the camera and centered the President's head on the monitor.

While Jenkins talked on the phone, the President slowly twisted his head around and tried to relax. A moment later, a communication lock icon appeared in the lower corner of the display and Jenkins gave him the thumbs-up signal.

The President, with suddenly weary eyes, swept his hand across his face a moment, and then looked directly into the hastily arranged television camera. He knew three hundred million American people were watching his every move, and more than ten times that number around the world. He blinked, then slowly blinked again, then spoke to the Nation and the world.

"Tonight, many of you watched as I was whisked away from my State of the Union address. Over the past hour, Washington has been attacked by terrorists bent on destroying America. From the reports coming in, I know they have already killed thousands in the greater metropolitan Washington, DC area."

"Bad as that is, there is more sad news I must convey to you all. Tonight the country has lost a great leader. An hour ago the Vice-President was killed when his helicopter was destroyed. I came very close to death, too. If it were not for a retired naval officer named Duke Ransom, I would already be with the Vice-President looking down on the city in flames."

The President reached over, picked up and gulped a full glass of water. Without looking downward, he replaced it on the edge of the podium, only to have it fall and crash onto the floor. The sound broadcast into every television set at the same time. The tension was there, and it was felt in every home in every nation.

"Unfortunately, the planes that spread devastation on our city also carried radioactive materials and avian flu. Of the two, the flu presents the greatest danger. It is a new variety, with the potential to spread death to every corner of the planet. From what I am told, there is no place to hide and no place to run. Nothing offers protection. The only hope the world and the rest of America has is for us to stop it here. Tonight!"

"Therefore, a few minutes ago, I gave the order to two Trident submarine captains to fire their missiles at Washington. It was the hardest thing I have done. I'm sure it will be the hardest order the captains have ever obeyed. But obey it they must, if they love their country. For without their commitment, the rest of America is doomed."

He paused, not in thought, but with a resigned look on his face. He closed his eyes and took in a deep breath through his nose. After holding it for a few seconds he opened his mouth and slowly let it out – then began to speak again.

"Without their commitment, the rest of the world is doomed. As The Bible says, the rain falls on the just and the unjust. I would ask you all to pray for your families and friends here and abroad. And remember the great sacrifices we are making here tonight. For those of you who live to see another sunrise, I pray you will work hard to unify the country and to further democracy.

"Tonight, I grant the State Governors special authority and increase their powers to act independently until a new federal structure is established. May God bless each and every one of you and may He truly bless America in this time of peril and need. Goodnight."

As he sat amid the somewhat subdued applause of those present, tears rolled down his cheeks.

●●●

Josh flipped up his glasses and saw his sister sleeping beside him. Reaching over, he lowered the volume on the television she had been watching. Although he hadn't been paying much attention to it, he had heard enough to realize his grandfather was in trouble.

"Josh, it looks like it's time to get our planes back to Foggy Bottom," Duke said, "I know I wouldn't want anything happening to my little beauty."

Josh felt helpless as he tried to figure out how to help his grandfather. "I don't want you to die, Pop-Pop."

"It's something we all have to do eventually. When it happens, it will be over in a flash," Duke said with a chuckle.

"Now let's get refueled and head south, while we have the chance." Maybe Ty or Sarah can figure out how to get my little jet back without crashing."

"Already got you covered," Sarah said, "after I top off Josh and Ty, come in and get ready for a tow."

Five minutes later, Sarah had the first two planes fueled as they headed south. "Okay, Duke, my man. Stick your nose into the refueling cone and cut your engine.

When his plane was attached to the tanker, Duke walked out into the front yard of the White House and sat down. The ground was cold, but he wanted to enjoy the feeling one more time before the missiles hit. "I love you, Josh. Tell your mother and sister. I'll miss them."

"I will. Pop-Pop. I love you, too. And don't worry, I'll never forget you," Josh said pulling ahead of the tanker and rocking his wings back and forth.

When Duke saw Josh's antics, he laughed and wished he had brought his controller with him. A second later, shooting stars filled the sky and a cool breeze rushed in from behind. An instant later a warm blue light surrounded him and he was sucked backward, but never felt the impact as he waited for his body to strike the ground. 'Strange,' he thought, as the world was suddenly silent.

Chapter 69
The Post-Game Show

Back in Jakarta, Mohammed raised his glass toward the television, "To President George Webber."

Fahid, Abdullah, and Dr. Ramadan stopped talking and chimed in. "George Webber."

As they finished, the scene on all the televisions switched over to the feed coming from the CNN news team just outside the White House fence. In the background, the sounds of sirens stilled until only the wind could be heard blowing against the reporter's microphone. The cameraman slowly began to zoom in on an old man sitting on the lawn wearing his Navy Dress Blues uniform as the picture turned to static.

Dr. Ramadan sat back down next to Mohammed. "It looks like they went for it. I kind of thought something would happen to spoil it all."

"Yes, we left so many loose ends, I'm a little surprised myself," Mohammed said patting him on the shoulder. "Who could have predicted, discovering that vial of flu we left in your lab would lead to this."

"Quite surprising when you realize it was the only sample that ever made the jump to humans. If they had done nothing, our little attack would have only killed a quarter of a million," Ramadan said, "remarkable! Quite remarkable."

"Well it just goes to prove what I've believed all along," Mohammed said settling back, "the only country that could ever destroy America is America itself."

Epilogue

Josh sat on the deck overlooking Delta Lake with his back to the house. Rolling his shoulders to ease the tension, he felt the warm summer sun break through an open patch of dark sky and enjoyed the warmth it brought to his face and hands. The hypnotic swish from the windmill blades was broken when Samantha, now ten, slid open the glass door behind him. "I put a glass of lemonade on the table for you. Don't knock it over."

"Thanks, Samantha," he said centering the joystick on the beat-up old controller in his lap.

"Is it time yet?" Samantha asked pulling up a chair beside him.

"Pretty soon. Go see if Mom got back from the fish hatchery yet," Josh said flipping up his virtual glasses and taking a drink.

After a couple of swallows, he put the glass back. "Those are the best lemons you've grown since we've been here," he said pulling the black glasses back down, "I hope she gets here pretty quick or I'm going to have to stall for time."

"I'll call you when we're ready," Samantha said returning to the house.

A few minutes later, Samantha called and Josh raised his glasses and walked inside and sat beside his mother, on the couch. "Are you ready, Samantha?"

"After all the practicing we've been doing, I'd better be," she said picking up her VR-glasses and switching her controller over to manual.

"How about you, Mom?" Josh asked.

"Don't worry about me," Amy said clutching a small controller herself.

Meeting and flying side-by-side, the model Phantoms passed over what was left of Baltimore and continued south. Ten minutes later they joined Ty and Sarah where the planes formed a diamond.

"Glad you two are on time this year," Ty said taking the breakaway position," I hate to keep our fans waiting."

Coming up on a large circular harbor that had been christened "Freedom Bay," the planes dropped down until they were flying a hundred feet off the water. As they did, two rows of a dozen fireboats began shooting streams of red, white, and blue water into the air to form an arch.

"This part always scares me," Samantha said as the formation flew under the water and emerged 1,000 feet from the Washington Monument that was straight ahead.

"You're doing great," Josh said.

Gaining altitude as they circled the spire three times and flew over thousands of sailboats below, the four planes finally leveled off and disappeared south.

Five minutes later, they returned and Amy pushed the button on her controller that opened the tanker's bomb bay doors. As they approached the monument again, Ty pulled his jet up into a steep rolling climb.

A tear streamed down Amy's face as she pressed the release button. "I love you, Dad,"

As the rose petals formed a cloud and floated towards the water, a giant American Flag was unfurled from the top of the monument. For a few seconds, it beat against the stones that had been bleached white by the blasts five years earlier. When a sudden gust of wind snapped it straight, the Armed Forces Band began to play and spectators who had come to celebrate another 4th of July joined voices and began singing the Star Spangled Banner.